Penguin Books
The Floor of Heaven

James McQueen was born in 1934 in Ulverstone,
Tasmania. He started writing in 1975 at the age
of forty, and has been writing full-time since
1977. He has won many awards for fiction,
including the State of Victoria Short Story Award
(1978, 1979), the Air New Zealand P.E.N. Short
Story Award (1978, 1979) and the Henry Lawson
Prose Award (1979, 1982).

He lives in Nabowla, Tasmania.

Also by James McQueen

The Electric Beach (stories) 1978
Escape to Danger (children's novel) 1979
A Just Equinox (novel) 1980
The Escape Machine (stories) 1981
Hook's Mountain (novel) 1982
The Franklin–Not Just a River (non-fiction) 1983
Uphill Runner (stories) 1984

JAMES McQUEEN

THE FLOOR OF HEAVEN

PENGUIN BOOKS

Penguin Books Australia Ltd,
487 Maroondah Highway, P.O. Box 257
Ringwood, Victoria 3134, Australia
Penguin Books Ltd,
Harmondsworth, Middlesex, England
Penguin Books,
40 West 23rd Street, New York, N.Y. 10010, U.S.A.
Penguin Books Canada Limited,
2801 John Street, Markham, Ontario, Canada L3R 1B4
Penguin Books (N.Z.) Ltd,
182-190 Wairu Road, Auckland 10, New Zealand

First published by Penguin Books Australia, 1986

Copyright © Panama Productions 1986

All Rights Reserved. Without limiting the rights under copyright
reserved above, no part of this publication may be reproduced,
stored on a retrieval system, or transmitted, in any form or by any
means (electronic, mechanical, photocopying, recording or otherwise)
without the prior written permission of both the copyright owner and
the above publisher of this book.

Typeset in Australia by Midland Typesetters, Victoria
Made and printed in Australia by
Dominion Press-Hedges & Bell

CIP

McQueen, James, 1934-
The floor of heaven.

ISBN 0 14 008869 5.

I. Title

A823'.3

for Barney Roberts

ACKNOWLEDGEMENT

The author gratefully acknowledges the assistance of the Literature Board of the Australia Council, which has given the greatest support to the writing of this book and earlier books.

CONTENTS

Part One   Jack Byrne – Inside, 1973   1

Part Two   Terry Byrne   61

Part Three   Jack Byrne – Outside   103

Part Four   Nancy Byrne   151

Part Five   Jack Byrne – Upside   171

Part Six   Martin Gogarty – Launceston, 1903   327

Part Seven   Jack Byrne – Down   411

'. . . Look how the floor of heaven is
thick inlaid with patines of bright gold;'

The Merchant of Venice, 5.1.54

PART ONE

JACK BYRNE – INSIDE, 1973

I'm lying on my back on the hard concrete of the path, the sun burning red shapes through my closed eyelids, another cigarette singeing my fingers, when the shadow moves over me, lingers, shutting out the brightness.

'Move a bit,' I say, 'you're blocking out my vitamin D.'

The shadow remains where it is for a long moment, then eases away, and the autumn sun crashes down on me again. I open my eyes, squint. It's Purple Brewster, neat and brown and sweating in little greasy bubbles.

'It's time for our talk, Mr Byrne,' he says in his high, sing-song, Paki-Paddy voice, teetering there in his mauve shoes. He's all in mauve today: mauve suede shoes, mauve socks, mauve tweeds, mauve shirt, mauve tie, mauve jacket. Some days it's royal purple, sometimes pale lavender, some days plain mauve. But always some brand of purple.

It's too much. I close my eyes again. 'Go away, you little turd.'

'It's time for our talk,' he says.

I can feel him still teetering there, fidgeting. 'Piss off, you bloody horrible little wog.'

'I take no notice of your insults, Mr Byrne. They are just a symptom of your illness.'

I open my eyes once more. His brown face is suspended above me, peering down, the pupils of his eyes aniseed black, the whites like dirty fried egg. 'What's my illness then, doctor?'

'That's what we must find out,' he says, and sits down on the garden seat in the shade of the big elm. 'Come over here out of the sun, why don't you?'

'I'm trying to get a suntan,' I say, undoing two more buttons on my shirt. 'It's all right for you, you're just about black anyway.'

'You are too flippant, Mr Byrne,' he says. 'You are a sick man. You wouldn't be here if you weren't.'

'Talk to me from there,' I say. 'If I got any closer I might lose my self-control and kiss you.'

'Why are you so miserable,' he asks, 'so depressed?'

'Do I look miserable?'

'Not now, perhaps, not at this very moment. But after all, one does not usually cut one's wrists when one is wildly happy.'

'Yeah? How long since you cut yours?'

He ignores this. 'Why did you do it?' he asks. 'We can make no progress until you will talk honestly about it.'

'I couldn't find any leeches when I needed them.' No, better keep off that line, it's a bit close to the bone. 'Well,' I say, 'to tell the truth, it just seemed like a good idea at the time.'

'If the policeman hadn't found you, you would have died.'

'He didn't *find* me, he *attacked* me.' That was good old Rod, the local sergeant, come to arrest me for assault and battery, dangerous driving, blasphemy, arson in Her Majesty's shipyards, Christ knows what . . .

'You did quite an efficient job,' says Purple. 'Most people flinch at the last moment, make several tentative cuts. But you, you cut very firmly, very deeply, and almost in the right place . . .'

'If you're going to do something, then do it right, eh?'

'But why did you want to do it at all?'

'I didn't.' For the first time in the month I've been here I tell him the truth. Let him puzzle it out.

He purses his lips. My God, they are really purple, a kind of dark bronze purple. 'That's an unusual statement,' he says.

'You'd better believe it, I'm a very unusual man.'

'If you didn't intend to kill yourself, then what *did* you intend?'

'Ah, that's the question, isn't it?'

'It's a little hard to accept, that you went to your office in the middle of the night, cut your wrist, and yet didn't intend to kill yourself . . .'

'You're the bloody expert, you bloody ponced-up pox-doctor,' I tell him. '*You* work it out.'

And I close my eyes, let the sun fry my bonce, burn into my skull. I decide not to talk to him any more, and after a while I hear him get up, hear the whisper of his brothel creepers on the gravel as he wanders away. I just lie there, smoking, eyes closed, thinking about that night. Going over it in my head, again and again. I can see his point of view, all right. It doesn't make sense any other way, not to him. I can see that. The answer's far too simple, far too obvious, for him to see it. Good. Because I'm not about to tell Purple Brewster, even if I felt like telling anyone.

The thing is, of course, that *I just wanted to let that blood out* . . .

•

Names, this place is full of names. They echo through the wards, the corridors, up and down the stairs. Mr This, Mrs That, Miss So-and-so . . . except if you're too sick or too mad and you have to be looked after like a kid, then it's Ernie, or Mavis, or Jill . . . or Jack . . .

No, that's not really true. If you're here a while and they get to know you, and if you're not too much on your dig, then they'll call you by your first name. Not the doctors, though, not old Purple Brewster. Why did I have to draw that great buffoon . . .?

Never mind, they're supernumeraries really, it's the patients that keep each other out of the observation wards. Most of the time.

And I don't have any trouble, really, keeping quiet about things to the doctors. The patients, well, most of them mind their own business. If someone asks, right out, you know they're twits, and you tell them: I have a slight behavioural problem, I suck wombats. And they leave you alone.

•

I wake in the morning to the sound of my room-mate, Old Benjy, trumpeting away on his back in the other bed. I get up, take a quick look out the window at the green lawns, the line of hedge that separates us from the road, the sky. Not much, but that's all there is to see. Have a shower in our private bathroom – just like a cheap motel, this place – and get dressed. Get in early for breakfast, before the old dears assault the servery, before the porridge gets cold and the hot water runs out.

In the dining room I sit at one of the small tables on my own. A few minutes later Petra comes in, planks down her cigarettes on the table, and goes to get her Weetbix. I find myself smiling like a born-again idiot. She comes back, looking all morning fresh, all golden and creamy, chestnut hair swinging, like something out of the best movie you've ever seen. Tall for a girl, and walks like one of those Egyptian queens must have done. I've never seen a straighter back.

She sits down with her bowl, looking at me with those greeny-blue eyes that you dive into.

'Have a good night?' she says.

'Not bad.'

She works on her Weetbix a while, then looks at me. 'What are you doing today?'

'Oh, I say,' I might jump on a plane, go to Melbourne, see a show or two . . .'

'Can I come?'

'How could I go without you?'
'After that?'
The morning collapses a bit. 'Purple Brewster, I suppose.'
'It's Thursday.'
'Oh yeah . . .' A day for rounds, when we get a quick visit from Johnny Cash.
'Want a game of table tennis after rounds?'
'Sure.'

She jumps up, leaves her bowl, her cigarettes, rushes off. She does that sometimes, not as often as she used to, but sometimes. Anyway, the day has a certain direction now. Johnny Cash, table tennis, lunch . . .

•

Waiting for Johnny Cash, sunlight bouncing off the scrubbed lino tiles of my room, I spend a little time watching the stranger in the mirror. Benjy's off making string sculptures, and we're alone. Over a month old, he is, a fine big broth of a boy, six feet and a bit, wide shoulders, curly black hair, eyes blue enough to break a nun's heart. Rough enough, though, not pretty at all, even ugly maybe. He holds his wrist up for me to see the scar.

The trouble is that he doesn't really look like a stranger. Except for the scar. I've seen the face every morning of my life almost, know the way the shoulders slope away into the arms, the way the left one is a bit lower where the collarbone set crooked, the hang of the balls, dressing to the left . . .

How they dangling, Jackie?

Plumb, old buddy, plumb magnolia . . .

And somehow the stranger isn't really there at all, but out here, on this side of the mirror. I know what I am, and I am what I wasn't before. It never occurred to me that other people could change you, just with words.

I take the new stranger off, go and sit in the armchair, wait for Johnny Cash.

I suppose I was about eight years old when I realised that I was a bastard. Oh, I *knew* before that, but I didn't really know what it was. Just a name they called you, like cow, or bugger, or something like that. No harm, just kids being naturally vicious at that age, not been taught the refinements yet. But about that time, when we were all queueing up outside Docking's cowshed to have a feel of Prissie Ward's twat, it started to dawn on me that it really meant something special and different. Not just not having a daddy – there were a few like that about for one reason or another (I was born in 1943). No, it wasn't not having a daddy: it was having a mother, a mother who'd done something sort of shameful and dirty in a special, secret kind of way that wasn't entirely unconnected with what went on in the cowshed with Prissie.

After that I learned soon enough that I didn't like the name. Not that it stopped them from using it. They just had to use it from a distance. And a few years later when I went to high school it had all changed again. Because I wasn't anywhere near the top of the heap then: I was on the bottom, and fair game for anyone.

So from then on it was Byrne the Bastard, and after a while I got tired of being knocked down by all the big kids when I objected. And one day I thought, OK, if that's the way you want it, then that's the way it's going to be. So that's what I was, that's what I *taught* myself to be – a bastard. I still fought a lot, but I didn't fight at being called a bastard. And I got very cunning, so that even when I lost I seemed to have won. And I went on for a year or two getting harder and tougher and more cynical about it all. And then when I was about fourteen I started to get my size, and I got it quick, and soon I was making the girls giggle and the old maids blush. That was about the time I started to play football in earnest, and I learned that if you were a bastard in *that* game, then you were a permanent yard ahead of the rest. And by my last year at school I was a big star footballer, with senior coaches trying to sign me up, and pictures in the paper, and all the rest of it. And they had already started to scream at me when I moved – Byrne the Bastard, they'd scream when I came out of a pack, or just the Bastard – and that's just the way it was.

So when I left school I went naturally to the Redlegs, the roughest team in the Union, a team *full* of bastards. And I said to myself, well, you might be only seventeen, cock, but before you're eighteen, you're gonna be the biggest bastard of the lot. And I was.

From where I stand now it seems that life was very simple then, just being the Bastard. And before I can think myself forward into the nasty bits, the complicated bits, Johnny Cash arrives, with a sister, two nurses, a clerk with a great trolley of files, and two learner doctors.

They wheel into my room and form a half circle in front of me, Johnny Cash in front. He's medium height with a pot belly and a straggly black beard and not much hair. And except for his white shirt, all his clothes are black. I swear to God, there's something very odd about the sartorial habits of the psychiatric class . . .

He stares at me for a while. He has this trick of not blinking for a long time, then closing his eyelids very slowly, leaving them closed a moment, then opening them again.

He puts out his hand to the side, without turning his head. The clerk slaps a file into it.

'Scalpel!' I shout at him, and he jumps a little, then almost smiles.

'You've found your sense of humour, then, Mr Byrne,' he says.

'Never really lost it, Doctor Cash,' says I. 'Just mislaid it.'

He looks puzzled for a moment. I don't think he's ever quite connected up with the Johnny Cash stuff. Then: 'How are you feeling today?'

'Tell the truth,' I say, 'I'm feeling like exercising a bit of mutual trust.'

'Oh,' he says, curious, 'and what form might that take?'

'A bit of oral sex with one of the nurses, maybe?'

'Ah.' He goes a bit distant on me. 'Dr Brewster tells me that you are being, ah, less than forthcoming about your . . . problems.'

'I don't have any problems,' I say. 'I'm young and fit and nasty. How could I have problems? What I have is a situation.'

'And how do you see this situation?'

'It's kind of like having to take a shit every day – I mightn't like it, but I'm stuck with it.'

'And what exactly is it that you're stuck with?'

'That's for me to know and you to find out.'

He sighs. 'You know, you seem to see us as detectives of some sort . . . we can't help you if you don't help us.'

'I didn't ask for your help.'

'You know what will happen if you're released now?'

'The pharisees will swoop on me and lock me up, charge me with all kinds of fancy stuff. But you won't let me go just yet, will you?'

He shakes his head sadly and turns away.

I sit there for a while after they've gone, thinking. I have to be careful. True enough, I don't want to leave just yet. And not just on account of the wallopers, but because . . . well, I just can't see yet how I can manage things . . . myself, the world, that stranger that looks out of the mirror at me every morning. There are too many things that I haven't sorted out . . .

I trot off along the corridor, past the trolleys lined up outside the door that's got no number on it, no name, nothing. All the trolleys are filled with little middle-aged ladies with bad depressions, already had their needles, waiting for the moment when they'll be connected up to the mains and the stars blaze for a second or two, and the circuits unblock in their heads. They'll come out of it with a bit of a headache and spend another few days not worrying too much about their ungrateful daughters or their mortgages or their unfaithful husbands or the thrips on their roses . . .

Into the kitchen and make myself a cup of coffee, take it into the lounge. Three dodderers and a pretty nurse playing five hundred in the corner, three old maids knitting, two teenage junkies, and a partridge in a pear tree.

When I sit down, one of the kids looks over at me. He's about twenty, can't walk properly, sweats all the time.

'Have you ever seen God?' he asks me. He speaks very slowly, as if he's got a mouthful of ice-cream.

'Don't know that I have.'

'He's big and red . . .'

'You seen him, then?'

He nods. 'Yeah,' he says. 'One night we were sitting in a car smoking grass, and I saw him up in the sky – really big and red he was . . .' He gets up and shuffles slowly away.

I never saw God, but I sure wrote his name. Wrote it in letters of fire – or at least orange Dayglo – on the stone wall of the Anglican church. Just before the sergeant busted in and rescued me from a fate worse than breathing. FUCK GOD I wrote. Didn't sign it. Blasphemious and obskene. Then I jumped into my car, careered off in all directions, shut myself in my office, cut my wrist with a brand new Gem that I was keeping for sharpening pencils. I never did like those sharpeners.

All right, I'm sharp enough. No pun intended. But I dress properly, shave every day – with an electric razor – and don't slobber my food. And I'm not really insane. Just went off the tracks for a few hours. Who wouldn't? So all I'm really doing is taking a little breather here, letting things settle a bit.

Trouble is, I can't really *see* myself any more.

It's almost as if everything I ever was has been taken away and I've been given a new me inside the old skin. No, that's not quite right, either, because it's the way I always was, really. I just didn't know. Good Christ, how can you go on for thirty years thinking that you're more or less normal, and then find out suddenly, in a flash, in a thunderclap, that you're not, that you're something different, something obscene, an offence . . .

That was the *reason*, of course. The wrist. *I just wanted to get rid of that blood* . . . Stupid, unreasonable, but I must have been in a state of shock.

Now what I have to do is get unsmart, make some kind of effort to swallow it all, to see if I can accept it. If I can't, then it's all over, anyway. I can't go back, I can't even go home, ever . . .

•

Visiting hours, and I'm sitting on the table-tennis table with Petra, drinking tea. No visitors for either of us. I haven't had one all the time I've been here, don't expect any, don't want any. Petra's mother comes once a week. It's a long drive and she works every day. The stepfather stays away.

Someone's using the red phone by the end of the table – a thick woman in a shapeless dressing-gown, shouting into the mouthpiece as if it was a tunnel.

'Why aren't you married?' says Petra.

'Why should I be?'

'You're old enough.'

'I'm old enough to shove my head in a meat grinder, too.'

'Someone asked *me* once,' she says.

'What did you say?'

'I said "no".'

'Clear and succinct.'

'It was another patient. Before you came.'

'Oh.' And I'm immediately bloody jealous! Oh, stupid! And I want to say, 'Listen, Petra, I'm in love with you, let's get out of here, let's go away, let's go down to my private suite, let's . . .'

The trouble is, she's had all this terrible stuff, months of shock treatment, awful hallucinations, all the shit she never asked for, never deserved, since she was fifteen years old, and what can you do? And she's chirpy and proud and she walks so bloody straight, and she's got so much guts and so much hope . . .

And I'm Byrne the Bastard all right, but I'm not that kind of bastard, am I?

But, all the same, I'm just about to say something very stupid when a nurse comes up and says to me, 'Mr Byrne, the front desk just called, your grandfather's out there and he wants to see you . . .'

And I freeze then, my throat gets so tight I can't swallow or speak, and I can see him there, tall as me, taller, in his good suit, his hair still black, shoulders still square, eyebrows bushy, eyes pale and cool . . . And I think, Oh Christ, how could you, and I want to run, run, anywhere, away . . . but I don't, I just shake my head at the nurse and get off the table and walk, very slowly, down the passage, round the corner, and when I'm out of sight, I grab the key from my pocket and dive down the stairs and head for my private suite . . .

All the black things are there again, and the blood that I needed so badly to get rid of . . . and I can't tell which is stronger, the fear or the revulsion, or even if they are really any different . . .

•

I lie secure in my private island of light, bolstered by gym cushions and old sacks and linen covers, atop the great billiard table. A narrow sea of green baize washes to the edges of my odd divan, and the old mahogany rails gleam dully. Except for the whirr and hum from the air-conditioning plant in the next basement, it's very quiet. I've been in more-or-less sole occupation for a week now. It took a little arranging. I found out almost by accident about the billiard room, which you reach through the woodwork shop. Saw the key on its tag hanging in the cupboard behind the nurses' station when someone left the door open. Asked about it, borrowed the key and came down and tried the table – a good one – took the key back, then thought about it a while. No one else seems to come to the room, and the woodwork shop is used only two mornings a week. So I borrowed the key again, had a duplicate cut on a rare trip down to the shopping centre to buy magazines, put the original back. Now I come and go as I please.

Despite the peace and quiet – or maybe because of it – I start to think again about the old man waiting in the foyer. If he is still waiting. I'll stay here until teatime, make sure he's gone before I come out. And I wonder a little what brought him, how he could bring himself to come . . .

The dimness here reminds me a bit of the deep shade under the pines, the path by the river upstream from the bridge and the hotel, from home. He used to walk with me there, when I was young, after church on a Sunday, both of us in our best, spick and span for the service in the little old church up by the rocky knoll behind the hotel. And that river . . . it seems to have been with me forever, to have run through my life like some persistent thread. When you live beside a river, you belong to it in some strange way. It starts forty miles back in the mountain, stays small and fast for most of its run to the sea, then in the last five miles it begins to broaden, turns brown and slow and amenable, except for those times in the depths of winter when it rises, floods its banks and spreads across the fertile flats of the valley floor. It runs under the road bridge, right past the weatherboard hotel with its high front wall, steep grey roof, narrow attic windows, under its high banks of blackberries and mallows and pungent fennel. A few hundred yards downstream willows begin to clog the banks, and the river spreads, widens into the shallows of the tidal estuary, rolls slowly under the railway bridge and out through the deep channel and over the narrow bar to the sea. It used to be navigable, and last century the timber ketches used to come right up to where the hotel stands now. There was a wharf, then, warehouses, a harbourmaster's office, cottages. All gone now. Only the hotel left, the post office, the little store, a dozen or so neat houses. The main road nowadays passes a mile away, and it's very quiet. But in those old days it was a busy riotous little backwater with seamen and timber-getters and Aboriginal harlots. Bushrangers too, for all I know.

He taught me to fish, the old man, down at the river mouth, spinning on the making tide for the big blackback salmon that used to run up the river to feed, that took your spinner like a train and killed themselves fighting, and flapped on the clean sand like dying angels, all silver and metallic blue . . .

I used to watch him as he fished, dropping the lure so neatly in the middle of the tidal rush – a big man, tall, wide in the shoulder, always clean-shaven, his long upper lip resolute, his hair still crisp and lightly curled. His eyes were very clear and grey, and his smile slow and white and rare, his hands solid and lightly calloused from his work in the garden. He must have been about fifty then.

He came to Melbourne, once, years later, to watch one of the matches. It was one of my very good days, a day when my feet seemed hardly to touch the ground, when the ball was bouncing just as if I had a string on it and I was a yard faster than anyone else and I was taking the bumps easily and laughing and breaking through every time and driving the ball downfield with great long raking drop-kicks all the way to the centre against the wind . . . and in the second quarter they moved me to the centre, I was going so well, and I was driving the ball into the square and even kicking goals . . .

He was in the stand among the St Kilda supporters; and all around him, I suppose, they were shouting for me, as they used to, come on the Bastard, the Bastard, the Bastard . . .

Later, after the game, while we were having a beer at the pub, before he took me to dinner, he said to me: John, it's never been easy for you, I know, and I'm very proud of you . . .

Lying here on the big green table under the hooded lights in this dusty basement, the sweat of the afternoon damp on my face, I can neither understand nor forgive, I am simply afraid to see him, afraid in case I begin to punch him and can't stop . . .

•

Small, furtive noises from the dim woodwork shop beyond the doorway. Soft shuffling in the sawdust, minute creakings, almost not there at all. I lie there on the table, cushioned like a pasha, and wait, knowing somehow who it is . . .

In a moment or two a shadow separates itself from the other shadows and there she is, tall and straight and a true gift, all brightness and courage. She's wearing a faded sundress, shoulder to knee, thin straps, and she stands, gentle-eyed, not moving, just watching me.

'You found me,' I say. 'Now you know my secret.'

She says nothing, merely smiles a little.

'How *did* you find me?'

The smile deepens, shows white teeth slightly crooked. There is no movement to the air, it's still as a tomb down here beneath the rattling, rowdy wards; yet her hair seems almost to move of itself – long, thick, tawny, some deep richness swaying slowly like soft weed in the currents of a tidal pool.

For a while after I arrived I was very cautious about her. Too attractive, too beautiful, too sexy. Yet she was the only thing alive in this place. One day I was alone in the therapy room with her, she still restless, wandering, coming back, losing matches, smoking in fits and starts. She got up suddenly, left, passing Paddy in the doorway. He came in clasping his battered guitar, wiry grey hair awry, eyes a little wild, half a century of ravages on his face. Sat himself down opposite me, began to strum his guitar.

'Listen,' he says, begins to sing. His voice is loud, rough, almost frightening.

'The trees in the forest, they bear strange fruit,
And only the blackbirds singing;
The leaves are all gone from the forest now,
And only the black fruit swinging . . .'

He pauses. 'You like that? I made it up . . .'

'Yeah, it's very good. It's bloody frightening, though.'

Leaning on his guitar, he peers at me. 'You want to be careful with Petra.'

'What do you mean, careful?'

'She's a very attractive girl.'

'Yeah.'

'She's very young.'

'So what?'

'I've seen you looking at her.'

'What about you? You do your share of staring.'

'It's different for me. That's all over for me now, I've drawn up my testicles . . .'

And he gets up, restless, and wanders away, twanging.

●

Now, as she stands in the shadows looking at me, I remember what he said. And it's true enough, you don't have to be a genius to see how vulnerable she is. But then, who isn't? And it's not like I'm an old man. The truth is that sexual tension runs between us like a tightly strung wire. I can't describe it really. But just the thought of her, the merest thought, makes a kind of raging in me . . .

'Well,' I say, 'don't just stand there, buy something.'

She looks blank.

I wave a hand at her. 'Come aboard.'

She approaches, smiling slowly, a little secretly, perches herself on the edge of the table, slips one hand into a corner pocket, pulls out a ball. Blue. Rolls it slowly under her palm on the smooth, green cloth.

'How did you find me?' I say.

'I watched you,' she says, voice low, the faintest hint of a stutter, a minuscule syncope in her speech. 'For the last week. I wondered,' and she raises her eyes, looks at me, 'I wondered where you disappeared to . . .'

And she stops rolling the ball under her hand, sits very still. The whole day seems to slow, slow, stop. The air itself seems to lose its value, as if the world is ending. Her eyes seem huge.

'Come here,' I say, and my voice is hoarse and flat, and seems to falter a little.

And, very slowly, she slides off the table, and begins to take off her clothes.

•

'Why did you do that?' she asks me later.

'What?' Spent, very drowsy. We're lying soft and slick among the strewn cushions.

'That,' she says, rising on her elbow, pointing down at the green baize. 'It's all right, you know, I'm on the pill.'

I look down at the stain of darker green on the baize. It looks vaguely like a map of Ireland.

'I'm making an atlas,' I say. 'Ireland for a start. We'll begin small, go on to bigger things . . .'

She looks at me curiously, a little sleepily, saying nothing. It seems impossible that only minutes ago she was calling, crying, over and over, Oh God Oh God Oh God . . .

17

'The continents may be too much for me, all in one go. I may have to do it State by State . . .'

'Why do you hate yourself?' she asks, quietly.

Once, on a very wet muddy day, I folded over a torpedo pass and the ball, hard and greasy, slid through my hands and hit me like a bullet in the balls. Dropped me. Now, just like that, a kind of paralysis falling on me from a great height, a freezing terror and an awful loneliness. I hide my face in the hollow of her throat, bury it in the sweetness of her hair, hold her very tight, and feel her small hands smoothing me, gentling me, as she might do to a very frightened horse.

And then, bugger me if we don't fall asleep, stark naked both of us, stark bollocky naked under the big lights on the wide, green atlas, just the two of us and the drying map of Ireland . . .

•

The next morning I sleep late, miss breakfast entirely. When I finally get up I trot along to the kitchen for a Maxwell House. In the corridor, at the top of the stairs, Herbie is on duty. Thin as an old tree root, about as grey. Pyjama top buttoned decently to the throat, daks down round his ankles, his lean shanks – and all the rest – exposed to the day. Likes to stand where the visitors see him first thing as they come up the stairs. I grab his trousers and reef them up, tie them in place. He resists, he's as strong as an old bull, obstinate. From a few yards along the corridor I look back. His daks round his ankles again. His jaw's tight and quivering. With laughter, maybe . . .

Someone's been into my coffee jar again, the level's fallen, and there are smears on the lid. Coffee, you buy yourself; tea is free. My God, my God, why hast thou forsaken me? *Mene mene tekel upharsim* . . .

Friday it is, yesterday a world away, dismissed, conjured away by the marvels of pharmacology, fish for lunch, fish and chips, and I eat two helpings. Always hungry now, wolf the first one, race in for the second. I get no exercise, I'm putting on weight . . . Go for a run maybe . . .

And I'm thinking of running, thinking of the old days and the start of training before the summer's even properly gone, and running, sweating in shorts and sandshoes, through the hot suburban streets, and no one even *thinking* we're mad . . . They knew who we were, nodded seriously, called after us with little family watch cries . . . we were the warriors of the tribe . . . pad, pad along on the hot footpaths . . .

So, I'm thinking of running, sitting at the little table with Petra and Paddy, when Rene makes her break. Talk of running, she moves like a good centreman, weaving through the packs, between the tables, past two wardsmen, feints at a nurse, out the door, down the stairs with all of them in hot pursuit. But she's got the break, five yards on them, ten as she hits the foyer, and they'll never take her alive. She's in her fifties – tiny, thin, miserable, with a face like a sad little dog – and this is her third break. Thinks that her husband will get a bill for her stay here, won't be able to pay, and they can't make her understand that it's all free. Personally, I think she just likes to run. She was away a whole day and a night last time. The pharisees found her five miles away in the scrub, right outside the city. Her legs are still bandaged from the cuts and scratches. The coppers are probably worse, stumbling in the dark through the prickly mimosa . . .

Paddy is restless, talking all the time. Can't seem to stop. Not really rubbish – it makes sense of a kind – just that he won't stop. Petra is quiet, maybe sensing that she's only a heartbeat off the action herself.

'Come on,' I say to her, 'let's go and have a game of table tennis.' We play for half an hour, and I beat her two out of three. When I first came here she used to beat me all the time. Not good, the Bastard can't take that sort of thing.

'I'm going for a swim,' she says at last, clattering her bat on the table-top. 'Want to come?'

I shake my head. I've seen her bikini hung on the line to dry. I'd love to see her in it, gives me a dry mouth just thinking about it. But I'm stuck here for the present. They'd let me go, probably like me to go. But I'm just not certain . . .

'No,' I say. 'I think I'll lie down for a while.' Then she's gone and the day seems suddenly empty, dull.

Two elderly ladies, demure in floral dresses, pass the table. Behind them is old Charlie, the castle's resident casanova. Round, silent, cheerful. He gooses one of the ladies, gently, smiling. She shrieks, her blue hair standing on end. Charlie, still smiling, disappears into one of the wards. The old lady looks at me indignantly, then at her companion.

'They shouldn't allow people like that in here . . .'

She turns away, still full of indignation. But under it all I'll bet she's excited. It's made her day. God knows what this place would be like if they didn't keep our libidos in order, saltpetre in the soup and so on. Everyone seems to think about it all the time anyway – Herbie with his daks down, Charlie goosing the ladies, the nurses telling dirty stories at breakfast time, Paddy watching me watch Petra . . .

In the dayroom someone tells me that Rene has been sighted near the City Mission. Police cars rushed to the scene, but I'll bet Rene has moved on already, disappeared into thin air . . . more power to her . . .

Find myself thinking of the outside again. Well, maybe it's getting closer. I'm actually thinking of the mechanics of it all. Money, transport, clothes, all that sort of stuff. The logistics of escape. One day I'll go . . .

•

'One day I'll go,' I tell Petra at teatime. The late sun beats in through the gaps in the dining room curtains, flashing off cutlery, chrome, bald heads. 'Just piss off.'

'Where to?' She is calm, cool, a little distant tonight. Her hair still damp from her swim.

'I don't know. Just do a geographical. Maybe Queensland. I know about one place up in the Gulf country . . . Carbine Creek.'

'Have you been there?'

'No.' I laugh. 'But I might have made it if I hadn't ended up in here.'

She looks puzzled, lights a cigarette.

'I worked for one of a group of companies, see, mining companies. And Carbine Creek's one of their mines. Copper. It's so far away, so bloody awful, so bloody isolated, that no one will stay there if they can help it. So, whenever anyone misbehaves in the other companies . . . drinks too much, screws the bosses' wives, punches the policeman once too often . . . well, they don't get the sack, they just get sent to Carbine Creek.

'Why do they go?'

'Better than the sack, I suppose. You see, there's a black book. You get your name in it, you never get a job again with any mining company in Australia. Serve your time at Carbine Creek, you get another chance . . .'

'Would you really go there?'

'I don't know. Maybe. Winter's coming on.'

She blows smoke out through her nose, not looking at me. 'Could I come too?'

I smile at her. 'How could I go without you?'

Paddy comes in, sits down.

He's getting worse, more nervous and restless, and at the same time more euphoric.

'God is love,' he says, 'that's the message.'

I look at him. Very twitchy. Petra looks at her plate.

'It's simple,' he says. 'You know, don't you? Christ is the answer, Christ gives love to the world, the world has to give love to Christ. Simple, isn't it?'

•

I watch Paddy carefully for the next day or so. I can hardly help it. He seems to be everywhere. He's stopped taking his pills, and he's getting higher and higher – you'd swear he was stoned, a kind of insane euphoria that grows and grows until he's sweating and trembling like a wire that's screwed up too tight, vibrating under its own tension . . . And all the time I keep thinking, well, this is Petra, without her pills . . .

He doesn't eat, he doesn't seem to sleep, just wanders about in short pyjamas and dressing-gown. His eyes get redder and wilder, and his hair sticks up on end. He smokes incessantly, the stubs trembling in his stained fingers, blistering his skin as they burn down.

Breakfast time, and he's there waiting when I go in for an early coffee, sitting at the table opposite the door, where he can pounce on everyone as they arrive. I sit down at his table. Poor bugger, you just can't ignore him.

'Yes,' he says, only half looking at me. 'Yes, yes . . .'

Then: 'Christ, the question and the answer.' Eyes suddenly swivelling to fix me full-on, knee jerking up and down, ciggie trembling in his burnt fist. 'You know that, don't you? Christ is love, love is Christ, simple as that, isn't it?'

'That's right, mate . . .'

Petra comes in, ignores us, sits at another table with Mrs Dell, who is getting the sparks for depression. She lives alone and worries because her son won't visit her, and because worrying is something to keep her occupied. This morning on the point of tears, mouth down in made-up face, pearly-grey hair immaculate. Nice, motherly lady abandoned in red-brick suburbia.

'Yes,' says Paddy, 'that's it, that's it.' He leans forward, aims himself like a pointer at Mrs Dell. 'Christ is love, love is Christ . . . that's the answer.'

Mrs Dell peers at him a moment, bursts into tears.

'For Christ's *sake*, Paddy,' says Petra, 'shut *up*.' She puts an arm round Mrs Dell's shoulders.

'Come on, mate,' I say, 'let's go for a walk.' I take him off along the passage. Herbie is standing at the nurses' station, trousers round his feet, frozen like a bloody statue. Paddy stops and moves in on him, puts an arm round him.

'Christ is the message and the messenger,' he says, mouth close to Herbie's ear. 'Love is Christ, and Christ is love, right? Simple as that.'

I leave them together and go back into the dining room. It's a dull, quiet morning. Everyone is on edge about Paddy.

I'm in the middle of my liver and bacon – I even eat *that*, I get so hungry – when Paddy comes back. Stands beside one of the long tables crammed with little old ladies, all depressed and sharing it round, and gives them the message for the day. They try to ignore him, grumble at each other: They oughtn't to let him go on like this . . .

Petra won't meet my eye. I fancy she knows what I'm thinking. No map-making today.

•

All through that day and the next it goes on. And on and on. No relief, no respite. He wanders everywhere, merciless, vocal and implacable. Building to some climax that doesn't even bear thinking about. One of the nurses tells me that people like him can really die of exhaustion if they don't hit their peak in time . . . He's trembling in earnest now, really shaking. There are cigarette burns all over his dressing gown, his eyes are red and wild. And the endless talking . . .

The awful euphoria of it seems to be tearing him apart.

In the night of the second day I can see him from my bed as he roams the corridors, drifts of smoke and ash and pain following him through the hours. By that time we are all just so tired of it that all we want in the world is for it to stop. I doze for an hour or so at a time, wake finally about six and it's just getting light. Know I won't get back to sleep, so I get out, get dressed, meaning to go along and make a cup of coffee. Then suddenly there comes the sound of scruffling, grunting – strange low animal sounds out in the corridor.

As soon as I hit the passage I see him. He's lying on the floor, groaning, twisting, shaking. One of the wardsmen is holding him, leaning down on his shoulders, trying to stop the convulsions. I stand there a long moment. He's shit himself, and his body is smeared with it, and for a moment his face is turned my way, eyes blind and hopeless, the black hole of his mouth stretched wide in a soundless scream. I turn away then, go back and lie down on my bed, my face buried in the pillow, trying to shut out the small, terrible sounds from outside.

By breakfast time the corridor is back to normal. The curtains are drawn over the windows on the observation ward where they have put Paddy. I peer round an edge and see him lying unconscious on his rumpled bed, still as death. One of the sisters comes up behind me.

'He'll be all right now,' she says. 'He's sleeping.'

The dining room is subdued, even the little old ladies seem to have forgotten their complaints. There's an air of sullen relief over everything. That awful voice has stopped. I think that at some time each one of us has wished him dead; then been immediately ashamed.

And I think: What in Christ am I doing in this place?

I know quite well, of course. At least, I think I do.

I hate the world outside because I have changed into something that disgusts me, while *it* has stayed the same.

I hate myself because, having made my peace with what I believed was reality, I find that after all these years there's another step down that I have to take if I'm going to survive . . .

And while I stay here I'm protected from the necessity of doing anything at all. I'm suspended in some sort of Hades.

But I know that I have to do something sooner or later. And Byrne the Bastard, the terror of the VFL rucks, the man who tamed big Kooka Lawes, is scared shitless . . .

But he knows that, if he is going to make it, he's going to have to make some kind of odyssey, see what the world looks like through his brand-new periscope . . .

Make no more green maps, then, but get on the real road . . .

And what about Petra?

Don't think about *that*, not right *now* . . .

Shit scared.

•

Lying on my bed, eyes closed, I find myself thinking about when I was a kid, before any of this stuff ever started. Somehow the landscape of childhood is stamped on us pretty indelibly. I mean, I've spent so little time in the valley since I was seventeen that you'd think I would have forgotten it. But it doesn't work that way – instead it gets burned deeper each year. And, of course, unlike most other places, it doesn't seem to change much at all.

It's hard to believe, what with the snags and silted bed, the weedy banks and the great blackberry coverts, that the river used to take schooners right up to the bridge where the hotel now stands, so white and solid. They would float or haul the logs down from the back country, load them aboard the ships with a great horse crane. Nothing slow or sleepy about it then . . .

Anyway, even if it was slow and sleepy when I was a kid, it was never dull. Only quiet. And in the big old hotel with its log, brass-bound bar, its wide fireplaces that would take four-foot logs, its enormous echoing kitchen, there seemed to be a kind of safety, a kind of protection. Apart from Mrs Billings the cook, Alf Yaxley the barman and yardman, and the part-time maids, there was only my grandfather and my mother, Nancy. And if Nance was a little taut and cool, a little unmotherly at times, a little removed from my noisy passions, there was – at least for much of the time – Auntie Cake.

Kate – Auntie Cake – was my dead grandmother's sister, which made her my great-aunt. But until I grew up she was always Auntie Cake and, after that, just plain Kate. There was little enough reason on the surface for her to have kept up her contacts with my grandfather; she must have been very different from my grandmother, by all accounts, and certainly she and my grandfather had barely anything in common. Yet she was always accepted as a family member, of right, and has stayed that way. I sometimes suspect – in later years, at least – that it may have been on my account.

She puzzled lots of people, Kate. She would probably have been more of a puzzle to me if she hadn't been there much of the time while I was growing up. She would appear every month or so, 'for a rest', stay a week or two, then be off again. She was born in 1906, and that made her a year younger than grandfather, so she must have been about forty when I first remember her. My God, that first recollection . . . The beach, the long sweeping beach to the west of the river mouth, bright tin bucket, wooden spade, a blue overall thing with straps over my shoulders, a yellow sunhat like a rag sou'wester. About three years old, I was . . .

Summer, and the beach bright, golden, dazzling. But not half as dazzling as Kate herself. Those were the days of modestly skirted and unflattering swimsuits for ladies; Kate wore a gold lamé suit so brief and so daringly unskirted that it was a scandal even years later, and she shone more brightly than the day. I remember thrusting my face into her golden groin, smelling the exotic perfume of her thighs, looking up into her smooth face, at her plucked and arching eyebrows, at her piled, golden curls. She smiled, smiled at me, preened, and – I swear – flirted with me. Even then. She needed, she always needed, maleness about her. Even now, when she must be what? sixty-seven, sixty-eight, she still thinks of herself, I'm certain, as a sex object. And in the days of my childhood, when she was a mere forty or fifty, she was in her prime.

She was no great beauty, I suppose. Good bones, and she looked after her body as if it were the crown jewels. But nothing startling. It was just that she took enormous pains. And she flattered men, charmed them, even mesmerised them. She believed, I suppose still does, that she possessed an incredible and irresistible beauty. I don't think she was all that promiscuous, then or earlier. Or later, for that matter. It was just that she was oriented to sex the way a pointer is to game . . .

There was a great scandal in 1942, the year before I was born, when a black soldier drove all the way from Launceston to pick her up . . .

Dear Auntie Cake, she always spoiled me. But I'm not at all sure she would have done it if I'd been a girl child . . . But, for whatever reason, she brought a warmth and a joy to my childhood that I probably never would have known otherwise.

•

For the next few days I'm depressed and irritable. Petra very quiet. I suppose it was the business with Paddy that started it. Once, on a hot sticky afternoon, we are lying on the billiard table, half-asleep, map-making over, and she starts to tell me what it was like for her, the first time it happened. Not map-making, the other thing.

'I was fifteen,' she says, 'still at school. One day I just started to get high. It was funny. I'd tried marijuana once or twice, but this was different – not like grass – sort of focussed, more intense, more real.' She pauses, turns a little, lies staring up at the light canopy. 'I was walking along the road beside the beach, and the air seemed to get brighter all around me . . . and my head was sort of twisting about like a turret, and I could see things that I'd never seen before . . . and this little dog was walking along beside me, and it had no head, just all bloody . . . and the day got kind of purple . . . Another time I just got lost in the city, because everything was covered in blood, even the camellias in the park were bleeding, and I couldn't find my way . . . I couldn't even cross the streets . . .'

She is quiet for a while, then: 'It can happen anywhere. Even sometimes in here. Once, after I'd stopped taking my pills I thought that the doctors and staff and everyone were Irish cannibals and they were getting ready to eat me . . .' And she giggles. I'm appalled.

'Is it always going to be like that?'

'I don't know,' she says. 'The doctors say that it just might go away some day, when I'm older. They've got some sort of graph, there's a pattern . . . but I don't know.' She turns to look at me. 'I can't ever have kids. I mean, I mustn't . . .'

There's no answer to that. 'What about the rest of your family?' I ask her.

'There's only mum,' she says. 'She's all right. My father died when I was little. Mum's all right, but I don't get on with Freddie.'

Her courage chills me. Or maybe it's my own lack of it. Four years she's had heaps of that kind of crap, and she's accepted it, goes on living with no fuss at all. Whatever's wrong with me I don't see headless dogs and Irish cannibals . . .

•

That night, lying in my bed, I realise that something has to be done. The old boy's stuck on a teenage schizo. Pinned at last, face it. How do you know? How *couldn't* you know? It's never been like this before, so don't kid yourself. All the high-class screwing in the big years, nothing. With Petra it's like another world; colours, sounds, smells, everything – on another planet, mate. And the sex is just the start of it.

So get out. Before it's too late.

Because one day, if you stay, you'll have to watch her the way Paddy was. And you don't want that.

But you're a long way down the tunnel already, killer. Get out, it's time to go.

So, down to the mechanics of it. Well, the pharisees may be waiting for me. No one's said anything about that. So best go gently. I know, quite suddenly, where I'm going. But how to get there? Money and a few bits of paper needed. Money, that's the difficulty. Can't go near my bank account, they'd be on me like a flash. About forty bucks in my kick from the money Kate sent me. A starter. Bits of paper, then. And I know where to get *them*.

•

Getting out of this place is simple enough. But I don't want to go with trumpets, not like Rene. Out through the laundry, then, into the backyard, over a couple of fences, through a couple of gardens, and you're in the street. I calculate that I need about four hours, and that's the sticky part. Most everybody in bed and tucked up by eleven o'clock, bar the late TV watchers, who wouldn't know if you were up them anyway. Shift change at midnight, again at eight in the morning. Best go after the incoming sister has done her round at midnight. This week old

Don the Weary Wardsman is on duty nights, so there'll be no between-time checks. A vehicle? Well, that will have to wait a bit. Could get one out of the clinic car park, but that's a bit obvious . . .

•

Next night the omens are auspicious. Well, I'm getting toey, too. Hate the delay now I've made up my mind. I've knocked off a screwdriver and a chisel from the workshop. Burglarious instruments, be arrested on sight. Also have a bit of metal foil from a ciggie packet. By twelve-fifteen all's quiet. I take up my position in the bed, huddled up, face turned away from the door, half-hidden by the blankets. A bit hot, but it won't be for long. Soon the wavering light of a torch from down the hall, and it's Sister Boone, built like a brick shithouse, going round her traps. Light briefly on my old mate Benjamin, gapping and snoring in the next bed. Then on me. A convincing mumble, bury my head deeper. The light goes away.

I give them a few minutes, then slip out of bed. On with my dressing-gown, tuck a small bundle of clothes inside my bosom, peep out into the corridor. Empty. Distant clinking from the kitchen, first cup of tea for the shift, all clear. If anyone sees me now, I'm just off to the crapper. But once past the end of the corridor, I'm committed.

At the corner, still all clear. Into the black laundry, bark my shins on an ironing board propped in the corner. It comes down with a great clatter. I wait for a couple of minutes, breathing slowly, but nothing happens. Out the back door and into the yard. Over by the fence under an enormous oak tree I shuck the dressing-gown, slip on jeans, dark sweater, runners . . . Bundle up the dressing-gown and pyjamas, stuff them in a hollow of the tree's roots. Then over the high paling fence I go, flying. A low wind moans round the building, through the trees. The moon is coming and going behind the clouds. There are enough night sounds to drown out my own. No dogs about, luckily. Cautiously through the side gate of the house and into the street. Mark the number for the return trip.

Down towards the city, padding along like a burglar through the dark streets. Autumn coming, chill in the night air. Four blocks away I find what I want. An old FJ that someone has done up. Locked, of course. But there was something about those old buggers . . . what was it? In a second I remember. Jump on the rear bumper and all the doors fly open. Holdens were always a bit idiosyncratic . . .

I look round carefully. It might seem a bit suspicious, dancing on an antique back bumper at twelve-thirty in the morning. No movement anywhere, no sign of life from the houses nearby, all blinds down.

A couple of cautious springs on the bumper.

Nothing.

A couple more.

Still nothing. Fuck it!

I take a running jump, hit it with all my weight. Sounds like Cobb & Co. on a bad day.

The doors don't fly open. But after a pause to see if any blinds have shot up, I inspect it, find that the nearside front door is sprung a little. Work carefully for a minute or two with the screwdriver, and I'm in. Lucky, and quicker than fiddling round with quarter lights and wire loops, which is a bit obvious to passers-by, anway.

I slip into the driver's seat, reach under the dash with my little bit of silver paper, fiddle it into place where the ignition wires meet at the back of the dash until the red dog's dick on the dash lights up. The gauge says the tank is nearly full.

I ease off the handbrake, let out the clutch. Luckily there's a gentle slope to the street. I run backwards, slip into reverse, bump her. Starts easily, the engine purrs away. Back round the corner. In the light of a street lamp I see that the car is a pale green, as anonymous as a French letter.

Seventy miles to go, and time enough. But I'm a little scared that in the next hour or so, on the lonely early morning road,

I'll have to think about where I'm going and what I'm doing. I begin to feel very nervous.

Forget the nerves, killer. Plant your foot.

•

Your mind tends to wander when you're driving on a familiar road. The well-known landmarks slip by, the hands and the seat of the pants guide the car through the bends, mind and imagination disengaged. It's odd that now I'm started I'm almost looking forward to the whole thing. Nerves still there all right, though. So what?

The night seems windier now, scattered clouds blown like puffballs across the bright, moonlit sky. The paddocks, the silent towns, the clumps of trees, all silvered and filigreed. Not much traffic, and soon a kind of bubble closes over me, and I can stop thinking for a bit.

But at last the final open stretch of paddocks ends, and I'm on the crest of the hill. Ease off the accelerator, swing down the old narrow bitumen that used to be the main road. The steep slope of the bank on the right, reaching up into the night, clothed in blackberry, hawthorn, wild box elder; downhill, to the left, falling away to the little creek winding bright as mercury in the moonlight, beds of sag and bulrushes, clumps of willows, the banks spotted with the caves of old rabbit-warrens. Near the bottom, the road stops winding, the slope flattens out and, the next thing, the brick post office with its neat tiled roof appears on the right.

The road spears straight ahead, across the narrow bridge, curves away across the rich river flats. A few Herefords stand still as statutes in the pastures by the river. On my right, the high walls of the hotel loom, I switch off the engine, coast to a stop in the shadows.

For a minute or so, I sit there waiting. To see if anything, anyone, is abroad. That's what I tell myself. Really, probably, to quieten the demons that are waking up inside me.

Off you go, killer . . .

The car door creaks loudly in the night air. I close it as gently as I can, pad quietly into the backyard. There should be a key – there's always been a key – on the third rafter along the verandah. I reach up, run my fingers along the dusty splintery beam. Key's still there. In a moment I have the back door open, and I'm in the kitchen. The old familiar smells are with me again, the smells of boyhood and innocence. Bon Ami, floor polish, roast meats, a faint tang of disinfectant, a whisper of stale beer from the bar. Moonlight through the big window over the sink floods the marble bench-top like water. The open doorway of the larder is a black cave. I find suddenly that I'm ravenously hungry.

I step into the larder, reach out and, as if by magic, put my hand on a plate of cold sausages. I take two, stand there in the darkness, chewing on the firm, spicy meat. I can even tell where they come from. Two miles east, along the road. Old Mac Kenny made them from wallaby, pork, tomato . . .

But I didn't come seventy miles and commit a number of crimes to eat cold sausages . . .

I wipe my hands on a tea-towel, still damp from the evening washing-up, and start out through the kitchen door, into the corridor. The stairs are to the right, a broad pale waterfall of light from the landing windows . . .

Remembering coming home late from a party, a date, up the stairs, trying to avoid waking anyone . . . knowing the old man would be awake and silent behind his door . . .

At the top of the stairs the corridor runs the length of the building, parallel to the river, with a dozen rooms off it. We always lived on the same corridor as the guests . . . like family they were, and that's how they were treated, unless they were noisy or drunken or indiscreet, and then the apparition of my grandfather would appear, tall and fearsome in the night, to quell them. They never argued . . .

At the far end, facing the river, my grandfather's rooms: bedroom, office, the two rooms connected. Then, across the corridor, my mother's, Nance's: two rooms again, bedroom and sitting room. Next, my own room, the room that was always kept for me, all through the years, even in the busiest times. Although those are long gone now . . .

Somehow I know that tonight none of the guest rooms is occupied. There is a quality about an unoccupied room that speaks as loud as words if you have lived much of your life in a hotel. A quality of emptiness . . .

I leave the shadowed brightness of the landing, set off along the corridor, pad, pad, pad . . .

The doorknob of my old room turns easily, the door opens soundlessly, and I'm inside. The moonlight almost blinds me, shining in like a floodlamp through the window that opens on to the yard, the climbing hillside beyond.

My eyes swing across the familiar room – the great heavy wardrobe, the captain chairs, the desk, dresser, bed . . . *bed* . . .

There's someone in the bed, and I freeze, begin to ease the door open behind me, ready to slip out again . . .

But there's something familiar about the shape of the head on the pillow, the spread of blonde hair more silver tonight than chemical gold . . . It's Auntie Cake, and my heart slows its thumping. I shut the door again.

My feet make no sound on the thick carpet as I cross to the bed. But as I look down at her, her eyes open and she lies there looking up at me, unsurprised and languorous as if I were an expected lover.

'What are you doing in my bed?' I ask foolishly, too loudly.

'Shhhh . . .' She smiles a little. In the clear moonlight the fine wrinkles about her eyes and mouth form delicate networks. 'I thought you might come,' she whispers.

'Why did you think that?' I keep my voice low, conscious of the other two sleeping so close.

'I don't know – I just did.' And she smiles. Her hands make small gestures of spurious modesty as she pulls the covers up about her breasts. I can understand why men pursue her; she seems always to move in a climate of desire. That she generates that climate herself, or mostly anyway, hardly matters. It's her ambience, and it has always been difficult to stay for long with her in a room without thinking about sex. She unsettles clergymen, I remember. I sit down on the bed, take one of her pale manicured hands, feel under my fingers the dry texture of her skin, smooth as silk.

'You're flirting with me, Kate,' I whisper. And she smiles a little, not denying it. For her, flirting is as natural as breathing. 'Why didn't you come to the clinic to visit me?'

'Would you have seen me?'

'I don't know . . .'

'Well, then.'

'How long have you been here? In the hotel?'

'Quite a while. Nancy rang me.'

'Did she tell you what happened?'

She nods.

I look at her for a bit, shaking my head slowly. I don't think anything would shock her. Certainly nothing to do with sex.

'All that silly business,' she says. 'Your wrist.' Why should any man want to cut his veins while Kate is alive and flirting?

'Did you know?' I asked her. 'Before, I mean?'

'Of course.'

'Jesus, and you're her *auntie* . . .'

She shakes her head impatiently.

'Christ,' I say, 'I'll bet you knew right from the beginning, when it was going on . . .'

She says nothing, just looks at me like a slightly frayed madonna.

'You're bloody disgusting, Kate.' I pull my hand away. The sickness is starting up again, and the room seems to be closing in . . . Kate's perfume, the sense of those two so close, the moonlight, the thought of other nights like this . . .

I stand up suddenly.

Kate raises herself on one elbow. 'Jackie,' she says, 'it just doesn't make any *difference*. You must *understand*. Knowing or not knowing . . . it can't make any difference to *what you are*.'

I turn away quickly, go to the other side of the room, to the desk, open the top left-hand drawer, pull out the big manilla envelope, check the contents, close the drawer.

As I turn back I look at her again. She's reclining there as if I'm some lover leaving her forever; forlorn, dramatic. I go back and kiss her forehead. 'Keep out of trouble . . .'

She smiles a little, pats my hand. 'Try and understand,' she says.

I close the door gently behind me and stand for a moment in the long corridor. There is no sound, no stir. But I am conscious of a strange presence pressing in around me, of old dry evils released, released when Nancy opened that door, the door that had stayed closed for so long . . .

Outside in the white night the pale gravel crunches under my feet. I look back at the great white box of the hotel with its steep grey roof and blind windows. The wind has dropped, and the only sound is the faint liquid chuckle of the river as it passes under the bridge. I jump into the car, coast down towards the bridge, start the motor, swing in a wide circle in front of the hotel, put my foot down and charge back up the hill. It is probably my imagination, but it seems that the curtains at one of the windows stir a moment, as if someone is watching . . .

After a mile or so I calm down a bit. I've got the paper anyway, and no one the wiser except Kate.

But as the road unwinds behind the car I find that I have difficulty shrugging off the thought of those two sleeping quietly at the end of the corridor. All those years . . . it gives me the horrors. I try to push the thought of the old man out of my head. Think of Nancy instead. She seems less threatening, somehow . . .

Nance . . . how old is she? Forty-seven, I think . . . seventeen when I was born . . .

She's what you'd call a handsome woman, I suppose – slim, a bit angular these days, but good bones; small, high breasts; long, dark hair, very soft, with a light curl to it . . . A beauty when she was younger, I guess . . . But something about her, something always checked, held in. She seemed always so totally contained, held hard on a leash of some kind.

Ah, hell, think of something else, killer, leave her behind with everything else, no room for passengers on the old geographical . . .

Somehow it seems almost appropriate in this mad world that my life should be ruined by no more than a belly ache. Would I have it the other way, now? Not knowing, the years piling up on me in ignorance? Christ knows . . . once you know, you can't imagine *not* knowing. . . . . And you can't uneat the apple anyway . . .

I drove up to the coast that day to see Fenton's solicitors, to see if there was anything to be done, his trial starting the next day. In the evening, deciding to stay overnight at the hotel, to leave for the three-hour drive back early in the morning.

So after tea we sat talking, the three of us – Nance and the old man and me – everything normal, nothing out of the ordinary; the old man smoking his pipe, asking questions about the job, about the strike just finished, about anything . . . Nance mostly silent, smiling quietly, slipping out occasionally to check on the girls cleaning the dining room, laying the tables for breakfast, washing up.

Sitting there, then, the three of us, drinking coffee, smoking . . . drinking coffee and smoking . . . boils down to that in the end . . . some joke . . .

I remember looking at the clock . . . five to nine. Then heard it, a kind of low groan, turned to find Nance leaning forward, looking a bit startled, anxious, fingertips of her right hand just touching her solar plexus.

'What's the matter?' It was the old man.

She shook her head slightly, looking preoccupied. Then, suddenly, she stood up. 'I'm going to lie down for a bit,' she said, and made off quickly. The old man was frowning. I don't think she'd ever been sick a day in her life.

In a minute he got up and followed her upstairs. Soon he was down again, filling a glass with water, taking the Dexsal bottle from the shelf. 'You'd better come up,' he said. 'I don't like the look of her . . .'

So I followed him up the stairs and into her bedroom, all silver and rose and regency wallpaper. She was lying under the grey Italian-brocade coverlet. There was sweat on her face, tiny beads on her forehead and upper lip, and she was groaning softly, clenching her hands.

'It's in her chest,' said the old man. 'I don't like it, I'm going to get the doctor . . .'

I sat down in the chair beside the bed, took her hand. I could see that she was biting her lip, trying to keep from calling out. But every so often a stifled groan would break out. Under the cover she was writhing slowly. I knew that the pain must be very bad, because she's something of a stoic. Once she drove a garden fork through her foot, then just pulled it out and washed and dressed it without flinching . . .

The old man came back. 'Parkie's not answering. He's probably next door playing crib.' Parkie is a retired and widowed doctor who lives alone three miles down the river road. 'I'm going to get him.'

I followed him to the door. 'What do you think it is?'

'Christ knows.' I could see how the lines in his face were deepened by concern. He looked suddenly almost a stranger. Then he was off, hurrying down the stairs again.

•

Stairs, those stairs, seem to haunt me all the way back to the clinic. Blue carpet – have you ever seen blue carpet in a hotel? Never; always red, dark brown, green . . . But ours is blue, thick and dense when I was a boy, thinner now from the passage of thousands of feet; but bright still, faint with forgotten patterns, brass rods golden against the unworn fabric of the risers . . . Feet – Nance, the old man, Kate, me . . . lovers, guests, strangers . . . the varnished banister smooth and dark and salty when I used to suck it . . .

Not far to go now, and only a couple of hours to dawn.

I drive sedately back in through the silent suburbs, down the long highway past the caryards and into the city. The gauge shows nearly empty, but I can't afford to leave the owner the money for a fill; it'll have to be his shout this time.

Turn in a block away from where I found it, run uphill past the spot, cut the engine, roll back silently and leave the car where it was parked before. Out quietly, ease the door shut. No sound, no lights, I've got away with it . . .

Envelope under my arm, back up the streets, hilly little side streets, until I find the gate I came through. Open it cautiously, slip down the path beside the house . . . roses, dusty oleanders, a big coprosma reflecting the streetlights like coins in its mirrors . . . over the fence, pick up my dressing-gown, pad across the gravel to the laundry door. It's still unlocked and I slip through. Head round the doorway into the passage. No one in sight. A clinking from the dispensary, that's all. Easy along the lino tiles, and into the dark room. Benjamin still snoring, trumpeting wide-mouthed at the ceiling. Traces of grey now in the night sky beyond the bars. The huddle in my bed undisturbed.

I'm remaking the bed, re-stowing my gear in the wardrobe, when I'm suddenly aware of a presence behind me. Look over my shoulder. It's the Weary Wardsman, leaning on the doorframe, belly bulging into the room.

'Where you been?' he asks, more interested than outraged.

'On the nest,' I say, 'Quick nick-in while her old man's on the night shift, eh?'

He chews on this a little. Then, still leaning against the jamb, raising his voice to carry over Benjy's snores: 'Could dob you in, I suppose . . .'

'Could do,' I say.

'Needn't though . . .' Pondering deeply. 'Not if it was worth my while . . .'

'Wouldn't bother, if I was you,' I say, ripping off my pants and climbing into bed. 'Someone might ask questions about all that scran that goes home in your black bag, mightn't they? Let's see, about forty pieces of fish last Friday, half a ham on the weekend . . .'

He sniffs loudly, stands a little straighter. 'I was only joking, you know . . .'

'Course you were.' Sheets tucked up to the chin. 'No harm done, anyway, is there? Everyone to his own vice, eh?' I turn away, pull my covers over my ears against the morning chill and Benjy's obligato . . .

•

Well, Benjy's noise drowns out everything except what's going on in my head. I'm tired, but I can't get to sleep. All tensed up, trembling a little after my criminal rampage. Theft of motor vehicle – or is it only illegal use? burglary – but I used a key; theft – but I stole my own paper, which I'd already stolen from someone else . . .

Usually I can put myself off, if I'm having a bad night, by imagining I'm in a football match, one I've really been in, play it all through, kick by kick, as much as I can remember . . . like a game of chess . . . soon drop off, seldom even make half-time . . .

But tonight, this morning, I keep drifting off the field, losing track . . . a funny feeling, almost as if I can feel his eyes on me . . . up there in the stands with the others . . . *him* . . .

He was always proud of my football, even when I was at school. I think he knew how hard it had been for me at times, and how I'd coped, and why I played like I did . . . he never said anything much, not to me, but I've heard him in the bar, when he didn't know I was there, heard him drop a word or two . . .

But it chills me now, the thought of those eyes of his, blue-grey, keen . . . they seem to look right into your head . . . watching . . . And that night, as he's gone down the stairs, that new thing, that awful thing in them . . . a kind of fear that he was trying to hide . . .

Christ, when I think of all those years of hiding . . . I try to imagine sometimes what it must have been like for him . . .

For her, too . . .

And remembering her again, that night, on her bed, writhing under the grey brocade, breathing faster and faster, hyperventilating, the sweat gathering in pools in the corner of her eyes, her hand gripping mine so tightly . . .

'Is he gone?' she asked me, just after he left.

'Yes,' I said. I'd heard the front door close, the car start.

'I'm going to die,' she said. And she must have felt the tightening of my hand on hers. 'No, no,' and her eyes opened, she squinted hard at me through the pain, 'don't talk, don't argue, just listen . . .'

She closed her eyes again, tried to stop the twisting of her body. 'About your father,' she said.

And, Oh Jesus, I thought, who gives a stuff right now . . . because all she'd ever told me over the years was that she'd loved him, but that there were reasons why she couldn't tell me his name, and anyway he was dead . . . So I squeezed her hand, and I said: 'It doesn't matter now . . . just lie quiet.'

'Your grandfather,' she said, and there was a high strained note in her voice, a heightened pitch, beyond the pain, as if she were reaching for something, some release . . .

'He doesn't know,' I said, 'he told me so long ago.'

And suddenly she reared up, her chest arched, her eyes staring, face twisted with some effort that had nothing much to do with the pain. 'Don't you understand,' she said, in a kind of whispered scream, *'it was your grandfather!'*

I stared at her dumbly, feeling my forehead crinkle up. Couldn't take it in, could you, killer? Is there a word for that? I shook my head . . .

'I'll kill him,' I said. It came out pat, like someone in a play. Nothing I really meant, nothing connected with me. And, just like in a play, I got up, let go her hand, started across the room towards the door. Moving quite slowly. At the doorway her voice pulled me round. This time it came out as a real scream.

'You fool! Don't you understand? I *wanted* him to do it! I *made* him! Can't you *see*, I *loved* him! I *still* love him . . .'

But I was gone by then, careering down the stairs, vomiting in little gouts all over the blue carpet, down the front of my shirt. Outside the front door I paused, looking back into the building, wiping my mouth. Wanting to do something, burn it down, I don't know. Then the sound of a car approaching from down the river road; and I couldn't bear the thought of meeting him, seeing him. So I jumped into my blue Volvo and roared off westward towards the mine and Christ knows what else . . . Screamed across the bridge, burned rubber in second gear going up the hill towards the little shop and the school, then set the bloody car at full throttle down the highway, concentrating hard on keeping the wheels on the ground. Nearly lost her on one left-hand bend, came out of it with one wheel on the gravel on the wrong side of the road, the throttle flat to stop her from tipping. Then I steadied down a bit, still driving fast, but a bit more carefully. Fast, though. Fast enough so that it needed all my concentration all of the time just to stay on the road . . .

Trying not to think of anything else.

Certainly not of Nance dying back there . . .

Which is a good joke, because – as I found out later – ten minutes after I left, she was right as rain. Nothing but a gastric spasm, said Parkie after he took a look at her. Very painful, but not serious. Not even fatal. Just too much coffee, too many cigarettes.

So much for deathbed confessions.

•

I hate going to sleep, because eventually you have to wake up. It's like when someone dies: you don't remember it in that first moment of waking, and then it all floods back worse than ever . . .

It's been like that. After the first moment I'm submerged again in nausea, horror, revulsion . . .

In the daytime I try to remember it all the time, what I am. So there's no sudden shock. Doesn't always work. Sometimes, with Petra, or reading, I forget . . . then it all rushes back, twice as bad.

That first night, driving like fury down the long, dark highway, the last couple of hours with only a few barely lit hamlets, only the darkness of the bush, I stayed in a kind of daze. I felt as if I wanted to dive into something, something that would wipe it all away, just dive in. But into *what*?

I've seen blokes do that when things go wrong – they make the big dive. Into grog, or sex, or drugs, or anything that numbs them for a while. But I had the feeling then, still have it, that if I made the dive, any dive, then I'd just be taking everything with me, that it would be there inside me all the time, and nothing would ever dull it, change it, numb it, even for a little.

Trouble was, I couldn't look at it then – the revulsion, the sickness, was too strong. It wasn't something I'd done, either, something that I could undo. Not something to be removed by confession, contrition. It was *me*, finally, irrevocably me, a fushion of genes as absolute as a gravestone . . .

It was late when I passed the mine. About one o'clock. The afternoon shift finished, the night shift started, the mine and the mill with only the night-time lights, yellow and lurid, a few scattered figures coming and going, a Wagner ore-carrier grinding up the long slope to the crusher. The admin block and offices dark. It had only been a couple of days, but it seemed then to me as if it was all years in the past, and no connection with me at all. I was just passing the town boundary when, slowing for the big curve, I remembered Fenton, and swung the car off to the right at the first turn instead of carrying straight on to my own place. I seemed to freeze up then, in a kind of gelid rage. Turning into the street where he lived, I remembered that it was already tomorrow, that it was the day he would stand trial.

The front of the house was dark, the familiar stereotyped company house, but there was a light burning somewhere in the back. I hauled the car into the drive and was out before it stopped rocking. Up the steps, punched open the kitchen door.

He was there, Fenton, tall and lean, thick dark hair gleaming under the single light, with his fat little blonde wife – who looked a whole generation older tonight – and his mate from next door. Waiting for something to happen, waiting for a miracle.

Well I wasn't a miracle, but I was a happening.

I hit him between wind and water, once, not too hard, because I didn't want it to be over too quickly. His wife backed away, hand over her mouth. His mate moved forward and I looped one to the side of his head. He sat down on the floor and blinked a bit. Then I hit Fenton again. Belly, belly, face. He opened his mouth to say something, his eyes filled with pain and puzzlement. And I hit him again. He went down on all fours, stuck there like a dog, sicking on the floor. I was disgusted then, disgusted with myself and with him, with the whole useless fucking world, and I went outside and hung on his porch a bit, sobbing away to myself.

I was staggering a bit by the time I made the car, feeling weak and light-headed. The truth was, I'd always liked Fenton, never believed it was true. Had taken the time off to go visit his solicitors to see if there was anything the company could do, that I could do. And that earnest young slizziter, all dark-suited and book-bound, had pulled out the file and shown me the girl's statement, his daughter's statement . . .

'. . . and he used to come into the bathroom when I'd had a bath or a shower and he'd take off his clothes and make me hold him . . . and he'd come on all over the towel . . . and when I'd done something wrong he'd say to me, what do you want, a beating or the other? And I'd always say a beating, but he'd take me out in the station wagon anyhow, out into the bush by the river and he'd get me in the back and he'd do it to me . . . sometimes he'd come inside me and sometimes he'd do it on me . . .'

And when I'd seen it, read it, I'd been sick and horrified . . . because, if it wasn't true, how could a fifteen-year-old girl know all that, what it was like, all that about coming on a towel . . . and then I knew that that was how a court would think, and I thought about that bloody fifteen-year-old slut, and about how many times I'd found her in the single men's quarters late at night, going from one man's room to another, and in the morning, naked and hiding in a wardrobe . . . and taking her home, and her mother making me promise not to tell Fenton . . .

And I'd really believed that Fenton was innocent, that that little bitch just had it in for him . . .

Then, suddenly, on that moment of passing the town boundary I'd known that he was guilty, that he *had* done it, that no matter how fat and ugly his wife was, no matter how depraved the girl, no matter what, he was guilty; he'd fucked his own daughter, and I wanted to kill him . . .

I found myself driving down the back road that led past the old church, the C of E, with its bare, grey, stone walls pale and blank in the night. And there was a spray can of orange paint in the glove box from the week before when I'd been spraying markers on my gateposts, and I hauled the car over, nearly going into the table drain, and I stumbled out and up the path and across the rank grass. And I made my accusation in bright Dayglo paint on the pale stone . . . FUCK GOD, I wrote, and then stumbled back to the car.

By this time things were piling up on me, and I was running fast through doors that I wouldn't be able to open again, heading for places there was no coming back from. The nausea was back again, in fits and starts, and I was choking and sobbing, and I wanted to kill someone, destroy something, leap out into the dark where there was nothing at all, nothing . . . but mostly I was just so sick at the thought of myself alive and healthy, all that tainted blood pumping through me . . .

Before I knew it, the mine entrance was coming up, and I was swinging off the highway and down the slip road. Inside the yellow aquarium that was the security office, lit like a refrigerator with the door open, sat old Aspro the Slow-working Dope, peering out at me like a groper under a rock. He waved at me, used to my comings and goings, and relapsed into coma, thick as two planks.

I ran my car into the general manager's slot, just because it was closest to the front door. Found the key on my car-ring, opened up, and went down the foyer, panelled and musty, filled with the stale traces of cigarettes and furniture oil.

There's something about an empty office at night. It seems to have a life of its own. All those little buzzings and clickings and tickings that you never hear during the day, and the sense of all those stupid machines crouched under their covers, haunted by the memories of all the mindless crap they've absorbed over the years.

The general office is as big as a tennis court, and about as cheerful, and at the far end are two offices, little glass cubicles – one the accountant's, one mine. I sat in my chair and looked back down the length of the office, down the passage that leads past the receptionist's desk and into the technical warrens of the geologists and mining engineers and surveyors. All dark, my own little cube the only place lit.

For some odd reason, habit took over, made me look first in my in-tray, riffle through the small pile of papers there. Stupid.

For a minute or so I sat there in my swivel chair staring at the blank primrose wall in front of me. My mind had been blank since I came through the boom gate. Now it all started to come back again. I opened the top left-hand drawer, rooted among the odds and ends of stationery. Gem blades, a whole pack of them, single-sided, all still in their cardboard wraps. I took one out, tested the edge. Then I took off my coat, hung it on the back of my chair. Lay my left arm on the desk. Rolled the sleeve up. As an afterthought, rolled the other one up as well. Then I took the blade between finger and thumb of my right hand, flicked off the cover, took a good grip.

Stopped for a moment, looking down at the blade, the wrist. I could hear the rising drone of a car engine somewhere.

OK, killer, I thought: Do it now . . .

A single deep cut that opened like a mouth, blood pulsing like semen. Very little pain. I sat, mesmerised by the blood that spurted, flowed all over my desk blotter, on to the steel desk top. Somehow there didn't seem to be enough though. I'd thought it would come like a fountain . . .

Looking at it, looking at the blood, thinking: That's the fucking stuff, look at it . . .

I almost forgot about the other wrist, just watching it escape, feeling cleaner, lighter, already, all that foul shit pouring out. Still, one more to go. Shadows seemed to move in the darkness down the corridor, beyond the spill of light from my office. Maybe going off a bit, seeing things . . .

I changed the blade to the other hand, turned the wrist to catch the light. The blade was a bit slippery with blood now, and difficult to hold. I stopped, squinted, trying to get a fresh grip. And out of the corner of my eye I saw him emerging from the dark alley of the corridor, moving fast now over the lino tiles, leaning forward as he came, sprinting, a big man coming very fast, like a solid half-back breaking free of a pack . . .

It was Rod Clifton, the local police sergeant. Big, dark, strong, about my age.

He careered through the doorway, hung there with one hand

on the jamb, his face pale and sallow in the flat lighting. He didn't say anything for a moment, just looked.

Then he ripped off his tie, moved towards me. 'That's enough,' he said. 'Quick, give us your arm . . .'

He reached out. It occurred to me that he must have been still on duty to have got there so quick, fully dressed and all. Tough egg. I've seen him put down some nasty drunken miners.

I pulled away from his hand, waved the blade gently at him. He looked down at the blood on the desk, at me again. 'You're bleeding pretty well, mate,' he said, 'we haven't got a lot of time.' He reached out again, and I pulled back again.

'Come on, Jack,' he said. 'Whatever it is, it's not worth this . . .'

I was trying to say something to him, to think of some smart answer, but my mind was slowing up a bit, the old clock not what it used to be, feeling a little distant about it all . . .

Then, suddenly, he was swarming over the desk at me like a fucking gorilla, one hand on my shirt-front, forearm across my throat, pressing me back towards the wall. I straightened my legs, came up out of the chair – very slowly it seemed – and slammed him sideways into the wall.

He shook his head. 'Jack,' he said, 'we haven't got *time* for this . . .'

Someone was breathing very hard. I think it was me. Maybe both of us.

Then he hit me with his left. He knows just where and how to hit you, the old Rod. I'm sure I could have taken him under normal circumstances, but I was feeling a bit – what's the word? – exsanguinated, and I hadn't even got my guard up when this ten-pound hammer hit me under the ear. Then, suddenly, I was lying on the floor and he was on top of me, kneeling on me, wrapping his tie round my arm, pulling it tight, grabbing me, leaning on me, holding me still. Whispering sweet and furious nothings in my ear, like: Stupid bastard, ya fucking idiot, and stuff like that . . .

I faded out for a bit, and when I came back the bright little office was filled with faces peering down at me: Aspro, Bandaid the ambulance driver, the GM (and I remember wondering where he parked his car), Rod, the doctor . . . . faces making a kind of family circle above me, looking down . . .

I cast a slow eye on my wrist. It was bandaged. My right sleeve rolled up higher, past my elbow, and a Bandaid in the elbow joint . . .

Faded a bit then, feeling a big pain in the side of my jaw where Rod hit me.

When I came to again I was in the ambulance and we were rocking and rolling along. In the dim light I could see the doctor sitting beside me, his hand on my good wrist. I could hear him talking to Rod . . .

'He's lucky, he just missed the big one. He took a good cut at it though . . .'

I turned my heard toward Rod, and found him looking at me.

'Christ, mate,' I said, 'you hit me a beauty there . . .'

He just shook his head. He was looking really concerned, the old Rod, and for a moment – just for a moment – I was sorry about it all. I looked up at the doctor.

'Haven't got a spare scalpel, have you, doc? I'll do a better job next time.'

The doctor ignored me.

'What are you going to do with him?' asked Rod.

'Well, I can't keep him down here . . . I'll sedate him, put him out till tomorrow. If he's all right then, I'll send him straight up to the clinic.'

And the next day, true enough, when I got to the clinic, who should be waiting for me but Purple Brewster, the barmaids' dream. 'God, you look sweet,' I told him. 'If you weren't a nigger I'd kiss you.'

•

I didn't do much in those first days except think of the old man. And I suppose that was normal enough. Because from the very beginning he had filled my world. Well, not filled it exactly – more like gave it flavour and meaning. It was as if everything I did as a boy, as a man even, had to be evaluated in terms of how *he* would see it. I never thought of Nance that way. Oh, I loved her, I suppose. She was always there, in her cool, self-contained way. But she didn't *share* my life, wasn't *inside* it, the way he was.

It's easy to think of him as a substitute father. But it wasn't that. Or maybe it was more than that, although he didn't really share all that much of my life in the way you usually think of sharing; he didn't take me camping, he never played games with me, or anything like that. He had the pub to run; and anyway, there was always that half-withdrawn quality to him, as if he'd retreated almost to the edge of life, and stood there all watchful and cautious. True, he taught me to fish, but not much else. Not that sort of thing. But he was always there, putting a value on things.

He didn't like some of the things I did, I know. But he wasn't critical, he just accepted it. For instance, he didn't like the way I turned myself into what I became. *Made* a bastard of myself. But he understood it, and the reason for it. He just felt – he never said it, but I knew – that I was too cold, too calculating about it . . . Once, when I was a kid, I asked him about my father.

'Dead and gone,' he said. 'Dead and gone, and we won't talk about him any more.' And we didn't.

I used to repeat that, later, when they'd say to me – at first cruelly, later just casually – Where's your father? or, What's your father do? Dead and gone, I'd tell them, dead and gone . . .

True enough, anyway. Gone, for certain. Dead, I thought. Well, alive for Nance still, I used to think, alive there in the circuits of her brain, his image still clear and sharp. And when she dies, I used to think, maybe they'll blank out and he'll be gone for good. Because he'd never been in my circuits, never touched me.

But the old man had.

He was in the circuits all right.

He never seemed to change much. He was tall, taller than me, and he never grew fat, despite his long days behind the bar or at his desk. His face, long and Irish, never grew lines the way other men's seemed to. His eyes were clear and very steady under the thick brows, very steady and very calm. Quiet, controlled, that was him. Smiled enough, but never laughed much. Not your usual publican.

He used to tell me the stories – on winter nights beside the fire, or walking in the pines on Sundays, or standing at evening by the tea-tree thickets at the river mouth – the stories about Old Jack Byrne, his father, who'd gone down into the West, to the country where I was to go later, gone there with his mate Gogarty at the turn of the century to find gold; how they packed their gear in through the rainforest looking for the creek, for the spot, their own cold creek; and how they'd spent the summer cutting firewood with crosscut and axe, stacking it in great piles – all myrtle from the forest, just like the pink and salmon logs we burned in winter in the bar and the upstairs fireplaces – and in the winter when the stream was swollen with the great rains they worked their creek, and nearly died of it; of how in the end Gogarty did die and Old Jack came out alone at last, came out again with forty pounds of gold in treacle tins on his back, came north and built the hotel the way he'd dreamed of doing; of how, until the day he died in 1939, the day that war broke out in Europe, he couldn't abide the sight of myrtle burning in the fireplace, and wouldn't have it on the woodheap or in the hotel, but would insist on stringybark or peppermint, because that lovely close-grained timber reminded him too much of that winter in the bush with Gogarty; and of how, when they wanted to floor the local hall with myrtle boards for dancing, he treatened to move away and close the pub, and made them change their minds . . .

The locals still spoke of Old Jack when I was a boy: Berry the Postmaster, who had grown up by the river, and whose uncle had been a harbourmaster; Grant the dairy farmer; and Tas Trebilco the carrier – they spoke of Old Jack as if he were the first settler or something, a biblical patriarch almost, which was nonsense, because the town was founded long before *he* arrived. But because he had been so much in their minds and lives, I was never just Jack, or Jackie, but *Young* Jack . . .

Years later, when I'd finished with football and gone down the West to work, I went to Tullah and found what must have been Old Jack's jumping-off place when they went bush. I stood there in the rain on a little wooden bridge and looked west towards the place they had gone to, one creek lost among a thousand others, and towards Gogarty's grave, who had stayed there; and it seemed then – as it did later, when I walked about that miserable old town, that ghost city that had been alive and booming when Old Jack was grubbing for his gold – that in some strange way it was just like coming home . . . But now, looking back, I think it was probably just a bad case of imagination.

God knows, it's not an impressive place, that town. The sky seems to hang lower there, mostly wet and grey. Only at the height of summer does that country seem to belong to the rest of Australia. Then it is hard and blue and brown, mud turns to dust overnight, leaves turn to tinder, sweat starts, skin burns. Summer lasts six weeks, two months, and for the rest of the year the land is submerged in one long, grinding winter. It starts to rain, and may hesitate briefly six weeks later. Water . . . water falls from the sky, spills from the bare hills of shale and gossan and gravel, flows in runnels over the greasy subsoil of the hungry gardens, streams down the deep, old gutters of the town. Water traces the town's veins, pulses through the arteries of the mine. From the steeply descending spiral of the main decline, it churns again to the surface, pumped perpetually against the weight of the world; surfacing, it rushes through stormwater channels, cascades into the rushing creek, pours north to the distant river, to the sea, where it is sucked up again by the great westerlies and dumped once more on the land, the town, the mine . . .

And the town is two towns really. The one you see first is the company town, a cantonment of brand-new cheap houses, asbestos cement and Colourbond and pig-wire fences, minimal gardens, damp kids and shiny cars. Suburbia, cut-price and makeshift. People go there for a year or two to make money, then they leave again.

The other town, the old town, is different. It's the bones of the old city, houses scattered at random over a map of streets that has been smeared back to anonymity by half a century and more of seasons and neglect; where thickets of houses stood, now there is only the scurf of the tea-tree flats.

When the ore ran out, when the market slumped, people just left. There were few clear titles to the land, and no one bothered. No good trying to sell – no market. Walk out, walk on, to the next job, the next town, the next mine. The houses that still stand are mostly water-rotted, rust-eaten, slumped; they smell of mould and neglect and time. The theatre where Melba sang is a hulk, a shell. Beside it, the hotel whose ornate dining room fed a hundred guests at a time, on white linen amid silver and crystal, is given over to mice and cockroaches. In the billiard room the great table is still there, as heavy as death, one leg dropped through rotted floorboards, its slate bed sound enough but the green baize ripped and rotted.

Why did I go there in the first place?

When I left the game it seemed to me that I was years behind everyone else, that I had to catch up. Not money – there was plenty of that – but the real business of life, of being somebody, of doing something. And there, in those places, that's where you *can* catch up, where you *can* move fast. The whiz-kids stay in the big cities, and if you can cope with the climate, the isolation, the natives, then the pyramid is easier to climb. A promotion every couple of years, good money, perks . . . and you can make things *happen*. That was the way I saw it then . . . get in, killer, show 'em how it's done . . .

If you think about it, it was just another way, a different way, for me to be a bastard . . . Byrne the Bastard is alive and well and living in Zeehan, Tasmania . . .

And it worked, for a while . . .

My gold was a little different from Old Jack's, not quite as bright and shiny, not quite as glamorous, but easier to pan, lighter to pack . . . even if it did carry a certain craziness as it's private curse . . .

•

It was the day after I arrived at the clinic that I first saw Petra. A bit unsteady on my feet, partly from general weakness, partly from some very heady dope that old Purple Brewster was pumping into me. But they refused to feed me in my cave, made me struggle along to the dining room. So I wavered out of my room in the middle of the day, propped myself against the wall in the corridor to get my bearings.

And this creature went past.

Smiled at me.

Good Christ!

I wondered what on earth she could be doing there. It was obvious that someone as beautiful as that wasn't – couldn't be – sick. A visitor, then, an off-duty nurse, Christ only knew . . .

It was her carriage that got me first, after the face, the eyes. Back like a ramrod, shoulders square, hips swinging. And that shape . . .

I didn't have enough blood left, I guess, for a good full-scale erection, but I sure as God had the tinglings and stirrings and all the rest of it.

I staggered along the passage, one hand on the wall, stumbled through the dining-room doorway; stopped, blinded by the glare from the windows. Shook my head, blinked. And she was there, sitting alone at one of the little tables.

I went at her like a homing pigeon, then, suddenly abashed, stopped, leaned on a chair-back. And she smiled at me again. I thought I was going to faint. A woman has that sort of impact on you, you know that there's something special about her.

'Sit down, young man,' she said. All of ten years younger than me.

I sat down.

'What are you doing here?' I said, my eyes on stalks.

'What do you mean?'

'Well, what are you *doing* here, in this place?'

'I'm a nut case,' she said.

'Oh.'

She laughed. 'I'm a schizophrenic, with a few manic-depressive complications . . . what they call schizo-affective disorders.'

'Oh.' Then: 'Listen, I don't know what I am . . .' And it

dawned on me that that was just the problem, and no more than the truth. 'But I promise I'll tell you when I find out.'

'Don't worry about it,' she said. 'Here, I'll get your lunch . . .' So she jumped up and away to the slide and brought me my plate. Don't remember what it was. Could have been pig-shit and I wouldn't have noticed.

I'd been kind of holding my wrist, my left one, turned over. I thought I'd better get it over with, so I turned the wrist up for her to see. Nothing much there, only a strip of Elastoplast.

'Gave myself a new orifice,' I said. 'Didn't work out so well.'

She nodded, not too interested. 'What's your name?' she asked.

'Jack,' I said. 'But you can call me Jack.'

She laughed a little then. 'Do you want a game of table tennis after lunch?'

'Christ,' I said, 'I couldn't hold a bat, I'm weak as a kitten. Lost too much of the old vital fluid . . .'

'Hurry up and get better,' she said. 'There's no one else here I can play with.'

I looked round the room. No one much under a hundred by the look of them. All heads down, agobbling. Mostly ladies, a couple of dismal little fellows in the corner, and a skinny old bloke with a Steptoe face. Two nurses holding him, a wardsman spooning custard into him. He's resisting, and there's custard ankle-deep on the floor.

'That's Herbie,' said Petra. 'He was all right when they brought him in. Some days he's better than others . . .'

I didn't say anything, a bit horrified at the sight.

Then suddenly she was on her feet, picking up her plate, her ciggies. 'I'm going for a swim . . .' And she was gone.

Later I staggered off back to bed, lay there staring at the ceiling. Suddenly horrified at my weakness – Jesus, something like that smiles at me, invites me to have a little game of ping-pong, and I can't even get a bloody *horn* . . .

Six foot and a bit, fourteen stone, thirty years old, and only yesteryear the terror of the packs . . . and I can't even get it up for someone like *that* . . .

Suddenly I felt almost cheerful.

Despite all the bullshit, I've been a bit cautious with the old Purple. Who knows what he knows? I do know that he's talked to Nance and the old man. Told me so. But they must have kept their mouths shut. Well, they've had plenty of practice. If they'd said anything the old Purple would have dropped on to me and hung on like a bloody leech.

So they haven't said anything.

Why? Well, obviously because they don't want anyone to know. Nance blew it when she told me. But they must be pretty sure I won't say anything. Or are they?

It seems to me that they might be a little unsure just what I might say or do. I guess I could discommode them quite badly if I snitched.

Well, let them bloody stew.

But, Oh Christ, I can't help thinking of those long winter nights, just the two of them upstairs in that big old hotel. Just thinking about it gives me the shivers . . .

Purple said to me on about the third day, 'You might as well go along to the group therapy sessions . . .'

'What for, old buddy?' He was in lilac, and doused in a kind of musky eau-de-wog.

'You may help someone else, even if not yourself.'

'How can I resist your invitation?'

At ten-fifteen we gathered, a sorry bunch of old ladies and broken squires, in a strange little room along the corridor. Quite empty except for the chairs we carried in and a couple of inexplicable black boxes and chrome tables. No number on the door even. Found out later it was where they plugged the little old ladies in.

We sat round in a circle, and old Purple got ready to take notes. There was a sister, the fat young social worker who smiled earnestly at everyone through her pimples, a couple of fidgety students.

Everyone stared straight in front, hoping not to be picked on.

'Well,' chirped the social worker, 'everyone ready? Well, then, let's start. I want you all to think of where you'd most like to be this morning . . .'

Oh, Jesus, how bloody awful . . .

She started at the other end. Old ladies wanted to be pruning their roses (do you prune roses *this* early, I wondered), wanted to be shopping in Myers, wanted to be visiting their grandchildren, wanted to be back on the farm . . .

One said she'd like to be asleep.

One red-eyed little man in the corner, hair awry, chain-smoking, cupping his butts in heavy, clawed, brown knuckles, said he'd like to be hunting possums.

Somehow I knew what the poor little bugger meant.

The fat girl simpered at me. 'And you, Mr Byrne? Where would *you* like to be?'

Chockablock up Petra . . . But I couldn't say that, because she was right there beside me.

'Fishing?' I said. It was the first thing that came into my mind. And it seemed somehow right. Because immediately there flashed into my mind that steep sandbank at the river mouth, and the heavy incoming tide all green and foam-flecked, and the silver wobbler flying and the vicious *fizzzz* of the line stripping and the soundless *plop*, and sometimes that heartstopping *lunk* on the line when the big blackback takes it, that *lunk* that seems to race through your nerves right to the centre, and then the strain of the line against the star drag, and the beginning of the heavy fight as the sun drops and the water turns violet, and the first sight of the fish's rainbow lights . . .

Somehow I seemed to be telling them all about it. No one took much notice (most of them wouldn't know a wobbler from a wobbegong) but the fat girl was smiling and nodding at me, and old Purple was scribbling away, and the possum-hunter – whose name was Sam – was looking at me with some odd recognition in his red-shot eyes.

Outside he sidled up to me. He came up to my shoulder, built like a small tugboat.

'You're Jack Byrne, aren't ya?' He sounded almost accusing.

I nodded.

'I seen ya in the Grand Final in '66. Seen ya on the telly.'

He looked up at me with an odd pleading expression. I wanted to say to him, listen, old possum-hunter, old Sam, I'm not that Jack Byrne at all, I'm someone entirely different, a different kind of bastard altogether . . .

But I couldn't, of course, and in the end he wandered off to hunt his own possums.

I saw him again, later that day, still red-eyed, and shamefaced now, bludging smokes in the day room. He had a thin pouch of Drum that he was guarding, maybe against the long night. Tried to hang himself in the woodshed, Petra told me. A council labourer, used to be a bushman. Doesn't seem entirely unreasonable.

I got one of the wardsmen to go over to the shop and buy me a carton of cigarettes. Tried to give them to Sam. He looked more shamefaced than ever, averted his eyes. Jesus, I hate to see a man without a smoke, the bloody last indignity . . .

His eyes were hungry, but he wouldn't take the carton.

'No,' he said, 'I've got a bit of Drum left, and me missus'll bring me some more tomorrow.' Then: 'Just give us a packet when I'm out, will ya?'

In the end he took two packets, and I put the rest in the drawer of my night table.

•

So all this and more bouncing round in my head while Benjy rips it off and throws it away. Tired, and sleep nowhere in sight. And then, bugger me, just as the dishes are starting to clatter in the kitchen, I go to sleep after all.

And when I come to, a couple of hours later, I'm so disoriented that for a minute or two I can't make out where I am. Unfamiliar bed, unfamiliar smell. I've been dreaming, dreaming of Sunday morning when I was a kid, and the walk up the hill, the three of us, to the little boxy weatherboard church among the big granite outcrops that look like scones, and the gentle boredom of the service, and grandfather's hand holding mine on the way back home, and milk to drink in the kitchen, thick and creamy, and fresh bread and blackberry jam . . .

Then *crash*, and the fucking awful world comes roaring back.

And I lie there thinking, this is the last day, killer – oh, maybe you won't go today, but this is the day when it finishes. Because I know I can't just go on here forever, shut away from the world, can't go on any longer at all now . . .

And it seems to me that over the past weeks I've made some sort of slow decision, a decision not to die, I suppose. I'm getting too comfortable here, though, because no one makes me face up. I'm not *me* in here, I'll never be me in here . . . I suppose that in some way I'm even grateful to old Purple and the rest, Johnny Cash and Herbie and Charlie the Philanderer, and Sam the possum man, even Paddy. Because they've given me time to settle down a bit, let the smoke clear. And not only that, but to see just how people can survive with all those terrible things on their backs and in their heads, Petra above all. Christ, it chills me to think of a fifteen-year-old girl struck with that lightning bolt, no reason, no sense, and to know that maybe you're going to be like that for the rest of your life, and have to *carry* it, Christ, *guts* . . .

I realise just how easy it was, all the years, all I've done.

Byrne the Bastard, tough man, killer . . .

So, you're a special kind of bastard now, killer – let's see if you can cut *that* . . .

•

Get out of the cot feeling a bit sad. Mostly at leaving Petra. No more map-making, no more ping-pong, no more coffee and talk, no more of that lovely walk, that proudness, that marvellous thing that seems to shine in her . . .

But I can't stay with her, not the way I am. Got to get the old act together, find out what makes the new man tick. Get moving, onward and upward, all that shit . . .

Better stop right there, killer. You've had it already, old fella, if you can't face facts.

Because you don't know if you can handle this thing with Petra, don't know if you can face it when she gets like Paddy, don't know if you can really put it all on the line. With Petra, the future might be a bit like snakes and ladders. Gutless all of a sudden, aren't you, killer?

Chills me a bit. Never thought I'd be like that.

But it's true. So suck on that, eh?

•

She's been for an early morning swim, and her hair's still damp, small tendrils clinging to her temples. Sitting across the table from me, smiling.

Just like any other morning.

But winter's on the way, and I've got to move.

Sunlight on cutlery, starched uniforms in the servery, Charlie tickling the ladies. Tuesday, so there's a bit of bustle about the nurses' station. Not many old ladies at breakfast – they're getting ready for their jolt from the HEC.

'Can I borrow your typewriter for a while?' I ask Petra.

'Sure. But I'll do anything you want – I need the practice.'

She's learning to type on a hired machine.

'Thanks, I'd better do it myself.'

She shrugs.

Well, I don't know . . . I want to say something, at least a hint that I'm off . . .

'You're quiet this morning,' she says. 'Are you all right?'

'I'm fine. Just thinking about these letters I've got to write.'

In a little while she gets up, breaks the awkward silence. 'I'm going to do some washing. Want anything done?'

I shake my head. She leans over and kisses me lightly on the forehead. Then she's gone, and I'm left cringing, while the tables empty and the noise and rattle of washing-up time comes from the kitchen.

I find Petra's typewriter in the therapy room, bring out my manilla envelope.

Inside is my collection of letterheaded paper. For some reason I've always collected a few letterheads from all the jobs I've ever had. Even a few prescription forms from the doctor's office. Kind of insurance. Proves that I'm basically dishonest, I suppose.

I pull out the ones from the mine. Figure that that'll be the easiest, I know the form there. They never give references, just certificates of service. Your name goes in the black book if you're a fuckup, but otherwise it's just the form letter; date started, date finished, reason for leaving, position held, all that crap. Signed by the GM. I know his signature well enough to have a go at it. I type up three certificates, very carefully, so as not to make any mistakes, trying with my two fingers to get the pressure even. Each certificate has a name, a different one, and a different job. And the names and jobs are real. I can remember enough of the employment records to pick them. Date of start and finish may be a bit off, but no one will worry too much about that.

When they're done I've got three fairly nondescript bodgies. Richie Todd, trades assistant. Len Flanagan, gardener. Michael Parsons, clerk.

Gives me a bit of leeway, pick and choose a bit. And no special skills required. Except maybe the gardener, and I reckon I can fake that. I daren't choose anything fancy, like a tradesman – I'd be spotted straight away.

I practise the old boy's signature a few times, scrawl it on the certificates, pack up my envelope, put the cover back on the typewriter.

I think about waiting until after lunch. But that's only procrastination. I go back to my room, put on my jacket, toothbrush in the pocket, envelope up my sweater, wallet in my hip pocket. Ready to go. Look around one final time. Old Benjy asleep again, and getting into his stride. I think about a last look at Petra, I can hear the washing machine faintly from downstairs. But that's no good. Feel suddenly chilled, nervous and lonely. That won't do . . .

Off you go, killer, out into the big world, into the packs.

Find that big mirror and see who looks back at you from the other side . . .

Go.

PART TWO

TERRY BYRNE

I spent the drive wondering just what I would say to him; how he would look, what he would reply. Mile after mile, small private plays in my head, dozens of permutations, each one without conclusion or finality. No matter how many times you rehearse the future, it is always different when it comes.

He refused to see me.

A kind of fear, I suppose, and disgust and shame. I don't know. He was never a coward, that boy. Yet this is very different, facing a thing so outrageous. I watched him when he was small, when the other boys began to call him a bastard. There were tears then, although he thinks I never saw them, that no one saw them. No one else did, I think. It was only that I watched him so closely, everything he did, always. And I saw him draw himself tighter, and hold back the tears, and fight and fight against shame, and build a shell that was almost impervious to the catcalls . . . until the catcalls stopped, or turned to something different, something almost admiring. He did it very well, and very steadily, and I was enormously proud of him, such a small fellow then . . .

From the time he was born, I just wanted to be near him, to touch him, to help him . . . he was so special.

But I was locked into an inflexible role within our strange and secret play. I was grandfather, and there must be a decent reserve, a distance. Yet it was hard, always hard. And later, much later, standing there in the middle of those shrieking thousands as they shouted at him *'Bastard! Bastard!'* and watching him swing through a pack – so fast, so sure, so damned *perfect* – it seemed that he was almost a god, one of those old-fashioned gods that lived for a while among men. It seemed impossible to believe then that this was the same small boy who stood big-eyed beside me at the river and asked me about his father, that soft-eyed boy who ran to me in the evenings in flannel pyjamas after his bath and put his arms around me, and smelt so warm and sweet and childish . . . *This*? This tall man who rose above the others by some magic and claimed the chorus of that vast communal throat . . .

But he would not see me.

Back at the hotel I parked the car in the yard and went in the back way through the kitchen.

Nancy was in the scullery rearranging her bottles of preserved fruit, standing on the small stool reaching upward. For thirty years I have not seen her once, not one single time, without that hard ache of wanting beginning to burn again inside me. And in thirty years I have not touched her once – except accidently at table, passing salt or butter, and then flinching from the contact. Not once in all that time; and yet the thing never dies in me. So I must live with the guilt – that is all I can do – and as well I must add to it each day by a new burst of lust that withers me a little further.

I turned away from her, then, from the taut, firm body stretching upward from the short ladder, the tiny patch of flesh in the small of her back where her blouse had pulled loose and ridden up. Turned away, tried to tiptoe across the kitchen and disappear upstairs.

But she heard me, of course, jumped lightly from the stool, came out into the kitchen, one hand brushing back a wave of dark hair. Strange, I find that the best thing in moments like these is to look her straight in the eyes, try to forget everything else about her, just concentrate on her eyes, until everything else dissolves, disappears . . .

'Well?' she asked.

'He wouldn't see me,' I said, blotting out everything else except the twin pools of her eyes.

'What did you expect?'

'I don't know. I thought perhaps . . .'

'Perhaps what? That he'd fall on your neck, cry with joy?'

I looked at her for a long time, the shape and expression of her face slowly crystallising round the edges of my vision. Since that night, the night she told him, there is something new about her, some defiant quality that I can't quite put my finger on, as if she is somehow glad that she has brought down the world about us, done what she has done to Jack . . .

'He'll get over it,' she said, turning away, moving back towards the scullery, her slight figure in its dark skirt and blouse an echo of the house's shadows. 'He'll get over it, there's nothing else he can do . . .'

'What's happened to you?'

'What do you mean?' And she swung round at the doorway, stood facing me foursquare.

'It's almost as if you *hate* him now – just because you've done what you have . . .'

'He's my son,' she said. And looked at me as if her equivocation was some sort of answer.

'Why *did* you tell him?' I asked her.

'I told you,' she said. 'Because I thought I was having a heart attack, thought I was dying . . .'

'Even so, why *tell* him? We agreed – long ago – *never* to tell.

For a moment she was silent, watching me. In the dimness of the afternoon it seemed as if there was a slight smile on her lips. A trick of the light perhaps . . .

Then: 'I had to, that's all. I just had to . . .' And she turned once more and vanished through the narrow door, back into her world of bottled greengages and apricots and pears, blackberries and quinces and raspberries . . .

I cannot comprehend her. No more than I could thirty years

ago. Love is not necessarily comprehension, of course, but still, it is difficult to live together and grow apart, while the strength of desire never wanes. She has taken on for me, takes on more and more each year, the quality almost of some abstract lust that will be with me to the end, growing stronger and more incomprehensible with every day that passes.

There are no answers, I know that well enough by now. No solution to our private enigma. Only endurance and eventually release. If there is release. There may be other pains beyond death, who knows? If there are I pray that at least they may be more comprehensible than these . . .

•

The next morning, I had just come upstairs from cleaning the beer lines and checking the spirit stocks, when I heard a car draw up outside. I wiped my hands and went to the window, displeased to be interrupted in the middle of my morning routine. From the window I could see that it was a taxi, a city taxi.

The driver was busy at the boot, removing luggage, and the passenger, a woman, was mostly obscured by his body. She seemed to be very close to him, and I could hear the sound of muffled laughter. Then he straightened, and I saw that the woman was Kate. She was dressed in powder blue, a kind of short-skirted dress and a top that left her throat and much of her shoulders bare. Her hair was bright gold in the sunlight – or gilded, rather – and curled and frizzed, and she wore harlequin sunglasses. As she moved away from the driver I could see that her shoes had enormously high heels, and she was tottering a little on the uneven gravel. Swinging a tiny handbag of blue leather with gold handles, she walked in front of the driver towards the front door. The driver, a young fellow of more than thirty, had a faint, slightly puzzled smile on his face. As well he might if he'd been sitting next to Kate all the way from the city.

I opened the door before she could press the bell, and she

waltzed past me into the hall, pecking my cheek as she passed.

'Pay the driver,' she said, 'there's a good chap, Terry . . .'

I looked at the driver, raising my eyebrows at him.

'Fifty dollars,' he said.

I shook my head, and went and got the money from the till. He took it, went back to his cab, and sat there for a moment looking towards the hotel before he started up and drove away. No doubt she'd had her hand on his knee for most of the drive.

I turned back and found her behind the bar pouring gin.

'A bit early, isn't it? Even for you?'

'Don't be a bore,' she said, hoisting herself up on the counter, twisting a little to face me, so that I had an unobstructed view of her upper thighs and a minuscule strip of blue pantie. 'I've been up since five . . . I got the early plane.'

'Why?'

'Because the later one was booked out.'

'No – I mean, why did you come at all?'

'Why didn't you tell me?' she asked, evading the question. 'About Jackie?'

'How did you find out?' Two can play at that game.

'Nancy rang me,' she said. 'That bloody girl.' Then: 'Get me another drink, there's a dear,' and she waved the glass at me.

I sighed and got her another drink. 'Why didn't you ring me first?'

'Because you'd have told me not to come.'

Which was true enough. Somehow, both of them in the one house, Nancy and Kate, are just too much.

'Why did she have to do it, Terry? Tell him?' As I handed her the glass I saw that her face was suddenly very serious, and for a moment the cultivated illusion of youth disappeared and I saw only the face of an old woman; powdered and painted and mascara'd, but an old woman all the same.

'I don't know.' I began to count out the float into the drawers of the till. Kate's taxi fare had disrupted the order of things and I might have to borrow change from the post office or the store. 'She thought she was dying. And so did I, she *looked* as if she was dying . . .'

'Yes, but *why*? Why tell him even then?'

I shook my head. I could understand it in a way, I suppose. But it wasn't something that I could put into words. Sometimes, when I think of dying, the thing about it that appalls me is that all the rest must die too, all the small joys of memory that are unique, that will simply cease to exist. Maybe something like that.

'You know,' she said, sliding off the counter, 'I really despise you two. You and Nancy.'

'Why?' She's known for thirty years. Sometimes she surprises me.

'Because you're gormless, the pair of you. You should have sold up when it happened, gone off, the three of you, to New Zealand or somewhere, and lived a normal life. No one would have known.'

As if it hadn't occurred to me.

And why not? For years, the first years, I thought of little other than the possibility of it. Maybe, looking back . . . but I thought that one day Nancy would find someone else, would start again, that it would wipe out what happened, for her anyway . . . but things just went on as they were. And slowly she became more ascerbic and sharp and taut. And then the other thing, of course, was that young Jack *belongs* here. Here in this valley, in this building that my father built with the gold he took, with such pain and difficulty, from the wild places in the west . . .

I think often of the old man in those last years, sitting so quietly on the verandah with pipe and stick and newspaper, gazing out across the flats, his feet planted so firmly and squarely, and I know that I could never take Jack away, that even if he went away for a while, he would always come back . . . always.

I'm glad of course that the old man died when he did, although it was a shock. He was only sixty, eight years younger than I am now, seven years younger than Kate. So sudden, a few moments of that strange, laboured breathing on the stairs, and that was all; a massive cardiac infarction, the certificate said, and I could hardly believe it . . . Then, a year later, I was out of the army, invalided out, with a weak heart . . . and I wondered then, worried for a while, if it was to be that way with me. And well it may yet. I have no fears of death, I think, but God knows I would like to see Jack again, once . . .

Kate finished her second drink and set the glass on the bar. 'I'm going upstairs. Which room?'

'Take Jack's,' I said. It was made up ready – we kept it that way, always. From the days when he was playing football, when he might fly home at any time for a day or so.

She went upstairs and I sighed and set about opening the bar.

•

We usually eat in the kitchen when we are alone, Nancy and I. But tonight, because of Kate, we took our meal in the upstairs parlour. Beyond the window, hanging over the hills to the east, was a heavy yellow moon, and we left the curtains undrawn. The meal was quiet until we were over our coffee.

'How's your love life?' asked Nancy, speaking to Kate. It was a harmless enough question, one that one of us always asks of Kate, sooner or later.

But Kate, with a couple of glasses of port under her belt, flew into an immediate tantrum. 'Better than yours, I'll bet, you little priss!'

Nancy flushed, the skin burning over her cheekbones. Her eyes widened, and her nostrils dilated a little. In the single dim light she looked much younger than her years, almost a girl again. And very beautiful, so beautiful that for a moment it seemed that all the blood was draining from my heart and I was going to faint.

She leaned forward, setting Kate like a pointer. 'You're a disgrace! Not only a disgrace,' she said, 'you're bloody ridiculous! You're not a woman at all, any more, you're just a bag of bones . . .'

Kate laughed, a little shrilly, and reached to refill her glass. 'I may be a bag of bones, but I still know what it's like to feel a prick inside me!'

We had been drinking white wine with our meal, and Nancy threw the dregs from her glass at Kate's face. Most of it missed, but a few spots stung her. She flinched and turned to look at me, then turned back to Nancy. 'Guttersnipe!'

Nancy hissed at her. It was the first time I've ever seen a human being actually hiss, and it was not a pleasant sight.

'That's enough,' I said. 'Both of you. Be quiet or I'll send you both out of the room.'

There must have been something in my voice, because they both looked at me sharply. Then Nancy got up without a word and stormed out.

Kate sighed, sipped her wine. She looked suddenly very tired, and not at all well. 'I'm sorry, Terry. Really I am . . .' She looked at me in such a ridiculously repentant fashion that I could hardly keep from smiling.

'It's Jackie,' she said. 'I'm just so worried about Jackie.'

'I know,' I said, putting my hand over hers. Her bones were as fine and fragile as a bird's, almost, her skin slack and wrinkled and tired. There was never much of her, Kate.

'I know,' I said. 'We all are.'

'*You* would have kept your mouth shut, right to the end, wouldn't you?'

'Yes,' I said. 'I think I would.'

'What can we do to help him, now?'

'I don't know,' I said. 'I just don't know . . .'

'Have you been to see him?' she asked.

'I tried. He wouldn't see me . . .'

'Oh, hell . . .' I could see the faint sparkle of tears in her eyes.

'Will you go up to see him?' I asked.

She shook her head. 'No. I don't think so. I'll just wait. One day, maybe, he'll come, or he'll call me . . . I'll just wait.'

'Yes,' I said. 'I suppose that's best. I suppose that's all any of us can do just now . . . wait.'

●

Kate, of course, is a foundation member of our conspiracy. In a sense she was the one who separated one thing from another; sin from guilt, passion from despair, life from the rest of living . . . No, that is too dramatic; but all the same, a watershed. She is a realist, a pragmatist – the ultimate pragmatist, perhaps, but one who has lived her whole life in a fantasy, an erotic world which she has created about her. Oddly, I have found her always curiously devoid of sexual attraction. Of the two sisters, so unlike – Kate and my Ailsa – Ailsa dark, plump and passionate, seemed always to hold the promise of a deep and earthy eroticism which she manifested with a lack of concern and consideration that made love for her a completely spontaneous joy. Kate – svelte, blonde, languishing, a year older – well, for her sex seemed a subject for conjuration and magic, the act less significant than the image. She has lived always within the bounds of a permanent sexual spider's web . . .

Kate was always the favourite of the old man, of old Jack. Oh, he liked Ailsa, even loved her; but Kate was the favourite. I think that she seduced him. Not literally, but to the point of looks and touches and whispers and smiles; and with promises that he knew were more than half-meant.

It was perhaps a touch, a taste, for him of the outside world, of the places he would no longer visit. For after the house, the hotel, was built here, well before the First World War, he never left the valley again except for a few rare visits to the town ten miles away. It seemed to me later – though in the days of my childhood such insularity was the norm – that he sealed himself off here, shut himself in, as another might have done in a monastery or retreat; as if he had committed himself for life – to some spiritual venture.

Yet there was nothing of the religious about him. He was quiet enough, but a smiler, a man who enjoyed a joke, his pipe, a drink, a woman . . . . My mother died a year after I was born and the hotel's hostesses were a series of housekeepers who invariably slept upstairs in the room next to the old man, and who – also invariably – were kind to me. They were all conscientious and buxom, and I have only fond memories of them . . .

But he never married again, as if his single legal union had fulfilled some long-nurtured plan, fulfilled it completely . . .

Of his days in the western forests he never spoke a great deal. When he did speak of them, it was usually to extoll the qualities of his companion, Gogarty. Gogarty, as I grew towards adolescence, became a kind of hero, a superman of the rainforest, a being so able, so gifted in the arts and mechanics of life that he stood like a giant in our small family hagiography. My father would see me reading the boys' books of which I was inordinately fond – Marryat, Kingsley, Defoe, Melville – and scoff a little at their paper heroes. He himself read little except the local newspaper, and would smile at my recitals of derring-do, compare the heroes, always to their disadvantage, with Gogarty.

The truth is that in time I became a little sick of this paragon of the manly virtues, and wished almost that he had been somehow less perfect . . .

And yet, for all his perfection, it was he who died, he who remained in the bush, he who occupied a lost grave by their lost river, while my father, the lesser man to hear him tell it, returned rich and prosperous.

'I do believe,' he told me once, 'that Gogarty could have done anything, become anything he wished . . .'

'Why did he get killed then?' I remember asking him.

And he was silent for a long time, staring from his seat on the verandah out across the rich green flats with their crop of lush oats. When he spoke at last his voice seemed to have lost its habitual certainty.

'Other people,' he said at last. 'It's other people always let you down . . .'

•

Ailsa died in 1927, of peritonitis, in great agony in the back seat of Sam Kenny's Whippet on the road to Formby and the doctor. I buried her soberly enough, then drew a thousand pounds from my bank account and sailed for Sydney. I stayed there six months, and don't like to dwell too much on the life I lived there. Why I chose Sydney I do not know, except that for us it had always seemed the most interesting and the most sinful place in the country. Whether it counted that my father had come from there, I don't know.

At the end of six months I returned to the valley. My liver had been a little damaged, I found later, by my diet of rum and meat pies, my weight was down by a stone, and I had a lingering case of the clap. But I was home again.

Waiting for me there were the hotel and my daughter Nancy, looked after by Kate – who had demoralised our local customers and seduced several of them. Nancy was two years old. A young daughter, a hotel to manage. At fifty my father was already retreating from the affairs of the hotel into his own private world that seemed to grow smaller each year. I needed a wife – I have never found celibacy easy or pleasant – but I could not bring myself to marry, somehow. God knows there was no shortage of farmers' daughters and timber-getters' widows; but I would not marry, and eased the more pressing discomforts of my single life with monthly visits to a quiet whore in East Formby.

And gradually, as the years went by, as I reached thirty and passed it, the local girls began to ignore me more and more, and I sank quite thankfully into a routine that I believed would carry me comfortably into old age.

Kate, of course, tried to seduce me each time she visited the hotel, which was at least twice a year. She never succeeded, not because I lacked interest in sex, but because I could never treat her seriously as a sexual companion. I would as soon have gone to bed with a clothes horse. But over the years we became better friends, and perhaps something more. It was, of course, between Kate and me alone. Nancy was not included; she was female, and thus by definition of little interest to Kate.

In the beginning, I was more than a little surprised at Kate's continued visits. I had thought that Ailsa's death would be the beginning of a withdrawal. I had never considered then that Ailsa must – being female too – have occupied the same position as Nancy in Kate's scheme of things.

I remember vividly one occasion, when Kate was about thirty, when she asked me: 'Terry, what's the population of this country?'

'I don't really know,' I said. 'Four or five million, I suppose.'

'Oh, God,' she said. 'Just think – over two million men – Christ, I'm glad I'm a woman . . .'

•

Jack has been back.

I knew this morning, as soon as I woke, that something had happened, that something was different. At breakfast Kate was noticeably pleased with herself, elated even. When she left the table I followed her back to her room, ignoring Nancy's look.

I went in behind her, closed the door, leaned on it, looked at her where she flung herself on the bed. Her skirt had ridden up to expose her thighs which truth to tell are quite good still, slim and smooth and pale. The legs, she told me once, are the last things to go . . .

'What's happened?' I asked her.

She said nothing for a moment, twining a finger in a wisp of her extravagantly yellow hair and pursing her lips a little.

'Well?'

'He came back last night.'

'Who?'

'Who do you think? Jack.' She cocked her head, looking at me almost coyly.

'Why?'

'To get something, I think. Out of the room.'

I couldn't think what he might want. Over the years most of his things had been shifted gradually to his other places. 'Is he all right?'

'I don't know. He's thinner . . . his face. And his eyes, there's something about his eyes . . . He doesn't seem to laugh any more.'

'What would he have to laugh about? Now?' I said bitterly.

She shook her head slowly. 'The trouble is, Terry, he's too much like you – he takes things too seriously.'

'You mean all this is just a big joke?'

She sat up, hands supporting her, on the bright bedspread. The look in her eyes startled me – it held a certain hardness, a scorn, that I'd never seen before.

'Just because *you* had to be a bloody martyr,' she said, 'you needn't have made him into one too.'

'It was Nancy who told him,' I said, and was immediately ashamed of myself.

'You should have gone away when he was born,' she said, and shook her head slightly, dismissively. 'All of you. Then he would have had a mother and father like everyone else, your lie would have been told once and for all and there would never have been any more to say . . .'

Was it true? That business about being a martyr? God knows I've wondered often enough myself . . .

But the going away, all that . . . no, there was an enormity, a perversion about it that I couldn't have undertaken. Our lie is limited here, and its effects circumscribed. A generation has passed. In one more, a couple of deaths, the lie would have been lost forever.

But now . . .

We have created him, and God knows when I think of him I can't regret it totally; but now we have disinherited him, cast him out, and he will know that he cannot come home again . . .

What must he have felt, coming last night like a thief?

We are the thieves.

Am I dramatising? God knows. The whole thing would almost be farcical if it weren't so terrible . . .

●

The evening bus left a parcel of books for Parkie, and I decided to walk down the road to deliver it. The main channel runs on this side of the river and the bank is steep and covered with blackberries, bracken and coppices of paperbarks. On the far side, to the west, the river spreads out, fingers of the estuary reach deep into the low flatlands that are sour and salty and good for nothing but an occasional crop of rape. When the tide is low there is water only in the main channel, and the estuary is an expanse of dun mudflats. But when the tide is high, as it was tonight, and there is no wind, the river seems vast, a great waterway. Small islets of reeds and tea-tree dot the still mirror of the water, and when the evening is calm it is hard to tell the reality from the illusion of the reflections. It has a tranquillity, then, that seems to carry some promise of peace and salvation.

Tonight the water was very high, reaching far across into the marshes. The sky was clear, and there was not a breath of wind. But there was a chill in the air, a real bite that promised winter. The sky in the west was that clear burnt-orange colour that comes only in the cold weather, a kind of chill glaze on the day's ending that looks both more glorious than the loveliest summer sunset, and far more threatening. It is the colour of fire, yet it freezes rather than warms.

A mile short of Parkie's house I stopped to look out over the river, resting my elbows on an old grey fencepost that marks some sort of ancient boundary between the road and the river. I put the parcel of books down at my feet, carefully propping it on a rock to keep the wrapping dry, and lit my pipe. Far out over the river, perhaps half a mile away, a single lone bird – a crane, perhaps, or a pelican, it was too far to see – was beating its way slowly, low over the shining water, towards the sea. I stood there a long time thinking of Jack. I can't see the river without thinking of him.

And I can't think of him now without a sinking feeling, as if my heart were hunching lower somehow in my chest. It is natural enough, I suppose, that he wouldn't see me. But there is still a deep disappointment. He has always seemed to me to be the kind of man – and earlier the kind of boy – who faced things squarely, even unpleasant things. Yet I can't blame him . . .

I remember watching him closely when he was a boy, a child,

a young man, to see if there were in him any signs of deficiency, any signal of his inbreeding gone wrong. But I found none. Frightened though I was by the tales of inbred horrors – apocryphal or not – that abound in country places, it seemed to me then, and still does, that the stock was strong enough, and that he was if anything a better man than those before him, better perhaps than even the other Jack, my father.

I took pride, God knows, in his skill at football, although before I had never thought much of the game. But what I took most pride in was his balance, his steadiness, because he knew that one day the football would end, that he would have to move on to something else. And while so many of the others were drinking and whoring and wasting themselves or simply ignoring the future, he was studying. His degree and diploma, things that he saw only as some rites of passage, I saw as something more, a mark of achievement that held an absolute quality, a recognition that he accepted in some measure the limitations of his physical scope. But I would have been just as proud, I think, if he had stayed in the valley with us. And I have always believed that one day he would come back, take over the hotel. He belongs here, more than any of us.

My father saw the hotel as a vision, almost, something of permanent worth; never just a grog shop, but something valuable to men. I grew up that way, thinking that way, feeling that way, and the task of hotelmaster fell naturally enough to me. For sixty years now our family has offered good food and comfortable lodgings to travellers; over the years many of them have become friends and still make the small deviation to stay with us when they pass. There are no sterile motel rooms in our hotel, no frozen foods, no artificial smiles. Only warm beds and feather pillows, and homemade breads and clean linen and the recognition that we are privileged to take friends for a little while into our home, to entertain, to be entertained, to reach somehow below the surface and touch common humanity . . .

Some may laugh, but for me – and I hope, for Jack, too – it is no laughing matter.

And if Jack would come back, it would be all right. If he *could* come back . . .

My pipe had gone out, and I shivered suddenly. The evening was darker, only the cold orange sky in the west as bright as ever. I picked up the books and turned away from the river.

And as I walked the last half mile of road, I wondered how long it would be before something happened. Jack could not stay in that place forever, and when he left, where else could he go but home?

●

Nancy went upstairs early to do some sewing. The bar was quiet, there were only two guests, and the house was silent by the time I had locked up, checked the till, taken the cash upstairs to the safe. I felt oddly tired and decided not to smoke a final pipe. The radio was playing softly in Kate's room – Jack's room – and there was a light under Nancy's door. I tapped gently, and she called out for me to go in. I opened the door, stood for a moment in the doorway. She was sewing at her worktable, the small lamp over her head leaving the rest of the room dark except for the glow of the dying fire. As she looked up at me, biting off a thread, the light caught her face oddly, and it seemed for a moment as though she were young again, young and innocent. And very beautiful.

'I'm going to have an early night,' I said, too abruptly.

She looked at me for a moment, then nodded, picking up the scissors, her face intent again. 'Goodnight.'

I turned away quickly, shut the door softly. Getting ready for bed, I felt suddenly very weary. But, once in bed, the sleepiness seeped slowly away, leaving only the tiredness, and the memory of Nancy's face in the dim, firelit room . . .

And despite all resolutions, despite thirty years of abstinence, I felt the small warnings in my groin, the tightenings, the beginnings of lust rising like yeast in me. I knew then that sleep would be a long time coming. In some small despair I turned on the bedside lamp, looked about the room as if the familiar surroundings – the heavy dark furniture, the plain soft wallpaper, the battered desk in the corner, the crowded bookshelf under the window – might somehow reassure me. But nothing was changed, and I took a book from the bedside table and tried to read. I can't remember what the book was. I know that I would read a few lines, and then the images, dreams, whatever they are, would intrude, interpose themselves between my eyes and the pages. But, although I could not read, I kept the book open, an excuse for wakefulness.

•

We have few storms here, few real storms, but when they do come, often in the equinoxes, they can be frightening. All the more perhaps because they are so rare. One of those storms brought Nancy to me the first time, and I still tremble when the high winds rage over the valley, when the pine boughs are stripped and tossed to the ground, when the lights fail and the roof rattles and the wind howls round the gables.

Jack was conceived in the autumn of 1942, and it was not an auspicious time if the omens of the war were regarded. The battle of the Coral Sea was to come, and Alamein, and in New Guinea only a handful of militiamen stood between the Japanese and an easy passage to the Australian mainland. We seemed under a threat, a threat that was close and urgent. Suddenly the small inconveniences seemed meaningless – we were faced with the actual possibility of subjection to an Asian race, a race which seemed to thrive on atrocity and repression. We began to see in a slightly different light the timid drills of the VDC, the plane-spotting sessions, the blackout regulations.

Till then, the war had not really seemed to touch any of us – except for those who lost sons, fathers, brothers. Humped gas-producers were perched over the back bumpers of cars, petrol was almost impossible to buy, and there were periodic shortages of almost everything. But, in the country, it all made little difference to us. The boys – many of them – were gone from the farms, true; but the older men and the women coped. We were better off for food than the towns, even later, when the rationing began; in those days rabbits were everywhere, and every second boy had a pair of ferrets. Wallabies were thick only a few miles back in the hills; there were plenty of fish – cock salmon, mullet, flathead, trout even. It was impossible to count every beast on a farm, and who was to know when a farmer might quietly butcher one for himself and his friends? Admittedly, it was harder for a hotelier, but still not impossible; our guests ate what we ate, and we ate well enough. Ever since my father opened the hotel there have been free snacks on the bar counter each day – small pies, thick sandwiches, cheese, pickles, and chutneys, small croquettes of beef, chicken, fish – and I would as soon serve a drink in a dirty glass as charge for them. The war made no difference to that.

My own service with the army was brief. I joined up in the spring of 1939, and spent a little time in the dismal creosoted huts of Brighton Camp, chilled and bored in my awkward, ill-fitting gigglesuit and stiff slouch hat. I could have stayed at home, as many did. But I was only thirty-four, was fit enough – I thought – and could not bear the prospect of the veiled sneers if I did not go. I had no desire to fight, only not to be shamed. I was stunned to find, weeks later, that a medical examination had belatedly revealed my rheumaticky heart. So back to the valley I came, to the peace and quiet and calm that I could never really believe would be shattered by anything. Not even in that bad autumn of 1942 when there seemed no prospect of halting the Japanese advance.

That night in late April, after days of cold, crisp weather that turned to yellow the final leaves of the chestnut in the back garden, and left frosts each morning on the grass, the winds swept in from the southwest, cold and vicious. By eight o'clock there were only a couple of customers in the bar, and they left soon after. We had no guests, and no breakfasts to prepare the next morning. A sheet of iron began to rattle on the shop along the road, and the half-dozen street lamps were swaying wildly in the night. By the time I closed the front door and checked the till, turned out the lights and went upstairs, the weather had grown worse. There was a final wrenching screech and the loose iron on the shop went, torn away, shied off into the darkness. The old hotel is well built and tight, and no harm would come to it, but all the same there was a sense of beleaguerment, of isolation and loneliness. Brief squalls of rain beat hard on the iron and rattled on windowpanes.

I went to Nancy's room to say goodnight. She was ready for bed, wearing nightgown and slippers, rugged in her thick, blue dressing-gown. Her face seemed paler than usual, and there were two spots of colour high on her cheekbones. But she seemed calm enough, even though I felt a small tremor when I put my hand on her shoulder, kissed her cheek. But I did not worry too much. She was a woman, seventeen, two years out of school, and ran the kitchen and the household as well as any older woman could.

My room was warm from the fire in the grate, and I fell asleep even before I knew it, into a deep sleep . . .

It was midnight when I woke, and I couldn't work out what had woken me. A door? Surely not . . .

The rain had stopped, but the wind was worse than ever, tearing at the high walls of the building, rattling windows, wrenching at the eaves. I was ready to turn over, go back to sleep, when I saw her, a pale motionless shadow by the door.

'What is it?' I propped myself up on an elbow.

She said nothing, but stood there by the door, her dressing-gown wrapped about her, arms hugging her chest, her face sharp and pale, her hair like a darker shadow in the dimness. She moved forward a little, stopped.

'Nancy, what's wrong?'

'I'm frightened . . .' She moved towards the bed, her shoulders hunched. She seemed to be trembling quite violently, and I sat up quickly.

'It's all right,' I said. 'We're safe enough. It'll blow itself out by morning.'

She sat down beside me on the bed, still hunched and shivering.

'What's the matter with you, dear?' I put an arm around her shoulder, pressed hard to try and stop the shaking, the shivers that seemed to grip her. She turned a little, slipped her arms round me, buried her face against my chest. Her hair was soft on my face. I patted her back, gently, feeling its smooth fragility, the delicate pattern of her vertebrae . . .

She lay like that for a little while, but she did not seem to relax. I began to move, to shift her so that I could look at her face, but she hugged me tighter.

'Please don't send me away,' she said.

'No, no, of course not . . . it's all right, it's all right . . .' All the years since her mother died, all the lonely years, we had been so close; oh, each of us independent, self-reliant – but without each other I think that neither of us could have gone on. Even since the time when she was a small girl, I had leaned on her strength and tried to lend her a little of what I found in myself.

So it seemed natural enough that I should pull back the covers, draw her into the bed, hold her close and warm, try to comfort and reassure her.

I swear to God, that was all that was in my mind.

We lay like that for some time, without moving. A log settled in the fireplace, and embers glowed a little brighter. It seemed very peaceful there, the two of us close together, safe and protected from the wildness of the world outside . . .

I don't know how long it was before she began to move a little, turning gently towards me until her body lay close and tight against me. I felt then, despite myself, the faint stirring in my groin, the automatic response to the warm smoothness, the closeness of her womanflesh. Shame engulfed me, and I tried to twist aside a little so that she would not feel me growing hard against her. But – by some chance it seemed – she moved at the same time, and we were pressed close from shoulder to knee and there was no way that she could not feel the hardness . . .

I lay in an agony of shame, yet so paralysed by my embarrassment that I could not seem to move away. I put my hands against her to move her gently away, to make some pathetic apology. But my fingers and palms met not the coarse flannel of her dressing-gown but the warm, smooth flesh of her breasts, and seemed to close of their own accord over them, the nipples like small ripe berries under my palms. I opened my mouth to cry out, to draw my hands away; but she raised her head a little, and I saw her face in the faint firelight. There seemed a sudden peace on it and the shiverings had gone.

She smiled, and said, 'It's all right.' And her hands covered mine, clasping them tighter against her body. Then they moved, inside my pyjamas, sliding down, down . . . and my own moved down her smooth back, under the rough cloth, feeling the sudden nip of her waist, the wonderful swell of her hips . . .

After that, nothing was clear until the moment when I found her beneath me, twisted somehow, her dark hair spread on the pillow, her mouth reaching for mine, her thighs spread.

I entered her then, in a single thrust of lust and need and wonder. And it was the end of any peace I might know in this life . . .

When I felt the surges, when the heart-stopping, agonising pleasure grew too strong, I tried to withdraw, to spend myself on the sheets, on her thighs, anywhere . . . but she cried out sharply, digging her nails into my back, her hands suddenly unbelievably strong – held me, clamped me with her thighs, and I gave up, surrendered, gave her my shameful seed . . .

Lying there beside her, panting, I expected that the world would end, must end; that the wind would batter the building down, that the roof would fly off, the walls crumble; that lightning would strike, fire burst out from the rafters, the floors char; I thought my blood must boil, my brain explode, my loins be cindered . . .

I began to weep, my head thrown back, tears pooling in my eyes, great sobs wrenching at my throat.

And she raised herself on one elbow, her black hair sweeping over my chest, the touch of her nipples like an agony on my skin. Her skin glowed in the faint light from the fire, her eyes were like large dark wells, and she was smiling softly.

'Don't cry,' she said. 'It's all right, it's all right . . .' And, laying her head on my chest, she held me very tight. 'I *love* you,' she said, 'so it's all *right*.'

I wanted to push her aside, climb straight out of bed, run to the river, throw myself in, be swept away in the rain and darkness. But there seemed no energy left in me, all of it expended in her softness, none left, nothing . . .

Except the beginnings of returning passion. My breathing had slowed but now began to quicken again, as the stirrings began once more, as she moved her thighs against me, as I felt my hardness growing against her. And before I could even think, it seemed, we were joined once more, the fire inside us mounting as she straddled me, her hair wild and dark as the raging wind . . .

Somehow, in the early hours, I slept.

When I awoke, the wind had stopped, and the sun was shining, breaking through the thinning cloud, spilling light across the windowsill and patterning the dark linoleum and the red carpet. For a brief moment it all seemed as though no more had happened than a strange and shameful dream. But then I was suddenly aware of my nakedness under the sheets, of the old, almost-forgotten smell of a woman's fulfilled body, of last night's sex; and the truth stabbed at me, the chasm opened beneath me. And yet, at the very moment when the shame and horror seemed greatest, my body betrayed me, and my groin stirred.

Then the bedroom door opened quietly and, soft-footed, clad again in her blue dressing-gown, the thick flannel of her nightie visible at throat and ankle, she came in with a tray of coffee. Her hair was caught back with a blue ribbon, and there was a softness, a fullness in her face that I had never seen before. God help me, she looked a little like her mother in those early days of our marriage. Yet her mother, although decidedly passionate, had never been like her in the night, never so wild, never so intent on erotic explorations, never so engaged with her own passion.

She came slowly towards me, placed the tray on the table, sat on the edge of the bed beside me. Leaned over, touched my cheek, leaned down to kiss me.

'Listen,' I said, taking her shoulders, pressing her back, away from me. 'Listen, Nancy . . . never again, this mustn't happen ever again . . .' My voice sounded pale and creaky, as if unused in a long time.

'Whatever you say,' she said, and sat back a little. I took my hands away from her shoulders quickly, tried not to look at her.

I had seen her naked often enough as a child, but not since she began to grow up, and it was as if a sudden stranger had invaded my world. I knew then that no one can ever keep children, that children change and disappear as they grow older, that they are just not there any more, that we must reach what accommodations we can with their successors . . .

But not this kind of accommodation.

'I'm sorry,' I said, the ache beginning to harden in my throat. 'I'm so *sorry*, Nancy . . .'

She shook her head, put a finger on my lips. Then leaned down, rested her head against mine. And the thought of her body, naked inside the soft bulk of her night clothes was a sudden agony.

Even now I cannot remember how it happened, whether it was my movement or hers, but she was in my bed again, her warmth close against me, her gown opened, her nightdress around her waist, my hands on her, her legs wide again . . .

Afterwards she lay close against me, sighing, moving her hands slowly on me.

'I love you so much,' she said. 'Terry, I love you so much . . .' She'd never called me 'Terry' before, always 'Father'. 'And I've waited so *long* . . .'

•

By the time Mrs Hemmings arrived to begin the day's work in the kitchen, we were up, bathed, dressed, about our jobs. I think – I am sure – that Mrs Hemmings noticed nothing. Yet my own voice seemed strange in my ears, stilted, false, and I was sure it must reveal everything. Nancy's voice was clear and calm as usual, but there was a kind of soft mischief in her eyes, which seemed larger, moister, more languorous than usual. We must have been an open book, yet no one seemed to read us.

It was another quiet day, the aftermath of storm lying like a broken fever on the land, with a lethargy that reflected my own. I went through the day hearing little, noticing little, absent-minded. I almost persuaded myself that nothing had happened; then, that it was a fluke, a strange once-in-a-world chance, that it had nothing to do with us, with the future, that it was something to be lost and forgotten in the multiplicity of the days ahead . . . But sudden hot flushes of shame and despair would strike at me, make me stop in my stride . . .

In the afternoon I called in old Fred Yates to look after the bar. Then I went walking down along the river where the stream, heavy with the rain of the night, swirled around logs and deadfalls, thick, yeasty and brown. The farther I walked from the hotel, the more difficult it became to believe what had happened. Near the railway bridge the smell of salt on the air seemed like a blessing, seemed to lighten me. By the time I neared the hotel again I had almost persuaded myself of the unimportance of it all. It had happened all right. But it must not be acknowledged, dwelt on; must be forgotten. Above all, though, it must never happen again. In the back of my mind, the thought that there must be other people who do it whom we never suspect . . . And behind that, like a worm in the kernel, the faint, smug satisfaction, the whisper of some pagan evil . . .

There were a few travellers for dinner that night, but none to stay over. In the evening, after I had closed the bar and locked the front doors, I hurried upstairs to my office, pulled out the ledgers, and began to go over my accounts. When they were done, I cleaned out the drawers of my desk, sorting, burning old paper and rubbish in the fireplace. I was procrastinating, I knew, but it seemed important somehow to keep busy. The evening, the night, would pass, and we could start anew. I knew that she had gone up to her room long before I had closed the bar, and I hoped that by the time I left the office she would be asleep, her light out . . .

Yet at the same time there was a kind of delicious apprehension in me, a trembling shadowy anticipation . . . would she come? I would lock my door . . . or would I? The tension grew and grew, and I lit my pipe, allowed it to go out a dozen times before I finally gave it up, turned out the lights and went to the bathroom . . . Did I brush my teeth harder and wash more thoroughly, more carefully, than usual?

There was no light under her door. Was it relief or disappointment that I felt? I can't tell, even now.

But I was subdued, the tension gone, a kind of melancholy on me as I opened the door to my own room.

I was a pace inside, the door shut behind me, before I realised that a light was on – the reading lamp by the bed, and she lay there, reading.

The soft light spilled on her hair, made it glisten as darkly as a crow's wing, touched the pale soft skin of her shoulders and arms. She put the book down, smiled at me.

'You've been a long time,' she said.

She threw back the covers and lay there naked, her arms stretching out to welcome me.

I had no thought then of turning away. Turning away? Nothing could have turned me away . . .

•

For a week we lived in two worlds.

The days were quiet, calm, orderly. The storms did not come back; there were sunny days and clear nights, frosty mornings. Business was slow, and we drifted on in our quiet routine, preparing for winter. I ordered another load of wood for the bar fire, great logs the colour of a salmon's flesh to blaze in the fireplace on winter nights. I called a builder to check the roof, the gutterings, the drains. I occupied myself with all the normal things. Above all, I kept myself from thinking.

Nancy seemed as she always had; efficient, orderly, pleasant; a little short sometimes with Mrs Hemmings, which was normal, when the old lady's slow country ways irritated her. She tidied cupboards, cleaned the silver, polished the brass stair fittings, shampooed the carpets. There seemed no difference, no change in her, except perhaps that she moved a little more slowly, a little more dreamily. But that may have been my imagination. Sometimes we would pass on our various errands, and smile a little at each other, sharing our secret . . .

I was lost then – we were both lost – in that hazy real world of the night . . .

After the doors were locked, the lights switched out, the fire in the kitchen riddled, we would go slowly up the stairs. We went together, unashamed now, and unhurried, the whole night before us. There was less urgency, more time; time for slow and sensual exploration, for looking long into each other's eyes as our hands and lips explored . . .

It was shameful, degenerate, blasphemous . . . all that and more. But it was passion. A kind of magic lay in her skin, in her eyes, in her loins, and I no longer cared about anything in the world but that . . .

•

How long it would have gone on, I do not know. There were so few customers, so little contact with the outside world, that there was nothing to break the spell. Had it happened at the busy season it might have ended as soon as it began. Indeed it might never have happened at all.

In the event it was Kate who broke the pattern.

She arrived in a rush of laughter and perfume a little before lunch on the sixth day. The first I heard was the low rumble of a motor, the crunch of tyres on the gravel. I went to the front door.

It was a taxi, a fawn Hudson Terraplane, just like Father Dowling's. The car stopped, and an American soldier sprang out, ran round to open the passenger's door. Kate got out slowly, put a hand on the soldier's arm, looked up into his face, smiling. He smiled too, and his teeth seemed very white against his very black face. She stood for a moment looking round while he got two bags out of the boot. In the cold, crisp sunshine she seemed to sparkle, almost. In her day, on her day, she could look quite beautiful, and she dressed expensively. Not always well, perhaps, but certainly expensively.

I met them at the door. The soldier was called David. He was very tall, very polite, and he called me 'sir'. I took them upstairs, showed them rooms, left them to wash. Nancy was in the kitchen making a great rattle with pots and pans, and hadn't come out to greet them, although I knew she had heard the car.

Kate's arrival left me a little bemused. The truth is that I was so dazed by then that I just couldn't take it in, see what it meant. But Nancy did. When I went into the kitchen for a moment, she was tight-lipped and angry, and she refused to look at me, or speak.

Kate and the soldier came downstairs and I made tea in the front parlour, where I could keep an eye on the bar. How long were they staying? I asked Kate. Only three days. David's leave ended then, and he must be back on duty.

Well, I thought, by now the word of Kate's black soldier would have gone the rounds, and I had no doubt the evening would see the bar crammed with locals, all hoping to get a glimpse of him.

They went off after lunch, to drive through the backroads, and came back in time for a late tea. Nancy didn't join us immediately, but came in later for coffee. She snubbed Kate for some reason, was quite rude to her, and was frigidly polite to the soldier. Kate seemed puzzled. They had never been exactly warm, but always on good enough terms. But the truth is, I never worried very much about it at all. The only thing I had on my mind was the night.

And, although I didn't sense it then, it was to be our last night.

In the morning Kate cornered me on the cellar stairs after breakfast. It was unusual to see her at that hour; she usually lay abed till mid-morning. She stood above me on the stairs, looking part-amused, part-concerned.

'What are you and Nancy up to?' she said, leaning against the wall, licking a fleck of cigarette tobacco from her lip. The smell of her Lucky Strike was heavy and acrid on the air.

I looked at her for a moment, quite stupidly. 'What do you mean?' My voice sounded as if it belonged to someone else.

She shook her head impatiently. 'God, Terry,' she said, 'I'm no prude, but, really, you're going a bit far, aren't you?'

I just shook my head, refusing to even consider that she might have stumbled on our secret.

Suddenly, she seemed quite angry. 'For Christ's sake! Ever since we arrived you've been wandering about in a daze, mooning at her! She's angry that we're here, and she can hardly keep her hands off you! And in the middle of the night we meet in the bathroom . . . You think I can't tell when a woman's been with a man? Christ, she *reeked* of it . . .'

There seemed nothing I could say. I just stood there drymouthed, aghast. That we had been so transparent . . .

And then, suddenly, the real enormity of it broke over me, the reality that I'd shut out for a week, kept at bay, never admitted. I slumped against the wall, closed my eyes, felt the sobs start in my throat. Then I felt her close, felt her arm round my shoulders.

'Come on,' she said, guiding me down the narrow steps. She led me over to the wall, and I slumped on a wooden crate. She perched on the edge of a barrel, shaking her head slowly. 'Listen,' she said, 'there's nothing very terrible about it, Terry. Half the girls in the world have a crush on their fathers, and more than you think do something about it. Or their fathers do.'

'Jesus Christ,' I said. 'I'm so *ashamed*.'

'Ashamed because you've been found out?'

I looked up at her then. Maybe there was something in what she said. 'I don't know what to do,' I said dully. The world seemed suddenly to have crumpled about me like old paper.

'You want my advice?'

'I suppose so . . .'

'Send her off on a long holiday . . . get her married to some young buck. That'll fix *her*.' She looked closely at me. 'Then *you* get married, too, Terry. And don't waste too much time; you've been alone too long.'

I shook my head again. Send her off, yes, if she would go. The rest? Yes, if she would marry, that would be best, certainly. As for me . . . I couldn't really see myself marrying anyone after what I had done.

I stood up, walked past her up the stairs, out of the old familiar gloom of the cellar into the hall, out into the front yard, across the road, and stood staring down the river. It was so sunny, so peaceful, so calm . . .

I turned, walked away down the road, walked all the way to the mouth of the river, sat for hours on the sand, watching the tide ebb, turn, begin to make again. I listened to the high, harsh calling of the gulls, the soft rush of the water, the shifting grumble of the shingle by the bar. It was late afternoon before I finally stood up and began the long walk home. Suddenly I felt indescribably weary . . .

We all ate together that night. The meal was a silent one, and no one seemed to look at anyone else. David was cautious, as if watching for pitfalls. Nancy was withdrawn, silent. I was tired and dull. The only normal one, it seemed, was Kate, who chattered away enough to drive me mad. Nancy was crumbling bread, and clenching her fingers. I stood up before the others had finished their meal, took a bottle of whiskey from the cellar and went upstairs.

In my room I locked the door, uncorked the bottle, lay on the bed in the dark, sipping slowly.

By the time I heard the front door close downstairs, the pain had started to retreat a little. By the time the footsteps came up the stairs – Kate and David first, Nancy ten minutes later – I had wept again, my eyes were puffed and my throat still ached, but I was passing into a sort of numbness at last.

Two hours later, when she scratched at the door, softly, gently, quietly, I was quite drunk – for the first time since my days in Sydney – and I couldn't have got off the bed to open the door if I'd wanted to. But the gentle tapping went on for a long time before it finally stopped and the faint footfalls in the hall faded into silence.

The next morning the house was quiet enough; yet it seemed haunted with tensions, tensions that lay like smoke in the silence. Kate and her black soldier left soon after breakfast, and she said no more than the usual polite noises of parting. Nancy was nowhere to be seen; later she came in from the back garden.

I wanted to see her alone, to speak to her, to tell her what had happened. But the day conspired against me. We were unseasonably busy, the bar took up most of my time, and when I was free Nancy wasn't. I felt a little ill after my drunken night and I kept dozing on my feet, snapping back to wakefulness at some sudden noise or movement. By midday I wanted desperately to go upstairs and lie down; but I knew that it was impossible. And all through it, spasms of suddenly realised guilt shook me. It seemed that for the first time I was seeing what we had done through the eyes of the outside world. And just as well too . . .

By closing time I had given up any idea of talking to Nancy. I had in any case lost interest by then; my tiredness had wiped out all my good intentions. All I wanted was to lie down, sleep, sleep . . .

In the end I locked up, staggered up the stairs and crawled into bed – after locking my door again. Within minutes I was deeply asleep, and stayed that way till morning. I would not have woken had a *regiment* of women scratched at my door.

When I came down to breakfast next morning I felt rested and pleasantly light-headed, as if from fasting. I sat down with a good appetite. Nancy silently cooked my eggs. She seemed not so much glum or angry as withdrawn, confused. We were alone in the house, with Mrs Hemmings not due for another hour.

'Sit down,' I said to her. She had been fidgeting about the kitchen, picking up forks and plates and cups, putting them down again, unable to stay still. She sat in the chair opposite me, hands clasped before her on the white cloth. Her dark-blue frock showed up the colour of her eyes. She said nothing.

I pushed my plate away, my appetite suddenly gone. I felt too ashamed now to meet her eyes. 'It's finished,' I said. 'No more . . .'

'Because of Kate?' she asked. And there was a hardness in her voice I had never heard before.

'No, not because of Kate. Because it's wrong.'

'I love you,' she said, as if presenting an outstanding account.

'And I love you. But not like that . . . not any more.'

'That bitch!' She was on her feet, pacing back and forth. 'It was all right till she came, her with her black buck . . .'

'Listen,' I said. 'Listen, now! It happened, we can't forget that.

But we'll never speak of it again, you hear? At least we can *pretend* it didn't happen . . .'

She didn't say anything for a moment. Then, quietly: 'You'd go to gaol if I told anyone, wouldn't you?'

I stood up, suddenly sick, and walked towards the door.

'Terry!' she called after me. 'Wait!'

But I was gone, on my way out into the bar.

I'm sure that I heard her weeping. But I could not go back into the kitchen. It wasn't that I didn't want to comfort her, tell her it would be all right. It was just that I couldn't trust myself. I knew that whatever happened, I mustn't touch her . . . because there was still that terrible magic in her, in her skin, in the way her body moved inside her clothes, in her touch . . .

I took a cloth and began to rub down the bar, one end to another, back and forth, back and forth . . .

•

She never came to my door again, not that I know of. I kept it locked at night, all the same, and have done ever since. It is as much to keep me in as her out, because nothing has changed in thirty years, and insanity is just as close to the surface as it was then, in that autumn thirty years ago.

•

After that, she would barely look at me. We would pass in the corridors, and she would avert her eyes. We spoke to each other when we had to, but no more than that. I told myself that the cloud, the misery would pass away from us in time, that it was just a matter of waiting. One day, I thought, she'll find some young fellow – girls do. And then she'll start to laugh again, and maybe get married . . .

And a terrible jealousy would take me by the throat when I

thought of that, of some local oaf fumbling her sweetness in the dark . . . I hated the faceless forms of those imagined lechers as I lay behind my locked door . . .

Autumn passed to winter, and there seemed nothing good or wise in the world. The war went badly, the locals quarrelled, the frosts came down harder than usual, the pipes froze and split, and I thought often of the fast, brown river and how it would solve things for me . . . but that was only a form of running away, and I've always felt that you need a better excuse than that . . .

And then she stopped me as I came downstairs one morning, stood in front of me, barred my passage.

'I want to talk to you,' she said.

I waited. Her face was paler than usual, but there was a curious sense of triumph about it, in the set of her lips, in the wide, blue gaze.

'I'm going to have a baby,' she said, her eyes fixed on mine.

I felt the old building rock a little under my feet, felt my jaw begin to sag. It wasn't that the news was such a surprise; after all, we had completed the implacable pattern often enough in that week . . . I had known, I suppose that it was possible. Yet the *reality* of it . . .

'Are you sure?' We ask it every time, needlessly. What woman isn't sure . . ?

She said nothing, just smiled a little.

There are certain things that you cannot avoid knowing if you are a publican – too many secrets find their way across the bar counter. And I knew that in the city there was more than one doctor who would oblige a girl in trouble.

'I'll find out,' I said. 'Find a doctor . . .'

She shook her head quickly, a sharp toss that sent her hair swirling, and I read a certain resolution in her eyes. She did not look like any seventeen-year-old I had ever seen, but a woman much older, much surer of herself.

'What do you mean?' I asked, knowing the answer.

'I'm going to have our baby,' she said. 'Our' baby . . . it struck me like a knife in the chest. 'Our baby' . . .

I turned away, knowing that what I felt was partly relief;

I hated the thought of abortion, always had: of the blood, the sharp instrument, the indignity, the finality of the loss, the cold-bloodedness of it all . . . Yet . . . yet, if she had shown any weakness I would have had it done . . .

I turned back for a moment. 'You're sure? You know what it'll be like? You single, with a baby . . .'

'I don't care,' she said. 'And don't worry, I'll never tell.'

And she didn't. Not till this year.

•

I wrote to Kate, asked her to come back for a few days. She was the only one I could turn to, and I needed someone. Uncertainty plagued me like a fever, and the strange minds of women seemed to mock me . . .

'Sell the bloody hotel,' said Kate. 'Pack up and move – New Zealand, Canada, anywhere . . .'

We were upstairs in my office. From downstairs came the distant clatter of dinner dishes. Nancy was looking after the dining room, Mrs Hemmings was mumbling over her pots, and Fred was in the bar. There was a light chill wind roaming up the valley from the south-east, the night was bright with stars, and by midnight the frost would be locked hard on the earth. The fire burned brightly and Kate sprawled on the sofa across the hearth.

'Why?' I said. 'No one will know, here. Not who the father is. She won't get rid of it, but she won't tell, either.'

'She doesn't have to,' said Kate. 'I'll bet that old biddy in the kitchen's got a good idea of what's going on.'

'Nothing's going on.'

'Well, what *was* going on, then. Besides, you can cut the tension with a knife when the two of you're in the same room. All that bloody electricity.'

'I've tried to get her to go away, have the baby in Melbourne, somewhere like that. Come back when it's all over. Maybe put the baby out for adoption . . .'

'You just don't see it, do you?' She held out her glass for more port. I filled it from one of the last pre-war bottles. The firelight shone on her hair and the rustle of her stockings was loud in the quiet room as she leaned back. God knows how she got her stockings, silk, nylon . . . I didn't like to think.

'What do you mean, I don't see?'

She sipped her port, shrugged lightly. 'Never mind, it doesn't matter . . .'

I didn't press it. I had the feeling that if I did, then she would tell me something I would rather not hear.

'What am I going to do, Kate?'

'I told you – sell out, pack up, get out now, before the baby comes. She isn't showing yet, you'll be long gone if you start now.'

Selling the hotel . . . it was unthinkable. And yet there was a certain perverse attraction about the idea. 'But what then?'

'What do you think? Set up house somewhere else. Just the two of you and the baby. That's what you both want, really, isn't it?'

Once it had been put into words, I realised that that was what I wanted, all right. It made me feel a little sick to think about it, but whether with revulsion or a kind of desperate longing, I don't know.

'Come on, Terry,' she said, lighting a cigarette. 'The sight of you two together, that's enough to tell me . . . it's your only chance, both of you – if you miss it, you're finished, one way or another. Either people will find out and you'll have to go anyway, or you'll be stuck here forever, the pair of you, and the whole place will be a kind of prison . . .'

I looked at her carefully. 'You haven't said anything about . . . you know, the *moral* side of things . . .'

'*Morals! Me?*' And she laughed. 'Christ, Terry, you're a scream!' She stubbed out her cigarette, turned to look at me, hands clasped over her slim knees. Then she sighed, and suddenly she looked a lot older. 'Terry,' she said, 'I've been opening my legs to blokes since I was thirteen, and I don't regret a single time. But the only thing that really matters in the end is waking up in the morning next to someone you love, putting your hand out, feeling the warmth, knowing that you've got it for another day . . .' She shook her head, slowly. 'If you get the chance at that,' she said, 'and you let it go, then you're the world's biggest fool, it doesn't matter whether it's your daughter, your grandmother, or McGinty's goat.'

I shook my head, looking away from her, into the violet core of the fire. I knew that I could never leave the hotel, the valley. God knows why, really. I haven't got a real reason that would stand up. But I couldn't leave it . . . and if I could, it would certainly not be to do what Kate suggested. There was a *wrongness* to it, a kind of ultimate self-gratification that would divorce us from the rest of the world, from all the weight of conscience.

But I would keep the suggestion to myself, all the same, not mention it to Nancy. For all I knew, she might accept the solution, and I would not like to think of that . . .

•

The weeks dragged on, the winter slow and quiet, the war news bad, the weather worse, business too slow to keep us occupied much of the time. I filled the days with odd jobs of maintenance that had built up over the past years, re-puttying windows on the weather side, replacing loose nails in the roof, re-levelling the old guttering, re-fencing the back garden.

Once the idea of the hotel as a prison had entered my mind, it seemed to lodge there, and I saw us both, Nancy and me, as prisoners, dragging through our days in a world of greyness and drabness and something almost like misery.

She was showing now, her waist thickening, although she looked better than ever, her complexion clearer, her eyes brighter, her hair glossier. Pregnancy agrees with some women. And she seemed to take no note of it, to ignore her expanding waistline.

But Mrs Hemmings didn't.

I walked into the kitchen one afternoon in my slippers. I had been upstairs reading by the fire for an hour, and they did not hear me come in. Nancy was cleaning ash from the big Aga stove, her face warm and sweaty, her hair awry. Mrs Hemmings stood at the sink, cleaning the mincer parts with steel wool.

'Who is it, then? Why won't you tell?'

'Because I choose not to,' said Nancy, sitting back on her haunches, wiping her hands on her hessian apron.

'Won't he own up to it, then?'

'He won't talk about it,' said Nancy, cocking her head at the old lady. 'Won't say a word.'

'Why ever not?' she turned away from the sink.

'Can't talk at all, can't speak,' said Nancy.

'Well, I never . . .' the old lady was consumed by curiosity. 'Who *is* it, then?'

'Oh,' said Nancy, picking up the scraper again, attacking the grate, 'it's Ertler's dog, I've got this thing about Alsations . . .'

The old lady turned away, rubbed as if to scarify the old metal in her hands, lips pursed. 'I dare say you're like a few others we know and can't say for sure just who it is . . .'

'That's enough,' I said, and moved into the room. 'I'll have none of that, Mrs Hemmings. Keep a civil tongue or go elsewhere.'

I knew that she needed the job too badly to leave. She lowered her head over the sink, jaw tight, mouth thin as a stitched wound.

Nancy started to laugh as I turned to leave. I could hear it all the way up the stairs. I stopped at the top feeling curiously light-headed, and found that I was trembling.

To my knowledge that was the only time, bar once, that she was taxed or sneered at or picked on for her pregnancy. The locals, after their first furtive looks, seemed even more polite to her than usual. I noticed a puzzled and curious look or two, but there was not a word in the bar. A publican, particularly in wartime, has a considerable influence on the drinking population of a town, and I knew that self-preservation was part of it. But something else, too. For Nancy had been a general favourite from the time she was a little girl, and I think that most people were more grieved than anything else that she found herself in such a predicament. There was a nasty incident one night with a drunken traveller, who tried to corner her in the passage, and sneered when she repulsed him. I came into the passage from the cellar just in time to see him try to grab her. I hit him with the bung starter I had in my hand, and although he was a month in hospital the locals all swore blind that he had been drunk as a tinker and had fallen down the front steps.

All this somehow seemed to distance me from her. It was almost as though, the further advanced her pregnancy, the further I faded into the background, the less involved I was. Sometimes it almost seemed as though there *were* in fact some other secret lover to whom she would not admit. No one so much as mentioned the matter to me, but I believe that the consensus of opinion was that he was most likely a married man from nearby, and that she was staying silent to save his family the disgrace.

The months moved slowly by, the seasons turned, and inside her the child grew larger. I tormented myself nightly with the thought of some gross deformity, some terrible affliction that would be the retribution for our sin, a burden that we would have to carry and that the world would jear at.

And when, at last, in the heat of late January, Jack was born, it seemed impossible that such a beautiful child should have been produced by such a blasphemous mating.

When they phoned from the hospital in Formby to tell me the news I almost collapsed, stood slumped against the wall by the phone, weak and useless, weeping helplessly . . .

And when I finally saw him, held him, watched him at the breast, there came that strange lightening of the spirit that was the last thing I had expected. I think it must be so for many men – divorced perhaps, or abandoned, or clamped in some hateful union – they must say to themselves as I did: Well, it was wrong, it was a mistake, it should never have happened – but when I see that child I cannot totally regret it . . .

•

In those days – it was only thirty years ago – the fate of the unmarried mother was that she was branded a slut. Few recovered, unless they married quickly. Anyone, as long as it was quickly. The few who remained unmarried and managed to wear down the brand on them had a thin time, and earned their recovered respectability the hard way. The price was high, and the smallest transgression, the lightest relaxation, was enough to lose it all for them again.

Nancy never faltered. For thirty years she has lived a blameless life, a life that would shame a nun. Swears a bit, I suppose, but not badly. If she has a fault, it may be a certain lack of charity . . .

I had hoped that she might marry, that she would take one of the locals – and there were several who would have married her like a shot if she had shown the slightest inclination. I was jealous of them, but that was just part of the price, and the least part. But she never gave them any encouragement, never flirted. She smiled, gossiped, laughed with them, but that was all. She went no more to dances, keeping her energies for the hotel and for young Jack. She was a good mother: he had the best of attention, always. Of love, well, I am not sure, even now. It's normal for children to grow away from their parents a little, but it seemed the other way with those two; Nancy seemed to grow away from Jack, and that right early. It never meant any lessening of attention, or discipline, or care. But it seemed to me that she became, as the years went by, a little more clinical about him. I could never understand it, but I had no right to criticise.

For myself, the boy was a small glowing sun that lit up the valley, illuminated my life.

But there is the old saying about prices, and eventually I have to pay. Now is the time, I suppose . . .

Nancy and I, we have both created and destroyed him. Now we must save him if we can. At least I must; there is an imbalance in the equation, any fool can see that: too many terms. I am afraid, at times quite desperately afraid, and grow cold thinking of it. But he belongs here, or if he does not, he has the right to choose his place, not to be forced away . . . My father, his namesake, traded only gold for this place, and had the best of the bargain. Jack must have his share, his chance at it. If he would come back and stay, perhaps he would wipe out what we have done, nullify a generation, make the family right again. How many times I have wished that he would marry, have children, repair the strain . . .

The only thing perhaps to say about dying is that it is right and proper that at the end we must leave the game to make way for the others, the newcomers, to see what they can do with their chance.

God forgive me for what I have done with mine . . .

PART THREE

JACK BYRNE – OUTSIDE

The alarm clock rattles, cheap and tinny, and I reach out an arm into the chill air to muffle it. There is grey light at the edges of the blinds, and I feel a hundred and seventeen years old. Beside me Claire stirs a little, then relapses into sleep, curled tight like a warm snail in the shell of tousled blanket. The room, high and dim and old, feels as still as a tomb.

I get up quickly – it's a bad idea to lie and contemplate at this hour of the day. Movement dispelleth melancholy, saith the prophet. Which explains my geographical. Which hasn't got me far yet. Never mind. I dress quickly, pick up my boots and go out into the kitchen. The blind rattles up when I touch it, and I have a fine and unobstructed view of our elderly neighbour clearing his sinuses into the petunias.

Turn on the griller in the antique electric stove with its green bow legs and red gauges. Pot of water on the stove for my eggs. If no one's pinched them. Into the bathroom for a quick dobie. No one in there for a bloody wonder. Told them that if they sleep in the bath I'll piss on them. It's the alkies, messy. The druggies are mostly OK. Quiet, mind their own business. But they sleep in unlikely places. One asleep now wedged into the cabinet dryer.

They back in on cold nights, turn it on to keep warm, then nod off, get stuck. If you've got washing to dry you usually have to pry out a jammed junkie first.

Back in the kitchen I plug in the jug for coffee, lace up my old boots, pour a mug of moselle from the flagon and drink it while the water heats in the pot. Fill the mug again, drink it while the eggs cook, the toast browns. Wine also dispelleth melancholy, especially at six-fifteen in the morning. Another mug while I eat the eggs. The flagon's getting low, must remember to buy another one tonight. Make coffee, add a generous dash of rum, hide the bottle again. Royal Swan's too bloody expensive to waste on transients. Cut some rough sandwiches and stow them in my crib box, put the box in my haversack. I give myself plenty of time in the a.m.s. Rushing is bad for all sorts of things: digestion, potency, temper, etc. The edge off melancholy, and I drink my second cup of rum and coffee at a nice leisurely pace. Melancholy? Melano . . black something? Black choler? Right on, buddy . . .

A quarter to seven, and my black choler is under control for the moment when Claire appears, pattering on bare feet to the bathroom. I go into the front room, pull the loose moulding off the fireplace and retrieve the stash, roll myself four joints. By the time I'm finished, Claire is back in the kitchen making toast. She's wearing jeans and a sweater, and her nipples stand out through the wool in the morning cold. She looks very pale and fragile, her eyes dark as bruises. I kiss her lightly, without speaking, and light the first joint, go and sit on the loo to smoke it. When it's finished, flush, come out and smoke the second joint in the kitchen. Offer Claire a toke but she shakes her head.

I tuck the remaining two joints into an empty cigarette packet. The grog and the grass are all that make the beginnings of the day bearable. And the rest of it, for that matter.

Seven o'clock. I kiss her goodbye and depart, both of us wordless in the godforsaken morning. It's only a fifteen-minute bus ride and I'm at the factory at twenty past seven. Ten minutes to spare.

The crib room is dim and cold, filthy as usual. Nearly everyone is there already. John, Mario, Terry, Peanut, Tony, Norm. Only two more to come. We sit talking in monosyllables. No one is wound up yet, all still slack and heavy with the frayed tag-ends of the night and sleep.

Five minutes to go and Mike the Mouth strolls in. He's dressed in bib-and-brace overalls, a black-and-yellow football guernsey, a red haversack slung over his shoulders. He sits down near the door and yawns. His great bush of black golliwog hair sticks out all over like a halo, his beak of a nose is pink with the cold. He has a big bruise under his right eye.

'Hullo,' says Norm. 'Who thumped you?'

'Ah,' says Mike, 'bloody king hit.'

'On the piss again, I s'pose . . .'

We sit in silence, yawning, blinking, scratching, waiting for seven-thirty.

One to come.

With a minute to go there is a confused clattering from the workshop outside and Hiroshima, the walking disaster, stumbles through the door wide-eyed. He always seems vaguely surprised to find himself here at all. He lives half a mile away, near the main road, but he won't walk round the footpaths: he insists on travelling as the crow flies. This means that he has to scale fences, invade backyards, cross the timber mill and a corner of the textile factory yard, and finally crawl under the bottom of the factory's back gate. He swears it's quicker. Not surprisingly, he's kind of bedraggled, as if he's been dragged backwards through a hawthorn hedge. Of course he never has time to wash in the morning, or to comb his hair. His clothes – torn jeans and filthy windcheater – are stiff with dirt. He stands, all five foot four of him, in the doorway, mouth open, looking around.

'Shit,' he says, 'I forgot me can of Coke . . . me girlfriend was still asleep . . . she should'a reminded me . . .'

John, a pot-bellied sixteen-stoner with a bald head and a red beard, hauls himself to his feet. 'Let's go,' he says.

We all stir. I take off my jacket, hang it on a nail, take my work gloves out of my bag, and follow the others out through the welding shop into the drum shed.

It's a high, galvanised-iron shed, maybe two hundred feet long by a hundred wide, with a concrete floor. Along one side runs the drum line – expander, roller, burrer, swager, seamer, tester, pre-dryer, spray tunnel, oven, stack-off conveyor. The other side of the shed is filled with packs of steel, shells, finished drums, pallets of tops and bottoms.

John switches on the oven and walks over to us.

'Right,' he says, 'off you go . . . two hundred shells to start with.'

We take up our positions. There are only three of us – all casuals – at the rough end of the line: me, Hiroshima, Mike the Mouth. Sometimes we go up the other end of the line when they're shorthanded or have a fast run, but mostly we stay down here. We each have our job: Hiroshima picks up the flattened steel cylinders, expands them, feeds them into the burrer; Mike swages them and rolls them on to the bench; I wipe out the insides with a rag dipped in thinners and stack them off three high. I'm bigger and heavier than the others, so drew the stacking job. They're only light-gauge forty-fours, and not heavy when you get the knack, especially before the tops and bottoms are seamed on.

Hiroshima punches the switches, the rumble and clatter begins, and we're away . . .

•

I'm sitting in this coffee lounge in the middle of town. They're tearing down a building across the road, and the wind surges round the shoulders of the buildings that are left, and down the canyon of rubble. I'm at the table nearest the door, facing it, back to the wall, just like John Wayne, and I keep shifting, edging away from the draught. Every time the door opens the wind slices in.

This town makes me nervous. Not that I've ever spent much time here – don't really know anyone. But it's a small place, Tasmania, a bad place for a dirty weekend; wherever you go you meet *someone* . . . If I had been just another player a few years out of the game, well, it wouldn't be so bad. Even if Tasmanians are nearly as insane as Victorians about football. But it was that bloody picture, after that it was never quite the same.

There are a couple of dozen of them, maybe more. They're everywhere: in newspaper files, living rooms, clubroom walls, football books. You see the picture in the distance and you know who it is. That *one* picture that after a while comes to represent the man. They all had them. Haydon Bunton, Pratt, Coleman, Hudson, Nash . . .

I remember that mark. But mostly because while it was still fresh in my mind the photo was in the newspapers. A big pack of Tigers, with Royce Hart up in front, and they're well up, toes down, reaching for the ball. And there's the old killer lying flat on his back about a foot above their fingertips, one hand – the left it was – stuck out above his head, and the ball just nestling neatly, securely, in the palm. I really couldn't believe it, that I'd got that high. But I remember I was a long time coming down. You see those things later, and you really *can't* believe it . . . But since then, that's the one, of all the years of photos, that's the one they always print.

People still come up to me in the street . . .

So, I'm a bit nervous. I suppose they've got the cops looking for me. But I don't guess they'll make too much fuss. I'm not really a criminal or anything.

It was easy enough getting away from the clinic. I just walked out through the laundry, jumped the fence to the carpark, wandered out into the street. No one saw me, no alarms. So I strolled down toward the main drag. And then it really hit me. For the first time in years. Nowhere to go, no objective, nothing. I began to sweat a bit then. Because I had this plan of a kind. Get some money, a temporary job, maybe, save enough for the air fare, head north. But once out in the streets, it just seemed to fall apart. I started to shake, and what could I do? I wanted a nice quiet room somewhere, a cave, a retreat. I wanted to hide from the world. But there was nowhere to go. An awful temptation to book into a hotel, lock the door, put the pillow over my head. But haven't got enough money for *that* sort of luxury.

So I compromise in the end by going into this coffee lounge, watching every new face that comes in, nursing my espresso, wondering where I'm going to put my head for the night.

Despite all this paranoid watchfulness, I don't notice her come in, just another anonymous gust from the door. She must have gone to the counter, because when I look up she is standing by the table with an orange juice and a plate of sandwiches.

'Mind if I sit here?' she asks.

'No, sure.'

I'm not all that good at women's ages. Looks about eighteen, nineteen. I try to avoid looking at her, watch the navvies on their picks and bars across the street knocking down the old dusty orange bricks. But I can see her out of the corner of my eye, and now and then I get in a furtive squint. She's pretty enough to intimidate me a bit.

'Excuse me,' she says, 'can you tell me the right time?'

I look at my watch. 'Twenty-five past twelve, near enough.' And they're lining up, Petra and the blue-haired ladies, for lunch.

'Thanks,' she says, 'I thought the clock was wrong.'

I turn, crane my neck, can't see any clock. But I've had a good look at her now. Pale skin, almost translucent, good teeth, good bones. Eyes that dark-grey colour, almost violet. Not much make-up. Long skirt, white shawl-necked sweater, brown cord jacket. She looks clean, almost scrubbed. And her small white hands are trembling a little. She has the coldest seat in the whole place: every time the door opens the wind spills in,
her like a wave.

'It's cold . . .' She's shivering. I watch her hands as they crumble one of the mean little sandwiches. She doesn't eat, just sucks her juice through the straw.

'It's crowded,' she says. 'Isn't it?'

I have this curious sense of dislocation. Our voices, our words, aimed across the table, are missing their targets, sliding off and away into the steam and the coffee smells.

As if we're blindfolded, trying to locate each other, uncertain.

'Where do you come from?' she asks. 'The mainland?'

Why would she think that? 'Sometimes,' I say. 'Here and there . . .'

'You're on your own?'

I nod.

'Where are you living?'

'Oh,' I say, 'I slept on someone's floor last night.'

'Don't you get lonely? Living like that?'

'Sometimes. You get used to it.'

She crumbles more bread, sucks more juice. 'Have you got somewhere for tonight?'

'I'm not sure.' Jesus, what's going on?

'I was going to say, there's this place where I've been staying . . . you could stay there.'

'Where is it?' And to tell the truth I just can't make her out. She just doesn't look the kind to go picking up blokes at midday in coffee bars.

'It's all right,' she says, fiddling with her straw, 'anyone can turn up . . . it doesn't matter, you can always crash there.'

I fumble at my pack of cigarettes.

'Have one of these,' she says. I take one. Mentholated, fucking awful, like a cough drop up your nose. 'Thanks.'

We seem to have found some sort of common wavelength at last. I look at her more closely. There are shadows, hollows, under her cheekbones that shouldn't be there. And she's still trembling.

'They're very good,' she says, 'the people at this house. It's going to be pulled down, and nobody worries about the rent. We're all on the dole, you know . . . I lost all my money yesterday, and they lent me sixty dollars . . .'

'Yes?'

'Yes,' she says, 'they're very good . . . it's just that sometimes I can't take any more . . . it's all right mostly . . . lots of junkies hang out there . . . and alkies . . . but it's all right, no hassles. It's just that sometimes it gets to me . . . like yesterday there was blood all over the bathroom . . .'

'A bit rough,' I say. Oh, Jesus, it sounds like fucking paradise, doesn't it?

'I went to see my parents last night. I was a bit of a mess,

I was pretty uptight, I started carrying on . . . so later on, when I got myself straightened out, then I went back and apologised, told them I was sorry . . . but I could never go back there, they're just . . . I don't know, it's another world.'

'You look a bit strung out.'

She smiles, her teeth very white. Her fingers are frantically shredding the last of the sandwiches.

'Yes,' she says, 'I'm meeting a boy at one o'clock down at the mall . . . a boy I know . . . he'll have something, I know he's carrying some hash . . . I'll make some cookies this afternoon . . .' She looks at me a little uncertainly, suddenly seeming shy. 'Would you like to come along?'

'Why not?' I don't want to go. But it's *somewhere*, a destination of *some* kind. And besides, I just can't bear the thought of her going alone into that horrible fucking world. She looks so fragile . . .

I look carefully at her eyes, at her pinched nostrils, at what I can see of her skin. Not smack. Speed maybe. Dry mouth, the shakes, no appetite, talking jag . . . I remember the days of benzedrine, dexedrine. 'What are you on?' I ask her.

'Oh, just grass and mushrooms . . .'

'Well, that's not too bad, you'll be OK . . .'

'Yes,' she says, twisting her straw, 'I'll be fine . . .'

She looks as brittle as a frozen flower.

'I'm going to have some more juice,' she says. 'I love orange juice.'

'Well, I'll have another coffee.'

We get up, go to the counter. She won't let me pay for her drink. Back at the table she is silent for a while. But she seems a little brighter now. And through the strange transparent sadness that seems to hang over her, something still shines dimly.

'My name's Claire,' she says.

'Mine's Jack.'

She smiles. 'We went out in the country at the weekend,' she says. 'We picked a big bucket of mushrooms. We're getting together tonight.'

Oh, Christ, *mushrooms* . . . But I'd like to slip a couple into old Purple's fricassee.

'You know,' she says, 'a couple of people I know have OD'd. The last one wasn't long ago. I went to the funeral, it really shook me up. I guess that's what started it, why I got so that I can't seem to take it any more . . . they were all throwing the stuff into the grave . . . you know, the syringes and stuff . . . I just stood there, and somehow it was all wrong, them doing that . . . you know, they should have been *thinking* about it . . . instead all they could do was throw that stuff in the grave . . .'

'Take it easy,' I say. She's getting the shakes a bit worse now.

'I'll be all right, I'm getting it straightened out . . .'

We sit silently for a little. Suddenly she speaks again.

'What time is it?'

I look at my watch. 'A quarter to one.'

'I'd better go . . .' And she is on her feet, gathering her cigarettes, matches, her handbag. She stops a moment, looks at me. Smiling, but a very tremulous, uncertain smile, something almost pleading about it. And it hits me then. Of course. She's just so bloody *lonely* . . .

'Are you going to . . . ?' she says.

'What?' Feeling a few bells ringing. Keep clear.

'Come back? To the house?' It's hurting her to ask.

Jesus H Christ, killer, who the fuck do you think you are to play hard to get? Byrne the Bastard. And worse. Pretend you're human for a bit anyway. 'Yes,' I say, 'of course. And thanks.'

Her smile flashes like a sudden light.

Walking through the dim tunnel of the arcade that leads to the street, the traffic, the stink and rush, I glance at her face beside my shoulder. In the open air it seems paler and gaunter, and filled with a kind of innocent and weary patience; with the patience of waiting for someone, for something, for afternoons and evenings, for mushrooms and speed and hash cookies; waiting to get it straightened out . . .

•

The shells clatter down the slope to the swager, a double hiss of escaping air, and Mike spins the first one on to the long metal table. With my gloved left hand I seize the burred edge, bare right hand dipping the rag into the bucket of thinners and wiping out the near end of the shell, spinning it down the bench as I go. Halfway down I flick the shell with my left hand to reverse it, and wipe out the other end. Pick it up, walk ten paces and stack it. Another shell is waiting. Grab it with my left hand, dip the rag in the bucket, wipe . . .

Not a very demanding job. My part in the great industrial process. Hour after hour, day after day.

By now we are submerged in the abominable noise of it all – all the varied hisses, groans, clanks and rattles, overshadowed by the harsh, high squeal of the burrer and the clanging of the shells going on to the stack. It's almost impossible to hear anyone unless they yell right in your ear.

I wipe and stack, wipe and stack.

Half an hour passes. The grog is fading now, just the grass carrying me. Without it, these mornings, these days, would be impossible.

Hiroshima sets a number of shells crooked in the burrer and they come out with all the flange at one end, none at the other. As they reach Mike, he takes one look and begins to tip them joyfully over the back of the machine. They bounce and clang madly.

'Hey, Cisco!' he shouts, waving at Hiroshima and pointing at the drums. Hiroshima shrugs, and feeds more shells into the burrer. Mike continues to tip them over the back, laughing. I sit down on the bench. Soon there are twenty or so rejects piled up. John rushes up and begins to harangue Hiroshima. Mike sits down beside me.

'Hard, eh, Cisco?' he says.

'Terrible,' I say, and we both laugh. You can't really take this shit seriously. Then I notice that Mike is a bit quiet and down. Says nothing for a minute or so. It's unusual; normally he hardly ever stops talking.

'What's the matter?' I say. 'You're quiet today . . .'

He scratches his ear. 'Got another bluey last night.'

'What for?'

'Maintenance . . . five hundred bucks. Haven't paid any for six months. Shit, I haven't had a job for six months. Not until this one came along.' He's only been on this job a couple of weeks, like me.

I know what's bugging him. He's saving to get his motorbike fixed. On the way south from Darwin with his girl on the back, he ran into a cow outside Maryborough. He and the girl ended up in hospital. Five hundred bucks will set his plans back badly.

'Just when things were looking up,' he says. 'June's got a job at the corner grocer's . . . all cash, no tax, she still gets her dole cheque . . . shit, if I had five hundred bucks and the bike I'd piss off now.'

Clang! Another shell hits the burrer. John is busy oiling a cam. We start to run again.

Wipe and stack, wipe and stack . . .

Now and then I roll one up the line and test it. They're all good.

Wipe and stack, wipe and stack . . .

Then Hiroshima starts on a new pack of steel, and the first shell splits on the swager. The seam cracks open. We go on running them. Now I test one. Most of them are leaking, and one in three bursts on the swager. We stop and call John. He runs round and waves his arms a bit. Tries them himself. No good. He sulks, because he doesn't know what to do. It's an urgent order, and he's panicked.

'Stop!' he says in the end. 'We'll have to wait for Herb.'

Herb is the works manager, and he won't be in for half an hour.

The area behind the machines is piled high now with rejects, maybe thirty or forty altogether. John's face goes slack whenever he looks at them.

Mike and I sit down, Hiroshima comes over and we all light up ciggies.

At last Herb turns up, his old mangy sheepdog trailing after him. He looks at the reject drums, swears. Talks to John. Then comes over to us. 'Keep going,' he says, 'put the rejects aside, we'll bronze 'em later.'

He wanders off towards the front office.

We start again.

Wipe, test, stack . . .

The noise flows over us, locking us into a voiceless void.

At last John waves at the clock. Smoko. We troop back to the crib room to drink bitter tea from scummy cups. Two and a half hours of the day gone.

After smoko Herb decides to spray and cook what drums are made up. There are a hundred or so from yesterday stacked near the oven. So we all move to the other end of the line. Mike feeds the drums into the spray tunnel, John sprays them, Peanut feeds them on to the conveyor, Hiroshima and I stack off at the hot end.

We sit on a couple of pails, Hiroshima and I, and wait. We have maybe ten minutes before the first drums come through.

He's kind of dim, Hiroshima, but I like him. He's twenty, small and wiry, with an ugly freckled face, long brown hair. Always cheerful.

'You married?' he says.

'No.'

'Got a girlfriend?'

'Yeah . . .' I suppose Claire qualifies, even if Petra doesn't. *Had* a girlfriend . . . Petra.

'She got a job?'

'On the dole.' Then: 'Your bird got a job?' I ask.

'No,' he says, 'she did have one at a bakery, but she had to start too early in the mornings . . . I couldn't get her out of bed. She's pretty young . . .'

'How old is she?'

'Soon be sixteen.' He gets up and wanders over to the oven doors. The first drum is showing.

Soon the double line of hot drums, painted bright orange, is edging slowly along the curve of the twin conveyors towards us. We have to take the temporary plugs out, purge the drums with compressed air, fit bungs and stack them off. The catwalk between the two conveyors doesn't reach the last fifteen feet to the oven doors. The drums are too hot to handle that close anyway. But Hiroshima is impatient. He walks along, reaching for them. And steps straight off the end of the catwalk, plunges down three feet to the floor between the lines. Drums spill from the tracks. I get down on my hands and knees and peer under the conveyors. He is lying on his back on the concrete floor looking surprised and vaguely indignant.

'You all right?' I'm reluctant to press the emergency stop button because that would bring John or Herb. And Hiroshima is already on warning for smoking right next to the paint tunnel, despite the two bloody great notices.

He blinks. 'Shit, that hurt . . .' He rolls over and crawls out, stands up and rubs his back. I pull up his sweater. There is a great red weal down one side where he hit a brace on the way down. He walks away muttering. But in five minutes he has recovered and is amusing himself with the air hose, poking it into his shirt, down his trousers, grimacing and laughing. Then he takes to putting the hose in the small bung hole of a drum, sealing the big hole with his hand, and when the pressure has built up, releasing it. He finds that the released air blows the sleeve of his jumper up past his elbow. He shouts, demonstrates this remarkable discovery, first to John, then to Herb. They both go away shaking their heads.

It's Thursday. Payday. The only good thing about it.
Another hour till crib time.

•

This house where Claire lives – a puzzler. It's like going into another world. In the middle of that bright, buzzing, clean little town, in the *middle*, you turn off the highway under the big hill, go up a little side street, the traffic noises still in your ears, and on one side of the street you've got inner-city suburbia, clean and brick and chee chee, and on the other this old house. Not so old. Just kind of *battered*. Like pieces seem to have fallen off it, and nothing fits any more. Beyond it, the new hospital complex is creeping closer, and soon it will eat up this house, like all the others. And in the mean time – a matter of weeks maybe, months at the most – it's in a kind of limbo, sold, acquired, but not needed. Tenants – I suppose one of these funnies is a tenant – well, they're there and no one is worried, no one can be bothered interfering . . .

What was once a garden, big old camellias and oleanders and twisted pencil pines, is littered with rain-softened cartons, cans, bottles, dogshit . . . you name it, it's there. The concrete paths are cracked, weed-seamed, tilted and crazy. The windowpanes are cracked, the frames skewed, the paint peeling, the roof rusted, the doors aslant . . . it's unbelievable that neglect, mere neglect, could bring a house so quickly to such a wreck.

Claire doesn't fit. Too neat, too clean, too young and too bloody fresh. Inside, in the musty dimness, she seems diminished again, dwarfed somehow by the tall, mouldy walls and wide, creaking floorboards. The windows are strange. Her small bedroom, along the corridor, past the twist of mottled water pipes and the dingy bathroom, has windows of a kind of stained glass. Red and blue, it's got the vague air of a church. The room is clean, tidy, a pathetic effort to hold the decay at bay. Neat counterpane, clean pillows on the narrow bed.

She takes me straight to her bedroom, as if there is nowhere else to go. I sit down on the bed, stare out the windows at the red and blue oleanders that scrape the stucco walls and tap on the glass in the wind. It's cold, and I'm embarrassed now we're here. But she smiles at me, seems more calm now, and content. And almost as if she has acquired weight and responsibility, a householder . . .

'Would you like a cup of coffee?' she asks.

'Sure.'

'I'll go and get it.'

'I'll come with you.' I follow her slimness down the narrow path of ragged linoleum that carries us over the grey, dirty boards. Someone has made an effort to clean the lino – probably Claire. In the kitchen she fills a cracked electric jug at a corroded brass tap and plugs it in. The kitchen is shabby, but not really dirty. The sink is old and iron-stained under the taps, and the electric stove is a monstrous antique. The window looks out on the path that runs beside the house. There are no curtains, only an ancient roller blind.

Waiting for the jug to boil, Claire is suddenly a little nervous again. Stands by the sink, smiling, twisting her hands.

'I'll have to go out for a while,' she says. 'Do you mind waiting? I've got to meet someone . . . the boy with the hash . . . he's a bit shy with strangers.'

'Sure,' I say. 'That's OK.'

The jug boils, the coffee gets made; no milk in the fridge. Sugar OK. I take the cup and we go back along the passage. The house has that deserted feel to it. I'm sure there is no one else there.

She moves round the room a little, edgily. 'I won't be long.' Anxiously: 'Do you mind waiting?'

'No, you go ahead.' I lean back against the headboard. 'I'll have a kip for a bit . . .'

She picks up her bag, backs out of the room, smiling edgily, still shaky, as if I might disappear while she's gone. I hear her footsteps diminishing quickly down the passage. Look round again. Nothing much to see. No pictures, no ornaments. Nothing personal showing but a scent bottle and a lipstick on the dresser top.

Well, killer, what are you doing here? Tell me that, eh? What's the new role, the latest one? Kept man, protector, friend? Brother, comforter, substitute father? How old is she anyway? Forgot to ask, didn't you?

And I don't really want to think about it too much. The truth is, I'm not as calm and collected as I make out. And I don't want to leave, to go outside again. Part of it – well, this is the ideal stop for me, who's going to come looking for me here? The rest of it? Well, that's plain funk, old boy. Shit scared, aren't you? Of the world out there. Just like her . . .

I seem to be finding out all kinds of things. About myself. Never thought of myself as a coward before. Took my lumps when I had to, never grizzled. Like with bloody Tommy Breck from Hawthorn, must be the hardest, roughest bugger I ever played on. Big, brutal and a three-way bastard. The only way to play him was to get in front, stay in front all the time, outmark him. And every time you did, you earned a fist in the ear. Hard. Every time. And you knew it was coming. So what do you do?

You fucking take it. What else can you do? I always figured that I was all right on guts . . .

But this stuff, this is different. I'm not The Bastard anymore, I'm just *a* bastard, and a special sort now, and things'll never be the same again. That's what it is, I suppose. But not only that . . . because I know now that I never was what I thought I was – I was something bloody disgusting and horrible, flawed and freaky and ruined before I started it all. It was all just nonsense, a kind of play-acting, even though I didn't know it was a play. As if you woke up from a dream of sunshine and laughter and realised that you were a war criminal or a fucking pervert or something . . .

Just don't hurt this girl, killer, don't take it out on her. Which means, don't let her lean too much, depend too much . . .

I drink the rest of the coffee, cold and bitter now. Decide to go exploring.

Out in the passage, I begin opening doors. Some rooms worse than others, some bloody awful. None as clean and good as Claire's. Scattering of sleeping bags, blankets, haversacks, duffle bags, old clothes. Biscuit tins, empty bottles, full ashtrays. Smell of dope over everything. One room, a stinker, the smell of vomit and urine, a nest of old bags in the corner. In the lounge room, an old armchair or two, cushions coming unstuffed. A bean bag leaking white beads, a couple of straw-stuffed palliasses. Bathroom not too bad. The basin cracked, the toilet pan a bit scummy. Like a moderately clean public bog. Newspaper squares on a string, kind of a rural touch.

While I'm in there, footsteps, footsteps approaching on the path outside. I come out of the bathroom as he comes in through the back door. A big young fellow, about twenty, long black hair, a single golden earring, hard eyes. Jeans and black rollneck. Looks at me carefully, not unfriendly.

He nods. 'Hi . . .'

'Hi . . .'

He passes me, goes into one of the rooms along the hall. Silence again, but complicated by the new presence behind the scratched door.

After a while, I go back into Claire's room and lie down on

the bed. It's chilly, but I don't like to pull the coverlet over me, looks too much like making myself at home. I lie looking up at the ceiling, a maze of fine cracks. Reminds me of maps. But the thought of maps makes me think of the big billiard table and of Petra, and there is a sudden hollow feeling in my guts and a warmth at the groin, and a great sense of loss, of something too bloody precious to even think about gone forever . . .

And trying not to think of Petra, I suddenly fall asleep, drop like a stone into some deep, black hole where there's nothing at all, no problems, no uncertainty, no pain . . .

And wake in late afternoon dimness to find Claire bending over me, her fingers touching me gently on the cheek. Her eyes have lost some of their darkness now, and she is smiling a little.

I smile back at her, without even thinking about it, and see small dimples form like tiny miracles at the corners of her mouth, almost invisible in the translucence of her skin.

•

Now, with the daylight going, there is a sense of people about us, as if the old house is coming alive. Not so much sound as a sort of presence. I get up, go down to the bathroom, splash my face with water, clean my teeth. The evening ahead – Christ, I suppose this is where I define my new role, as someone, like old Purple would say.

Outside, in the living room, there are several people now. The dark young fellow, a gingery blonde without a bra, a pale and flaky-looking bloke with shoulder-length fair hair, a thin dark girl with enormous eyes and olive skin. She is well dressed, just as if she might have come from a day in a city office. The radio – a tranny in the corner – is turned down low, and they're all smoking grass, saying nothing, just passing the joints around. No one seems to be enjoying themselves much. Claire and I sit in the corner on a couple of ragged cushions, and take our place in the chain. When the joints come I take a toke and pass them on. Never done much for me, old mary jane. I think that, like

121

a good Irishman, my drug is booze. But anything for peace and quiet. The dark boy opens a tobacco tin and begins to roll more joints. The bra-less girl reaches out and takes the dark girl's hand. They don't look at each other. Nothing happening, no one saying anything, the music low, the grass smell high and sweet, and I begin to fall into a not-unpleasant half-doze. Claire is close beside me, leaning a little.

Then I begin to feel hungry. But I don't like to say anything. I'm the outsider here. I think of the old folks queueing up for the evening meal. Maybe roast beef, vegies, steamed pudding, bread and butter. Belly rumbles a bit. To take my mind off it, begin to think about a job. Don't want to go to the CES if I can help it, leave traces, even with a shonky name. And too many people in and out, might recognise me. And I'll bet the philistines have given them my description . . .

There is a sudden clash of gears, the roaring of a motor in the street outside; the slam of car doors, squeak of the gate, heavy footsteps on the broken concrete. The back door bangs open, and the footsteps approach. I watch the doorway.

The most hideous man I've ever seen comes in. Behind him is a quiet little man, middle-aged and mousy, carrying a great paper bundle that steams and gives out the aroma of fish and chips. The little man clasps it to his chest, and hunches in the doorway. The hideous man smiles – an awful sight – and looks about him.

'Me chickens!' he says, and suddenly they are all smiling at him. He's about five and a half feet high, freckled, with gingery sparse hair, a non-existent neck, a gut hanging over his belt inside the dirty green sweatshirt. His teeth are yellow and snaggled, and there are old faded tattoos of anchors and snakes on his bare fat biceps. His eyes are brown and opaque, his nose squashed flat; his ears stick out like swinging doors. There is an odd, mismatched appearance to his features. But all the same, for all the hideousness, he seems to exude goodwill . . .

He gestures towards the little man behind him. 'Feed my lambs, Paulie,' he says. 'Feed my sheep . . .' His voice is a surprise – pleasant, almost cultured.

The little man comes forward, kneels down sacramentally on

the centre of the warm carpet, lays down his bundle, carefully unwraps it, exposing a great steaming pile of golden battered fish and crisp chips. Everyone draws slowly closer, sliding down off chairs and cushions. Only Claire and I stay where we are. But no one touches the food; they all look with a kind of expectancy at the Hideous Man. He leans forward, seizes a handful of chips, sucks them into his gob, mouths through the mess: 'Fall to, fall to . . .'

And they begin, timidly at first, but with increasing boldness, to dig into the pile. Claire moves forward, kneeling beside the white paper, urges me forward too. But I don't really like to take anything. Always paid my way, never bludged, and it's a bit awkward.

The Hideous Man pushes in beside me, takes a large chunk of fish, begins to gnaw. Between mastications he looks at me.

'What's your name, friend?'

'Jack,' I say. Then: 'Jack Todd.'

He regards me carefully, coolly, for a moment, then nods. 'I'm Wingnut,' he says. Seems to see my puzzlement, turns a little as he squats until he is full-face towards me. Gestures at his ears with the remnants of the fish. 'Me ears,' he says. 'When I was about five or six, me mother sent a picture of me to me old man, who was in Korea. He showed it to his mate, and his mate said, "Christ, he's got a head like a fucking wingnut" . . . just stuck from then . . .' Dives for chips. 'You with Claire, then, are you, Jack?'

I nod.

'Nice girl,' he says, just as if she wasn't right there beside me. 'Bit fucked up, but a nice girl. You look after her, then, or I'll bite your balls off.' Quite friendly about it all. 'Go on,' he says, 'feed your face before these bludgers scoff it all.'

So I do.

Beside me, Claire picks at a few chips.

Silence, but for the gnashing of teeth, a stray burp. At last the pace slows, and only the thin dark girl and Wingnut are eating, brushing together the last crumbs. The little man who carried the chips has returned to a corner, begins to roll a ciggie from a packet of Drum. Lights up, no smell of grass. I notice his hands for the first time. Pale, long, fine-fingered. I recall that he wore gloves when he came in, thin dark leather ones. Now that the cigarette is rolled and lit he puts the gloves back on. Wingnut sees me looking.

'That's Paulie,' he says. 'You got a strange sexual disease, a touch of piles, anything like that, you have a word with Paulie – that right, Paulie?'

Paulie's eyes, deep-set and darkish grey, muddy, swing towards us. He nods, almost shyly.

'Paulie's the resident medico,' says Wingnut. 'Struck off years ago for laughing gas and various misfeasances, but he still knows a thing or two, eh Paulie?'

Again Paulie nods.

Everyone slowly retreats from the paper. Paulie stirs himself and wraps it up carefully, goes back to his corner.

'Take it outside, Paulie,' says Wingnut. 'Put her in the garbage, mate.'

Obediently, Paulie gets up, goes out. A clatter of metal and he's back, wedged into his corner again.

Claire moves a little closer to me on her cushion, but doesn't say a word. The inevitable joints begin the circuit again. Wingnut waves one away when it reaches him. So do I. Claire leans back, takes two or three deep tokes. Wingnut seems deep in thought. Then he turns to me. 'Come for a walk,' he says. 'I'll buy you a beer, we'll have a natter.'

I look at him a moment. Under the layer of lard and freckles his expression seems friendly enough. So I stand up, look down at Claire. 'Won't be long . . .'

'All right.' She's been very silent since we came to the house, after all the talk in the coffee bar. Maybe she's regretting bringing me home? Maybe just as nervous as I am . . .

And I haven't heard another word about that bucket of mushrooms.

Thank Christ . . .

Wingnut waves Paulie back into his lair. 'You wait there, mate, I won't be long.'

Outside in the street he turns downhill toward the highway. 'Only a couple of blocks,' he says.

Far away, down the valley, the river is visible, a winding track of tidewater that reflects the orange of the western sky. At this time of year, on the calm still days, the evening seems to burn . . .

We turn in at the Sportsman's Arms, a dingy tile-fronted pub on a ratty corner near a fish shop and a Greek mini-market. Inside, the air is thick with tobacco smoke and stale beer fumes. There are maybe forty or so people, all men in working clothes, crammed round the two sides of the small bar. The barman, a wizened little ape with red eyes and great conk, brings our beers. Wingnut pays. Takes a long draught. Turns to me.

'Won't be staying long, will you Jack?' It's neither a threat, nor a question. He wipes his mouth with the back of his thick paw.

'I don't suppose so. But why not?'

'Ah,' he says, 'you're just not one of them, that's all . . .'

'Who are "them"?'

"Oh, you know,' he says, 'the ones that gotta be looked after . . .' Drains his glass. I put some money on the counter, finish my glass. He looks at the money.

'You afford it?'

I nod.

'All right then,' he says. 'Where you heading?'

'I don't know . . . north maybe . . . bit of a geographical.'

'Ah . . .'

Silence a minute or two.

'On the dole?' he asks, not looking at me.

I shake my head as he looks up.

'Don't want to go on the list, show your face?'

'Something like that.'

'Want a job then . . . temporary, that kind of thing?'

'I guess so.'

He sniffs, takes a deep breath. 'Might be able to find you something.' Ponders a bit. 'I know a place is putting on a few temps just now . . .'

'What kind of job?'

'Does it matter?'

'Not too much.'

'Making drums. You know, forty-fours.'

'Sounds all right.'

'I'll give you a lift in the morning, show you where.' Looks sideways at me. 'Claire's got an alarm clock. We'll leave about seven . . .'

He empties his glass, buys another beer. 'What you been doin' since you gave up the footie?'

'Oh, shit,' I say.

'Don't worry,' he says. 'None of those other buggers down the house'd know a football from a lump of nannygoat shit.'

'Who are they, anyway?'

He shrugs. 'Just . . . people . . . you know. Got off the track a bit, like the rest of us, haven't got back on it again.'

'Need looking after?'

'For a bit.'

'And you look after them, right?'

He shrugs again, grimaces. 'For a bit.'

'What do you do for a crust?'

He grins at me then. 'This and that . . .'

I laugh, and so does he.

On the walk back to the house he tells me a little about the others. Jenny is the gingery, double-gaited girl without a bra, a junkie, like her mate Fran, the dark one. He thinks they're both hawking it in their spare time. Reg, the thin fair boy, is a junkie, too, but not too strung out. Chris, the dark boy, is just a gentle doper, hiding from the coppers over a GBH.

'Ah,' he says, 'they're all right, this lot. There were a few roughies about a week or two back, but they've gone now. There's still a couple of drunks, but they don't get home till late, and they don't generally make a fuss.'

Just before we go in, he stops at the gate. Looks at me carefully. 'Let her down light,' he says. 'You know, when you go.'

And I nod. But how do you let anyone down light, how the fuck do you do *anything* light, because there's really nothing in your life you can control. Not even yourself, not even what you are . . .

Still, light as I can . . .

Inside, the room is almost empty. Paulie is crouched in the corner still, hugging his knees with his gloved hands, staring at nothing. Chris is gone, so are the two lesbians, so is Claire. Reggie is lying on his back, eyes closed. A trip to the battery charger, I guess, while we were at the pub.

Wingnut smiles at Paulie. 'Come on, mate, time to shift.'

Paulie scrambles to his feet. Wingnut winks at me. 'Got to go round me traps. See you in the morning . . .' And they are gone. Reggie doesn't stir, and I walk quietly up the passage, tap on Claire's door.

'Come in.'

She is sitting on the bed, looking thin and miserable, and very young. 'I thought you weren't coming back . . .'

I go and sit beside her, put an arm round her shoulders. 'Of course I was.'

'What did he want? Wingnut?'

'Just fitting me up with a job, that's all.'

That sudden, lovely smile flashes over her face. Her eyes are almost violet in the light from the dim bulb overhead. 'Really? When do you start?'

'In the morning.'

'That's wonderful!'

'He said you had an alarm clock.'

She nods. 'It's in my case. I don't like to leave it round. It's not that anyone's dishonest, but you never know who comes in while you're out . . .'

'No.' Still uneasy about the night, uncertain. 'Listen, where do I doss down? I'll just borrow your clock.'

And suddenly she's crying, tears running silently down her face, and her shoulders are shaking, and she's huddling forward clutching herself like an old woman in grief. And I curse myself for being so fucking clumsy. Just take her and hold her, hold her tightly, until the sobbing slows down.

'Listen,' I say. 'I want to stay with you . . . of course I do . . . but I thought you mightn't want me to . . .'

She doesn't say anything, but seems to burrow closer. And after a while, when the sobbing is gone, and she is lying quiet and soft and very small against me, I put out the light and we go wordless to bed.

For a long time we lie still and twined, her face buried in the crook of my shoulder. All strangely sexless. She seems to need warmth and closeness and comfort more than anything else. No bloody wonder. And I don't really mind. Because there *is* a great comfort in two naked bodies resting quietly together, skin on soft skin, contours accommodated, fitted – a completeness . . .

It occurs to me that I've never really been in love, whatever that is. Sex, plenty of sex, and some good sex. Because I learned pretty early not to make love with anyone unless I liked them. No matter how sexy she is, if you screw a bird you don't like you'll get nothing but a mouthful of ashes and a dirty taste. But lust, just lust, that's very human and very natural, and as long as you're both willing and you like each other and you're not hurting anyone else, there's nothing much wrong with it, and a lot right with it. Not that it was an easy lesson. No one ever told me about sex. Nance certainly didn't. The old boy, Terry, well, he gave me the facts, straightened me out on the technicalities all right. But the emotions . . . well, I suppose we all have to learn that for ourselves.

I've never felt any urge to marry. Never felt that way about any woman, never felt I wanted monogamy, fidelity. Maybe there's some woman somewhere that it'll be different with, maybe then I'll want no one else. For a while, I thought maybe Petra . . . don't know . . .

And the memories of Petra begin creeping round the edges of my mind – her eyes, her straight walk, the slight swell of her belly . . . one of the only women I've known where the soft hair creeps up in a sweet thin line almost to the navel . . . indescribably sexy . . .

Claire stirs against me in the darkness, her hands moving, her lips on the skin of my shoulder . . .

And the old body betrays me again . . . after all, if you're naked in bed with a pretty girl, you can modify the behaviour, but you can't change the nature of the beast . . .

She opens to me sweetly and gently and we move easily into the old dance, the pattern that our bodies are made for. It goes on for quite a long time; but gently and slowly and without any kind of urgency. She murmurs a little at last, makes small sighing groans deep in her throat and I let the explosion overtake me, slow, pulsing, deep . . .

And lie at last, spent and done, and relaxed and at peace. Before I know it, Claire has slipped gently into sleep as we lie, still entwined. And it is only then, as sleep begins to overtake me too, that I realise that I have spent my seed in her, without a thought, without a tremor of guilt or self-disgust . . . something I could never bring myself to do with Petra . . . and even now there is no revulsion . . .

Drifting off into the darkness of sleep, wondering at what she has done, what gift she has given me, to make it possible, and what I can give her in return . . .

•

I wake some time later, I don't know how much later, pulled back to the surface of the night by alien sounds.

A light shines under the door, and there are bumpings, rattlings, gruntings . . .

Claire stirs a little beside me, but does not wake. We are curled comfortably together, spooned; and, feeling her back under my hand, I am struck with wonder at the slimness, the fragility of her body. She would break so easily . . .

There is a great bump, as if someone has fallen, and a loud muttering. I ease out of the bed, pull on my trousers, pad softly to the door. Open it, look down the passage. A door is open on the other side, light streams out. The sounds begin again. Then, from another door, Wingnut emerges, wearing – oddly it seems to me – striped flannel pyjamas. He doesn't see me, but goes to the open door. There is a further thud, a thump – I know *that* sound: someone's been thumped – and a scuffling, a bit of heavy breathing.

I move out and down the passage, closing the door of Claire's room softly behind me.

Inside the other room – I see it's the smelly one with the nest of bags – Wingnut has a headlock on a big bloke in a mismatched suit coat and trousers. He seems to be very drunk. A sherry flagon is lying on its side on the bare floor, half of its contents spilled and soaking into the dry, grey boards. I can see, as the two swing about, grunting a little, that the man has pissed himself.

Wingnut catches a glimpse of me over the man's staggering twisting shoulders, shakes his head wearily.

'You want any help?' I ask.

'I don't think so,' he says. He's not nearly as tall as the other man, but much heavier. 'I can usually get him settled down.' He pushes and shoves until the man is backed into a corner, pushes him upright, lets go his headlock. The man looks about fifty, but he's got that seamed, pickled look of the long-time alkie, the metho man, and he may be quite a bit younger. His eyes are wild, mad, and he swings his head about like a punch-drunk fighter. Wingnut pushes him in the shoulder with his left hand to straighten him up, then wallops him under the left ear with his other fist: a long, looping punch with all his weight in it. The drunk slips down the wall, until he is sitting on the floor. His eyes are still open, but he's not taking much in.

Wingnut sighs deeply. 'Give us a hand,' he says.

Together we lay the man on the heap of bags. He's closed his eyes now and he's breathing deeply, raggedly. Standing over his body I can smell an almost overpowering stink of unwashed body, metho, cheap plonk and piss.

Wingnut stands looking down at him for a minute. Scratches himself. 'He'll be OK now . . . won't wake up till the morning, won't remember anything about it. Never does.'

'How often does this happen?'

'Oh,' he says, 'a couple of times a week. Sometimes he sings when he's in the rats. Sometimes he prays – that's a bloody sight worse.'

'Who is he?'

'Christ knows – they call him Harpic, 'cause he goes right

round the bend.' He stands the sherry flagon up within reach of the man, and moves towards the door. 'Come on, back to bed.'

'Why do you do it?'

'What, punch drunks?' He grins.

'Look after them. All this lot.' Which includes me, a nice thought.

'Someone has to.'

'But why you?'

'I'm a fucking philanthropist . . .' He turns away down the passage. 'See you in the morning, seven o'clock.' His door closes behind him.

I go slowly back to Claire's room, close the door, slip in beside her. She turns over, cuddles up to me.

'I thought you'd gone away . . .' Her voice is blurred with sleep.

I don't say anything, just put my arms round her, stroke her gently until she goes back to sleep. Then I lie there for a long time staring into the darkness. Thinking about Wingnut, about all the others, the drunks, the junkies, the deadbeats, this weird old house . . . the last month I've really come to see that we're all living somehow on a knife edge, that there's no certainty, no security, anywhere, in anything. I know too bloody well that I've come close to slipping off that knife edge. And it seems that some of these people have an even worse grip on the world than I have. Surely Harpic's already gone? Reggie nearly gone? Claire going? Just drifting away from life. What's it like, I wonder? What's it like for Harpic, say? The truth is that Harpic has ceased to exist already. Because maybe he no longer *sees* himself at all. He's just a hunk of agony, a bundle of physical needs, needs that jerk him round the world like a galvanised frog. Because without a vision of yourself, you're dead, although you're still moving. Even if you hate yourself . . . well, you're still alive, surviving. Even if you're a failure, you can dream of success, still see yourself as a trier. Even if you can still see yourself *only* as a failure, then you're still alive. Maybe it's not so bad to hate yourself, despise yourself. As long as there's *some* feeling left, you're still teetering on the knife edge . . . Hate but not despair? Disgust, despair, where's the dividing line . . ?

With the unfamiliar alarm beating in my ears, I wake from a confused dream of childhood. Standing in Hearps's river paddock, in short trousers, clutching a battered football in my dirty hands. The old man leaning over the bleached rail of the fence saying: Your great-grandfather came out of the bush a changed man . . .

I disengage myself gently from Claire's warm presence, get dressed and go out to the kitchen. Wingnut is already there, dressed. The house is quiet. Without speaking, he pours a cup of coffee and passes me a joint.

Ten minutes later we leave in his old twin-spinner Ford for the drum line.

•

Herb signs me on. The others are already working on the line. The noise seems appalling. There is one other new recruit, a fat youth with no front teeth, direct from the CES.

Herb glances up from the cards. 'What's your name?'

'Jack Todd,' I say.

'You want a bodgie name?'

'I've got one.'

He bends over the cards, scribbles, then takes us both off to draw work gloves, inspect the amenities.

I've got a job, easy as that.

I go to the door. Wingnut is waiting in his car. I give him the thumbs-up, and he drives off in a cloud of smoke. Herb takes me over to the line, gives me a rag and a bucket of thinners, and I've joined the nation's workforce again.

•

Today the crib room is indescribably filthy. Someone is detailed to clean it up every week or so, but within hours it's just as bad again. It seems an immutable law of nature: filth is a natural condition, and it just reinstates itself when you turn your back. The sink is scummed and filled with tea-leaves, the scarred laminex tables sticky with spilled tea, sugar, jam, tomato sauce. Cigarette butts overflow the tin lids and mingle with crusts and scraps of paper that cover tables, chairs, the dirty linoleum of the floor. The walls are smeared and greasy.

I sit down near the back of the room, against a wall, and open my crib. Mike is toasting his sandwiches on an old hotplate. Hiroshima is gone, scrambling home for lunch over and under the fences. Terry and Peanut savage each other's crib boxes, stuffing food into their mouths, punching each other, spilling tea. The fat boy who started on the same day as me is gone, lasted only one day. John leans his chair back against the wall and spoons baby food into his mouth from a can. He's on some sort of diet. He belongs to the Salvation Army, doesn't drink, smoke or swear, and the story is that he's been warned that at the first sign of a sermon he'll get the bullet.

Herb comes in. He's about fifty, thin, short, with a bony face and bulbous blue eyes. A failed building contractor. The dog follows him and settles under a table.

'What you got to eat, Herb?' says Peanut.

'Nothing, fuck you,' says Herb, but he throws Peanut a couple of biscuits. Peanut bolts them immediately. He's voracious, insatiable. He's about nineteen, thin and snake-hipped, with a delicate degenerate face that's almost pretty.

Norm, one of the fitters, starts to feed his lunch to the dog. She eats anything – tomato sandwiches, fruit – anything.

The conversation, once appetites are blunted, runs the usual course: money, cars, sex, in roughly that order. After this, any new business. Today it's Mike's bruised face, then his bluey. He gets varied advice.

'Shoot through . . .'

'Get legal aid . . .'

'Pay twenty bucks and hope for the best . . .'

'Cut her fucking throat . . .'

'Bitch,' says Mike. 'Her old man owns three butchers shops – she doesn't need the dough . . .'

'Have a talk to her old man, then.'

Mike grins. 'We're not talking since I knocked him through the glass door at the Globe.'

Laughter.

'What did you do that for?'

'I found out the old bastard had given two blokes fifty bucks to do me over. So I got in first.'

Someone starts to bait Herb. He hates Abos, all kinds of foreigners.

'See the Abos are after land rights . . .' One of the local Abo leaders has been hassled by the police. It was in the paper yesterday.

'Bloody Abos,' says Herb. 'They should'a polished off the lot of the bastards when they had the chance.'

'They didn't do a bad job . . . there's no Tasmanian Abos left now.'

'No,' says Herb, 'they're all those bastards from the Islands now . . . won't work, the bastards, useless.'

'Yeah, but Jesus, it was pretty crook what they did to the old Tasmanian Abo . . .'

Herb leans forward and bites into an apple. His eyes have that fierce boiled look. He starts to stutter a little.

'L-look. It wouldn't have made any d-difference . . . a friend of mine, a professor, t-told me they were decreasing anyway, and by now they'd have all been g-gone . . .'

'Ah, bullshit.'

'N-no, it's right! They never ate any protein . . . all they ate was f-fish.'

Norm catches my eye and grins.

John, our resident Christian, speaks up. 'Ah,' he says, 'they were only boongs, anyway.' He slurps up more homogenised banana custard.

'Never mind,' says Norm, winking again, 'we've got plenty of New Australians to replace 'em.'

'Bloody wogs!' says Herb. 'They ought to s-send the whole b-bloody lot of 'em back to where they came from and b-bury the b-bastards.'

Mario sits at the far end of the table, saying nothing, smiling to himself. He's an ex-pug, used to fight with Harry Paulsen. He's just had two months off on compo after a phantom drum fell on him. While he was off he worked in one of the city pubs as a bouncer. Herb is too scared to brace him in case he gets thumped.

I finish my sandwiches. Herb is still ranting on about wogs, his stutter getting worse. I get up and go outside, sit on a pallet in the yard and smoke the two joints I've brought with me.

Only another three hours.

•

The days merge into one another, uniformly horrible. I try to think what it must be like to be committed to this sort of work for life. Can't imagine it. Worse than anything I've ever dreamed. If I can stick it for a month I'll have enough to move on. But wherever I go, I'll have to earn money – I can't go near the bank. And that means a job, and a job seems to be bloody misery. It was never like this before, I've always managed to find something that interested me, challenged me. It was different in the Melbourne days. Insurance company work was dull, but I was spoiled – off early for training, and they didn't care if I never processed a claim; it was enough that I'd get my pickie in the papers regularly. The managing director would take me to lunch once a month at his club, and talk football – he'd played for the Melbourne seconds long ago, and wanted to play the games over and over again. And to get all the inside gen on the current season. Such bullshit. And the job, clean and warm and safe, and pretty girls and long lunches and days off when I wanted them. Then, later, the mines . . .

One night Claire asks me about the past, where I've come from, what I've done.

She's not smoking so much dope now, no mention of hash cookies, seems calmer, less ragged about the edges. The house is much the same, a few new faces, a few old ones disappeared. I contribute to the common food requirements, buy a bit of plonk. The grass just appears from nowhere. I think most of it must come from Duncan, a part-Aborigine, part-Chinese, who has a plantation on the east coast and drives an old FJ. All the seats are stuffed with grass. He visits occasionally and, when he stays, pins up a bloody great Japanese flag in his room. He seems confused.

This night we've been walking round the ghetto – a dozen square blocks of inner city where the old folks are dying and the houses are being pulled down and replaced with warehouses. Bright moonlight, quiet, black shadows away from the street lights, a chill breeze, a few leaves rustling in the gutters. Winter not far away. She holds my hand, talks about her parents.

'It's just,' she says, 'that they seem to live in another world. Dad's never been out of a job since the war. He thinks that all you have to do is try hard enough and you'll get one . . . Mum's all right, but she's never worked since she got married, she gets her housekeeping money every fortnight, goes to bingo, weeds the garden, does the housework, that's it, that's her life . . . there must be more to it than that, surely?'

'You got any brothers and sisters?'

'One sister. She's older than me . . . she's worked at K Mart ever since she left school . . . she even smells of it now . . . you know, a kind of stuffy, powdery, dry smell?'

'You ever had a job? Any kind?'

She shakes her head. 'I was never very good at school . . . all the cleverer kids got jobs, I didn't . . . I don't know if I could cope now . . .'

I think of the drum line. I'm bloody sure I couldn't cope with *that* for long . . .

'Tell me,' she says, 'what sort of jobs did you have? Before you came here?'

'Oh,' I say, 'nothing interesting. In offices mostly.'

'Were you some sort of boss?'

'Sort of.'

'I'll bet you were good at it.'

'Yeah, I was. I was a real killer.'

'Don't say that,' she says.

'What?'

'That you were a killer.'

'Well, it's only . . . you know, just an expression.'

'I know what you mean, but you could never be like that, you're too gentle . . .'

'Me? Gentle?' I can't think of anything to say. Maybe it's old age creeping on, maybe I'm just tired.

'Have you had many girls?' she asks suddenly.

'A few.' More than a few, I suppose. When I was younger, before I learned the great secret, I'd fuck anything wet and warm, shove my dick through a knothole if there was nothing better round.

'I've only been with three boys – you're the third. Lots of the girls used to do it with everyone, but I never really wanted to . . . it always seemed to me that it was something special . . . nice, but special, so that you saved it up, and then when it happened it was like a birthday, or Christmas or something . . .'

I take her hand, wishing I'd been as wise as she was when I was her age.

'It's getting late,' I say. 'We'd better go home.' I take her hand, and we turn down the hill.

'You'll be going soon, won't you?' she says.

'I guess so.' Not something I can lie about, not to her.

'It's all right, you know. I never expected you to stay with me . . . you know, for long . . . I knew you weren't ready to stop anywhere . . . not with people like us, anyway.'

I feel like crying, feel tears prickling in fact, and want to put my arms round her and tell her I'll stay with her forever. But I can't, of course. 'Listen,' I say. 'There's no such thing as "people like you". There's just *you*.'

She smiles a little, and I wonder if she believes me.

'Look,' I say, 'you're not going to spend the rest of your life with those no-hopers. It's just . . . well, time out. You'll get it together, get back to things, you'll see . . .' And while I'm saying it I'm not really sure that I mean it a hundred per cent. Because, let's face it, there are people who survive and people who don't. You can't always pick them, but I wondered about Claire, whether she has the . . . I don't know . . . the strong filament somewhere that, no matter what happens, keeps you saying I *will* . . . She's got a gap or two, I know, because it takes one to know one. Not sure about myself any more . . . No, that's not true. What frightens me now is that I *will* survive, and I don't know how I'll handle it . . .

We come round the last corner, turn towards the house. And there are sudden prickles at the back of my neck, raising the hair a bit, alarm signals. Four motorbikes parked by the kerb, a faint spill of light in the yard from an open door, a mutter of voices. Queer types aplenty in that old house, but we don't run to bikies. And these are bikies, by their mounts. Chopped hogs, all of them . . .

Claire notices my sudden tension. She hasn't noticed the bikes. I press her back against a fence, motion her to be quiet. Advance in my runners, soundless on the old asphalt.

As I reach the corner of the house I can see them.

Four greasy hobos in leathers, long hair, with chains and iron bars, gathered in front of the low porch. One standing a bit apart, behind, looks like the leader. German helmet. On the porch, at bay, is Wingnut, holding a pick handle at the port. While I watch, one of the greasers, wearing a red headband and tattoos, laces his chain through the air, cutting down at Wingnut's head. Wingnut catches the chain on his pick handle, jerks, and Headband has to tug hard to get it back. The other two move a pace closer. German Helmet, slight, dark, long beard, says something, and the others jump at the porch. Too many, they get in each other's way. And Wingnut's doing all right – he's good with the pick handle, doesn't use it like a club, but like a quarterstaff, catching the blows from the bars, deflecting them, giving sharp stabs and lunges with the handle ends. But it's only a matter of time. Sheer numbers will get him in the end.

I look around for a weapon, because there's no way I'm going unarmed into that little lot. Time's slowing down now, the way it always does when things are happening fast. All the time in the world. There's a five-foot steel star post driven into the remains of the nature strip with an old NO PARKING notice fastened to the top. Flex my knees, take a good grip, straighten the legs, and the post comes free. I go through the gateway very fast, very quietly, getting a nice swing up with the post, aiming to take Headband in the kidneys with the edge of the sign. But he hears me, or some instinct works, he turns towards me and the chain goes back. So I alter the angle, swing the post like a baseball bat and give him the flat of the notice across the face. There's a satisfactory thunk, and he falls away against the wall, blood spurting. But I've overswung, and I see the one in leather helmet with skull and bones swinging a bar. Then Wingnut drives forward with the butt of the pick handle, takes Leatherhead in the small of the back, and he groans, his eyes roll and he sways aside, collapses against the wall. An iron bar wielded by the thick one takes Wingnut a glancing shot on the shoulder and he yells. But now there're only two left, the leader facing me and the thick one facing Wingnut. I make a feint at the leader, who has a nasty-looking knife out now, and swing hard with the post at the Fattie's knees. I scythe him down, and he flops heavily, arse first, on to the broken concrete of the path. Everything stops a moment. Wingnut and I look at each other, look at the leader, who's getting nervous. Headband isn't stirring, but Leatherhead is climbing slowly up the wall, looking white under the scum of grease, but reaching for his iron bar.

Suddenly there's a screech of brakes and the smell of burning rubber from the street, and a pale-blue EH rocks to a stop outside the gate. From the rumble of the engine, there's a V8 under the bonnet. There are four blokes in it. I see their silhouettes against the light. They look awfully hairy and rough. Bikie kind of rough. I look at Wingnut a bit anxiously, ready to take off, or get the old back to the wall. No sign of Claire, and that's a relief. But Wingnut's got a tight little grin on his ugly moosh, a reassuring little grin.

The two in the front seat of the car stay put. From the back seat emerge two large and really horrible bikies. You can just about smell them. One has got a sawn-off pump gun under his arm, the other a kind of sledge, looks like a bloody twenty-pound spalling hammer. The shotgunner moves towards us. He ignores Wingnut and me, motions to one side with the barrel of his gun.

Three of our bikies – Leader, Fattie, Leatherhead – get themselves somehow off to one side. The shotgunner stands over the fallen Headband, who's looking very sick and bloody.

He pokes the barrel into Headband's ear. 'Move, turkey . . .' Turkey moves.

They disregard Wingnut and me; we don't even exist for them. Shotgunner saunters over to our Leader, who looks very pale and unintrepid. Nods his head towards the car. 'Move.'

Leader drops his chain, moves very reluctantly towards the gate, out into the street, approaches the car. As he reaches it, the front passenger window of the car is wound down, a finger beckons. I can see Leader flinch. But the shotgun is still there. He pokes his head through the window. Into the bloody mousetrap. A hand reaches up and grabs his hair, and suddenly the window is going up like a guillotine. He's jammed tight by the throat. A fist begins to hammer at his face in the dimness of the car. The engine roars, rubber burns and the car fishtails away, dragging him with it, his boots dancing on the road as he tries to keep up, his hands clawing the car, at the doorhandle, at the roof channel, trying to get a grip. The car disappears into the night. We hear it screech round a corner.

The bloke with the hammer, all sixteen hairy stone of him, moves towards the four gleaming bikes by the kerb. Lightly, almost delicately, he toes each one over so that it crashes to the deck. Then he proceeds, calmly and methodically, to hammer shit out of them with his giant sledge. He doesn't worry about the frills, goes for the engine blocks, the transmissions. A fork or two, a set of handlebars gets in the road, but it's the guts he's after . . . within a minute or two the four bikes are reduced to scrap.

By the time he is finished – and it doesn't take long – the EH is back. It hauls to a stop, the window winds down, and our boy slips quietly to the road. He's bleeding badly, breathing in hoarse gasps, and he's unconscious. Some of his hair seems to be missing.

The shotgunner herds the other three out the gate, nods towards the body by the car. Sullenly, heavily, like very tired old men, they lift it, drape arms round shoulders, stagger off drunkenly down the street towards the highway. The shotgunner and the hammer man get back into the car. No one looks at us. With a throaty purr, the car drifts off into the night.

Wingnut and I stand and stare after it. I find myself shaking a bit, with that empty, shivery feeling in the pit of the stomach, that horrible trembly weakness that always comes after heavy action. There's blood running down my hand, I find that there's a thin shallow gash on my left forearm. He must have gotten closer than I thought with that knife. Wingnut is holding his arm where the bar glanced off. We're both breathing heavily, and it's not just the exertion.

Slowly, very timidly, Claire steps out of the shadows by the fence and walks a little unsteadily towards the gate. She doesn't look at the wrecked bikes, but keeps her eyes on us, stumbling a bit on the uneven path. She must have seen most of it from the shadows. I take her arm, not saying anything, and we follow Wingnut into the kitchen. I turn on the tap, run water over my arm. The cut is very shallow, hardly more than a deep scratch. I'm glad of that, because stitches would mean questions. Claire goes off up the passage, comes back with some Elastoplast, doctors me up quite neatly. She's still pale and very quiet. Wingnut opens the dilapidated, rattling old fridge and dredges out three beers, rips the tops, hands them round.

'What was all that about?' I ask him. 'What brought the goons down on us?'

'Bloody freelances,' he says. 'The ones that tried it on. Looking for dope. They know there's a supply somewhere.'

'What about the other lot, the hard ones?'

'Oh,' he says, 'they're our protection. Duncan keeps them in grass and they keep the bandits away. They were a bit slow on the uptake this time.'

He wipes his face with his hands, blinks, sighs deeply. Guess he's feeling the same after-effects as I am. Tiredness beginning to roll over me, weakness starting in my legs. Claire gets up, leaves her beer half-drunk, goes off up the passage without looking at us.

Wingnut looks at me. 'Thanks,' he says.

I shrug.

'Bit different to the big packs, isn't it?' He grins.

He's right. I grin back at him. 'You take it pretty calmly.'

'Shit,' he says, 'I grew up with it . . . facts of life, you know . . .'

We sit quietly, finishing off our beer. I leave him, go off to Claire's room. It's nearly midnight.

The room is dark, and in the faint spill of light from the blind I can see her slight figure lying straight and neat in the bed. I undress, slip in beside her, put my arm round her. She moves a bit closer, brings a hand up to touch my face.

In a minute I say: 'You all right?'

Feel her nod against my throat.

'Upset you a bit, did it? That bloody fracas?'

'Not really.' I think it's the first time she's spoken since the fight. 'I thought you were going to be hurt. I saw the blood.'

'Much of this go on? Fights, that sort of thing?'

'Now and then,' she says. 'I try never to take any notice.'

'They ever bothered you?'

She shakes her head.

The silence stretches out, and gradually her body relaxes, settles against mine. After a while she says, sleepily, 'I don't really mind you going, as long as nothing happens to you . . .'

Then, suddenly, she is asleep, breathing quietly and very softly in the crook of my shoulder. And I lie there awake, feeling sad, now, and shaken, and pissed off with the whole bloody business. It's very different from the ritualised violence of football – this is so casual, so easy, so bloody murderous . . .

It shocks me, I suppose, that people accept it so easily. Fighting's nothing. I learnt very early that there're far worse things than taking a hiding. But when you know there's death in someone's eye, and they don't really care one way or another – that you might have to kill someone yourself to survive – well, that's another story, and by Christ, it gives you a new perspective on things. Poor bruised kids like Claire, fucking philanthropists like Wingnut, even the harmless junkies up the hall – they live in a world that's failed them, that's waiting to cut their throats. There's got to be something better than that . . .

It leads me back to think about me . . . I've become kind of submerged in this little subculture, and, God help me, I've stopped thinking about myself, what I am, all that. Good? Maybe, but maybe it just proves how easy it is to get strangled by this kind of life. It seems to take all your efforts just to get by, and it's a battle even then . . .

I've lost all that's gone before, anyway. The last weeks have turned into a kind of buffer, somehow shutting it out . . . I can function all right, but that's all. I'm not really getting anywhere, I'm still so bloody afraid, so disgusted . . . and beginning to realise how much I've lost . . . knowing that I can never go home again . . .

And I drift off to sleep, wondering what is happening in the little town by the river, what *they* are doing . . .

And realising that winter is coming, that it is nearly time to move again . . .

•

Payday, so we're all in the pub – Mike and Hiroshima and Peanut and me. It's past six o'clock now, and almost dark. Getting a pleasant buzz on. Peanut has disappeared round into the ladies' lounge, and Hiroshima's playing eightball. Mike and I are at the bar.

'Jesus,' says Mike, 'I hate the cold weather. Wish I was in Darwin.'

'What about work?'

'Walk into a job just like that.' He clicks his fingers. He's a brickie's labourer.

'What are you going to do tonight?' I ask him.

'Get a few cans, get in the cot with the bird and watch telly.'

Another round.

'What's Peanut up to?' he asks.

'Don't know – he was cuddling up to some blonde piece in the other bar half an hour ago.'

Mike cranes round the corner. 'Not there now.'

143

'Maybe he's scored.'

I'm conscious then of someone standing close beside me at the bar. I turn my head and see this heavy-set bloke about my age. He looks tough, but he wears, a bit incongruously, very thick pebble glasses. A nasty, mean look about the mouth. He reaches across, picks up my beer and drains it. Looks at me.

'What are you going to do about it?' he says.

Feel suddenly very weary and sick of it all. The last thing I feel like doing is fighting. 'Christ, if you're that thirsty I'll buy you another one!'

'Smart bastard!' He starts to edge in on me.

Suddenly Hiroshima is there beside him, tugging at his arm. 'Ah,' he says, 'come on, Ray, he's a mate of mine . . .'

Ray looks at me for a long moment, then shrugs and turns away.

'Who the bloody hell was that?' I ask Hiroshima.

'Me brother,' says Hiroshima, and goes back to his eightball game. I've heard about his brother. He offers you outside, and when you get there you're likely to find a couple of his mates waiting.

Mike and I have another round or two, and Hiroshima finishes his game and drifts over. Half an hour passes.

Across the bar I see the back door open and Peanut's head appears. He looks round quickly and sees us. Comes over. He seems nervous, and when he gets closer I can see that he's got the shakes.

'Listen,' he says to Hiroshima. 'That's your brother, isn't it? With the thick glasses?' Hiroshima nods. 'Yeah, well, I walked this bird home . . . I didn't know she was his wife . . . I was just talking to her at the gate, and he walked up behind us and came at me . . . I didn't like the look of him so I pulled a picket off the fence and laid him out . . .'

'Jesus,' says Hiroshima, 'you'd better get goin' before he finds you.'

Peanut doesn't seem to hear him. ' . . . he's still there, he doesn't look too good. There's blood coming out his ears . . .' He blinks. 'Listen, I won't be at work tomorrow, I'll stay away for a few days and see what happens . . .'

He leaves quickly without saying any more, going out the way he came.

'I better go and have a look,' says Hiroshima.

'Come on,' says Mike. 'Let's get out of here. I'll split a taxi with you . . .'

The evening crowns the day . . .

•

For some reason I am reluctant to go back to the house. But there's nowhere else to go. So the house it is. Leaves are clogging the gutters now, and the nights are colder. Another month and the frosts will be here. Like a bloody swallow, I want to go, want to fly away.

The broken gate creaks, and I seem a stranger, more a stranger than ever. The evening has an alien quality to it now, a dead tag end, lost . . .

In the kitchen, Wingnut is sitting at the greasy table. Across from him is Paulie, gloves and all, looking ratty and cadaverous as usual, between them a torn bag and bun scraps, spots of grease and tomato sauce. Paulie seems to have been eating his hamburger with his gloves on. He's so bloody odd, Paulie, yet you don't really want to find out more about him, why he's here, why he's what he is. The answers would be too bloody depressing.

The bulb throws yellow light down in a hard circle. Wingnut looks tired. But he grins, pulls another stubby from a pack and hands it to me. Paulie drains his bottle, pushes back his chair, slips away down the corridor. From a room somewhere up there in no-man's-land there is the sound of a flute – weird, dissociated phrases that fall sadly on the night. There is the familiar smell of marijuana drifting on the air.

I sit down in Paulie's chair, open the bottle. Neither Wingnut nor I say anything for a little.

Then: 'Claire here?' I ask.

He shakes his head. 'Gone off. To see her mum and dad, I think.'

'Reckon she'll go back to them?'

He shakes his head vaguely. 'Dunno.' Pauses. 'Hope so – she's not cut out for this stuff, doesn't belong. You know?'

I nod.

'No more than you do . . .'

I raise my eyebrows, and he shakes his ugly great head again, squints at me. I know what he means. Whatever I am, whatever I've come to, it's not this . . .

The edges, the sharpness of it, have begun to wear off. But there's still that shock in the mornings, wakings, that revulsion . . . The thing is . . . all the things I've been, all the things I've done . . . well, it's as if they've been done by someone else, not me at all. A kind of pretend person. Not real any more. Someone I made up, imagined, put through the paces. It's impossible that the fellow in that picture, lying flat out above the hands of the pack, impossible that he's me . . .

Who am I? Now? It seems to me that I'll never find out living in the same world as that bloke. Not here, not in the clinic, not at home.

Still drawn to all those old things, those old people, those memories. But the only chance is to press on, in some new place, some new life . . .

'Will she be all right?' I ask Wingnut. 'When I'm gone?'

He squints at me, his face a gargoyle's in the harsh overhead light. 'Oh, I think so,' he says. 'She's a lot better now. Steadier. It's not just you . . . she had a rough trot . . . too much speed, too many freaks here . . . Trouble is, she hasn't got much . . . you know, *gumption*. Know what I mean?'

I know what he means; there's a peculiar lack of resolution about her, as if her soul was as pale and transparent as her skin. I love her, but I don't *love* her . . . No, the truth is, I *pity* her . . . and that's an awful thing, that's probably the real reason why I have to leave her . . . Even when I knew how bad Petra had been, what she's been through, might go through again, I *never* pitied her . . . I was *proud* of her, I *admired* her, I *smiled* when I thought of how tough and good she was . . .

'I'm going north,' I say to Wingnut. 'Soon. Maybe Queensland.' Then, out of the blue, surprising even me: 'Why don't you come with me.'

We both look a little surprised, I guess. But I realise that I mean it, that I'd like to go with him, that there's some quality in the ugly frame, the grotesque face, that inspires a sort of affectionate confidence.

He smiles, shakes his head slowly. Rubs his face with a grubby, freckled hand, tries to flatten his unruly hair with a palm. 'Christ,' he says. 'Best offer I've had today . . .' Then laughs. 'I couldn't, Jack.'

'Why not? Because you've got to look after your bloody strays?'

He clasps his hands on the table, stares at them. 'It's not really like that,' he says. Frowns. 'This is my patch,' he says. Looks up at me, suddenly. 'I know this town like my own . . . in a way, it's *grained* into me . . . I *know* it, everything: every wrinkle, every con, every villian, every fucking *rubbish* bin . . . I *know* it . . .' Smiles a little helplessly. 'It just wouldn't be the same anywhere else.'

I suppose the bugger's trying to tell me he loves it.

He's looking at me a little sadly. And I bloody-well *envy* him, envy him his scrubby city, his mean little life, his bloody *roots* . . .

'Good luck, anyway,' he says. 'And don't worry about Claire, we'll look after her.'

I stand up, clap him on the shoulder and traipse off up the passage past the flute sounds and closed doors and go into the dark of Claire's room, lie down on the bed, boots and all. Decide to try and sort it all out in my head. And go promptly to sleep.

Two hours later I waken to find Claire sitting on the bed beside me. In the light from the door I can see that she is smiling.

I stretch, yawn, run my tongue round my furry teeth. Realise my boots are still on, sit up and begin to unlace them. Look at Claire again. Still smiling.

Rub my stiff neck. Pat her knee. 'Why so happy?'

She seems to be bottling something up.

'I might have a job,' she says. 'Not certain, but I might . . .'

'Great, that's great.' I kiss her cheek. 'Where?'

She snuggles closer, hugs me. 'It's only in an office. My auntie works there, she thinks she can get me in.' She squeezes me. 'I've never had a job before, I told you that, didn't I?'

Christ, so excited over a bloody job? What's the world coming to? Poor little bugger. I smile at her. 'Let me up, I'll have a shower, we'll go down to the Bloodhouse, have a drink, celebrate.'

'It's not certain yet,' she says. 'It mightn't happen . . .'

'Of course it will, and if not now, then next time.'

'I'm glad it happened while you're still here,' she says.

Nothing really to say. I kiss her on the forehead and grab a towel, head for the bathroom.

Later that night, or early in the morning, home from the pub, we lie very tightly clasped in the darkness. After we make love we both lie awake for a long time, both of us pretending sleep. I think that both of us are impatient, somehow, for the future to happen . . .

•

No breakfast this morning. Couldn't be bothered somehow. Apart from that, it's just like every other morning. But colder and greyer. Frosts closer.

Peanut isn't at work.

Mike and Hiroshima and I start making shells. Mike is subdued. During a short spell while Hiroshima is breaking out more steel, I walk over to him and ask him how his brother is.

'He's in hospital – he'll be all right.'

'Coppers looking for Peanut?'

'No – Ray didn't tell them anything. But he'll be looking for Peanut when he gets out.'

Clang! A shell hits the burrer. I go back to my place.

Wipe, test, stack.

Wipe and stack.
Wipe and stack . . .
I look at my watch. Only five to eight.
Somehow this morning the noise seems louder – almost unbearable, and the pace faster. The air seems thick and heavy. A feeling of disgust and despair wells up in me. It seems impossible, quite impossible, for me to stand this awfulness for another seven and a half hours. The smell of the thinners seems to bite at my sinuses, and the screeching and clanging echo in my head.
Wipe and stack.
Wipe and stack . . .
I look at my watch again. Half past eight. Only half past eight! It seems that the single hour has stretched to fill a whole day, days, days on end . . .
Suddenly I've had enough.
I've got enough in my kick now to move on. Air fare and a couple of hundred left over.
I leave the line, walk out of the shed. Not worth waiting for the two days' pay they owe me. Just can't stand another minute.
In the crib room I drop my gloves on the table, put on my jacket, pick up my bag, walk out of the building. The long, double-lane highway stretches towards the city a mile away. I walk along the verge, my boots sinking deep into the soft, wet grass. Free at last. There is no sun, and a chill breeze carries a faint rotten smell from the muddy river.
Halfway into the city I see Herb's car coming towards me. He sees me, pulls over, leans out. 'Where ya going?'
I shake my head at him, keep going. In a moment I hear his car move off. Soon the sound of its engine is lost in the thin traffic. I keep walking, feeling as if a terrible weight had been lifted off me. When I cross the bridge, I turn left, head for the city centre where the airline offices are. I know where I'm going, all right.
Carbine Creek.
That distant purgatory in the Gulf Country where all the bad boys go . . .
Purgatory?

Don't think about it, killer, just flash your cash and fly away . . .
Carbine Creek? Why?
I don't really know. Maybe there's just nowhere else to go . . .

PART FOUR

NANCY BYRNE

Clay on my shoes from the cemetery, the only place within miles where you find that particular yellow clay. On my black shoes. I left them at the front door, went upstairs in my stockinged feet. Got out of my black hat and dress, put on my dressing-gown, lay on the bed, closed my eyes. I knew that the night would be a big one in the bar, that I would have to make a ceremonial visit before closing time. No one told me, but I knew. As if it had been bred in my bones I knew what was proper . . .

My mother was a fool I thought, dying when she did. I didn't care what it was, she shouldn't have let it happen. You don't die when you've got a man like him . . .

I hoped that Jack, God curse him, would never come back, would get lost, something so awful happen to him that I can't even imagine it . . . because if it hadn't been for him, Terry would still be alive . . .

We made him, but he had no right . . .

Am I to blame? For Terry, everything?

I wonder sometimes why I told him that night . . .

I know really. I tell lies to other people, but not to myself.

I told him so that he'd be *hurt*. Why should we be the only ones? But I really thought I was going to die . . .

In the beginning, Terry so big and hard inside me and his seed spurting, not that I could feel it, but I could tell when he did it the way he tensed, and all I wanted was it inside me forever, him and his seed . . . And if not the seed, then his baby . . .

I got that wish all right. And never regretted it. Those months with his child inside me seemed like heaven, the best time in my life. It didn't matter how much others laughed or sneered or poked fun at me, it just didn't seem to matter . . . My life was bound up with what was inside me . . .

Then, after he was born, it seemed gradually to matter less. Because Terry never came back to me again, wouldn't. I used to give him all the chances, try to meet him after my bath, touch him, look at him, be near him . . . and nothing. I knew how he felt, you could see the hunger, it was like my own, I *knew* . . . but he locked his door, and he wouldn't touch me . . .

It was strange, but when Jack left this time, and it seemed that he would never come back, then I thought that maybe Terry might come back to me . . . And I hoped that Jack would stay away, would die if he had to – it didn't matter what – I didn't care, get married, or go blind or lose his memory or . . . it doesn't matter now.

Terry is gone.

Outside the sun is almost down, the day almost finished, and I'm lost totally . . .

Terry is gone, because of Jack, and there is some terrible irony at work that I can't begin to understand . . .

●

I woke in the evening, surprised that I had dropped off to sleep. In the bathroom I showered carefully, looked at myself in the mirror. My body is still good, useful, firm. My breasts don't sag, my bum is tight and smooth, my waist trim enough. A bit of muscle tone gone – but I'm forty-seven, after all. But it's a good body, all soft now from the shower, and damp and pink and *unused*! I could cut my throat thinking of the *waste* . . .

But, but . . .

It was *never* for anyone else but Terry, that was the trouble. It never *worked* with anyone but Terry. It doesn't even work for me, and I've tried, God knows, all the warm baths, all the fingering . . . It doesn't work . . . And years ago I tried, I went away for a holiday, all the way to Sydney, the big city, the big smoke. How old was I? Twenty-two, twenty-three, and full of despair by then . . . And I stayed at the Mansions Hotel in King's Cross. In the evening, the first evening, I found a man, quite a good-looking man, a stranger, and I went upstairs and did it with him; and the next night with another man, and the next night with a third . . . and all *nothing* . . . I went through the motions, but *nothing* . . . and I knew then that I was bound forever to Terry, and that if he wouldn't love me then I would be unloved . . .

I dressed carefully, navy blue this time (black is a slut's colour behind a bar). White blouse, no lipstick. Young Peter Kenny, helping out in the bar, tried to get near me, rub up against me, and I'd have let him if it would have done either of us any good. There's something about funerals, about death . . .

The bar was full, all the locals. Quiet though. Just a constant heavy undertone, the thick country beasts retailing Terry's worth, over and over . . .

What would they think if I came out with it? Raised my voice, drowned out their mumbled tributes. 'He was the best fuck in the world . . .'

They wouldn't hear, wouldn't recognise, wouldn't believe . . . Poor girl, they'd say, she's under strain . . . It used to be a nervous breakdown, before all the pretty new names came in.

I wonder what they made of Jack, up there in the fancy clinic with its fancy doctors? The only trouble with Jack is that he's so sane he's frightening. Now he must be frightening himself . . .

If he would stay away, and Kate would go away, life would be easier. And, I suppose, duller. I wonder if he'll come back? Can he resist it, coming back to gloat, with fifty-one per cent of the hotel?

Oh, Terry, Terry, Terry . . .

I tell Peter to give everyone a drink on the house, and I go upstairs. The level of the noise seems to rise after I've gone.

Kate was upstairs in the sitting room, painting her toenails. She looked up as I came in.

'What are you going to do about Jackie?'

'What do you mean?'

'About finding him.'

'What can I do?' I shrugged and sat down by the fire, not looking at her. She didn't go to the funeral, said she never went to them, that they depressed her, she'd go to her own and that was all . . .

'A bit more than you *are* doing.'

'But *what*?'

'I don't know dear. Hire a private detective, or something.'

'Oh, God.' I couldn't help laughing. 'Do they really have such things?'

'All very well for you to laugh . . .' She finished one foot, propped the other one up. Her thigh beneath the skirt was white and stringy like a boiled chicken leg. Gave me the creeps. 'But he *does* own the hotel . . . well, the majority of it.'

'I've been managing it this long, I can manage a while longer.'

She cocked an eyebrow at me. 'Does it worry you, Terry leaving it to him?'

Of course it did, but the last thing I was going to do was let her know. 'Of course not – it was always understood Jack would get it one day.'

'But after you'd gone, eh?'

'What's the difference?'

'Why do you think he did it?'

I was getting tired of her harping. 'Does it really matter? Really, Kate?'

'He never did anything without a good reason, Terry.'

I said nothing. I knew why as well as she did, but I wasn't going to admit it. As for finding Jack, well, he'd come home in his own good time, if he wanted to. If he didn't I'd just go on the way I was. Not that there's much to look forward to now. Some sort of light has gone out.

'Where do you *think* he went?'

'God only knows . . .' God and that bloody little girl of his, the mad one from the clinic. *She* knows, I could see it in her look. Got the hots for our Jack, that one. Much good it may do her . . .

Kate said no more, and I sat watching her finish off her toes. Her hair that ridiculous shade of yellow, her low-cut dresses, her high-heeled shoes, her make-up – God she looks ridiculous. Even when she was young there was that look about her, a kind of dressing-up-for-fun look. But more business than fun, perhaps. Even in the worst days when everyone else was painting their legs with that kind of suntan lotion or going bare-legged, she always had nylons . . .

Sex, sex, sex . . . and yet there has always been something queer, something not quite right about it . . . Oh, not that she didn't get it, didn't like it, but as if it was only the *excuse* for something else. The dressing up maybe, the eternal games, the flirtings and the teasings . . . In fact, I doubt if she ever really *needed* sex – just sex, for its own sake . . . I think I can tell when it's like that with a woman . . . and so I should, God knows . . .

I'm sure she tried once to seduce Terry, and it wouldn't surprise me if she'd tried Jack too . . . even if she did bath him when he was little . . .

Oh, Jack and his bloody women . . . He used to make me so mad . . . coming home with a different one each week, sneaking them into his room at night, and thinking we didn't know . . . those sounds from his room . . . *those sounds* . . . and Terry lying awake along the corridor . . .

I hated Jack then for having what I didn't. Do I hate him now? I thought that after the football was over he'd be just another has-been, would settle back in the rut and I could despise him, we could be friends . . . But instead, he becomes a brilliant young executive, up another rung . . . and Terry so full of him, talking, talking, talking about him . . .

The truth is, I only wanted Jack while he was a link between Terry and me. Does that sound unnatural, unmotherly? But then I suppose I'm hardly a natural woman . . .

'Do you want a drink?' I got up from the chair. Actually, I

was glad of Kate's company that night, glad of any company at all. I wanted to sit up late, have three or four drinks, not go to bed till I was tired enough to sleep . . . there were things I didn't want to have to think about . . .

I gave her the glass, took my own back to the fire.

'I was right, wasn't I?' said Kate. 'You should have gone away, the pair of you, all those years ago.'

'Of course you were bloody-well right,' I said. One of the few times we'd agreed on anything. It's odd, she's been almost like a big sister, sometimes: a woman when I needed a woman. When all those things that happen to a girl happened, she was there. But we always squabbled, as if we were set right from the beginning on different sides, engaged always in some sort of quiet warfare . . .

The trouble was, you could laugh all you liked at her, about her, but she *knew* things. She seemed to know them instinctively, sense them. I'm sure she knew a minute after she walked in that time, about Terry and me.

'Kate,' I said. 'Was it *so* terrible what Terry and I did?'

She lay back, her head against the chair cushion, and closed her eyes. She looked quite old and tired. 'No,' she said, 'not so terrible.' She opened her eyes a moment, looked askew at me. '*You* don't think so, do you?'

'No.'

'No. Well, some children kill their parents.' She smiled suddenly, eyes still closed. 'Make love not war, that's it, eh? No generation gap with you two, was there?' And she laughed, quite coarsely. Opened her eyes, looked at me. 'Don't look so bloody *prim*.' Then she closed her eyes again, and she really *did* look tired, and not very well.

'Are you all right?' I said.

She nodded. After a minute she sighed. 'It's sad,' she said. 'It's all over now.'

'What do you mean?'

'Somehow,' she said, 'I know I've had my last lover,' and there was an enormous weight of sadness in her voice.

'And so have I', I said.

And suddenly, in a moment, I was across the room, on my

knees, my arms round her, feeling very frail and weak against me, she was clasping me tight, and we were both weeping. And I wondered if we were, after all, weeping about the same thing . . .

•

I woke in the morning to bright sunlight flooding into my room. For a moment I lay there listening to the sounds of the morning. Bird calls from the garden, the gentle clash of dishes from the kitchen, the hum of an early car on the highway, the faint rippling of the water under the bridge. Waiting for the familiar footsteps as Terry came back up the stairs to shave and shower before breakfast.

Then I remembered, of course, and the thought that I'd evaded successfully enough the evening before, in tears and alcohol and sleep, the thought came back to then, striking like a great dull blow, the thought of his body lying there cold in the cold coffin, under the cold yellow clay, and beginning already the disgusting processes of decay . . . Gone, gone, what was, what used to be, what could be . . . the warmth and the strength and fire . . .

Nothing left, nothing at all.

Widowed twice, once thirty years ago, once the day before yesterday . . .

God curse men, and women, and all the world . . .

•

By noon it seemed that I must get out of the place or explode. Kate showed no signs of leaving again, even seemed to be entrenching herself as if for a long war. War? Perhaps rather attrition, endurance . . . She didn't look well; she seemed paler, older, less committed to life. She's not that old, but she seems worn out. She drifted about the hotel like a harlot's ghost, never seeming to settle anywhere. Her presence upset me somehow that morning, and it seemed that every time I came on her – on the stairs, in the garden, in the sitting room, the kitchen – she seemed on the point of collapse . . .

In the end I could take it no more. I saw to the menus, then went up and changed into a tweed skirt, jumper, walking shoes, and set off down the road. A mile towards the river mouth, I turned off to the right, took the narrow overgrown track past the sign that said BRADY'S LOOKOUT. Everywhere you go in this State, there seems to be a Brady's Lookout. He must have been a very busy bushranger, climbing every hill in sight to take in the view . . .

The rutted track ends half a mile from the top of the hill, and there is a sort of stile over a fence, and a foot-track across one of Cameron's paddocks. The grass was green and thick after the good autumn rains, and the mild weather had brought on the mushrooms. Everywhere underfoot were the rotting turrets or the spoiled gills where children had kicked and plundered. At the top, where there is a small seat and a fancy noticeboard with a varnished face, I stopped, leaned against the rail, looked out over the land. From there you can see fifty miles along the coast as it curves in a delicate broken cusp around the focus of our river's mouth. That day the world was clear and razor-edged, sharp as hedgehogs' quills; and clouds, light and puffy, lay in ranks across the distant range of mountains where the west really begins for us. The sea was flecked a little, delicately stroked by the light wind. Neat hedges, ranks of manuka, tea-tree, stands of pine and, further back up our valley, the heavy olive grey of the deep forest, fading in the distance to soft pearl.

Sometimes that is the only place, there on the hill, where I can find any kind of peace. The wind is strong and clean there, and it seems to relieve a strange pressure that gathers and builds inside me.

I would have liked, years ago, to have played golf. God knows why. Except that it meant a kind of orderly escape from things for a little. One could dress up as if for walking, and walk, taking the excuse of a little ball. And as well, see other people, talk, gossip, drink a little, socialise . . .

But it was all quite impossible. Now, perhaps, it might be different. Now people don't seem to care so much for respectability. But then, it was the work of every waking hour to brace myself so that I could look people in the eye. I did it by staying as much as possible on my own ground; or on neutral ground. But I knew that golf was the enemy's ground, that there I would lose every battle. And never win a war. They had their wedding rings, that was the trouble. They were adulteresses, shoplifters, slanderers, thieves, bankrupts, drunks and morons . . . but they were protected by their little annular talismans.

So instead of golf I began walking. For twenty years, more, I walked. I know every road and track and field and coppice within ten miles of the hotel. And I'm as slim and neat, as trim and well muscled, as I was at twenty. Not that that matters any more. But it kept me sane through all those years. Wind, free air, and physical weariness, they made life tolerable. But I never forgot that I was useless. I could manage a house, but could do little else. No ear for music, no hand for the artistic skills. Knit, sew, bake, clean, scrub. Yes, that was me. And household accounts, and throw out a drunk if need be, and swear at a truck driver, and laugh with a traveller, and still keep private and clear of it all. And *unused*, no man to use me gratefully, exhaust love and energies on me . . . Well, there was only the one man, and now he is gone . . .

I turned away, began to walk down to the bottom of the hill. I couldn't stay away too long that day – there was too much to do, after the slack days of death and funeral arrangements . . .

I never stopped, never paused in my walks, in all those years. Nod and speak to the faces I passed, yes, but never stop for a cup of tea, a talk. If I did, I would be a loose woman, accused of trying to steal the men of the country, to seduce and corrupt them in their own ricks and yards. Corrupt *them*, cow-fuckers and child-rapers and drunkards and wife-beaters . . .

Corrupt *them* . . .

If you listen, if you listen carefully, and if you live there for a long time, you find out just how much corruption exists in the good, clean, green world of the country.

Approaching the old white building again along the pale gravel of the road, I couldn't help remembering those arguments with Terry, almost domestic in their quality, the closest we ever came to it . . .

After the main road was moved and we were left in our backwater, after the profits began to slip, after we saw the new shiny motels spring up and take our trade, I tried to talk him into modernising, putting in holiday cottages in the acre at the back; advertising; having a little music, cabarets; maybe fishing vacations, anything to gain back some ground . . . But for him, it was always the old ways, the ways established by his father, that old bore who bludged forever on the basis of a single year in the bush when he'd been lucky . . . An unemployed gravedigger who brought back a lucky poke of gold from the bush, and suddenly was the arbiter of all things . . . Terry would see nothing good in change, would insist on all that free food on the counter each day for the scroungers who came ten miles to buy a portergaff and stuff themselves with our food . . .

I longed to turn that old place inside out, get rid of all the wallpaper and panelling, the endless dadoes and heavy timbers and brass . . . to let in light and air, and maybe a little profit . . . at least to *try*, to exercise the small skills I have . . . But no, it was as sacred as the ordering of an altar to gods that are too young to be tolerant . . .

Now, with Jack in control, Christ knows what . . .

I suppose we will sell, and not much of a price we'll get. I can't see anything else except a continuation of the past. He won't change anything. For him Terry was the master of the house and probably always will be. For me, Terry was the master of my world, but I saw his faults. I wanted him more than anything in the world, I wanted to feel him between my thighs again, but I wanted some kind of partnership, too . . .

And I think that what Terry wanted in the end was a kind of sad and dignified guilt . . . If he'd been less moral we would have been happier . . .

I think sometimes I should have married Alf Wellard, who at least was strong and cheerful, and didn't care a curse for morality, wanted only a hard day's work, a wife at home to cook his tea, a warm body in the bed, and a pint or two on payday . . . I nearly did take him once, in despair, after he'd asked me, as he did once a week without fail for seventeen years . . . I liked him, so I would have done it . . . But he only wanted marriage.

Oh well, Alf is gone, and Terry, and Kate looking dim enough to fade away, and Jack disappeared into the wild blue yonder in chase of God knows what, and I'm the only one to keep things going here . . .

Maybe I should let it all fall to pieces, let someone else pick up the bits.

By the time I got back to the hotel that day I was feeling easier, better than I had for days. I went upstairs, knocked on Kate's door.

'Come in.'

She was lying on the bed, eyes open, staring at the ceiling. I said to her, 'Kate, don't you want something to eat? You've had nothing all day.'

She shook her head.

'What's the matter?' I went over and sat on the bed beside her. Her hands were crossed on her chest as if she were dead already and lying in state.

'What is it?' I asked.

'It's nothing,' she said wearily, not looking at me.

But there was something all right. 'For Christ's *sake*,' I said. 'What's the *matter* with you?'

She sighed. 'Just a bit of palpitation . . . I've got pills for it.'

I was stunned. It had never occurred to me that she really might be sick.

'How long have you been like this?'

'A couple of years,' she said.

I said nothing for a bit, thinking it over. I don't know . . . Kate and I, well, God knows, we're at loggerheads often enough, and I've never pretended to understand her. But we're family, the two of us. And the house is very empty now . . .

'You'd better stay for a while, Kate,' I said. 'Rest a bit.'
'Yes,' she said. 'I think I will . . .'
That surprised me. I'd expected her to protest, at least a little. And her voice seemed low, weak, not like the old raucous Kate at all. But, oddly, I felt relieved, reassured that I wouldn't have to spend the winter alone in this mausoleum.
'What about your flat?' I asked her.
'I gave it up long ago,' she said.
'Why?'
She smiled a little, turned her head to look at me. 'Why do you think? Flats cost money . . .'
It had never occurred to me that she might have no money . . . Kate as an old-age pensioner? It hardly seemed possible . . . God, the lovers and the money, all gone now. What a bloody cruel and lonely world it is.
'Never mind,' I said. 'You're welcome here, as long as you want to stay.'
'I'll stay,' she said, 'till Jackie comes home . . .'

•

I left her to doze, thinking I'd take her up a snack later, a cup of tea, a brandy. That was supposed to be good for heart patients wasn't it? God, Kate a *heart patient* . . .

Stay till Jackie comes home, she'd said. I stopped halfway down the stairs thinking of what it had been like all those years ago. Jackie. Getting conceived, getting born, growing up, playing football. Jackie . . .

He was so *long*, I thought he was never going to get born, the doctor kept pulling him out, and it seemed never to stop, he seemed to be so *long* . . . And through the pain, which I didn't really care about, because that's all it was, through it all I was worried that because he was so big he'd stretched me, that I'd be too big down there, too slack, to take Terry again, to clutch him inside me, tight and hard and smooth . . . That's all I wanted, by then, to get the baby out of the way and be ready for Terry again . . .

Because I had fooled myself over those long months that it was only the baby that was keeping him away . . .

For a year after Jack was born, more I think, I was a bit mad . . . When he didn't come back, when I couldn't make him, I wanted to drown myself, anything . . . it was just the thought that maybe he *would* come back in the end . . .

I went on down the stairs, and for some reason began to think about Jack's girl, the one who'd come to see me. Young, quite young, not much older than I was when I had Jack, not pretty, but almost beautiful. A bit too . . . genuine. She'd be easily hurt, and I wondered if he'd hurt her yet. Soon he would, anyway, if not already. We're good hurters, we Byrnes . . .

I took him for granted, Jack, until he began on the football, that idiotic game. Suddenly he and Terry disappeared into a world of their own where I couldn't have followed even if I'd wanted to . . . The stupidity of it . . .

And Jack flying home for a holiday, a bloody hero for everyone, strangers, people we hardly saw once a year flocking to the bar, and him standing there with his limps and bruises and gashes, laughing, laughing, telling them the stupid stories of this player and that, and all the scandal and the politics of that bloody circus . . . And they lapped it up, and Terry standing there like a proud father . . .

I hated them both then.

•

When the bar was closed, the last of the few guests off upstairs for the night, I went into the kitchen for a final cup of tea. The wind was getting up, clouds scudding heavily across the moonlit sky. The night seemed haunted somehow, and I could hardly bear to be alone. Especially in the kitchen, the sight of the floor damp from the mop, smooth and sheened, the wet draining-board, the lamp hanging lit above the sink . . .

By the time I'd found him he'd been dead for no more than a few minutes, I suppose; but already he was gone, there was nothing there but a pile of old clothes and a waxy face that looked somehow older . . . And later, in the room upstairs, his room where I'd never been in thirty years, he lay, after the doctors and the undertakers had been, and his face was yellow and empty, and the cloth they'd tied up his jaw with and knotted on top of his head gave him a strangely childlike look. I'd given him a final light kiss on the forehead, the only kiss in thirty years, and thirty years too late, and his skin had been cold and clammy and I'd felt suddenly sick . . .

How could he have done it? To himself, to me?

I think that he'd never quite realised, never accepted, that I'd seduced him, and never the other way around . . .

At seventeen I'd long been grown, long been feeling the deep and urgent longings . . . I'd thought for a year or two that it was just for a man . . . any man I liked . . . until one day when I'd slipped on the wet slate steps in the back yard as we walked there together, and he'd caught me, held me a moment, and I could smell, feel him . . . I knew then that it wasn't any man, it was *him*, it *had* to be him . . . I would watch him then, and find myself growing moist, down there, when he was near . . . I spied on him, taking furtive glimpses as he shaved, changed his shirt, washed at the garden tap . . .

And on that night, *that* night, I'd been so tired of waiting, so achingly empty . . . I'd gone to him, and made him take me . . . and he filled the emptiness, and suddenly I knew that as long as I lived I'd never want, never need, anyone, anything but him . . .

Sin? *Sin*? If *that* was sin, then I've longed to sin every day of my life, still long to, even now it's finally over. *Sin*? Paradise . . .

Hardly a night passes when I don't dream that my thighs are wet from him again, and I wake and weep . . .

●

Terry's room is cold, airless, depressing. There has been no fire there for weeks, and today there was no sun. Only the wind: a low, sighing wind from the west, breathing dullness and late autumn chill over the house . . .

I lit the fire, went and got a cardigan, sat down with my cigarettes and a cup of tea to go through the desk drawers. A job I'd been putting off. In the event, nothing to be afraid of . . . everything in such order, neat, tidy, up-to-date, that it seemed strangely anonymous, despite the familiar, round handwriting that even after half a century still carries the discipline of the classroom . . .

Cancelled bills, accounts, bank statements, correspondence from the solicitors, accountant, liquor suppliers, brewery, butcher, baker, candlestick maker.

There was really nothing to do, only a few files to locate for the solicitors, things about probate. But in the bottom drawer – filling the whole bottom drawer – folders of old newspaper clippings. All of them about Jack and his football career . . . I ruffled through them, the old ones yellow and fragile, pictures of him at fifteen, still not filled out, leaping high in the air, posing at training, kicking a ball, his long leg high like a dancer's . . . Those were the days when they started to call him The Bastard openly . . . funny, it wasn't anything he did after he moved to Melbourne, just the carry-over of his childhood nickname . . . I think that if young Rafe Dilger hadn't gone to play for Footscray at the same time it might have been forgotten . . .

Nothing about me in the drawers, the files, nothing. Jack's whole career, but just a blank for me . . .

In a sudden rage I pulled all the old clippings out of the drawers, threw them on the fire. They smothered the flames and the room filled with billows of smoke. Coughing, I crouched down with the poker, stirred the old newsprint until the pages began to char and burn. I opened a window, stirred and stirred, and soon there was nothing left but ashes . . .

The Bastard. I remember him coming home from school with that white look about his face, and how I knew that the kids had been at it again, calling him those names. But I never tried to comfort him, knew that it would be best if he learned to handle those things himself, grew callouses as young as he could, that it would be doing him no favour to coddle him . . .

And it worked, even if it took a long time. Years of bloody noses and scraped knuckles and complaining parents, who got short shrift from either me or Terry . . .

Tell him to hold his tongue, said Terry to one mother about her son, if he wants to keep his teeth . . .

I knew that part was finally over one day when Jack was about fourteen . . . Two boys carrying a football down the road towards the paddock where they played, running, punching the ball back and forth . . . One of them saying to the other: Gunna get The Bastard? And the other saying, Yeah, let's get him . . . and calling loudly over the garden fence, Jack, Jack, come and have a kick . . .

Then, it was clear, the abuse and nastiness were over, and he'd survived in his own way, and the label was no more now than that, just a badge that was part of him, that he answered to, that no one thought about any more . . .

And I envied him a little, then, because he'd made a *place* for himself among the chaos of the world, and he wouldn't feel lonely, ever, as long as he stayed in that place . . .

Why did I tell him?

I try to be honest. With myself, anyway. I really thought that I was going to die that night. The pain began so quickly, starting as a little cramp in the pit of my stomach, and then within minutes it was a terrible iron claw gripping my insides, my breathing hard, the cold sweat breaking out, my fingers tingling . . . I'd never even *suspected* pain like that, pain that never relaxed, never . . . I *knew* I was going to die . . .

But *why*?

Perhaps because he had taken Terry from me, had made a little world for the two of them that excluded me . . . I don't know. Maybe it was just that if I was going to die, if all the imprints in my memory of Terry, of joy, of love and loving, were to be lost forever, then I had to pass part of it on, somehow, some part of it, even if it was nothing that anyone could understand or share . . . Someone must know, remember, that we had been lovers for that short time, that short time that was really all the life I ever had . . .

Surely love deserves some kind of immortality?

When I went to close the window, the last of the smoke drawn out in the chill afternoon, the clouds were darker, thicker, and the wind was rising. The trees on the far ridge were tossing their branches, waving quite wildly, and I knew then that winter was close, that it would be on us within days.

And somehow it seemed that the rest of the world was fading away, leaving nothing but two women in an old hotel in a backwater, waiting the winter out, waiting for something, some ending, some proper termination, to take place.

Kate was waiting for . . . what? Jack? Death?

What was *I* waiting for? Not death, my body knew that it was not ready for that . . . Not Jack, surely? Not *Jack*, with his mad girl and his faded clippings and his scarred wrist, surely?

What, then?

Some sort of resolution, perhaps, some sort of final reckoning? Forgiveness?

Surely not that . . .

I turned away from the window, stood riddling the ashes with the long brass poker. There would be time; the winter would be long enough to think of all that, all that and more . . .

And I found myself shivering as the room grew colder . . .

PART FIVE

JACK BYRNE – UPSIDE

I prop myself up in the Rodeo Bar, drinking slow beers. Arriving in Mount Isa so pissed I can hardly stand, jeered off the plane by a tribe of shrewish hosties. Not the fitting thing to show up at Carbine Creek in a state of advanced inebriation, so I decide to take a day off, recover, see the sights. Some sights. Big, smoky, hot, dirty, another company town, just writ a bit larger. But different all the same. Abos in riding boots and cowboy shirts and Akubra Silver Spurs wandering about boozing up, playing eightball.

The flight to Melbourne is all right. Done it so many times in the past. It hits me, though, at Tullamarine. Nowhere to go now. And I can't hit my old haunts. Not so much that they might be looking for me, but I'd be . . . somehow out of place. I'm not The Bastard anymore. Not *that* bastard, just a different one. They'd look right through me as if I were a pane of glass. So I sink a few in the Jackaroo Bar, sink a few more in the city, find a room in a cheap-and-nasty, sink a few more. By then the nervousness has turned to paranoia, and I retreat to my bed with a bottle of whiskey, lock the door. A long night, with the city noises going on outside. I have this sensation of all my old life being replayed outside, around me, like an old movie endlessly replayed, with the scenes all mixed up. Feel haunted by the city, but afraid to go on. North is strangers' country for me. For a while I even toy with the idea of going back, getting an early plane, sneaking back to the house. A vision of curling up in that narrow bed with Claire. Who turns into Petra, and I realise I'm on the edge of a dream, half in, half out. But I can't go back.

I sweat the night out, get the bus to Tullamarine. On the plane I'm still sweating. Coming into Brisbane it's raining, the airport's closed. We circle round, and it opens. Then it's closed again. Down below, through a break in the clouds, I can see Eagle Farm, puddled with water. I can see the fucking aerodrome, but the bloody gutless pilot won't put us down. Round and round and the bar's closed. I'm pretty-well tanked, and the hosties disapproving. Used to be different when I was that *other* bastard. All over me like a bloody rash, then. Another drink, Mr Byrne? Another coffee, Mr Byrne? Wipe your arse, suck your cock, Mr Byrne?

Never bothered with them. Fucking airborne waitresses with all those airs and graces. Bet they hate having to shit . . .

Bumping round the circuit, waiting, I wonder what Claire is doing. I never saw her to say goodbye. Left like a bloody thief in the night. She'll understand. Nothing to say, anyway . . .

On the ground at last, in a terminal that's all tiles and philodendrons and rain-washed glass, I find there's no plane for Mount Isa till the next day. So into the wet dismal city. Get off the bus and book into the Gateway. Save trouble in the morning, no traipsing round to terminals and so on. The air is thick enough, wet enough, to swim in. Not normal, not bloody civilised. Fucking *foreign*. The wogs begin at Brisbane. A few beers and I lie down in my room.

•

The further north I get, the lonelier it seems.

After dark I go out and buy a bottle of whiskey, lie in my room, drinking slowly. Go to sleep eventually, half-pissed, and twist and turn restlessly all night.

In the morning I wake to bright sunlight, feeling queasy and hungry from missing dinner. Breakfast arrives, and I get the first hint of what food is like in a foreign country. Eggs and sausages. The eggs are like hotel eggs anywhere, not quite hot, overcooked, tasteless. But the sausages – Christ! – hard-packed, mottled, tasting like over-spiced sawdust. I eat half one, and get instant heartburn. I shower, pack the rest of the whiskey in my suitcase and head off down to the lobby to wait for the airport bus.

Sitting there in the anonymous lobby I wonder really why I bother with it all. It just doesn't seem worthwhile any more . . .

Back towards the airport, tracking along beside houses on stilts and unfamiliar banana trees. Shorts and long socks everywhere. Feel overdressed in my desert boots and jeans.

The airport hasn't changed overnight. Neither have the hosties. A thin blonde one with a sharp nose sneers at me when she brings my first drink.

Once we're up in the clouds there's nothing to see. Air travel's got to be the most boring human activity known. Jammed tight in a too-small seat with no leg room hour after hour with nothing to see, nothing to do . . .

It seems to go on forever, today. Hour after bloody hour. Only now it begins to dawn on me just how vast Queensland really is. I booze the time away. Carefully. If I misbehave in the slightest, they'll cut me off. But I smile nicely in the face of the sneers and dull the edge of that feeling I have of flying forever into nothing. And the further we fly, the more certain the feeling that I really belong in the valley, in the white pub; and that I can never go back there . . .

By the time we land at Mount Isa I'm nicely charged, but still walking straight. Collect my suitcase, take a quick look at the skyline – a mine, a town, a mining town – and head into the Copper Bar for a beer. It's all done in copper – copper ornaments, copper ore, smelted copper, copper, copper, copper . . .

It's crowded with shorts and long socks, shorts and short socks, shorts and thongs . . . loud . . . in a corner a great throng is clustered round a short bloke with a round face and frizzy greyish hair, dressed in shorts and long socks. He's holding forth, waving his glass.

'Who's that?' I ask the bloke next to me, a thin rail of a bloke in shorts and long socks.

'Bob Katter,' he says, looking at me with pity. 'Member for Kennedy.' Drains his glass, 'He's a good bloke.' He looks at me carefully. 'You live in the country, in a mining town, you've got to vote Liberal . . .'

'You're a fucking idiot,' I tell him.

He looks at me, frowning, sidles away.

I go out, find a phone, look up the number of Carbine Copper.

Operator's voice starts talking to someone over the buzz. At last I get a woman with a pommie accent – broad brummagem – who puts me through to the employment office. A girl answers.

'Any jobs going?'

'What sort of job are you looking for?'

'Well,' I say, having rehearsed my lines carefully, 'you see, my mates and I are at the Isa, just arrived. There's three of us, one's a TA, one's a clerk, one's a gardener . . .'

'We've got two positions for TAs at the moment. Nothing for gardeners. I think there'll be a clerk's job coming up in a couple of weeks . . .'

'Well, I'm the TA, my name's Ritchie Todd . . . could I come out and see you?'

'Yes, sure,' she says. 'When will you be here?'

'How often do the planes fly out?'

'Sometimes once a day,' she says, 'sometimes twice. You'd better check with Bush Pilots at the airport. If you get a job here we'll reimburse the fare.'

'OK,' I say, 'I'll check in as soon as I get there.'

What happens if you don't get a job, I wonder . . . I suppose they'll let you stay till the next plane, give you a bed? Christ knows, this is a foreign country, mate.

I wander round the airport until I find the little cubbyhole with a notice that says 'Bush Pilots'. There's a girl in the background rustling through papers, a young bloke in shorts and shirt who seems to be manager, baggage boy, maybe pilot too . . .

'Can't take you today,' he says, brusquely. 'Full up. Take you tomorrow morning, ten-thirty. Got any luggage?'

I lift the case and show him.

He nods, 'That's all right. Not much space in the planes if there's a full load of passengers. Sometimes we have to leave the luggage behind. You'll be right though . . .'

I pay the girl thirty bucks and get a ticket. I find a taxi, book in at the first motel we come to, the Overlander at the edge of town. It looks like any other small-town motel. A bit pretentious, but everything slightly askew.

I pay in advance for a room, dump my bag, go for a walk. It's a sunny evening, quite hot. I walk past the drive-in movie place, heading for town. Dusk is starting to fall. Suddenly, through a gap in a hedge, I see a sports oval, green and lush. Strange, familiar sounds fill the air. Grunts, thudding of boots, the unmistakeable dull empty *thunk* of a kicked ball . . .

I stop, peer through the hedge. A couple of dozen blokes, all dressed up, despite the heat, in woollen football guernseys, are at practice. I stop, shocked, because they are playing Aussie Rules. Stabbing, marking, hand-passing, shooting for the familiar double sticks . . .

A great wave of homesickness floods me. One thing I *never* expected to see up here . . .

Night closes down quickly, and the yellow of lights springs to life as the road stretches out before me, the city grows . . . I walk on slowly, the sounds of footie practice fading slowly behind me.

•

Half an hour later, into the Rodeo Bar for a few beers, then an early night, an early start in the morning, sober and bright-eyed. I stroll away from the big island bar towards one end where, behind a waist-high railing, a dozen young blackfellows are playing eightball. Most dressed in stockman's gear, a few in jeans and sandshoes, dark shirts. I watch for a couple of games, leaning on the rail. There's one young Abo in a red shirt who's pretty good. I say as much to a sullen-faced young boong standing near me.

'He'll get done,' he says, hardly glancing at me.

'Dollar says he doesn't.'

'You're on . . .'

Another black comes over and joins us. He's light brown, actually, tallish, white shirt. He nods, watches the game.

Red shirt wins.

'You owe me a dollar,' I say to the boong.

'Like buggery,' he says, sneering a bit.

'Go on,' says the bloke in the white shirt, 'pay him, for Christ's sake!'

'Mind your own fucking business!'

'Go on, pay him! It's cunts like you that get us a bad name . . .'

The young bloke wanders away, still sneering at us.

'Sorry,' says the bloke in the white shirt.

'Not your fault,' I say. 'A dollar's neither here nor there. But I'll bet he'd have expected me to pay if I'd lost.'

'Come on,' he says, moving towards the bar. 'I'll buy you a beer.'

So we stand and yarn and drink a couple more beers. His name's Vince and he works at the airport, luggage handler, regular job; he's been at it three years.

Closing time, and he looks at me a bit anxiously.

'Listen,' he says, 'do us a favour, will you?'

'What?'

'Just go out the door with me, walk a couple of blocks.'

'Why?'

'Ah,' he says, 'the cops'll be waiting outside . . . they'll lumber any of us they feel like . . . unless we're with a white.'

I shrug. 'All right. You're not pissed, though . . .'

'Don't have to be pissed,' he says. 'Just black.'

The lights are being flicked off one by one, and the crowd at the bar and the tables breaking into small clots, drifting towards the side doors. Outside the night is clear and velvety blue, the lights of the town giving it a soft yellow blush.

There's a paddy wagon parked near one door, a handful of policemen in their checkered caps and short-sleeved shirts standing idly by the kerb, watching. The blacks keep in small groups, sidle quickly along the walls towards the corner of the street. Now and then a copper will beckon one over. Jerks his head, into the wagon. No rough stuff, no arguments.

Vince keeps close to me, on the side away from the road. One of the coppers looks hard at me as we go past, but doesn't say anything.

I walk a couple of blocks with him, till we're away from the pub area and the coppers. We say goodnight quickly, shake hands, and he slips off into the darkness. I go looking for a taxi to take me back to the motel.

Before I go to bed I drink a big glass of water. It's got a strange, foreign taste in my mouth. I don't know, maybe not the water at all . . .

•

The morning is bright and clear and hot. By my standards, anyway. The girl at the motel desk has a thick cardigan on, and clasps her arms as if she's cold. I suppose the temperature's fallen below eighty or ninety . . .

Out at the airport I present myself and my ticket at the Bush Pilots counter. The bloke, a different one, crosses my name off the list. 'Be a little while yet, Father Carey's a bit late this morning.'

I wander off. The airport's a bit quieter this morning, the Copper Bar still closed. I go and stare out at the hot, flat land outside. All reds and ochres. The dusty oleanders seem vividly green by comparison.

Finally the bloke comes and collects me, and we track out on to the tarmac, the pilot, me, bit of a kid about twelve, and Father

179

Carey – shorts, long socks, open-neck shirt with gold crucifixes on the collar tabs. We carry our own luggage.

The little Beechcraft looks very fragile and tiny, and I begin to feel a bit nervous. The pilot stows our luggage in some mysterious place behind the seats, shows me where to put feet, and we clamber in; the kid, blond and tousled, up front with the pilot, me and the good father in the back. Full load.

I've always been nervous of little planes. I suppose they're safe enough, but I still get nervous. Father Carey grins at me, starts to say something, but the roar of the engine cuts him off. He shrugs, grins again, opens his little plastic briefcase and starts going through a bundle of papers. We lunge off down the runway and before we've got up any speed we seem to be airborn. Flying along, it seems to me, at a good fifty miles an hour. But up we go, heading west, leaving the town behind, flying over the railway tracks, pointing off into the distance.

Oh, that bloody country . . .

Within a few minutes I've forgotten all about my nervousness. The country down below spreads out as we climb, and by the time we level out it seems to reach away for ever. It's just so *vast*, I've never imagined anything like it . . . it just goes on and on . . . and all the *same*, the same pattern repeated endlessly. And not just the distance, the vastness . . . it looks so *ancient*, like some old terrible skin, cracked and eroded and dead. Not desert, it's scrub, bush of a kind I suppose, a kind of olive scurf on the land. And the land itself is broken into an endless series of worn flat-topped ridges, each with its crown of low trees, each with its gullies plunging away . . . it fills me with *awe*, that's the only word for it. God, it's a terrible place . . .

I tear my eyes away from it, and lean back in my seat, resting my eyes by staring into the bright, pale sky beyond the pilot. Something wrong up there, I realise. The pilot is reading an old copy of Time, turning the pages idly, eyes cast down. Autopilot?

No bloody fear. I realise with sudden terror that the *fucking kid next to him is flying the plane*!

I freeze, look sideways at the priest. He beams back at me, offers me a lolly from a packet. I take one, a jelly bean. I've got the black one . . .

I calm down a bit. I suppose the kid's a squatter's son, and they all have planes up here. I suppose he learned to fly before he could walk. Anyway, it's out of control, out of my control.

Relax and enjoy.

All those stories about bush pilots . . .

Ah, well . . .

The drone of the engine has a lulling effect, and the little plane is steady on the air. I'm calming down a bit. I turn my head and begin watching the land again.

Half an hour later the priest touches my arm, points out his window. 'You can see Carbine Creek,' he says.

I crane over. Far away, miles away, to the north, is a faint patch that looks a shade, just a shade, greener than the rest of the land. For a moment I think I can see the pale flash of buildings, then it's gone.

Below, the land is definitely greener; a kind of low knoll a little higher than the surrounding plain with the flash of water somewhere beyond. A lake? Here? There's no sign of the creek itself, which according to the map flows north to join the Leichhardt, but there's a thread of green in the dry landscape that suggests a hidden watercourse.

The plane drones lower towards a red-dirt airstrip. The colour has nothing of the rich chocolate red of the south; it is harsh, arid, primary earth. And the greens seem paler, flatter. The plane touches down, bumps a little, stirring clouds of red dust, swings wide, turns, and taxis back towards a gaunt tin shed. Down now on the surface of the earth, perspective shows a few contours, low hills to the east, a slight rise in the land to the west, the crown of a rocky bluff to the south. The plane stops, the engine noise cuts and dies, and the silence closes in. The pilot jumps out, opens the door. I climb stiffly out on the wing, careful to place my foot on the black patch, and step on to the ground. Look around. Have the sense of being in the middle of a great blank map, with immeasureable distances stretching away on all sides.

The pilot hands me my luggage, nods towards the shed. 'Better wait over there in the shade – there'll be a bus soon . . .'

Then he's gone, the plane is taxiing away, dust trails following it as its speed mounts. It leaves the earth, climbs steeply, circles, heads west towards some station or mine. I go into the shelter, look around me. The shed is pretty basic: three galvanised walls and a roof, earth floor, a couple of rough benches. Outside the pool of shade the sunlight is bright and harsh. There is nothing else but a few patches of spiky dry spinifex and some strange livid vines clawing the earth, clustered with little melons the size of cricket balls. They look succulent and cool in the dry land. I decide there must be something wrong with them.

From the west, behind the shed, I hear the mounting sound of an engine. I get up, walk out into the sunlight. In a minute or two, from the direction where the mine must be, there appears an ancient green bus. When it gets closer I can see that it's an old Reo, panels sagging, door gone, two or three of the windows replaced by hardboard. It grinds to a halt beside the shed. It's empty except for the driver. He gets out, leaving the engine running, steps down, nods at me, grins gummily.

He's about fifty, tall, stringy, leathered, with short black hair greying at the edges. All his teeth are gone. His hands are the size of small shovels. He's wearing dark-blue trousers, a white shirt with the sleeves rolled, cracked black shoes.

He grins again, pulls out the makings. 'Sorry,' he says, 'I'm running a bit late today. Been delivering lunches, and the fuckin' cooks didn't have 'em ready . . .'

He rolls the smoke, an incredibly thin racehorse, sucks it into the corner of his mouth, cups his hands round a match to light it.

'Where you goin'?' he asks, round his cigarette. 'Employment office?'

'Yeah.'

'Right,' he says, 'we'll get goin' then.' Pauses. 'Name's Tom.'

'Jack.'

'Right. Let's get movin' then.' He swings himself back up into the bus, and I follow him, sit in the seat behind him. The engine revs, and he swings the old bus round the shed, off along the red-dirt track.

After a few miles, we turn left on to a metalled road, quite a fair one for the bush, that leads westward.

'This joins up with the Barkly Highway,' says Tom. 'Goes all the way to Darwin. Lots of road trains go through here.'

'Not much of a road for a bloody highway . . .'

'Oh,' he says, 'it's not bad for the bush.' Then: 'For Queensland, specially. Not too hot on roads up here . . .'

The rocky crest is rising on our left, the scrub on our right thickening into light bush. Bottle trees bulge pregnantly here and there beside the road. It looks foreign, the trees all strange to me. They're recognisably Australian, but odd, different. At home, even if I never knew the *names* of the trees, I knew the *feel* of them. These are different.

We pass a track, red dirt and gravel, that branches to the right. 'That's the road to the township, the quarters,' says Tom. 'You'll see all that later.'

We swing suddenly round a bend and with a shock of surprise I see a stretch of water to our right. A lake, a real lake . . .

'Lake Leichhardt,' says Tom, turning his head a little, eyes still on the road. 'Town water, water for the mill, even water-skiing . . .'

'That's to the mine,' he says a few minutes later, as we pass a road to the left. There's a grader parked by the roadside, and I see a quick glimpse of orange down the track. An ore carrier. We must be near the adit.

Then, coming slowly in third gear to the crest of a deep cut, we turn into a wide flat valley, and there it is before us. Carbine Copper.

Across the valley, on a shelf carved out of the red hillside, are the offices, low and white. From where we are, they look modern, cool, pleasant. To our right, on this side of the valley, is the processing plant, a great barn-like building only half-enclosed with galvanised iron, girders showing everywhere. I can see the shapes of ball mills, a crusher, what look like banks of flotation cells. An overhead pipe leads to a concentrate dump.

The wide flat floor of the valley is given over to workshops, stores compounds, generating plant, fuel storage – everything runs on distillate here, power for the mine, the office, the town. To the north, the valley wall rises to a low bund, and beyond that is nothing but sky. A hundred miles beyond is the Gulf.

We slip down the road into the valley, crawl up the winding track to the offices. Close-up they look less impressive, paint peeling, garden beds dry and cracked, a few straggling bushes half dead. The dust follows us up the hill like a red shadow.

Tom pulls up at the end of the building. 'Turn right as you go in for the employment office,' he says. 'Leave your case in the bus. I'm goin' back to the quarters in half an hour. I'll pick you up.'

'You reckon I'll get a job?'

He grins, wide and knowing. 'You can't get a job here,' he says, 'you'll never get one nowhere . . .'

Then he's gone, the bus bumping off down through the dust to the road again. And I turn towards the buildings.

•

The offices are built in a hollow square round a bare patch of earth that used to be a garden. A single dry poinciana struggles there now. The walkways are concrete, cracked a little and dusty. Inside the windows I can see an accounting office, a telex, and what look like geological offices. There are a few people coming and going, men in shorts and shirts, a few women in light frocks and sandals.

Inside the employment office an air-conditioner whines, and the air is cooler. The air-conditioner is one of the cheap evaporative types. I know the story of this place. It was built – with all mod cons – by the VAM group during the mining boom. When they went broke, our group took it over as a joint venture with the Japanese. Now, not yet paying its way, everything done on the cheap. There's a girl at the desk in the employment office. Young, scrubbed, ponytailed, blonde. Thinnish, with a hard look to her pale-blue eyes. The employment officer's out, she tells me; I'll have to wait. Goes back to her payroll. There are no spare chairs, so I go outside, stand in the shade overlooking the valley.

I'm not comfortable here near the offices. The fact is, there are two or three blokes who've been transferred here for their sins, and I'd know them, they'd know me. One for certain, Barry Carver, who got caught screwing a mines inspector's wife. Very cheeky. So I stand in a corner, out of the way. After a while a cream Holden wagon pulls up outside and a thin balding guy in the mandatory shorts and long socks climbs out and bustles inside clutching a bundle of papers. He's wearing blue-tinted specs over his weak, brown eyes. I know the type – unscrew his ears and his arse'll fall off . . . He looks at me – a quick, darting look. Goes into the office, speaks to the girl, looks out at me. Beckons me in.

'Sit down,' he says, going behind his desk, pointing to a chair.

I sit down, pass him my certificate of service. He reads it carefully three or four times, doodles with his pencil.

'Why did you leave the last job?' he asks.

'Family trouble,' I say. 'My old man was crook, I had to go home and work on the farm.'

'Mmmmm . . .' He asks a couple more questions, ones he already knows the answers to from the scrip. Not game to ask too many, I might pack up and leave, or he might have to refuse me a job. He doesn't want that.

'Any firearms?' he says suddenly.

'What?'

'Firearms. A rifle or anything. If you have I've got to lock them up . . .'

'No,' I say. 'No firearms.'

'Got your union ticket.'

'No, I let it run out.'

'Sign this,' he says. It's a deduction authority. Union dues. I sign.

He passes me a stores requisition. 'Safety hat, safety boots,' he says. I take the paper.

'Authority for the quarters,' he says, passing me another. 'Start in the morning with the town gang. Housing maintenance and so on. That all right?'

'OK.'

'Can you get a ride into town?'

I nod.

'Eight o'clock then. Report to Mr Chugg. Someone at the quarters will tell you where . . .'

I get up, start to go.

'Payday's a week away. You want a sub?'

I shake my head. They've both got their heads down again. I shrug, go outside to wait for Tom and the bus.

•

The bus turns off the highway on to the track leading to the town. Various buildings, mostly glorified tin sheds, start to show up, spotted haphazardly here and there in the scrub. A low hill looms behind, sparsely dotted with trees, covered in dry, pale spinifex.

Tom labels the sheds for me as we go past.

'Carbine shop . . . groceries, toilet stuff, kind of general store . . .'

'Library . . . open Tuesday nights and Sunday mornings . . .'

'Sports centre . . . that means badminton twice a week. Dance occasionally . . . squatters bring their ugly daughters in . . .'

We grind to a halt outside the post office, set behind a pool of dust, framed by two twisted, stunted gum trees. Tin shed, like everything else. Off to one side is a big single-storey fibro building.

'Mess,' says Tom. 'Find the contractor in there, this time of day.'

Behind the mess, stretching down a slope towards a deep gully, I can see row after row of dongas – portable camps that look like old railway carriages, each divided into half a dozen cubicles. They're mostly painted black, stained, scuffed, weary. Each is connected to the power lines. Beyond, up the far slope, half-hidden behind a great blushing screen of bougainvillea, is what looks like a modern motel building.

'What's that?' I ask Tom, standing in the hot dust, holding my port.

'Staff quarters,' he says. 'Out of bounds except for Saturday nights when the bar's open.'

'Bar only opens Saturday nights?' I can't believe it, not here . . .

'Oh,' he says, grinning his gummy grin. 'The canteen's open every night.' He nods towards the roof of another tin shed, just visible over a rise beyond the mess. 'That's where the serious drinkin' gets done . . . Got to go now, good luck . . .' And the bus grinds away along the track, churning its cloud of red dust.

I'm sweating inside my thick shirt now. The sun's burning down, not a cloud, not a breath of wind. And this is bloody winter . . .

Inside the mess hall I find the contractor, a wiry little Italian, talking to his mess manager, a heavy hard-looking bloke in dirty whites with a doughy, bruised face and the look of the drinker about him.

'Lunch is over,' says the contractor when I give him my docket. 'You wanta sandwiches, eh?'

I nod, and the manager goes into the kitchen, opens a big fridge door, tosses me a packet of thick sandwiches through the hatch.

'Come,' says the contractor, whose name is Ettore, 'I show where you live . . .'

I follow him out again into the brightness, the heat, clutching my port and my sandwiches, and down the hill we go towards the dongas. Home sweet home . . .

Ettore pulls a piece of paper out of his pocket, reading as he goes down the track. He has a wide, black moustache and a big bald spot. He's not sweating. We stop outside one of the dongas near the end of the first row. He pulls open a screen door. The interior seems black after the brightness outside. The window at the far end is a hard, bright square. I step up, inside. Two bunks on each side. The little room seems impossibly full. Four bunks, two wardrobes, a couple of suitcases, clothes hanging on makeshift lines, frayed pictures of naked women on the scarred plywood walls. Ettore follows me in.

'That one,' he says, pointing to the right-hand side, where the bunks seem less densely populated with clothes and magazines and rubbish than those on the left. 'Two men to a room . . . us'a top bunk for clothes, you know?'

I nod.

'You in with young Hansen, he good boy, no trouble . . .'

'You get much trouble?'

'No much trouble . . . bit fighting, bit gambling, much drunken, you know?'

'I know.' I put my case down, start to clean up the bunk, toss the detritus on the other side. 'How many coppers you got here?'

'Coppers?' he says, leaning on the doorpost, lighting a cigarette. 'No coppers . . . if very bad thing, then coppers come from Mount Isa . . . You know? But no coppers here. Young copper come once a month from Kajabbi for half a day . . . driving licence, that sort, you know?'

'Yeah, I know . . .'

'Other troubles we look after ourselves. Look,' he says, pointing to a torn notice taped to the inside of the door. 'Here camp rules . . . mealtimes, no women in units, no loud noises in night, all that. You know? No firearms.'

'I know. Where's the toilet block?'

'Ah,' he says, 'two lines over, down the hill.' He butts out his cigarette on the sole of his shoe, turns to go. 'You gotta problems, you see one of mess committee . . . names in mess, you know?'

'I know . . . thanks.'

Then he's gone, and I'm alone in the cell. Christ, that's what it's like. Nasty, British and small. But as Jock said as he emptied the can, the money's clean . . .

I lie down on the bunk, suddenly very tired. Outside the screen door, the day seems white and washed out, lost in a kind of pale overexposure. Suddenly I'm conscious of that map again, with me in the middle of it, lost and far away from everything, everyone . . . It's a kind of loneliness that's an ache, an almost unendurable ache . . .

•

I wake up a couple of hours later, from a dream of the valley, the white hotel, scones and jam on a winter afternoon, Kate painting her nails in front of the fire, and the lingering smell of the old man's pipe tobacco. And the heaviness comes back, a feeling of abandonment. Starting out in life all over again, with a port full of nothing, and this strangeness inside, and can't just accept it, it eats at me like acid . . .

How could someone fuck his own daughter?

Right down deep inside, in the very core, is this horror at what he did, at the *impossibility* of it, at the impossibility of being what I am . . .

Why did she *have* to tell me? If only I didn't know . . .

Hang on right there, killer: are you crooked because of what he did, what he made you? Or at her for *telling*? At him for letting her, for not making sure she didn't? If you're going to get up again, then everything's got to be square, right?

The truth is, I don't know. I've thought so much about it, and I'm just tired and confused, and don't know which way is up any more . . .

Outside, the day seems less leached with light; the shadows of the trees between the lines of dongas are lengthening. It seems warmer now, in here, as if it's been storing the day's heat. No air-conditioning. It must be bloody impossible in the *hot* weather . . .

I can hear stirrings outside, footsteps approaching, passing, as the camp begins to come alive. The figures pass. No one looks in.

Suddenly the screen door is flung back and someone steps inside. Against the light, a tall figure, dark against the day. It stops at the sight of me . . .

'Oh . . .' The voice is light, boyish.

'You must be Hansen.'

'Oh, yeah . . . Stretch, that's what they call me.' He must be six-two, six-three, but young, no older than maybe seventeen, eighteen. And built like a good light-heavy – long, strong legs, a wide ledge of shoulder, narrow waist. His hair is longish, over his ears, fair and fine. A good face, regular and handsome. If it belonged to a girl, she'd be more than pretty. But nothing feminine about this one.

'Jack,' I say. Then remember about Ritchie Todd. 'Ritchie really, but everyone calls me Jack . . .'

'Ah,' he says, sitting on the bunk across from me. 'Sorry about the mess, if I'd known anyone was moving in, I'd have cleaned up a bit.'

'Not much room, is there?'

He blushes, as if it might somehow be his fault. 'I'll clean up a bit after I've had a shower . . .'

'I didn't mean that – Christ, I haven't got enough gear to worry about.'

'Oh.' He's still at that awkward age when he doesn't quite know how to handle strangers. 'Listen,' he says. 'I'm goin' to have a shower. You want to come along, I'll show you the works?'

'Fine.'

'They give you a towel?'

'No.'

'Useless cunts,' he says. 'You get two a week, they change 'em Wednesdays and Saturdays. Never mind, we'll pick one up for you.'

Outside the evening has begun. There are people about, men in shorts and shirts, shorts and blue singlets, shorts and nothing else. All with short socks. I'll have to buy some shorts and socks, I can see that . . .

We pick up a towel from the laundry behind the shower block. He shows me where the washing machines are, the clothes lines, and we strip and get under the tepid water. I notice that he's hung like a bull.

'Where do you work?' I ask him. 'What part of the business?'

'Town gang,' he says.

'Me too.'

He smiles, and it seems to light up his face. His teeth are very good, very white and regular. 'Terrific,' he says.

'What's it like?'

'A fuckin' bludge,' he says. 'Except the shit run . . . you know, collecting garbage once a week.'

'What's the trump like?'

'Curly? He's all right. Bit of an old woman, but all right. Piss in his pocket, he'll follow you anywhere . . .' And he laughs.

'Where you from?' he asks a little later, rubbing his wet hair with a towel.

'Down south.'

'Yeah, me too. South Queensland, that is.'

'Ah . . .'

'Listen, you want to go up to the canteen and have a beer before tea?'

'Why not?'

'Come on, then . . .' He pulls on a pair of jeans and a T-shirt. I drag my boots on and we go out again into the slowly cooling evening. Up the dusty pot-holed track, past spindly trees and thorny shrubs.

A scattering of men strolling towards the big barn-like shed at the crown of the ridge, most of them newly showered, clean-dressed, with wet hair. Converging slowly on the evening's goal.

A few cars and station wagons, a Mini Moke or two, a couple of Toyota Landcruisers. Behind the canteen is a cleared area, a sort of rough beer garden with benches and tables. It's sparsely occupied, mostly by women in summer frocks and cardigans. Staff, I guess; maybe wives.

I stop for a moment at the door of the canteen and look west. The sun has gone, dipped below the ragged ridge that dominates the skyline. The shadows are a deep hollow purple, flooding like ink into the valley below. The evening has a kind of scented air to it, even if it is mostly the scent of warm dust and cooling leaves.

I follow Stretch inside.

It is a single gigantic room, unlined, the galvanised iron bare everywhere. It's hot inside, but more with the heat of packed and sweating bodies than of the sun. The air is thick with the buzz of talk and the drift of cigarette smoke. At one end is a bar that runs the width of the building, at the far side a door that leads outside to the toilets and the beer garden. Behind the bar, a refrigerated beer store. Everyone seems to be drinking cans of Carlton Draught, nothing else in sight anywhere.

'Want a whitey?' asks Stretch, and I nod. He pushes into the crowd by the bar, comes back in a minute or so with the two white cans.

I step back to lean against the wall, and almost stumble over a dog. A dog?

A sight.

It's enormous, dusty black and pinkish white, bloated, dewlapped, drooling, disgusting. Bloodshot eyes peer up at me with tired hostility, the ghost of a snarl curling lips to show yellowed teeth. Slack balls dangle on the concrete floor.

I realise with a shock that the dog is drunk as a pig.

Before him on the floor is a deep plastic bowl, half-filled with beer. A plate beside it holds the crumbs of potato crisps.

I look at Stretch. 'What the *fucking* hell is *that*?'

'Shhh . . .' he nudges me in the ribs. 'Careful what you say . . . that's Bully.'

'What the bloody hell's Bully? Apart from disgusting?'

He looks around carefully. 'Watch what you say about him,' he says. 'You can buy a fight saying things like that.'

'Who with?'

'Any of the miners . . . he's a kind of mascot.'

'Jesus. Does he spend all his time here, in the bar?'

'No,' says Stretch. 'They put him on the bus every morning, take him down to the mine. He sleeps in the office there every day, and they bring him back here at night, give him his chips and beer.'

'Oh, Christ . . .'

'Hangover every morning,' says Stretch. 'Mostly they have to lift him on to the bus. He usually makes it down to the street on his own, but they have to lift him on . . .'

'Come on,' I say. 'Let's get over the other side away from it.' I'm halfway between amusement and disgust. How bored do you have to be to make a bloody alcoholic out of a dog? Don't even know what sort of dog – his breed's obscured by all that beer.

'There's Vic and Jimmy,' says Stretch, and changes direction slightly.

'Who are they?'

'Oh,' he says, 'they're our neighbours – they live next-door to our donga.'

We push our way towards the far wall, towards a short bench where two men are sitting. One of them takes the eye at once. He's sitting there like a big, very tough Buddha. An inch or so taller than me, maybe; fifty, sixty pounds heavier. Dark hair cut short, all visible skin tanned dark, thick chest and heavy shoulders, a big belly that looks all muscle and is carried high, not an ounce of sag. Hands like mauls. His eyes, above a broken nose, are brown. Most brown eyes are soft eyes, but when they're hard they're the hardest eyes in the world. His are like that. There's a static quality about him, but a strength too. Know I'd hate to tangle with him, even if he is pushing fifty.

The little fellow beside him could hardly be more different. Short, lean, knotted; a pale face, all angles, and washed-out blue eyes. His brown hair seems to stick up at every imaginable angle. Tattoos on both arms: MOTHER and various anchors and daggers and snakes, made a long time ago. His nose, too, is broken, maybe more than once. Lots of scar tissue – knuckles, cheekbones, ears, lips. He seems nervous, all the time jiggling, shifting, shrugging.

They're both dressed in clean shorts, blue singlets, sandshoes, and look like some sort of crazy Mutt and Jeff. And something else. Well, face it killer, they look bloody intimidating. Break rocks on either of them. I notice the little fellow's legs. They're like those you see on Belgian bike riders, knotted, lean, carved out of ironwood.

'This is Jack,' says Stretch, 'he's moved in with me.'

The big man gives me a long, calm look. Leans forward, reaches out one of his hands. 'Vic,' he says. 'Vic Cotton.' Turns his head, 'This is Jimmy.' No other name. I take Vic's hand. It's warm, hard, dry, and his grip is surprisingly gentle. Jimmy's, when he offers it, is the way he looks: strong, tense, nervous.

Vic pulls a packet of Drum from his hip pocket, starts to roll a smoke. While he rolls, he watches me. Seems to watch me for a long time. No hostility in his gaze, just a certain assessing quality. Finally he lets his eyes fall to his ciggie. 'Where you working, mate?'

'Same place as Stretch.'

'Ah,' he says. 'A soft cop.' Raises his eyes again. 'Money's not as good as for the shift-work jobs, but a soft cop . . . you'll be right.'

'What about you?' I ask him.

'Oh,' he says, turning to smile a little at the man beside him, 'Jimmy and me work in the mill . . . on the float cells . . . three shifts, a quiet life, good money. Not as good as down the hole, but we don't like it much down the hole, do we mate?'

Jimmy shakes his head, shrugs his shoulders, grins a bit. Says nothing.

'Buy you a beer?' I ask.

'Next time,' he says. 'I'll buy this one.' He gets up easily, despite his bulk, and moves towards the bar. Like lots of big men, he's light on his feet, and people seem to get out of his way, too, so that he finds a clear path to the bar. I'd bet my balls that both him and Jimmy have spent a lot of time in the ring; they've got that look about them, the shape, the hands, the eyes.

'How long you been up here?' I ask Jimmy.

He looks at me quickly. 'Three four months,' he says. 'We come in at the end of the last wet.' His voice is a little hoarse, and kind of flat, as if he's taken one too many in the voice box.

'How long you reckon you'll stay?'

Jimmy looks past me. Vic is suddenly there with two handfuls of cans. 'Oh,' says Vic, 'Till we've got a stake. Enough to buy a few acres somewhere . . . somewhere down south.'

'Where it's quiet,' says Jimmy, 'quiet and cool . . .' There's a strange anxiety in his voice and his eyes, as if he's looking for reassurance.

'That's it,' says the big man as he sits down, passes the beer round. 'That's it, mate . . .'

The anxiety seems to leave Jimmy's eyes, and he settles back with his fresh beer.

Stretch has been looking round the room. He says suddenly, to no one in particular, 'Be back in a minute.' And he's gone, drifting quietly through the crowd. I see Vic's eyes following him, so I turn a little, follow his progress. It seems aimless. He stops for a word here and there, waves to someone in the back of the room, sauntering idly, just drifting. But his course, I notice, is taking him towards the far corner of the bar, where half a dozen men and three women are drinking in a group. The women are in their thirties, clerks in the office, maybe, or just workers' wives. They're nondescript to the point of plainness, except for one; she's taller than the rest, a striking brunette with short, wavy hair. She has the air of some experience, of having gone a mile or two down the track. But attractive, all the same.

Stretch drains his can, pushes in to the bar to buy another. As he moves away from the bar again, he brushes against the dark girl's arm, seems to pause a moment, say something close beside her ear. You'd miss it if you weren't watching closely. A few minutes later and he's back with us.

We talk idly for a while, drink another round. I'm getting a nice gentle buzz on, and it's dark outside now. For a while there has been a drift towards the door. Hunger is stirring.

Suddenly, Stretch, with an air of nonchalance that fools no one, looks around and says, 'Think I'll go for a bit of a walk . . .' He nods vaguely at us, his thoughts somewhere else, and drifts off towards the door.

Vic laughs gently, calls after him: 'Don't be late for tea.'

Stretch waves without looking back. There is a hint of purpose in his walk now.

'He's got a meet on,' I say to Vic. 'That dark piece.'

Vic nods. 'He'll fuck anything female, Stretch will.' He grins a little wryly. 'And there's something about him . . . I don't know, he just has to look at 'em . . .' he shakes his head. 'Come on,' he says, 'let's go and eat.'

The mess hall is crowded. Rows of wooden tables, rough and stained. A constant stream of men moving between servery counter and tables. Steam and smells, strong tea, gravy, frying food. We go through with the queue, take our plates to tables near the rear. The buzz of conversation is loud.

Soup, roast beef – brown and stringy – vegetables, among them curious, stringy things that must be some kind of yam. Tinned fruit and custard.

I find I'm ravenous, and put it all away. Halfway through, Stretch comes in, fills a tray, sits down and begins to plough into it. He looks a little flushed and dishevelled. Vic raises an eyebrow, winks at me, but says nothing.

When we've finished eating, we sit for a while over cups of tea and cigarettes. The hall empties slowly. There's a strange feel about all this. I've run a mess like this, supervised contractors, kept order, made the rules. It's rather eerie to be on the receiving end: the other side of the mirror.

'Not much of a mess,' says Vic, rubbing his butt out in a saucer. 'No?'

'Food not the best, everything a bit sloppy. For the best tucker you've got to get into construction camps – that's where they treat you well.'

'Been in a few, have you?'

He grins. 'Too many.'

We stretch and stand up. As we reach the door, someone begins to push past, coming in. A wiry, red-headed bloke, freckled. Never seen him before. But he stops, peers at me.

'Christ,' he says, 'I know you . . . you're Jack . . . Aaaaaah!'

Vic is fast, very fast indeed. He's got his great hand clasped round the redhead's arm just above the elbow, fingers digging in deeply. The redhead's face is a grimace of pain.

'You got a big mouth, Blue,' says Vic, not releasing his hold. 'Haven't you?'

'Yes, Vic, I've got a big mouth . . . now, for Chrissake . . .'

Vic lets go and the redhead stands aside, rubbing his arm ruefully. He shakes his head at me. 'No offence, mate . . .'

'She's jake . . .

'Thanks,' I say to Vic when we are out in the dark. 'But it's not really important enough to break bones for.'

'Do him good, anyway,' says Vic. 'He *has* got a big mouth, Blue . . .'

Later that night, Stretch and Jimmy in their bunks, Vic and I sit for a while on the donga steps. The night is very still, almost cool, and the stars are very clear and bright. Vic's bulk looms dark and somehow reassuring.

Breaking a long silence, he says: 'I saw you play in the Grand Final . . . when was it? sixty-seven?'

'Sixty-six,' I say.

'I'm a Sydneysider,' he says. 'You know, rugby and Resch's. But I had a few years down south. Almost got caught up in that nonsense. Like a bloody religion in the south, isn't it?'

'That's what they say.'

'What's it like on the inside?'

'Not religious.'

He laughs.

'To tell the truth, Vic, I don't think it's really religious – what it is, it's more like a kind of tribal warfare. Each tribe picks its best warriors, and they all do a kind of ritual battle. Can you imagine what it'd be like if all that bloody violence was bottled up? Instead they've got their gladiators.'

'See what you mean . . .'

'You ever get mixed up with rugby? You've got the build . . .'

'No,' he says. 'I was always a bit of a loner. That's what made me a pug. All on your pat, you know?'

'Yeah, I know.'

'Never any good, though.'

'No?'

'No. Usual bloody bullshit for a year or two, new white hope, all that. But I never quite had it. Ended up doing the rounds with Harry Paulsen's troupe . . . you know, round the shows and carnivals.'

'Yeah, I know . . . used to go and watch when I was a kid.'

'That's where I met Jimmy.'

'Was it? He doesn't look the type somehow. I mean . . .'

'Too nervous? Yeah, I know what you mean. But he wasn't always like that. No, he just turned up one night when the show was at Swan Hill, looking pale and hungry – just come out of the bluestone college I found out later – and broke. Jumped up on the platform, lookin' like sixpenn'orth o' nothing. We laughed a bit. Then we went inside and Jimmy cleaned up quite a nice middleweight. Hit him about six times, just almost casual, like swatting a fly, and the middleweight lay down and went to sleep. Harry signed him on that night, but he wasn't cut out for the life, went through in about a month.'

'Was he really good, Jimmy? Not just bullshit?'

Vic is silent for a moment or two. 'He could have been the welter champion,' he says at last. '*Could* have been . . .'

'What happened?'

'Oh,' he says, 'the usual thing. A prick for a manager, after the quick quid. Over-matched too soon too often. Got his brains scrambled. Inevitable. That's the sort of fighter he is . . .'

'How do you mean?'

'Well,' he says, 'he just won't give up. You really can't keep him down, he just keeps getting up again. It's mostly his legs. He's got this incredible set of legs that just keep him goin' when he's really out.'

'There's more than that to a fighter, though, isn't there?'

'Oh, sure,' says Vic. 'He's incredibly fast, really fast, and he punches very, very hard. But really, when it's all boiled down, he's got that thing that Dempsey and Robinson and Carruthers had – he's a killer. Know what I mean?'

'Yes,' I say. 'I know what you mean.'

He laughs a little, quietly, amused, in the darkness. 'I thought you might . . .'

I begin to feel tired then, and the day has been long, and I really want to get my head down.

Vic stirs, getting up. 'Just one thing,' he says. 'The young bloke in there, Stretch, he's a good boy, but he's a bit young, hasn't got himself quite set yet, know what I mean? Keep an eye on him, eh?'

And, lying in the cool darkness, listening to Stretch's soft breathing from the other bunk, I grin a bit to myself. At the end of the day, the first day in this fucking horrible place, I've got myself a mate . . . and a bloody charge. You can be lonely, I suppose, but you can't be *dead* lonely unless you're dead . . .

Then sleep drops on me like a great black shroud . . .

●

Curly Chugg is bald, of course. A thin little moon-faced fellow, brown as a nut, including bald head, with a harried, worried look to him.

Eight o'clock, and the town gang is foregathered at the depot, a big tin shed filled with timber and tools, cement and machinery, workbenches, water pipe, fibro-cement sheeting, bits of this and that. Curly's desk is a table in the corner, covered inches deep in old time sheets, job cards, requisitions, lunch papers, Coke bottles, overrunning ashtrays, pipe fittings and general rubbish.

The shed is on the back road, the loop between the quarters and the town, which is hidden beyond a small rise. The creek flows across the road a hundred yards back towards the quarters, curls northward. I haven't actually seen the town itself yet. But I guess it's only houses . . .

The other members of the gang are sorting themselves out, piling gear and materials into a Bedford truck and a Landcruiser. A Holden ute stands outside in the bright sunshine. Hot already.

Curly, sorting through job sheets, looks harrassed. He clearly doesn't know what to do with me. 'Well,' he says at last, 'you can go with Stretch today, clean up the GM's garden . . .'

Stretch goes into a corner, winking as he goes, grabs a bundle of gardening tools, throws them in the back of the ute. He points to a motor mower behind a pile of rubbish. 'Grab the mower, will you?'

We load the tools, lean against the tray, waiting. In a few minutes Curly comes out and gets in the driver's seat. We squeeze in beside him, Stretch curled up like a big grasshopper. Curly starts up, turns the ute out of the yard, heads back towards the quarters. A few hundred yards in, we turn up a red-dirt track, past the staff quarters – which look like a motel, and probably started out that way – past a deep gully overgrown with tangled weeds and vines, towards a building half-hidden behind an enormous bougainvillea. It's a large, single-storey house, concrete brick and fibro, with empty twin garages, a wide dry garden and a scruffy lawn.

Curly pulls in through the gateway. We get out, unload the tools.

'Stretch knows what to do,' says Curly. 'See youse lunchtime.'

When he's gone, Stretch yawns and looks round. 'Bit of a bludge today,' he says. 'Only take us a couple of hours, we can have a spell later on . . .'

I look at the house. Blinds drawn, no movement, no sign of

life. I nod towards the place. 'No one home?'

Stretch picks up a pair of shears. 'No one been home for a couple of months . . .'

'Where's he gone? The General Manager?'

'Pissed off, resigned.'

'Why?'

'Oh,' says Stretch,' his wife was on the piss, and his daughter – she was about fifteen – was fucking one of the Alimak crews.'

'What. The whole crew?'

'Yeah. Plus a bit of casual stuff.' He starts to snip at the bits of bougainvillea that are creeping out, trespassing on the front verandah.

'When's the new GM coming?'

'Christ knows – they can't get anyone to take the job. There's been half a dozen come to have a gander at the place; but one look, and that's it, they're off like cut cats.'

'Who's in charge?'

'Don't really know,' he says, snipping lazily. 'I think it's the Mine Manager . . . for the time being.'

I'm starting to sweat already. 'Look, I've got to get some shorts and stuff – don't want to wait till the weekend.'

'We'll go over tonight,' he says, 'when we knock off. Get Curly to drop us off. Listen, you want to cut the lawn? We've got to do that, rake up, weed the beds, water, that's about all . . .'

So I start the mower, begin wheeling it over the thin, dry grass outside the silent house. It's quiet, bright, hot. Peaceful.

By ten o'clock Stretch has finished trimming the bushes and hedges. He picks up the rake, then looks at his watch. 'Smoko,' he says. 'Let's go and get a drink.'

'Where?'

'Over the staff quarters . . .'

We walk slowly back down the track towards the low, long building, painted pale yellow and looking cool and quiet.

'Soft cop up there,' says Stretch. 'All air-conditioned, waitresses in the dining room, shower and bog in every room, just like a motel.'

'Rather be up there?'

'Bloody oath – except it must be bloody dull . . .'

We approach the back of the staff quarters. There's a flyscreen over the closed kitchen door. Stretch goes up to it, taps, calls out. 'Anyone home?'

A girl comes to the door, opens the screen. Young, thin, blonde. Quite pretty, a wedding ring on her finger. Smiles at Stretch.

'What are you doing up this way?'

'Bloody horticultural,' says Stretch. Nods at me. 'This is me mate Jack. Any chance of a cuppa?'

She smiles at me. Quite nicely, but without the warmth that Stretch gets. 'Come on in,' she says.

Stretch hesitates. 'Not supposed to go in there . . .'

'Don't be silly,' she says. 'They don't like it, they can find another waitress.'

We sit down at a clean laminex table in the spotless, stainless-steel kitchen. Beyond the small hatch in the wall, I can see tables laid, with white cloths, shining utensils, glass; and there's carpet on the floor. It's cool, and there's a thin background hum from the air-conditioner.

The girl puts a plate of cakes and pastries on the table, looks briefly at me. 'My name's Shelly,' she says. 'My old man's a fitter.'

Got the form, Shelly. 'Nice to meet you,' I say politely. Take a cake.

She brings the teapot, three cups. With saucers. Sits down, pours, lights a cigarette.

A little small talk. I don't say much. She spends a lot of time smiling at Stretch.

When it's time to go – ten minutes has extended to half an hour – she says: 'Come back at lunchtime – there's no one in today.'

Then, on the doorstep, to me: 'You come over any time you're working up this way, Jack, always a cup of tea on . . .'

I smile politely. 'Thanks.' I must have passed some sort of test. Or maybe just being Stretch's mate is enough . . .

Back to the lawn mower.

An hour later Curly turns up, brings our paper bags from the mess. He looks about a bit vacantly at what we've done, nods a few times, heads back to the ute. 'See y' about four then . . .'

I open my lunch bag. An apple, an orange, two great thick sandwiches. Bread stale, meat stringy, drenched in pickles. Oh, well . . .

'Come on round the back,' says Stretch, 'we'll have a kip for a couple of hours, then go back and see Shelly . . .'

Round the back, in the shade of a nameless thick shrub, we settle down, eat our lunch, drink from Stretch's lukewarm Coke bottle, stretch out, smoke a bit, talk desultorily, fall quiet . . . doze . . . sleep . . .

I wake later to find the sun far to the west. Three o'clock. Stretch is yawning. 'Come on,' he says, 'let's go and find a cuppa . . .'

It doesn't seem, at that moment, such a bad life . . .

•

The evening has a dark, soft, velvety quality.

Vic and I are sitting on the donga steps drinking whities. Stretch has gone marauding, drifting off quietly into the night. Jimmy is inside the donga, in his bunk, reading a comic.

'You know mining towns?' says Vic.

'Yes,' I say. 'One, anyway.'

'Yeah, well,' he says. 'You know what it's like. They're all the same. Only this one's worse.'

'How? Worse?'

'I don't quite know. The isolation, the climate . . . but mostly it's the women . . . well, lack of women.'

'Yeah?'

'Yeah. See, in a construction camp, there's no women at all, right?'

'Right.'

'And everyone's in the same boat. You know you're only gunna be there a while anyway, then move on. But here,' and he pauses, takes a long swallow, crushes the empty can in his fist, 'here there *are* women. Trouble is, there's just a few of them, and they're mostly taken – married whatever – and the few available ones crack the whip . . .'

'They're all hard on marriages,' I say. 'All these bloody places.'

'Yeah, well . . . mostly the married ones keep to the village. Just go to the store, the library . . . into the Isa once a month to shop . . . you know. And their husbands try to keep close. Not that that helps if they want to try a bit of foreign stuff. There's blokes in a line a mile long . . .

'It's not even sex, really,' he says. 'It's the bloody *idea* of sex . . .'

'What about the birds up at the staff quarters?'

'There's only three of them. Margaret, the nursing sister, she's got a regular boyfriend, one of the mill foremen. Sue, the one in the office, she's got a steady miner. The other one, Nell, she just won't be in it, not interested.'

I've seen the nurse: plain, pleasant, brisk. Sue – well, Stretch pointed her out in the canteen: plain as a pikestaff, freckled, forty-five, legs like a chippendale chair. Her young miner's twenty-five, big and good-looking, showing her off as if she's the bloody queen.

'What about Stretch, then?' I ask.

He laughs. 'Stretch's a different kettle of fish.' Shakes his head. 'Don't really know how he does it . . . but he just has to look at them . . . maybe they just want to mother him . . .'

There's a long pause. A faint drift of sound filters through the night from the canteen. There's an intermittent traffic between there and the dongas and the showers. It's lazy, quiet, almost soporific.

'You know how old he is?' says Vic. 'Stretch?'

'What, seventeen? Eighteen?'

'He's fourteen,' says Vic.

'*Fourteen*!'

'Hard to believe, isn't it? He's a big boy.'

'But *fourteen* . . .'

'He's older than that in the head. Doesn't talk much about it, but he's seen some bad times, has Stretch.'

'Jesus, but *fourteen* . . .' Hard to believe. Physically he's a man all right. And there's none of that silliness about him that you connect with fourteen. 'Don't people *know* about it? Don't they *do* anything?'

'A few people know about it. But people mostly mind their own business up here,' and I see his sly look at me. 'Well, they look after him a bit, you know . . .'

'What if he gets caught – you know, shagging about?'

Vic shrugs. 'He'll get thumped. Takes his chances like everyone else.'

I have to laugh. 'Oh, Christ, fourteen . . .'

Inside, the sound of Jimmy's feet hitting the floor. He comes out, skin pale despite the sun he gets. One of those blokes that neither burn nor tan, always stay off-white. He seems nervous and edgy tonight. Refuses a beer.

'Goin' for a walk,' he says, and wanders off.

'He's not going prowling too, is he?'

Vic smiles. 'No,' he says, 'not Jimmy. He just gets edgy sometimes. Christ, this place would make anyone edgy, wouldn't it?'

'How badly scrambled is he?'

'Not too bad,' he says. 'Well, not good, either, I suppose. Wasn't all in the ring, see? Coppers did a bit of it . . .'

'Oh?'

'It's that thing of Jimmy's see . . . not staying down. A bad time once, before I met him. Canberra, of all places. Jimmy's in a pub, see, just havin' a few quiet beers. Police sergeant comes in, knows Jimmy's form, says to him: Listen, cock, soon as you step out that door I'm going to have you . . .

'Why? says Jimmy. Because, says the copper, I've got a heap of wood to be split and a bloody great hedge that wants trimming . . .

'Jimmy stays in the bar till closing time. Reckons he's safe by then. But sure enough, as soon as he hits the footpath, the sergeant grabs him. Into the lock-up . . .

'Well, Jimmy split the wood on the first day. The second day the sergeant put him on the hedge, then got called away. Bloody great cypress hedge, old, slow-growing, you know? Well, Jimmy wronged 'er, wronged 'er badly . . . Looked like a snake's nightmare when he'd finished. The sergeant came back, took one look and went for Jimmy. Jimmy ripped half his tunic off, and jumped clear through the hedge.

'Well, that buggered the sergeant because on the other side of the hedge was Commonwealth property, and they had to get the Commonwealth police to get him out . . .

'When they finally got him back in the cells, they went for him, the sergeant and three or four young coppers. Hammered him, kept him down by pure weight of numbers.

'But Jimmy was cunning. He'd lie in there doggo, waiting until they'd all gone but one. Then he'd spring up and do the copper left in the cell. The others would rush back, flatten him again. He'd lie doggo, then up and do one copper . . .

'It went on too long . . . didn't do him much good. Hasn't been able to stand bein' shut up ever since then. Had a year in the bluestone college a bit later, nearly killed him. Just can't stand it . . .'

We sit in silence for a long time. It seems like another world altogether. Violence . . . well, the old football's violent enough. And you can get hurt right enough too. But it's a kind of ritualised violence, almost controlled, expected, and limited . . . In all the years of football I've never had a single punch-up off the ground. Just once it nearly happened; some mug mistook me for someone else, someone who'd been screwing his wife. Three of them waiting outside the ground in the dark after practice. A palm in their faces, and I took off. Used to run close to evens in those days and they never looked like catching me . . .

But *this* world – Vic's world, Wingnut's world, the world of Hiroshima and Mike and the others – this *casual* violence, violence that they live with, *accept* . . . is *this* the world, the real world? Am I *that* fucking innocent?

'Listen,' says Vic, draining the last can, 'Jimmy and I have got our days off this weekend. A few of us are going out to the Corned Beef Holes Saturday afternoon. Want to come?'

What the fuck are the Corned Beef Holes? Never mind. Anything's better than being alone . . .

'Love to . . .'

•

The Corned Beef Holes are a different world.

Ten miles to the west of Carbine Creek, another creek crosses the highway. This is Corned Beef Creek, flowing north towards the Gulf. A hundred yards or so south of the highway are the holes – three linked waterholes at different levels with small waterfalls between.

We drive in along the track to the first hole: a wide, still pool perhaps fifty yards across, surrounded by tall trees and grassy flats. At the southern end bushes grow tightly about the low falls, dry now, where summer rains spill the creek downhill.

The old utility grinds to a halt near the water and we clamber out. There are six of us: Stretch and I in the back with Ray Nermutt, a dark and cheerful mill hand; Vic and Jimmy in the front with Ice-cream Peters, who owns the ute. Ice-cream is a lean and laconic croweater, a motor mechanic. Cartons of beer and sandwich packs are stacked under wet bags to keep them as cool as possible. The day, like every other day, is warm – hot – without a breath of wind or a cloud in the sky. Strange how quickly you get bored with perfect weather.

We all gather in the shade for the first beer of the day. It's well past noon now, work done for the week. This has the look of a well-used place, a picnic place. The turning circle is churned deep in the red soil, and there is the inevitable litter about – empty cans, papers, lolly wrappers. While we drink, a Landcruiser drives in and parks well away from us. Bloke and his wife, two small kids. Waves to us, but they keep well away, a private family group.

First cans finished, we go about our recreational pastimes. Ice-cream brings out a stick wound with nylon monofilament, and baits his hook with a bit of meat from his sandwiches. He casts his line, reclines against a tree, beer and cigarette to hand, ready to doze away the afternoon.

'Ever catch anything?' I ask.

'Never,' he says cheerfully, his eyes half-closed.

Vic has found himself another tree, and sits, back against it, gazing out over the water with vast serenity. Jimmy and Ray have wandered round the edge of the waterhole, idly skimming stones and bits of bark into the water. Stretch strips off to his underpants and wades in, begins to swim slowly through the dark water. I pull off my thongs and dangle my legs in the water. I've now adopted the uniform of the place, bought a couple of pairs of black football knicks. My knees, a bit pale still, are like old friends.

I watch Stretch. I'm used to swimming – or was when I was a kid – in those dark-brown river swimming holes where you couldn't see the bottom, but this water is darker, seems heavier, more menacing, somehow.

'Is it safe?' I ask Vic. 'To swim?'

'Safe enough. A bit muddy on the bottom.'

'Fish?'

He looks towards Ice-cream's reclining figure, grinning. 'They reckon.'

'Anything else?'

'Odd water snake maybe. Croc . . .'

'Croc?'

'Just the little Johnson River ones . . . real shy . . . won't hurt you . . . not like the big salt-water jobs . . .'

But I don't really feel like swimming anyway.

It's very peaceful here. I know now why they make such a big fuss of oases. This place – well, back home it wouldn't rank a mention, pretty ordinary. But here, in this godforgotten place, it's a miracle. What the old Abos must have felt about it . . .

There is a sudden tug on Ice-cream's line and he springs into action, yanks it out of the water. Nothing on the hook but the bait. A moment later Stretch surfaces by the bank, laughing so he can hardly stand on the muddy bottom.

'Bastard!' shouts Ice-cream, and leaps in on him, clothes and all. They wrestle in the shallows for a moment, then collapse sideways, locked in mutual embrace. When they surface, Stretch breaks away, swims out into the middle of the pool. Ray stands waist-deep in the water, clothes sodden, raging at him good-humouredly. Then he climbs out, drops his line in the water again, opens another can, flips water from his hair and face, settles back against his tree trunk.

Sometimes – at times like this – I feel almost happy. At others I can hardly bear being alive. A great ache of desperation will suddenly rise out of my chest and close my throat, and I'll get a hard pain behind the eyes. It just seems to me that I'm lost, abandoned by both the world and myself . . .

I no longer seem to think of home, of Nancy and the old man, or Kate. They all seem part of that lost world I can't go back to. Kate though . . . it strikes me how much at home she'd be in a place like this . . .

Strange, I've always felt more warmth in Kate than in Nance – my own mother . . . half-sister . . . Oh, Christ, how *could* he have . . .

Let it go, let it go, another world . . . Anyhow, he's got to look after his own bloody problems. I've got mine . . .

But I wonder how they *saw* each other . . . I can understand, maybe, what he saw in *her* . . . there's a lean, suppressed kind of sensuality in her; I suppose I've always recognised that. Not the way you should think about your mother, though, is it? Mother, Christ, seventeen years older than I am . . .

Him, though, what did she see in *him*? True, I can never understand what any woman sees in any man – ugly, functional beasts that we are . . .

But *together* . . . The thought chills me . . .

So bloody don't think about it.

I stand up. Stretch is out of the water now, towelled dry, back in his shorts and thongs, and I notice again how wide his shoulders are, wider than mine, how perfectly proportioned he is. No wonder the women . . . yes, I can understand women seeing something in *him*. If you used words like that about men, well, you'd have to admit that he's beautiful . . .

'Want to climb up to the next hole?' he says, running fingers through wet hair.

'Yeah, all right.'

We walk round the thick undergrowth at the end of the pool,

push our way through to the rock wall. It's not too steep, a series of almost overlapping layers. Our thongs slip on the rocks and loose vegetation, but in a few minutes we are standing on the top, looking down into the middle pool. It's disappointing. Small, deep, choked with brush and overhung with small, stunted trees.

We both look towards the rocky decline that leads to the top hole. Wordless, we pick our way to the bottom, begin to climb. It's harder than the last one. Damp in patches, slimy where a thin seepage runs, steep. But we persevere, helping each other, stretching harder, working a little bit. At last, pushing through a crown of dry vines, we come out into the open. And stop as if struck by lightning.

It's one of the loveliest places I've seen. A great wide pool, almost as big as the bottom one, but shallower, clearer, the water reflecting the overhanging branches, the red rock, the sky. And everywhere blue waterlilies, thousands of them, cornflower blue, blue against blue, rich, delicate and succulent. It's very quiet, nothing stirs except the insects above the surface of the water.

We squat on the soft grass by the bank, not speaking. It seems some kind of miracle in this dry land. And no one comes here. There's no track. It sits up here, waiting, quiet, lovely . . . and they all stay down below drinking whities and telling jokes . . .

'I didn't know it was like this,' says Stretch, something new in his voice.

For a long time we just sit in silence. I pull out my tobacco, roll a smoke, offer the bag to Stretch. He shakes his head.

'What you thinkin' about, Jack?' he says after a while, picking up a pebble and tossing it into the still water. The ripples widen and take a long time to die.

'I don't know, mate. Home probably.'

'I never think about that any more,' he says. 'Just bloody glad I don't have to go back.'

'Well, I don't think I *can* go back.'

'You want to?'

'I don't really know . . .'

He lies back, folds his hands behind his head. 'You heard of a place called Scrubby Creek?'

'Only in that song . . .'

He laughs. 'Yeah, well, it really does exist. Down near Gympie.'

'That's home?'

'Not any more,' he says. And there's a load of bitterness in it that seems impossible in a boy so young.

'Bad?' What is there to say?

'I was a fucking Cinderella,' he says. 'You know? Only I had a bloody stepfather. In love with his bloody fist, he was. Used to bash us all the time . . .'

'Who's *us*?'

'Mum, me sisters, me . . . the dogs, the goat, anything that moved.'

'Pisspot?'

'Nah, he just liked it . . .' He rolls over on to one elbow, picks a grass stem, sets it between his teeth. There is a faint sheen of sweat on his forehead. But then it's warm here, even lying in the shade. 'The truth is,' he says, 'he really wanted to fuck my sisters, but he wasn't game to try . . .'

'How old were they?'

'One nine, one twelve . . .'

'What happened in the end?'

'I got big enough to do him.'

'And did you?'

'No. I knew he'd just take it out on the others. So I told him – you know, touch me once more and I'll kill you.'

'He leave you alone then?'

'Caught him next day tryin' to sneak up behind me with a Dutch hoe . . . so I thought, oh fuck it, you can't win . . . so I just pissed off . . . that was two years ago . . .'

Silence for a while except for the insects.

'You like it up here?' I ask. 'Carbine Creek?'

He grins suddenly, and seems even younger. 'Like it? It's bloody *paradise* . . .' Suddenly his grin disappears. 'Not for you though, is it?'

I shake my head.

'Why don't you go home?' he says.

'I can't. Not right now. Not ever, I don't think . . .'

He looks at me, a little puzzled. Then shrugs. 'Want to go back down? Those buggers'll drink all the beer . . .'

At the edge of the rocks I stop and look back. The pool is still there, placid, still, the waterlilies blue, blue, blue . . .

Then off down the track again, following Stretch's lead . . .

•

We leave the Holes as evening is falling, and by the time we reach the camp it's full dark. The mess hall is emptying, everyone showered and shaved and mostly already half-pissed, ready for a night at the canteen or the pictures.

When we've finished eating – chicken and chips, apple pie – I don't feel like doing much. Stretch and the others go to the picture show, Vic and I head up to the half-empty canteen for a few beers. I'm in bed by the time Stretch is back from the pictures. He yawns a little as he comes in, kicks his thongs off, slips out of his gear and into his bunk.

'What's the matter?' I say. 'No tracking tonight?'

'Too tired,' he says. 'Anyway Saturday's a bad night . . . too many people about . . .

'That was a good day,' he says in a minute or two, settling back against his pillows, picking up a comic. 'Out at the Holes. Wasn't it, Jack?'

'Yeah, a good day, mate.'

'You know,' he says, 'I was telling you about home . . . down near Gympie?'

'Yeah?'

'I reckon they're mad down there,' he says.

'Why?'

'Well,' he says, 'they've got a good bit of land, say. Forty acres or so. A bit hilly probably. Right?'

'Right.' I roll over, look at him. He's staring at the ceiling a couple of feet above his head.

'Well,' he says, 'they grow pineapples, see? But after a few years the soil's buggered, eh? Very hard on the soil, pineapples are . . .'

'What happens then?'

'Then,' he says, 'they grow beans . . . you ever hear that song – The Gympie Bean Picking Song?'

'No, don't think so.'

'Yeah, well . . . Anyway, they plow straight up and down the hills, don't they? No bloody contour plowing for them. Guess what happens when it rains?'

'But why do they plow straight up and down?'

'I've often wondered,' he says. 'The only reason I can think of is that they're clearly and purely fuckin' *stupid* . . .'

'You've picked a bean or two, have you, Stretch?'

He gives me a quick look, the one you get from spud diggers and berry pickers and scallop splitters when you mention their curse. A little wry, a little bitter, but mostly tired. 'I never want to see another fucking green bean in my life,' he says, and opens his comic again.

I lie there reading my book for a while, or pretending to read. There seems to be an empty space in the day, a part of the pattern incomplete. For some reason I begin to wonder – not for the first time – why the hell Nance didn't sneak off to Melbourne for a year; that way it could have been kept quiet . . . can't see an abortion in those days, not for Nance . . . but she could have put me in an orphanage, put me out for adoption, something like that . . .

'You know, I'm a bastard,' I say, suddenly, out of the blue.

Stretch looks up from his comic. 'Yeah?' he looks mildly interested. Surprisingly, he laughs a little. 'What? You mean . . . *really* . . . not just a nasty shit?'

Can't help laughing a bit, with him. 'Yeah, a *real* bastard.'

'I'd never have guessed,' he says, 'you look just like an ordinary bastard to me.'

'No,' I say, 'not an ordinary bastard at all.' And, horrified, I hear myself going on: 'My father was my grandfather . . . slept with his own daughter . . .' And it's as if the whole bottom has fallen out of the world, saying those words, out loud, to someone else, as if finally I've destroyed myself, any pride, any self-respect I have left . . .

'Go on,' says Stretch, a little more interested.

'That all you got to say?'

'Well,' he says, 'there's a bit of it about. But if it's good enough for racehorses and Royals, well, I suppose it's all right . . .' And, incredibly, he goes back to his comic.

Still, I tell myself, he's only fourteen, he doesn't *realise* . . . Stretch? Not realising? Don't kid yourself, killer, Stretch is probably the ultimate realist . . .

You opened your mouth, anyway, didn't you, killer? Had to tell him, didn't you? What if he tells someone else? Well, what if he does? You wouldn't fucking *like* it, would you? You want to *choose* the people who know that stuff . . .

Well, I tell myself, Stretch is not a great talker, so just wait and see, don't worry . . .

But I lie awake for a long time, all the same, long after the light has gone out and Stretch is asleep. Thinking sometimes I just *make* problems for myself . . .

•

But, waking in the morning, showering, eating breakfast, walking with Stretch across the hill to the library to get some books, it doesn't seem quite as important. He never mentions it, it doesn't seem to have changed anything . . . not for him, anyway.

Sunday passes slowly, drowsily; reading, talking, dozing.

And, on Monday, the week begins again, the small cycle starts over; and the never-changing days, the sun, the dust, the heat and thirst, seem to iron everything out into a round of somnolent monotony.

We go about our business, fixing roofs, clearing blocked drains, building sheds, collecting garbage, felling trees, putting up power poles, rehanging doors, easing windows, replacing broken panes, fixing air-conditioners, unblocking sewers, laying pipes, hauling gravel . . . Days pass almost unnoticed, interspersed with nights at the canteen, open-air picture shows, trips to the Holes, out to the lake to watch the water-skiing; playing cards, reading, listening to Stretch's radio, talking, talking . . .

And suddenly two months have gone, and I'm slotted in as if I've been here all my life. The faces are all known, and people nod to me, and I'm just one of the crowd.

And one day I come face to face, at the library, with Barry, the metallurgist taken in flagrante delicto and banished here to purgatory. And we smile a little carefully at each other, and nod. 'Hullo, Jack,' he says.

And: 'Hullo, Barry,' I say.

And that's all: we pass on our respective ways. But there has been a small acknowledgement behind the words and the nods, a quiet undertaking that the past will stay buried for both of us, no questions asked. As it should be in all purgatories . . .

The thought occurs to me that purgatories are no more than places where you have to wait . . .

•

September comes, the thermometer rises in the daytime to 110, but the sky is still clear, still no wind, no cloud, and the air is bone-dry. And it feels no more than a warm eighty. But the wet is coming, and then the humidity will go up. I hear stories of the year when it reached 124 on Christmas Day, and the miners were vomiting, and everyone was gulping salt tablets like lollies . . .

And I wonder what it must have been like for the two old Afghan brothers who mined the surface ore sixty, seventy years ago, hauling the ore into Cloncurry by camel . . .

•

There are no real seasons here, only the wet and the dry, otherwise I could blame it on the spring. But as the temperatures rise, as the days lengthen, a strange restlessness grows in me. In the evening the dongas are like ovens and I can't bear to stay inside. I walk at night along the roads, the tracks, round the camp, watching the stars, incredibly clear and sharp, against the warm, soft darkness of the sky. And a great ache fills me for all the places, all the people that I have lost. That terrible feeling of loss sweeps over me sometimes with the power of a great storm and leaves me empty, abandoned.

Vic notices – I suppose the others do, too – and says to me, 'There's a caravan full of pros sneaked in from the Isa. They're down in the park – why don't you go down and get yourself fixed up?'

But it's not that sort of fixing I need. Oh, I need that, too, I suppose, but not at the end of a queue of drunken miners grunting on some tired harlot . . .

One Sunday morning I set out westward, sandwiches and a couple of bottles of soft drink in a haversack. I walk down towards the edge of the lake, where the earth is a cracked, grey flood plain, I drive great clouds of grasshoppers before me, like a prophet driving devils. They rise like a curse, a wave of mindless energy in the heat, settle, rise again, their dry clatter an echo of the desolate land . . .

By the lake a kingfisher with an azure back breaks from the dry scrub and spears the sky like a small miracle, his back a badge of heraldic colour.

By noon I am far north, past the spinifex plain, into an area of dry rocky gullies and broken plateaux. In one ravine, a big kangaroo breaks from cover and flees, pounding away incredibly fast . . . On a rock, a flat dry stove plate, a three-foot goanna, yellow as the rock, frilled and dragonlike, gapes silently at me, then slips away . . .

My mind is filled with admiration for the Aborigines who managed to wrench a kind of living from a land so harsh, filled with incredulity that it could seem anything but hellish to a white man, even a hungry Scot like Kennedy from the slums of Edinburgh . . .

By mid-afternoon I am back once more in the land of spinifex and scrub. I drink a can of warm cordial sitting on a hot rock watching the tiny ta-ta lizards as they dart here and there, pausing every few feet to stand on three legs, waving a forepaw . . .

The second can is gone long before I sight the lake again. I'm sweating hard now, my shirt and shorts soaked, and I begin to realise how quickly you can die in this awful country . . .

The last few miles are pure slog, and as I swing on to the road again, half a mile from camp, I'm beginning to get an awful feeling that I'm on the edge of collapse . . . vision going dark in waves, cramps beginning, a truly awful thirst . . .

I slam into the empty donga, glad that it *is* empty. There are three cans of lemonade on Stretch's bed. I drink them all, one after the other, and collapse on my bunk. Within a few minutes I can feel the liquid moving back into my dehydrated cells, feel the awfulness easing . . .

In half an hour I get up, take off my wet clothes. I sniff at the sodden shirt. It smells not of sweat but of ammonia, heavy and pungent. I go and shower, drink several glasses of water, lie down again. And I know, with enormous certainty, that I can never be at home in this terrible place, not if I live here all my life.

•

We go down to fix one of the fibro roofs at the mine office. It's the first time I've been to the mine. Stretch is with me in the ute, and Hickey, the carpenter. We turn south off the road, past a grader, a big compound where mechanics are servicing the Wagner ore-carriers. There is a steepening slope, and at the bottom I can see the black hole of the main portal.

Outside the office, a ramshackle dusty building with a lean-to porch in front, we pull in beside a couple of dusty diesel Land-rovers.

In the shade of the porch I nearly stumble over Bully, lying bloated and hung-over in the shade. He opens one bloodshot eye and sneers at me. His belly is hanging, greyish pink, in layers of flab, and he's panting hard in the heat. There's a permanent halo of flies around him.

I shake my head, and Stretch laughs cautiously.

Inside, we stand in the middle of a slew of mine maps, charts, filing cabinets, cap lamps and dirty gumboots. There's a great hole in the roof. Someone for some unknown reason has been walking on it, and put a foot through. We get lethargically to work and replace the broken fibro sheet.

On the way back to the town, I say to Stretch, 'That dog's on his last legs.'

'You reckon?'

Hickey, thin and laconic, tanned dark as teak, flips his tiny butt out the window, spits. 'The day he dies, the fucking mine'll close down . . .'

'You reckon?'

'For sure. Be like a national holiday. Day of mourning, you know.'

'What if someone killed him? Ran over him or something?'

Hickey shakes his head slowly. 'Get fuckin' murdered . . .'

Stretch and I look at each other and smile a bit. But I'm not so sure that Hickey is wrong.

•

It seems almost too great a coincidence.

The next day, the gang is spreading gravel in township driveways. It's like a real village, almost, an enclave, a cluster of fifty or sixty houses, concrete brick, low, air-conditioned, half-hidden by lush shrubs and trees. There's plenty of water here, piped from the lake, and garden sprinklers run almost continuously. The houses all have a private, closed-in look. The housewives, most of them, don't venture far away. They go to the library, the store, a few with their husbands to the canteen, or they visit each other. But mostly they stay home. Beyond the houses, a few hundred yards further on, is the caravan park, another village, with half a hundred vans tucked in a fold in the ground. Most of the vans have gardens, shrubs round them; some have potted trees, arbours, trellises. It's staff in the houses, the daily-paid in the vans, and never the twain shall meet . . .

We work our way along the streets, dumping gravel, spreading it on the driveways. Occasionally a woman, sometimes with a kid or two, comes out to watch. They might nod, but they seldom speak to us. Rabid, sex-starved wage slaves, that's us, waiting for a chance to rape them . . .

But I notice that a few of them smile at Stretch, wave a little surreptitiously.

Late in the morning, Curly comes by in his ute, looking harried as ever.

He stops and gets out, looks the job over, kicks anxiously at a pile of gravel, stares at us bleakly, as if the end of the world is here.

'The mine's shut down,' he says. 'For today, anyway.'

'Oh, yeah?'

'Bully's crook,' he says.

'Been crook for years,' says Bert, the truck driver. 'Bloody permanent hangover . . .'

'No,' says Curly, 'this is serious . . . he's really crook . . . they've chartered a plane to take him into the Isa to the vet. Everyone's up the canteen waiting for news.'

It's true enough. When we get to the canteen in the evening, showered and changed, it is crammed with drunken miners, stiff in their filthy overalls and shorts. There is an air of crisis, of unconcealed tension in the air. Not a lot of noise, but a steady buzz below the currents of conversation. Mostly, they are talking quietly, or staring at their cans.

We get our whities, settle in a corner, out of the way. We are almost ready to leave for the mess when one of the shift bosses comes in, stands at the door. He waits until all eyes are on him, till the buzz has died down.

'Listen,' he says, and his voice seems to echo through the shed. 'We've had the vet on the radio, and Bully's OK. They've had to amputate the crown jewels, but he's all right, and he'll be back by the weekend.'

Immediately there is a great collective sigh, a sudden frothing of questions, a babble of talk. One of the miners near us speaks to another, one of the Alimak crew: 'Old bugger's got no use for 'em anyway . . .'

His neighbour drops his can and punches the speaker in the head. He drops and someone else strikes the striker, and in a moment the room is a battlefield. We sneak quietly out by the side door and into the beer garden to finish our drinks. Inside, the battle rages gloriously, happily, unabated as we wander off down the track to tea.

•

It's funny – I don't seem to miss the people back home individually. Not in particular. It's just a great sense of total, overall loss. Am I missing *them*? Or the *places*? Or *me*, the way I was?

I don't know where all this is leading. I do know that something has been knocked out of me, some of the stuffing, some of the fire. Maybe it's a good thing; I used to be a terrible smart arse . . .

I wonder how long it went on, the old man and Nance. How many *times*, how *often*, how *long* . . .

That *is* fucking sick, now . . .

I can't forget it, though, always have it with me. Better get used to it, killer, learn to live with it . . .

But it can't last forever. Who knows, maybe one day someone will buy me an indulgence, and I'll graduate from purgatory. But to where?

•

It's getting hotter. Today, halfway through October, the temperature up to 117. But still bone-dry, and not even really unpleasant. Except that every night when I knock off work I want to lie down and sleep . . .

Have to wash my hair, shampoo it, every day or it stinks.

Never really cool, not even at night, and in the darkness the air is full of insects. The screen doors are thick with strange sticklike things, some kind of mantis maybe . . .

Tonight a big green python, harmless enough but frightening, crawls into Jimmy's bunk next door, and it takes two hours and half a dozen cans to calm him down. Their light is on all night . . .

•

Coming back about nine o'clock from the library, over the hill that separates the two roads, along the steep narrow track, the half-dozen of us from this donga are going our quiet way when the lights go out. Generator failure somewhere, and every light in the universe disappears. No moon, only the stars, and it's black as a gin's tit. We stagger down the hill in the dark, wandering off the track, going arse over head in the bushes, dropping books, cursing. By the time we reach the bottom of the track the lights come on, and Flake Jackson, a tractor driver, is missing. We find him halfway up the hill, out cold, his head split on a rock, blood everywhere. Margaret, the nursing sister, puts a few stitches in, and he's good as new . . .

•

I go to every picture show that's on, see everything, anything. The open-air theatre is up behind the quarters: a painted metal screen set behind the fence, a strip of grass, a gravel parking area, a wooden projection shed in the middle of it all. Vehicles park on the gravel, people sprawl in aluminium chairs, banana lounges, deck chairs, on the grass, on lilos, complete with eskies, whities, potato crisps; dogs fight and chase each other furiously round the screen. Kids in pyjamas and dressing gowns crow and yell. No breeze, no cloud, stars as thick as a light dusting of snow, the air so warm you take your shirt off . . .

Smells of beer and insect repellant and freshly showered bodies . . .

Tonight they show *Catch 22*, mixing the reels as usual. Halfway through the third reel, which comes on second and seems to make just as much sense that way, Ted Suzuki gets up, wanders away shaking his head, muttering . . .

'Too much crazy . . .'

What the fuck am I doing here?

•

Waiting for the wet to arrive is like waiting for some kind of revelation. Or maybe a bit like waiting for the dentist: you know it won't be pleasant, you don't quite know in what way it will be unpleasant, but – maybe – you'll feel better afterwards.

In the south, waiting for winter, there is a sense of preparation, of girding the loins, laying in the firewood, caulking the cracks before the storms strike. Here there is nothing but an increasing torpor and lassitude, a kind of dumb acceptance. Everyone sits around clutching their tinnies and talking with a kind of gloating about how horrible it'll be; the old hands tell horror stories, the new chums sneer.

The temperatures continue to climb as November comes, but the air is still so dry that there is little sense of heat. And, of course, it changes so gradually, day by day, that you settle easily into the groove gouged by the rising temperature.

We go up one Saturday night to the bar in the staff quarters – Vic and I, Stretch, Jimmy and Ice-cream Peters.

It's in the middle of the long, low building, between the two wings, and it's a kind of dimly lit, deeply carpeted pit, with a small but very professional bar and soft muzak. Seems strangely out of place out here in the mulga. Looking at it, I can see why VAM went broke.

The bar is crowded, and the room full. Mostly they are staff people I've hardly seen. The employment officer is there, shorts longer than our fashion, as hesitant as ever. There are a few women in the crowd. I've seen some of them round the town, wives from the village.

We don't stay long, just have a round or two and go. It's not the place for us. Not that anyone is nasty; largely they ignore us. It's just that it's not our kind of place. Not *my* kind of place any more . . .

We buy a carton from the canteen and sit outside the donga. It's calm, peaceful. Jimmy and Stretch and Ice-cream are playing five hundred by the light from the doorway. Vic and I sit in the dimness across the path, under a couple of scrubby trees.

'How much longer you going to stay, mate?' I ask. 'You and Jimmy?'

'I don't know,' he says. 'Maybe till Christmas time.'

'Where you headed?'

'Not sure,' he says. 'South, somewhere.' He pauses. 'I'd like to stay a bit longer, get a bit more dough together . . . but Jimmy doesn't like the wet.'

'You got something in mind? For when you've got enough money?'

For a moment he's quiet. When he speaks his voice has dropped to little more than a whisper. Across the track they are playing a very vocal and noisy game. 'Get a few acres,' he says. 'Maybe an old house on it. Somewhere way up the back country, maybe northern New South. A cow, a few goats, a bit of casual work when you have to . . . you know . . .'

'Sounds all right.' Sounds bloody awful, really. Rural poverty . . .

'Yeah.' He swills the beer round in his can, peering down at it. 'Not much of a life, wandering about, you know. I've been at it since I was sixteen.' He sighs, drinks the rest of his beer, crumples his can absent-mindedly. 'Big family, we were, small house, small income, you know . . . I was on the road early.

Found I could fight a bit, earned a few bob . . . years of that, then I got in with Harry Paulsen . . . that's the closest I've had to a family life since I was a kid. Sylvia, his wife, she was a kind of mother to all the boys. Not much older than most of us, she used to do the oriental dancer bit, snake lady, you know . . . Bloody old Harry led her a bit of a life . . . but she looked after us, saw we were fed, clean, all that . . . and respectable . . . you know, no swearing, no dirty stories, nothing like that . . .' He pauses and grins at me. 'More like a bloody parsonage than a boxing troupe . . . but it was home.

'Jimmy didn't fit in, though,' he goes on. 'After a while he started to get very edgy, wanted to move on . . . so I went with him.'

'How long 've you been together?'

'Nearly ten years.'

'Never wanted to settle down, get married, either of you?'

He looks at me a little oddly, out of the corner of his eyes. 'Didn't you know? Me and Jimmy – we're as queer as a pair of corkscrews.'

Oddly, I'm not at all shocked. Hardly startled. I suppose that sort of thing sinks in some way without you knowing. 'I suppose I did know, really. Just never put it in words.'

He nods. 'Nothing much else for either of us . . .'

After a minute I say: 'Jimmy wouldn't make it on his own, would he?'

'No,' he says, looking across the track at Jimmy, who's peering intently at his hand, grinning, as Ice-cream abuses him for being slow. 'No,' he says, 'I don't think he would. He's got that thing, you know, he gets in trouble . . . he'd end up inside again, and go right round the bend.' He looks sharply at me. 'Don't think it's all one way, though – Jimmy does his share – you'll see one of these days maybe . . .'

The card players abandon their game. Ice-cream yawns and wanders off to bed. Stretch drifts off into the darkness, headed for God knows where. Jimmy comes across and sits down with us, clenches hands round knees, smiling. 'That bloody Peters,' he says, 'he's got those frigging cards trained . . .'

Vic smiles at him affectionately. 'You're a rotten card player, mate. Almost as bad as me.' He turns to me. 'Never see anything in it myself . . .'

We sit smoking for a bit.

'You gonna stick it through the wet?' says Vic idly.

'Don't know,' I say. 'Haven't got anywhere else to go. Nowhere in particular, anyway.'

'Don't drift too long, Jack,' he says. 'Gets into your system, it's hard to get out sometimes.'

'You reckon?'

'Sure of it.'

'May be the best thing.'

'No, mate,' he says. 'Don't make *that* mistake. It's not the best thing for *anyone*. It's just that it's all some people have *got*. All they'll ever have.'

'I can't go home again,' I say. 'Things have changed. There's some stuff there I just can't handle . . .'

'Well,' he says, 'sometimes it's marvellous just what you *can* handle when you have to,' and I see his hand creep out and rest for a moment on Jimmy's shoulder.

There isn't much to say to that, so I say nothing.

The night is quiet now, and very peaceful, and there's a gentle feel to it, and I'm sure it's not so much that magic tropic night, but the presence of those two beat-up old queers beside me.

●

I'm doing a crossword puzzle – that bored – when the wet begins.

For days at the tag end of November the temperature has wavered, steadied at about 110; clouds have dragged sullenly over the horizon, the humidity has crept up until any movement at all is uncomfortable, and the sweat starts at the slightest exertion. It seems as if the whole world is aching for some sort of break, some relief. As all this is going on I'm thinking that it will happen slowly, the beginning of the wet, at some sort of reasonable pace. But it's not like that at all; there's nothing rational or reasonable about this country.

Sitting on a banana box just inside the door of our donga, I read the clue to 3 Down – *My father's brother on the terrace(Span.) (5)*. There is a faint, dusty pattering on the roof of the donga, and I look up. The first heavy raindrops are falling on the dry paths, the thin grass, the roof. I look down, think a moment, write '*patio*' under 3 Down, and look up again. And sit locked in a kind of horrified wonder.

Because, while I have looked away, thought a moment, pencilled a single word, the world outside the door has been deluged. The track is a sea, a river of red mud; visibility is perhaps fifty yards, and the rain is bouncing in a pale explosion from the wet earth. The sound on the roof is a cannonade, the air filled with sound and water. Suddenly, I know exactly how Noah felt.

Stretch gets up from his bunk, moves to the door. I can't hear his movements – there is no sound in the universe but the rain. He stands looking out through the screen door for a minute or so, then turns, smiling, a kind of innocent pride on his face, along with the pale beads of sweat. 'It's started.'

'Jesus Christ! Surely it doesn't go on like this for three months!'

He laughs again, happily, with a kind of proprietorial air. 'No,' he says, lifting his voice to be heard above the battering. 'It'll probably stop for Christmas Day . . .' And climbs back into his bunk, grinning.

But half an hour later the rain stops as suddenly as it began; the sun comes out, hot, hot, hot, the steam rises from the wet earth. And I sit watching, amazed, the crossword forgotten. There's something unnatural about it, something perverse; and, despite the heat, I feel a sort of chill, as if the awful onslaught of the past half-hour is only the prelude to some great disaster. For a while I even forget my own small one . . .

•

The rain starts again in the late afternoon, and almost everyone seems to get soaked. Rain runs off them, and they are smiling. In the mess they eat tea in sodden shorts and singlets, the atmosphere strangely hectic.

'Reckon the strip'll be closed?' asks Jimmy, chewing on his gristly steak.

'Maybe for a day or so,' says Vic.

'What about the road between here and the Isa?'

Vic looks at Ice-cream. 'What you reckon?'

Ice-cream shakes his head. 'Not yet,' he says. 'Oh, she'll be closed for a bit by and by . . . week at a time maybe . . . won't worry us.'

'Mmmm . . .'

'What do you reckon?' says Jimmy to Vic, his pale, nervous face creased with concern.

'Oh,' says Vic, 'we'll chance her till Christmas, eh?'

Jimmy nods, not very happily, and goes on chewing in silence.

'For Christ's sake,' I say to Ice-cream, 'how long does it last?'

He scrapes the last of the gravy from his plate with a crust, pops it in his mouth. 'Late February, be finished by early March.'

That seems, right now, a very long time.

•

It's a quiet night. Vic and Jimmy are on shift, and Stretch has gone off alone. I lie in the donga, trying to read. But I'm unsettled by the strange wet smell of the earth, the banging, more insistent tonight, of the insects against the screen door.

Back home, it would still be the occasional fire, and down the west coast even maybe a frost. Hailstorms at Christmas weren't unusual in *that* bloody place. Bloody, yes, but all the same, civilised in a way . . . at any rate, a *place* for civilisation, not like this . . .

Somehow I doze off for a couple of hours, and it's nearly eleven when I wake. I blink, my mouth foul, sweat pooled in the corner of my eyes. I look at my watch, think of getting up and showering.

Then the small scratching sound that must have woken me is repeated. It's at the screen door, a kind of clawing. I raise myself, look out. Nothing. The rain has stopped, the night is clear and soft. I can see the glow of lights in the other dongas, stars.

The noise again.

The screen door shivers a little, begins to gape.

I sit up quickly.

A hand, filthy, coated with red mud, is wrenching at the bottom of the door; and beyond it a dim shape, dark and slug-like, lies across the step. My hair stands on end for a moment. Then I'm out of my bunk.

I push the door open, reach down and drag Stretch into the donga. In the light he looks terrible. His face seems . . . kind of crushed. His eyes are closed under a mask of blood and mud, his left eyebrow cut loose and hanging, showing bone. His left hand is swollen and misshapen, his bare legs gashed and smeared. When I move him his left forearm seems to have an extra joint.

I lift him carefully, lay him on his bunk. I find I'm breathing in a strange, ragged fashion, realise it is mostly anger. This is no fist job - someone's used something very nasty here . . .

One eye opens and looks at me. Very blue, the white startlingly white. His puffed lips move a bit, and I bend closer.

'Don't move,' I tell him. 'I'll get the sister . . .' I start to move towards the door. But something in his look pulls me back. I put my ear close to his broken mouth. When he moves his lips I see that there's a bloody gap behind the swollen lips where some teeth are gone.

I have to listen very carefully to make out what he's saying. He repeats it. Seems for a moment a complete non sequitur.

'Shit meself,' he says.

Suddenly I know what he means. Got to clean him up before I get the sister. So I take his shorts and underpants off, get a wet cloth, clean him up, throw the dirty stuff under the bed. He faints some time while I'm doing this. I cover him with a sheet.

'Thanks, mate,' he says, when I bend over him. I find I'm almost crying with rage.

'What did he use on you?'

'Garden stake,' he says, trying to smile. I know what he means, a six-foot length of some hard local wood, about an inch and a half thick.

'Who was it?'

He tried to shake his head.

'Listen,' I say, 'I've got to go and get the sister. You be all right?'

Faint nodding motion.

I don't dare wait any longer, can't tell what's broken inside him, so I tear away, out into the night, kick off my thongs, fly down the track. The sister has a room in the staff quarters, another room next-door as a kind of dispensary. It's about a quarter of a mile.

It seems to take forever, although it can't be more than a couple of minutes. I feel the stones under my feet, a few rips and tears here and there from trees and fences, but they don't seem to touch me. The lights of the staff quarters seem a great distance away, and not getting much closer. And I think: he's crawled all the way home, through the mud, a mile at least, some bastard's done that to him and left him to crawl home through the mud . . . And I begin to get very tight and icy cold inside then, and I make my legs work faster, lungs pump harder, just to take my mind off it . . .

I go past the front door of the quarters at full pace, mud to the knees, trip going up the steps to the verandah, recover, hammer along past the dozen or so doors to the end of the building. I know where it is, I've been up with Ice-cream to get a boil lanced . . . The big yellow bulk of the Toyota ambulance looms like an armoured car outside her door.

I don't bother to knock, fly in. The door bangs against the wall, and I stand there in the middle of the room panting and fighting for breath, looking down at Margaret and her boyfriend on the bed. They're decent enough, fully dressed, just having a bit of a cuddle. He jumps up, Beagle Boy, a good enough bloke, jumps up swinging.

'What the bloody hell . . .' I hit him once between wind and water, and he goes down. I grab him, lift him, put him back on the bed. Poor bugger, he's gasping for breath, red in the face. Margaret is sitting up looking at me fairly calmly. She's taken off her white smock, and she's wearing a T-shirt and yellow shorts.

'Sorry . . . about that.' I pat Beagle Boy's shoulder. 'Be all right. Someone hurt . . . hurt badly . . . gotta come . . .'

'Where?'

'Down the dongas . . .'

They must see something in my face, because she doesn't say any more. She gets up, goes through the door, comes back with the keys to the ambulance. 'Come on,' she says, stooping a moment to whisper to Beagle Boy, who's recovering a little, and looking at me carefully while he holds his middle.

I get into the ambulance, climbing up the steep steps to the cab. Margaret starts the motor, switches on the lights. The track is thick mud, and she engages the low set in four-wheel drive. The lights sweep across the clearing as she turns.

On the way down the track she asks me what has happened. I tell her as best I can. Can breathe a little easier now, but the cold anger still there.

Stretch is lying just as I left him. She looks carefully at him for a moment. Glances at me. 'I'll have to get the mud off so I can see what's what.' She bends over him, raises his eyelid. 'Can you hear me?'

There is a faint motion of the head.

She speaks clearly, slowly. 'I'm going to have to clean you up a bit, find out what the damage is . . . I don't want to give you anything till I find out . . . if the pain gets too bad, let yourself go . . . faint. OK?'

Again the slight movement.

She looks at me. 'Get a bucket of warm water, a basin, some towels.' She sits on the edge of the bed, takes his wrist between her fingers.

When I get back with the water from the ablutions block, a basin from the kitchen, someone's towels off the wash line, I find Jimmy out on the path, and Vic inside with Margaret. They have his clothes off. I see the muddy, bloody T-shirt on the floor, slit neatly. Stretch, his body looking very pale against the red mud on arms and legs and face, is very still. While I watch, they ease him over on his side, Margaret holding the broken arm carefully in the air, Vic turning the boy, handling him as if the weight were nothing.

There is a gasp from someone – it could have been from me or from Margaret – at the sight of Stretch's back. It's covered with great weals and bruises, beginning now to flower into obscene livid colours and shapes. Nothing like that on his chest and body; and I know only too well what's happened: he's gone down, and while he's been on the ground someone's got stuck into him, boots, Christ knows what. Curled himself into a ball, protected the vitals, so there're no marks on his front.

Vic sees me from the corner of his eye. When they set Stretch down, he moves over, takes me by the shoulder, moves me reluctantly towards the door.

'Listen,' he says. 'You wait outside . . . I'm used to this kind of thing, you're not . . . go and keep Jimmy company.'

So I find myself out in the hot, damp darkness, looking up at the closed door of the donga. Feel myself shaking with something that's not quite anger, not quite pity, not quite hate . . . but a mix of all of them. And realise that it's not a new feeling; I've been shaking like that for a long time . . .

A gentle touch on my shoulder. Jimmy. Something new in his face, something I've never noticed before.

'Come on, mate,' he says, flicking his head a little towards his door. 'Sit down, that's what ya need . . .'

I follow him into the donga. His and Vic's. The small space is tidy, ordered, neat. I sit on an old trunk, take the ciggie that Jimmy offers me, the light. Sit, smoking and shivering.

A minute or two later Ice-cream puts his head in the door. 'What's up?'

Jimmy tells him, and he takes a quick look at me. 'Know what you need, mate, a good hot cuppa tea . . .' and he's gone.

In five minutes he's back with a big enamel mug. Christ knows where he got the tea, who made it, but it's strong and sweet, and laced with rum. He squats beside me, thin, dark hairy fingers lightly on my arm. 'Don't you worry, cock,' he says, 'we'll get the cunt that done it, don't you worry . . .'

I look up at him, at the narrow eyes in the leathery face.
'*I'll* get him . . .'
'That's right, cock,' he says, 'you'll get him.'
And we sit, a silent trio, waiting for the other door to open, for them to come out and tell us something . . .

•

It's nearly an hour before anything happens. At last the door opens, we hear heavy footsteps, and Vic looks in through the screen.

'Give us a hand with the stretcher.'

We troop out, getting in each other's way. A few heads stick out of other doors. No one seems to be asleep. We wrestle the stretcher from the ambulance in through the doorway to our room. Inside, the air smells of unidentifiable chemicals, a vague hospital smell. Stretch is cleaned up and looking very pale. They've put clean underpants on him. His left arm is in a cast and a bandage wraps his chest and shoulder tightly. His head is bandaged too, and his stitched eyebrow and lip are dark with iodine. His left eye is puffed shut. He's conscious, but only just.

Vic and Ice-cream lift him, very gently, on to the stretcher.

When they have got him out through the door, I look at Margaret, who is packing up her gear. She looks very tired, and there are fine lines about her eyes and mouth.

'How much damage?' I ask her.

She stops her work, puts her hands in the small of her back, stretches. 'Broken arm,' she says, 'broken collarbone . . . he'll knit quickly at his age. The gashes on his face aren't serious . . . the stitches'll be out in a week, he'll be scarred . . . nose broken, I've set it as best I can . . . It's the bruising round his kidneys I'm worried about . . . there may be internal damage . . . we'll just have to wait and see.'

'Where are you taking him?'

'Up to the dispensary where I can keep an eye on him. There's a bed there.'

'Can I stay with him?'

She shakes her head. 'There's nothing you can do . . . I've given him something, he'll be asleep by the time we get him there.'

'I'd like to come, anyway.'

'All right. Don't disturb him, though.' She picks up her bag. 'I'll get on the radio to the doctor in the Isa in the morning, see what he says. But there's nothing we can do really except wait and see.'

'Can you get him into hospital? At the Isa.'

'No, even if the strip was open, we couldn't put him in one of those little planes . . . and the road . . . even if we could get through . . . too rough. Best leave him where he is for the moment.'

I get in the back with Vic and Ice-cream. In the dim light Stretch looks battered and older than his years, and very sick.

After we've settled him in the dispensary, snug in the white cot, the light turned low, we all go out into the hot, quiet night.

'Do you report this kind of thing?' I ask Margaret. 'To the police?'

She shrugs. 'I've got to log it. I'll give a copy to the constable when he comes next time. But God knows when he'll be able to get in . . . Anyway, there's not much he'll be able to do. The boy'll be gone by then, probably.' She looks at me. 'What happened, anyway?'

'I don't know. He'll tell you tomorrow, I suppose. But I reckon he fell down a gully in the dark.'

She looks hard at me for a moment, then gives me a tired grin. 'Go home to bed.'

'I want to stay with him.'

Suddenly she's cross. 'Oh, all right, bloody well stay then . . .'

But, after the others have gone, and I'm settled in the armchair in the corner of the dispensary, she comes in, in her dressing-gown, and brings me a cup of cocoa. 'Drink that, it'll help you sleep.'

'Listen, I'm sorry about Beagle Boy . . .'

'Better tell him that!' But she smiles a little as she goes back through the door.

It's very quiet in the room, with only the gentle battering of insects against the flywire screens and the hoarse rasp of Stretch's breathing. His face is half-hidden in the shadow, and no longer truly recognisable.

I drink the cocoa slowly. Well, the wet has started; and there seems to be a growing shadow over the camp, a shadow that has nothing to do with the heavy clouds. It seems somehow to be deepening, as if this business were only the beginning. I feel a great temptation to pack and leave as soon as the strip is open. But I haven't got any idea where I want to go. And anyway, now there is Stretch, and I couldn't leave him here alone, the way he is . . .

The room seems to waver a little in the corners, to recede and come back, and I feel my head nodding . . . thinking maybe she put something in the cocoa . . . slipping, slipping . . . sleeping . . .

I half-wake once to see Margaret bending over the bed, her dressing-gown obscuring Stretch's figure. I want to wake properly and ask if he's all right, but my eyelids sag, close again . . .

•

When I finally wake it is bright morning, sun streaming in through the window. My head is thick and muzzy, and it is a minute or so before I can work out where I am, what I'm doing . . .

Then it all comes back with a jolt, and I swing my head to look at the bed.

Stretch is awake, his one good eye – now a little bloodshot – watching me. I stand up, stiff as a poker, and stalk over to the bed, look down. Although he's cleaner now, he looks worse. The swelling is worse, his face is hideously distorted, the cuts wet and ugly, the bruises deep and livid.

'Jesus,' I say, shaking my head, 'you're a handsome sight . . .'
The corners of his mouth crack a little, and he winces. His

good eye blinks, or winks. The door opens behind me.

'It's nearly eight o'clock,' says Margaret, bustling in in her clean starched smock. 'You'll be late for work.'

Fuck work, I think, standing there like a gawk.

'For God's sake go and get some breakfast,' she says. 'Go on, get out, I want to examine the patient . . .'

I leave, stand alone and kind of at a loss on the verandah. The sun is already bright, not a cloud in sight. I can almost see things growing. The greens are vivid after the rain, fresh and vital . . . everything that I'm not. I head off heavily down the track towards the mess hut. It's almost deserted, the cooling food in the bain-marie – eggs, kidney, bacon, beans – greasy and unappetising. All the same I'm famished, and eat a great plateful, hardly tasting it, washing it down with two big cups of coffee. I'm the last to leave, except for a few blokes off the night shift.

As I move outside, stand a minute or two on the steps, Curly's ute turns up, drifts to a stop. He gets out, his boots thick with red mud. But already the ground is drying again to dust. He pulls off his hat as he stands looking at me, and his bald head shines in the morning.

'You coming to work today?'

'No, I'm going back to stay with Stretch.'

'Yeah, right . . .' he seems almost uncomfortable. 'Listen . . . anything he needs . . . you know, anything . . . well, you see me.' He's suddenly loud, almost angry. 'Just see *me*, right?'

'Righto . . .'

He turns away, begins to get into the ute. Pauses, half in, looks up at me, frowning horribly. 'I'm not gonna dock you for today,' he says fiercely, and jumps in, roars away.

I stand there a minute, shaking my head, looking at the ute as it bores off down the track.

●

Stretch dozes most of the day.

Margaret comes in every couple of hours, takes a quick look

and leaves again. After lunch it starts to rain again, and keeps on all afternoon. It has a soporific effect, and I doze over my crossword. About five o'clock Margaret brings in a mug of broth from the kitchen and a straw.

'Give me a hand to lift him up,' she says.

He's awake, more or less, and I put my arm round his shoulders, lift him while she slips another pillow behind him, and she feeds him a little of the broth.

'Outside now,' she says. 'I'm going to give him a bottle.'

I go outside and stand watching the rain. If it wasn't for the heat, the lushness, the plants almost growing while you look, I'd think I was back in Zeehan.

A quarter of an hour later Margaret comes out.

'There's no blood in his urine,' she says, 'and that's a good sign.'

I don't say anything, stand watching the rain.

'He's gone back to sleep,' she says, 'and I'm going to keep him sedated till the worst of the pain is over. So for God's sake go away, Jack. You can come back every night and see him, but you're just in the way here.'

I nod, sigh.

'He's not going to *die*, you know. He's a big healthy boy.'

'I know, Margaret . . . and thanks.'

'Go on, you big lug,' she says. 'Go and get your tea . . .'

•

Vic and Jimmy and the rest are waiting, and we go to the mess hall together. After I've told them the latest news, there doesn't seem much to say, so we're a quiet group at the table.

'You been up the staff quarters,' says Ice-cream to me at last, making conversation. 'You see the new bird?'

'What new bird?'

'The one come in on the last plane before the strip was closed.'

I shake my head.

'Ripper,' says Ice-cream. 'Working at the post office – you know, old Marjie's off crook, and the girls from the office been looking after it. Now this new bird's on the job.'

'What's she like?' says Vic, pushing his plate away, taking out the makings.

'I told you,' says Ice-cream. 'She's a ripper. A real looker. The blokes were so thick round the post office you could hardly get in to buy a stamp . . .'

I don't send letters or get any, so I never go near the post office.

'You didn't see her, up the quarters?' insists Ice-cream.

'No, didn't see her . . .'

'Want to keep your eye out,' he says. Then, a little morosely: 'Not that it's likely to do ya any good – be a queue a mile long at her bloody door, and you can bet your balls all the staff blokes'll be in front . . .

•

After tea Vic and Jimmy walk up with me, through the rain, to see how Stretch is. We drape old sacks over our heads, folded like hoods, and we must look an odd trio in the rain. Jimmy hops round us, silent and intense, kicking at stones with his bare feet. There are yellow haloes round all the lights.

'Your shoes gone mouldy yet?' asks Vic.

I look down at my thongs.

'Not *those*, ya nong,' says Vic. 'The ones in the cupboard – the leather ones.'

'I don't know – I haven't looked.'

'You better look.'

'All right.'

There is no one in sight at the staff quarters. A few vehicles are parked in the mud of the car park, in front of the narrow strip of grass and the tall oleander bushes. Lights show behind the curtains in the rooms, small warm glows. We can hear the hum and rattle of the air-conditioning.

Before we reach it, the door of the dispensary opens. Margaret comes out. She closes the door behind her, gently.

'Listen, fellas,' she says, 'he's asleep. First real sleep he's had, you know, no drugs. Let him sleep, huh?'

'Sure,' says Vic. They're both almost whispering. 'Listen, you want to come down to the canteen and have a beer?'

'Love to,' she says. 'But I'm really clapped out, and I've got paperwork to do yet, and a call to make up the village. Some other time, eh?'

'Right.'

'Listen,' I say, 'how is he, though?'

'He's all right,' she says. 'I'd tell you if anything was wrong.'

'How long's he going to be up here?'

'Another couple of days, maybe. There's no sign of anything wrong inside, and he'd be better off down there with somebody to talk to. The only thing is, there's air-conditioning up here, he'd be more comfortable for a bit.'

'Ice-cream's got an air-conditioner,' says Vic. 'We'll move him in there.'

'All right,' she says, 'we'll move him as soon as he can walk to the bog and back. Now, I've got to go. One of the good ladies down the road has a bad case of vaginal thrush . . .'

'How do you treat that?' says Vic. He looks interested.

'Paint her crutch with gentian violet,' says Margaret. 'Women shouldn't wear pants in this bloody climate . . .' And she's gone.

'Hear, hear,' says Vic. Absently, 'She's not a bad old girl, the old Margaret, y' know . . .'

That reminds me that I have to find Beagle Boy and apologise. On the way back down the track, the rain slowly fading to a drizzle, it's Jimmy who raises the question that's been on my mind.

'Who done it, do ya think?' he asks. 'You know, to Stretch?' He's hunched under his sack, slouching along between the puddles.

'Yes,' I say, 'that's what I'd like to know.'

'Yeah . . .' says Vic, and steams on for another fifty yards. 'It's a wonder,' he says finally, 'that we haven't heard, one way or another, before now . . .'

'I don't think Stretch is going to tell us,' I say.

'No,' says Vic, 'I don't think he is.'

'Well, then . . .'

'Listen,' says Vic, '*nothing* in this godforsaken hole stays a secret for long. Some time, somewhere, someone's goin' to say something, someone's going to notice something . . .'

We trudge in silence through the drizzle.

Near the dongas Jimmy hits it right on the nail. 'They shouldn't have used that stake on him,' he says. 'Fists, that's fair enough. But they shouldn't have used that stake.'

'Don't worry,' says Vic, calm as a buddha, 'she'll all come out in the wash.'

•

I'm going through the tools in the workshop, sharpening spades, fitting new handles, grinding chisels, cleaning out tool boxes, when Curly comes over to me. The others are all out on the job. It's not raining, but heavy and humid. The temperature's dropped to under 100 degress, but it seems hotter than ever. Sweat runs even when you're not moving.

'Listen,' says Curly, his chin thrust forward, his expression grotesquely aggressive. 'Listen, Jack, you saw the accident, didn't you? When Stretch fell off the truck?'

'What's up?'

'Gotta fill in an accident report – the workers' comp.' He waves the form in my face. 'You saw it, didn't you?'

'Yeah,' I say. 'Of course. But let's have a look at what you've written – just to refresh my memory.'

He gives me the form. It's double-sided, the usual insurance company bumph. He's filled it in with so much verbiage and double talk that it reads like an act of parliament. There are maps in three colours, showing where the truck was, where it was going, who was on it, how big the bump was, why Stretch was standing up – to stop the lawn mower bouncing off, what time it was, the state of the weather, the visibility, and a very neat compass rose in the corner of the sheet.

'Christ, Curly, they won't pay out on *that*.'

'*What*?'

'They'll fucking *frame* it!'

He snatches it back from me, glowering. 'Well?'

'Of course I saw it Curly.'

'Good, I'll put you down as witness . . .' He retreats to his cluttered table, mumbling.

I get on with the tools, working the file across the ends of the shovel blades, slowly building a bright edge of raw steel, taking some kind of pleasure in the sight of it; keen, hard, straight. And sharp.

•

After tea I pick up my sack, still wet from the last rain. Poke my head into the room next-door. It's empty, and I remember that Vic and Jimmy are on afternoon shift. So I head up the track towards the quarters. There are rumbles of thunder from the north, and it has begun to rain again.

There's no light in Margaret's room, and the ambulance is not in its place. I tap lightly on the dispensary door, and go in. Stretch is awake, lying propped in the bed, a comic on the sheet over his knees. He looks bloody awful, his face all the colours of the rainbow. The swelling is down, but he looks truly wrecked. I feel like crying when I think of how he was before.

He smiles a bit – more an awkward lift to the corners of his mouth.

'How you going, mate?' I ask.

'All right . . .' It's a kind of lisping mumble, his lips not moving much. He's lost an incisor and the tooth next to it on the right.

I pull up a chair and sit by the bed.

'Anything you want?'

He shakes his head.

'Want your radio?'

'No – Marg's got a spare she lent me.' Jerks his head towards the bedside table where there's a trannie standing beside the empty plate.

'You been eating solid stuff?'

He nods. 'Baby food – eggs, custard, you know . . .'

'That's an improvement.'

'Listen, Jack – I can get to the bog and back now. She says I can go home tomorrow if I like.'

Home! That fucking donga . . .

'That's terrific, mate. Listen, I'll come and get you after work.'

He grins, a bit lopsided. 'I won't be much trouble.' He pauses. 'One of the girls in the kitchen's gunna bring me tucker.' Has the grace to blush a bit.

'Haven't lost your touch, then?'

'She offered . . .' There's a silence.

'You going to tell us who it was?' He lowers his eyes, shakes his head.

'We'll find out, anyway.' He looks unhappy. 'You worried about the bird?' I ask. 'What he might do to her?'

He nods.

'Don't worry about that, he won't touch her . . .' But he just looks down at his hands.

'All right, let's forget it. Get you back to the donga. Hey! You know Curly's put you on compo?'

He smiles, almost widely. 'Yeah. He came in yesterday.'

'Good old Curly!'

'Good old Curly!'

We sit and talk for a while, small stuff, the latest round the camp, the wet, the job. I turn on the radio after a bit, and we listen to the news. We're not the only ones to get flooded. Seventeen inches of rain at Innisfail overnight, Boulia flooded, tourists stranded everywhere.

A bit after eight I notice that he seems tired, so I get up to go. 'See you tomorrow, cock . . .'

He nods, smiles, eyes heavy.

I turn off the overhead light, leaving just the lamp glowing by the bed.

Outside, the thunder's rolling, closer, but the rain has eased a little. I stand for a moment on the verandah, rolling a cigarette, thinking of nothing much. Three or four doors down the verandah a light goes off, a door opens, and someone comes out, closes the door behind them, turns away toward the other end of the walkway. A woman, longish hair, pale dress, I can see that, nothing more.

Then suddenly a streak of lightning flashes across the night, and close thunder rolls again. In that brief second the figure down the verandah is frozen in the glare. I seem to stop breathing, the match unstruck in my fingers. I can't move, incredulous, paralysed . . .

She senses my presence, turns, craning a little to see me. She moves forward a pace, steps into a pale flood of light from a window. The light touches her hair, her face . . .

Petra!

'Jack?' she says, uncertainly, moving slowly forward, out of the light again.

I seem frozen there with my stupid unlit match.

'Jack?' She seems surer now, getting slowly closer.

I drop the match, the cigarette, find myself moving at last. In a moment we're together, our arms round each other. I can't believe it, but the feel of her, the smooth shoulders, the straight back, the soft curl of her hair . . . I've hardly thought of her in weeks; I seem to have shut all that out of my life . . . but suddenly, feeling her pressed against me, smelling the old familiar smell of her, it's as though I've come home again.

'What the *hell* are you doing here?'

She keeps her face pressed close to my chest. 'That's not much of a welcome . . .'

'Petra – what are you *doing* here?'

'What do you think?'

I stand there, unable to think any more, unable to connect, unable to speak. Shock. Petra doesn't *belong* here, not in this place . . .

But where *does* she belong? In that bloody clinic? With Purple Brewster and Paddy and Eric and the old ladies? With the pills and the shock therapy? Why *shouldn't* she be here?

'Come inside,' she says, pulling away, taking my hand, opening the door behind her.

She turns on the light, stands holding my hand, looking at me while I look at the room. Just like Margaret's, the image of a motel room anywhere, complete with en suite bathroom, green curtains, prints on the wall, built-in cupboards, a bedside table, smooth lino tiles on the floor, venetians at the window . . .

What the *fuck* am I doing taking inventory at a time like this?

I take both her hands, look down at her. She's smiling faintly, but a little uncertainly.

'Listen, tell me . . . really. How did you get here? Whose room's this?'

'It's mine,' she says. 'I've got a job here . . . I'm looking after the post office . . .'

'*What*?'

And it all starts to come back with a flash, what Ice-cream said . . . a new bird on the last plane . . . a ripper . . . queueing up . . . *a ripper* . . .

Petra . . .

'How did you find me?' My voice sounds harder, rougher than I mean it to. I haven't even kissed her yet. Oh, I'm some lover, I am . . .

She lets go my hands, turns away, stands looking at the blank wall. 'You told me once . . . about this place. A kind of purgatory, you said. It was the only real place you ever mentioned. So I thought maybe you might have . . .'

I'm struck dumb.

'Jack,' she says, 'I've got some bad news. I'd better tell you now.'

'Bad news?' I seem to be an accumulation of disconnected circuits that won't lock together.

She sits down on the bed, watching me a moment, before she speaks. 'It's your grandfather,' she says. 'He's dead.'

'*What*?'

She sits looking at me, very still. Suddenly everything is wiped out. The world is a smeared sheet; the past, the present, everything, everyone, everyone I've ever known, every thought I've ever had, smeared into each other, smeared all over the white wall of my mind, swirling and shifting . . . After what seems a very long time, it all seems to settle again. I can see straight, think straight, but the world is different, as if a focus has changed, as if the quality of the light is new, foreign . . .

I go and sit on the bed beside her. Take her hand.

'What happened? Tell me.'

'It was an accident,' she says. 'He was changing a light bulb, and he got a shock. His heart . . . you know,' she looks at me suddenly, 'he had a weak heart . . . something he had when he was a kid?'

'Rheumatic fever . . .'

'That's it.'

'And he was *electrocuted* . . . changing a *light bulb*?'

'It was in the hotel kitchen . . . the floor was wet.'

'You're joking!' Him, electrocuted changing a bulb? Wet floor? Listen, the old bastard was so careful about electricity he wouldn't . . . 'When?' I say. 'When did it happen?'

'Just after you left,' she says. 'Just a few days later, after you left the clinic.'

A sudden thought strikes me. 'How do *you* know all this?'

She turns to look me full in the face. 'I went to see your mother.'

I look at her open-mouthed. Can feel myself gawping.

'I wanted to find out if she might know where you were.' She pauses. 'Even what was wrong with you . . .'

Suddenly I feel cold as ice, despite the heat. All the same, I feel the blood flooding to my face. 'What did she tell you?'

Petra is still looking at me. 'Nothing,' she says. 'Nothing at all.' She sighs, looks down at her hands. 'I don't think she approved of me . . .'

'*She* didn't approve of *you*?' I find myself giggling, it sounds horrible. Let myself fall back on the bed, put my hands over my eyes. All I want to do, suddenly, is go to sleep . . .

My mind seems to be bouncing back and forth like a bloody ping-pong ball – between Petra and the old man, the old man and Petra . . . back and forth . . . as soon as I start to fix my mind on one, the other one gets in the way . . .

It seems impossible that I should have come this far, and still be so close . . . Petra has become a sort of link, stringing everything together. Thank Christ Nancy didn't tell her anything . . .

But why not? Why shouldn't Petra know?

The old man . . . an accident? Like bloody hell. But why? Because I wouldn't see him when he came to visit me in the clinic? I can't believe it . . .

And Petra? 'Are you all right?' I ask her, not looking at her. 'How long have you been out of the clinic?'

'Six weeks,' she says. I can feel her looking at me. 'I'm still taking my pills, but I'm all right.'

'Listen, if you thought you knew I was coming here, why did you go and see Nance?' I have this odd feeling that she has intruded too much, it's stupid . . .

'I wanted to know what was wrong with you . . .'

'And you didn't find out?'

'No . . . oh, she knows, I could tell . . . but she wouldn't say.'

'Did you see anyone else?' I'm thinking of Kate. It'd be just like her to say something.

'No. I was only there half an hour.'

I haven't touched Petra since we sat on the bed. I don't understand why, unless it's . . . I don't know, it's not that I don't want to see her . . . more that, well, Carbine Creek was my own, my retreat, and I felt in control, and now someone else has broken the spell . . .

I sit up. 'Listen, I've got to go . . .' She says nothing. 'It's the old man . . . and . . . well, everything.'

'It's all right,' she says.

I get up and go to the door. 'Look, I'll see you tomorrow night.'

'Yes.' She doesn't look at me, sits there as still as death on the bed, looking very small and lonely.

I go out, shut the door very softly behind me, feeling like some sort of murderer. Back in the quiet donga I drop on to the cot, and within minutes I'm in a black sleep that lasts till morning, no images, no dreams, no threats, nothing . . .

•

Rain, rain . . .

I drag through the day somehow. Saturday, and we knock off at midday. In the afternoon I lie on my bunk. I should be tidying up the donga ready for Stretch, but I can't seem to break this terrible lethargy. Maybe it's some kind of grief for the old man, but I don't think so. The truth is that, despite all the memories of him, he seems now like someone I knew a long time ago in another country. His death doesn't seem to have meaning. Although I'm certain that it wasn't the way it's supposed to be . . .

But why? *Why?*

The old man . . . sick? No, there wasn't that sort of weakness in him, of taking the easy way out . . .

Petra, I feel so wretched about treating her like this . . . And I wonder what she expected, hoped for . . .

Love Petra? I don't know. Something wrong with the equation. One term – me – undefined, won't work out. I seem to be just as big a mess now as when I came here, months ago . . .

The rain has stopped, and the sun is out, hot and bright. I remember Vic's words, and get up, look in the cupboard. My shoes and Stretch's are both covered in mould, thick, greenish-grey. I pull them out. Jackets, slacks, everything the same. I rake everything out, take it outside. The line outside the donga is half full with stuff belonging to others. I peg my stuff up to dry, stand the shoes in the sun.

Petra will have finished work in the post office. I should go and see her, but the thought hits a rawness in me, and I can't seem to bring myself to it.

In the end I go up to the canteen and drink several whities, sitting alone in the shade at the back, looking out over the acres of stony wilderness that is supposed one day to be a golf course. Whenever there's no work for us, we take the tractor and trailer and pick up rocks . . .

Like Hitler's hopes, the job will last a thousand years . . .

Get a buzz on, and instead of feeling sober and miserable, feel half stung and miserable . . .

Tea over, Vic and I and Jim and Ice-cream walk up to bring Stretch home. I'm a bit nervous, because we have to pass Petra's room, and I don't think I want to see her. But when we get there, no one is in sight, her door closed, no light on. And I wonder – a little jealously, God help me – where she is . . .

Ice-cream is on his dignity a bit, because Stretch won't let him move his air-conditioner to our room, and won't move into Ice-cream's room. He's adamant.

Stretch is up, sitting in a chair, wrapped in someone's dressing-gown. He's looking quite chipper, but in obvious pain as soon as he starts to move. Those bruises are deep, and they'll hurt for a long time. I remember well enough . . .

But his cuts are starting to heal, and the colours round his eyes are starting to lose their rawness and to take on that livery, livid look. There's a decided twist to his nose now, and that will never be the same again. Finger my own, which has been broken twice, but high up, and reset straight. I can only feel the slight irregularities now in the bone and cartilage . . .

'You gonna lie down on the stretcher?' asks Vic, as we stand around him.

'No . . . Sit up.' He is speaking a bit more clearly now, and there's a slight mushy sound to it, because of the puffy lips and the gap.

'We'll put him in the front,' says Margaret. 'Come on, get him outside.'

Ice-cream and Vic pick him up, chair and all, and cart him out to the ambulance. I wonder how we are going to get him into the cab; but Vic simply lifts him – all six foot four or whatever – out of the chair like a baby, deposits him, gentle as a puffball, on the seat. Margaret gets up, starts the engine. We crowd in, Jimmy beside Stretch, and the rest of us in the back.

Margaret parks at the end of the row, and Vic carries Stretch into the room. Margaret comes in, settles him, sniffs at the room – which I've tidied after a fashion – leaves some pills in case he can't sleep. And a stainless-steel bottle and a bedpan.

Stretch frowns at them, and I tuck them out of sight under the bunk.

Then Margaret is gone, and we're all clustered round the bed, feeling awkward and not knowing what to say.

Ice-cream goes out, comes back in a minute or two with half a dozen cold cans from his little refrigerator. Grins slyly at Stretch, 'Reckon you could handle a whitey without a relapse?'

Stretch grins at him, and suddenly his face takes on the old shape and boyishness again. 'I reckon . . .'

And everything is back to normal again.

I switch on the radio, Ice-cream and Jimmy get out the cards, Vic and I and Stretch sit and sip our beer and talk. Quietly, easily, just the way it used to be . . .

An hour later the room is getting a beery fug to it, the radio is turned low, and Vic is entertaining Stretch and me with tales of his days with Harry Paulsen. I don't notice for a minute or two, but the voices of the card-players have faded out. Silence seems to seep into the room, and a kind of stillness. Vic's voice drones to a halt, peters out, and I see him looking over my shoulder towards the door, a puzzled look on his big brown face. Stretch too is looking at the door, and looking as if he's seen a ghost. I turn round, and there's a woman in the doorway, standing quite still, watching us. For a split second I think that it's Petra. But it's not, and suddenly I recognise her. It's Sigrid who operates the telex up at the main office. I've seen her before – the day I arrived, and several times since at the canteen, usually with her husband, a big gingery South African geologist.

She takes a hesitant step inside the room, letting the screen door swing behind her. We're all a bit stunned, mainly because women never come here, aren't allowed here, and most of them would be too scared anyway . . .

She doesn't look scared, just pale and determined. She's a slight woman, about twenty-seven or twenty-eight I'd guess, in a thin, black dress and sandals. Face triangular, wide forehead and narrow chin, good features, tanned skin that looks a bit sallow, good thick dark hair with a tinge of auburn. Her arms and legs are slim, almost thin, but tanned and shapely, her breasts small and firm.

She looks round at us, darts a glance at Stretch, addresses the room at large. 'I'd like to see John . . .'

I find myself frowning. John? Surely she can't mean me? I haven't been called John since I was a kid. Then it dawns on me – *Stretch. His* name is John . . .

Stretch . . .

And suddenly it all clicks into place.

This is the one . . . *this* is the one . . .

And her *husband* . . . Van Erkelens . . .

Him . . . Find myself breathing deeply, my nostrils flaring like a bloody stallion in rut . . .

'Please,' she says, her void light and slow, an accent I can't quite pick . . . not South African . . . maybe Dutch or German . . . 'I'd like to see him alone . . . if you don't mind . . .'

'You shouldn't be here, you know,' says Vic, his voice light and friendly.

She doesn't say anything, just stands there looking at Stretch. And he's looking at her. And I know that there's no one else in the room, just then, as far as they're concerned. All sorts of questions and answers are flying back and forth through the air, some swift current of understanding that we can't grasp.

Vic gets up, and moves towards the door. We all follow, sidling past her to get out. From outside I look back. She's sitting on the edge of the bed holding his hand. They're just looking at each other.

We go down the row and sit on some empty boxes outside Icecream's room. Stars are out and the night is soft and gentle, and none of us wants to talk much. So we sit smoking and sipping our beers. Everything is quiet – most of the blokes are up at the canteen or at the films. It's only a bit after nine o'clock, and there's a sense of time stretching out a long way in front of us. Oddly, there's no real curiosity about what's happening in the room; we all seem to know that whatever it is, it is very quiet and very gentle and good, and we don't want to interrupt.

A little later there is a crunch of footsteps from the direction of the mess. In a moment or two Ettore, the contractor, comes into view, his bald head shining in the light from the overhead lamps. He seems agitated, stops as he comes level, looks at us accusingly.

'There is a woman here,' he says, his voice rising a little. 'Someone has told me . . . a woman here.' He looks accusingly at me. 'In your room, Mr Todd . . .'

Mr Todd . . . I feel like laughing.

'Just a visitor for our invalid,' I say. 'No harm done.'

But he is on his way, rushing up the row towards the door of our room.

'Oh, shit . . .' We're up and after him in a flash.

I'm half a pace behind him going through the door. Stretch and Sigrid are exactly as we have left them; they don't seem to have moved.

Vic does move fast for a big man. He's past me in the narrow space and on to Ettore, an arm round his shoulders, engulfing the little Italian with his bulk, and sweeping him back past me and out the door.

Stretch and Sigrid watch silently, and I follow Vic outside, bemused. He has Ettore ten yards down the path, his arm still round the white-shirted shoulders, head bent, talking softly into an ear. After a minute or two, Ettore starts to nod slowly, then more quickly; then, suddenly, Vic releases him and he's off down the track, not looking back.

Vic comes back, winks at me.

'What did you say to him?' I ask.

'Nothing much,' he says.

'But what?'

'Oh, I just told him that, you know, it was just like a hospital visit . . . no harm.'

'What else?'

'Oh, just that it looked like being a long wet, and I was sure he wouldn't want a riot in the mess . . . you know, maybe if they found a rat in the soup, something like that . . . he's a reasonable man, the old Ettore . . .'

I can't help laughing.

We go back to the boxes. A couple more blokes have drifted up, and there's a kind of festive air about the place. Except that, like the others, I'm a bit nervous about Sigrid, even if Ettore has gone . . .

But it's still peaceful, the night still soft and starry, and I start to relax. Ice-cream turns the radio up, and there is cold beer, and the world isn't such a bad place, maybe . . .

Ice-cream is telling us a long, involved story about how he was sleeping on the luggage rack on the old Transcontinental, and bounced off as the train went over a set of points, on to a copulating couple on the floor. He's just getting to the interesting bit when I see Vic looking hard up the track towards our room. He seems to tense a little, beginning to rise. I look round and see the big South African emerging from the dark end of the row.

Van Erkelens, Sigrid's husband.

Vic and I both move at once, but he's inside the door of my room before we've gone more than a couple of yards.

I get to the door, catch the flywire door before it slams. There's a sharp *crack*, and I see Sigrid hit the far wall, the imprint of the big man's hand on her face. Stretch is struggling to get out of bed.

'That's enough!'

He doesn't take any notice of me. Ignores Stretch, too, after shoving him back on the bunk.

'You bitch!' he says. His voice has that hard rasping Afrikaans accent. He's a big man, as tall as me, heavier, thicker, with gingery fair hair in a tight, wiry brush. His skin – all you can see: legs, arms, neck, face – is red-brown. His calves look like small trees. His hand goes back to hit her again. I grab it.

'I *said* that's enough!'

'Let me go . . .' He still doesn't look at me. Seems to forget, after a moment, that I'm holding his arm. 'You fuckin' slut,' he says. 'I'll kill you when I get you home . . .'

Everyone seems frozen for a moment. Then Sigrid steps away from the wall. She stands up to him, looks him in the eye.

'I'm not coming home,' she says.

'What? You'll come home when I fucking tell you!'

I feel sorry for him in a way. All this in front of strangers. Then I think of that garden stake.

Suddenly she spits in his face, a good gob fair in the eye. He starts to surge away towards her and it's all I can do to hold him. He half turns to look at me.

'Who are you?' he says.

'Never mind who I am,' I say. 'This is my room, and you're trespassing.'

He looks suddenly concerned, as if this were a very grave impropriety. 'I'm sorry,' he rasps, in that terrible voice. 'But I've got no choice, man . . . I'll take her home.'

'I told you, I'm not going.'

He turns back to look at her. 'Listen Piet, I'm never coming home again. I've moved my stuff, all that I want . . . I'm finished.'

He starts to look puzzled, a little unbelieving. 'You're my bloody wife, you'll do as I say . . .'

'Wife!' she says, her voice full of scorn. 'Only men have wives . . . *You're* not a man, you're a big baby. John – ,' he looks quickly at Stretch as she mentions his name, 'John, he's twice, ten times, the man you'll ever be . . .'

He's starting to tremble a bit and I wonder if he's going to go berserk. She's not making it any better, and Christ knows what will happen if he gets loose in here. I can feel the little tremors all the way down his arm.

She spits at him again. It's not a habit I like, and I get some of it this time. By now Vic is inside, and Ice-cream is behind him, the others clustered outside the door.

Van Erkelens looks slowly around him, and it seems to dawn on him that we're not about to let him murder her.

'Listen,' he says, to all of us. 'This is personal, this is between my wife and me . . .'

No one speaks.

'It's my right!'

Sigrid laughs, a little shrilly, and he wrenches round towards her. 'Whore!' he shouts, trying to hit her. I manage to hang on.

'Listen', I say in his ear. 'I told you, you're trespassing. You don't get out now, I'm going to fucking brain you . . .'

He looks at me a little blankly. He's breathing hard, and a

little raggedly. I jerk my head towards the door. Suddenly all the tension seems to leave him, and he seems to lose six inches in height. The others make way.

We stand out in the dark, the yellow light spilling out the doorway on to us. I've still got his arm, but he still doesn't seem to notice. Suddenly he looks a bit empty, almost beaten, haunted, and I think for a minute that he's been punished enough, what with the way she's abused him in front of us and all. But then I think of that bloody garden stake, and how he needn't have done that at all, he's plenty big enough to have handled Stretch with his fists. And I think of the boot marks on Stretch's back, and the coldness starts to build inside again, that hard icy anger. And I remember Stretch the way he was before and Vic saying to me, look after him . . .

'We've got some business together, you and I,' I tell him.

He looks at me blankly.

'You shouldn't have used that stake on the boy,' I say. 'He's my mate.'

He doesn't say anything, looks puzzled.

'You hear me?'

'I caught him,' he says. 'I *caught* him . . . he was . . . you know, with my *wife*!'

'I don't care if he was fucking your grandmother . . . you shouldn't have used the stake on him.'

'Keep out of it,' he says. 'None of your business.'

'It's my business, all right. You don't believe me, you're going to find out the hard way . . .'

By this time the others are clustered round us, a couple with torches. More doors open, more light spills out, and I can see the faces clearly. They're all deadly serious, not a grin anywhere, none of that excited light-hearted look that often comes when there's a punch-up in prospect.

'Keep out of it,' he says again, but he's looking round the circle now, and I think it's beginning to dawn on him that he's in for something.

The light from the doorway is suddenly dimmed, as Sigrid steps on to the top step. 'Kill the pig,' she says, quietly, looking at me.

While I'm turned to look at her he hits me.

Because I've already started to turn back the fist misses my face and hits me on the shoulder, glances off. I can feel a lot of muscle behind it. There's a different look on his face now, kind of hard and desperate, and vicious too. His face is broad and freckled, and there's sweat on it, and his thickish lips are curled back a bit.

'You fucking asked for it,' he says. And I guess he's going to try and take it all out on me. So I give him a little more needle.

'You're all talk, you bloody squareheads . . . no use without a bloody waddy.'

He just snarls a little.

'Too used to bashing kanakas, aren't you, squarehead . . .'

He looses one off then, a roundhouser that I just manage to duck. But it's close, and I feel my ear start to puff.

'Go on,' says Vic from behind me. 'He's all yours.'

So I go for him.

It's a pretty dull fight, I suppose. At least for the onlookers. Neither of us is an expert, not by a long chalk; and we miss as often as we connect. And the light's not too good, so we don't see each other too well, and the onlookers don't see us too well either. It goes on for a long time. You get two good bruisers that know their business, and a fist fight's likely to be over very quick. But not us; it seems to go on and on.

There's a lot of grunting and heavy breathing, and our feet stirring the gravel of the path, and the solid thud when one connects; but not too much real damage. A lot of blood, but none of it serious blood.

The squarehead tries a rush now and then, and once he almost pins me against the wall of the donga. For some reason when he's got me there he stops punching and grabs me by the throat. That's an easy one, and I break it the way they taught me when I was a kid in the learn-to-swim campaign; arms between his, up and out. Give him a good knee in the guts to be going on with, and slip away from the wall. He's blowing a bit now, and so am I, but my legs are still OK. So I decide it's time to move in on him a bit.

The next time he rushes I let him in, let his head drop, because

I know he's going to try and get his arms round me. So when he reaches I slip right in and give him three good ones, hooking hard and low, catching between wind and water, and his head comes down further. So I lace my fingers behind his neck and bring my knee up.

He staggers back then, and there's a lot of blood on his face. His nose is gone, and his lips are kind of split. So for a minute or so I hit him in the face, hard as I can go. His head goes back, his hands come up, and I drop my shoulder and let him have one very low, so low it'd be foul if there was a referee, and his face goes pale under the blood, and I know that I've got him.

No mistake though, I've been copping it while all this is going on. He's a big boy, not much older than I am, and fairly fit, and those big freckled fists have been hammering away at me.

But now's the time, so while he's clutching his affairs, and wheezing, I step in and chop him a couple of times under the ear. Then I grab him, haul him upright.

'Listen,' I tell him, finding it surprisingly hard to get the words out between breaths, ' . . . listen, squarehead . . . this's where you get what's coming to you . . . gonna cut you up a bit, squarehead . . .'

So I start to hit him then, pretty well wherever I want to. But I want him upright. Punish his face for a bit, hitting him under the eyes, round the nose and mouth. But it's awfully hard on the hands, so after a while I think, oh bugger it, and I hit him a good one, all the way up from the floor, that takes him right over the heart. He goes down then, legs moving as he lies on his side, head out of the pool of light. His hands move and I see that he's reaching for an old steel-star post that's lying by the donga, left over from some fencing jobs. Pulls it to him, gets to his knees, ready to swing it at me. But someone – Ice-cream I think – takes it from him, quite gently, and suddenly he falls flat on his face. There's still something working, because he curls up, knees tight into his belly, head down, waiting for the boot.

And right then I start to feel sick again, because, let's face it, I've got this bloody compulsion to kick him hard in the crutch, lift him on his way. So I just stand there, holding it in, until the urge goes away. After all, there's got to be some difference between us and animals like him, even if it's only a difference you make yourself . . .

He stirs then, and starts to crawl away, into the darkness, and I'm tempted to let him go, make him do it the hard way, the way Stretch had to . . .

No one else's stirring; they're all just standing as quiet as if they were in church, as if they're waiting for me . . .

So I go and grab the squarehead's arm, try to pull him up.

'For Christ's sake,' I say. 'Give us a hand!'

So they move then, and Ice-cream and Triple Jackson take him.

'What we gonna do with him?' asks Ice-cream.

'Yeah, yeah, yeah,' says Triple, who always says everything three times.

Vic is standing beside me. 'Lug him up to the staff quarters,' he says. 'Someone up there can look after him.' Then he turns to me. 'How you feel?'

'Fucking awful . . .' It's true. All that adrenalin has been used up and I've got the usual aftermath, trembling muscles, sick stomach, chills . . . My legs seem to be on the point of crumpling.

'Come on,' he says, and shepherds me into his room. As I go past our door I see that Stretch is out of bed, hanging on the doorframe, propped up by Sigrid. Their faces are in shadow and neither of them says anything . . .

Vic and Jimmy get me on to a bunk, and I close my eyes. There's a small rattling, a stirring, and a cool damp towel on my face. I open my eyes to see Vic's heavy brown face bent over me, his black hair haloed by the ceiling light.

'Take it easy,' he says, 'we'll clean you up.'

He mutters and tuts over me like an old lady. Something stings me hard and jerks me half up. He pushes me down again, brandishes the styptic pencil. 'Never done much pugging, have you Jack?'

'No.'

'Neither's the squarehead. Lucky for you. More muscle than science, both of you. Jesus, your hands are a mess . . .'

Styptic pencil, iodine, tape. Eventually it's over, and I feel a little better. Stung and bruised, but better. Still sick, though, and a bit sleepy . . .

I feel their hands on me, undressing me, rolling me over. Then Vic's big paws go to work on muscles, legs, back, shoulders, and gradually the kinks come out, and I feel my muscles settling back into their proper places . . .

'Christ, mate,' he says, 'you're going to be stiff and sore for a day or two.'

'Did I hurt him?'

'Sure, you hurt him all right. Didn't do any real damage, but he'll be a lot sorer than you are.'

'That's all right then . . .'

Then it's quiet for a while, and I think maybe they've gone. But when I open my eyes Vic is still there. I flex my hands, but they're badly swollen now, and the fingers seem like those sausages that split when they're fried, and lose their stuffing . . .

'Vic?'

'Yes, mate?' He's sitting on the other cot, smoking.

'Get some clothes for me, will you?'

'What for? You can stay here tonight. Jimmy'll sleep in your bunk.'

'No . . . I've got something to do.'

'Can't it wait?'

'No.'

'OK.'

I close my eyes, hear his soft footsteps go off into the night. In a couple of minutes he's back. He's got a clean pair of shorts, underpants, a shirt with buttons down the front. Thinks of everything. Don't think I could have managed a T-shirt . . .

He helps me dress, and then I get to my feet. It's not so much that I feel old, rather as if I've been through a bad rock fall, and every part of me is bruised and screaming. I move slowly over and look in the mirror on the end wall.

I look bloody awful. My nose is swollen, and I wonder if it's gone again. There's a strip of plaster across the bridge. My mouth's all right, hardly cut, just swollen. Under my eyes great bruises are already coming up, and there's a crust of blood on one cheek where the squarehead's signet ring caught me. Eyes bloodshot, one eyebrow thick with caked blood. Everything mottled with iodine, a nightmare . . .

'Lend us a torch, will you?'

He finds one on a shelf and gives it to me. 'Sure you'll be all right?'

'Sure.'

Once I'm down the steps and on to the level it's not so bad. The little crowd has gone, and I can hear voices from the direction of Ice-cream's room. The stars are being shut out in patches by drifts of cloud, but it's not raining. Yet. As I pass the door of our room I see that Stretch is back in bed. Sigrid's sitting beside him, and they're still holding hands, not talking, not looking at each other.

Hobbling up the road I start to warm up, move a little easier. By the time I get to the staff quarters I'm moving fairly freely, but still feeling sick and empty. It seems that ever since it all began I've been living on top of a rising wave of violence, and at last it's swamped me. And I hate it; I just can't live like this. The trouble is that, despite everything – all the bravado and bullshit, all the make-believe of the football years, all the kidstuff of schooldays – I'm not a violent man, I never have been . . . we put on these disguises, and people take them at face value . . . he's a hard man, the Bastard, they say, he'll take his knocks and give back better than he gets . . . And it's true, I suppose, you can't let people get away with too much in that world, or they ride all over you . . . but *that* was a kind of pretend world, and you could walk out of it when you wanted . . . and I did. But this world . . . Oh, God, they seem to live by it, and it eats them up . . .

There's a light behind the heavy green curtains of Petra's window, and I knock softly at the door.

In a moment or so it opens, and she's there, dark hair spilling down on to the shoulders of her old blue dressing-gown, the one I remember from the clinic. She sees who it is, pulls the door wide, takes my arm, gets me inside. I sit on the edge of the bed.

'Sorry it's so late . . .'

'What *happened* to you?'

'Nothing, just a fight.'

She looks at me for a long moment, her eyes very large and dark and deep in the dimness. There's only the one small reading lamp above the bed. 'What is it, Jack? What's wrong?'

I feel it all begin to well up, then, all the pain and fear and disgust, all the shame and secrecy and violence, and it seems more than I can bear.

'Listen,' I say, 'there's something I've got to tell you . . .' She's kneeling in front of me, hands on my knees, her eyes never leaving my face.

And I tell her, I tell her the whole bloody thing, about the old man and Nancy, and what I am, and what I'll always be . . . And her eyes are still on me, and they never falter, and when I finish, drift off to a halt, she doesn't say anything, just gets up, and moves away. And I think dully, well, that's that, you've fucked that up, too . . .

But she's only gone to turn out the light. And then she's back, and I hear in the darkness the soft sound of her dressing-gown and nightdress coming off, slipping to the floor, and then as my eyes grow a little accustomed to the gloom, I can see the tall pale candle of her body in front of me. Then she's undoing the buttons of my shirt, helping me out of my shorts, pulling back the sheet . . .

And we're lying there together in that narrow bed, held close in each other's arms in the hot night, and her hands are moving softly on my back, and my face is buried in her hair, my lips against the softness of her throat. Suddenly I find that I'm crying, tears squeezing out of my shut eyelids, running down my cheek, on to the pillow and the dark hair. It seems to go on for a long time, a very long time, until eventually the hard ache in my throat seems to ease, and I stop crying at last. And I move my bruised hands to her face, and feel her tears too . . .

And then, very quickly it seems, too quickly, I'm slipping away into the well of darkness, and sleep covers me like a warm and familiar garment . . .

●

In the morning, I wake to the sound of rain drumming on the roof, feel the unfamiliar warmth beside me. I lie there for a few moments, eyes closed, trying to remember where I am. It all comes back in a flash, with a kind of surging lift, a great sense of relief, of a great load gone. Slowly the presence of Petra's body sends out its messages. Sex hasn't worried me unduly, and apart from a few furtive wanks, I've just forgotten it, set it aside, during the time I've been here . . . but now . . .

She's lying with her back to me, and slowly I feel myself harden against the silky skin of her buttocks. She moves a little, beginning to turn towards me. I stir, turn a little to put my arms round her . . . and groan at the sudden pain. I'm stiff and sore in a hundred places, and my face seems double its usual size. My hands are clawed in a kind of cast of broken skin and swelling and plaster. It doesn't seem possible that I can accomplish anything useful, despite my suddenly urgent prick . . .

But Petra moves easily, widening, opening, hands on me, pressing me gently back, finding me, slipping me in, and the warm sweet silkiness makes me groan again, and she moves so gently, so sweetly and my aches are forgotten and I move a little too, and then we are both making the small animal noises and the hotness and the . . .

We lie there for a while, not speaking. The rain seems louder now, and the light through the blinds is dull and heavy, and we're both sweating a little, and cooling now. Soon she moves, slides away, out of the bed, smiling at me in the dimness, her hair wild and heavy, her eyes soft. I watch the strange dimples at the base of her spine as she moves towards the bathroom.

I hear the shower going, above the rain sound, and in a little while she comes out towelling, slips into jeans and a shirt.

'Stay there,' she says, 'I'll get you some breakfast.'

In ten minutes she is back with a tray. Orange juice, cereal, toast, coffee for us both. 'Is that enough? Or do you want eggs?'

'No – that's fine. How did you get it, though?'

She shrugs, setting the tray down on the bedside table. 'Lots of them don't come into the dining room on Sunday morning, just get a tray and go back to bed . . . I just paid for the extra breakfast.'

I eat, and the food tastes different this morning.

'Listen,' I say, sipping coffee. 'I'm sorry I haven't been up to see you before.'

'It's all right,' she says. And smiles. 'You don't have to explain anything. Ever . . .'

We smoke in silence for a bit. But it's not an awkward silence, and we smile at each other a bit. At last I sigh and begin to climb out of bed. The aches and pains are back again. But they don't seem so bad any more. Petra helps me into the shower, and under the hot water most of the worst aches fall away. It almost feels like old times, those Sundays years ago after a hard match, when the bruises are deep and the bones hurt . . .

I dress slowly, comb my wet hair, try to stick down my damp dressings.

'Will there be trouble? I mean with me being here all night?'

She smiles. 'I don't think so. I don't care, anyway . . .'

Petra.

Then the thought of the old man . . .

The trouble is, I can see it, see it so clearly, what happened. I can see the early morning kitchen, the dull light from the window above the sink, the floor still a little damp from the mopping of the previous night. He comes down the stairs barefoot in his old blue-plaid dressing-gown, and plugs in the kettle to make coffee. Flicks the switch to put on the light over the kitchen sink. The light comes on. He switches it off again, takes an old burnt-out bulb from his pocket, lays it on the sink. Reaches up, takes the good bulb from the socket. Turns the switch on again. Stands there a moment, looking out the window. Maybe sighs a little. Face blank in the dimness. Moves away, finds the mop bucket, tips it over so that the bit of water left in it pools in front of the sink. I'm sure he sighs then. He's probably tired, I don't know if he slept or not. But he was never one to put things off. So he steps forward into the little pool of water in his bare feet, picks up the new bulb in his left hand, reaches up and steadies the lampholder with the same hand. Maybe then takes a deep breath. Then, steadily, deliberately, forces the fingers of his right hand into the live light socket . . .

The fuses go, and the kettle begins to cool . . .

How do I know? Because, I suppose, that's just what I would have done. If I'd wanted to do it . . .

Why? *Why* did he do it?

Petra touches my hand. Something must be showing in my face.

'What do you want to do this morning?'

'I don't know.' I have difficulty in getting rid of that image of the old man in the kitchen. 'I'd better walk, or something, move, get my muscles working or I'll seize up . . .'

'Let's go for a walk, then.'

The rain has stopped. 'OK.' We smile at each other and the other image fades a bit.

Outside there is no sun yet, but the clouds are lifting, and there are small patches of blue sky. As I wait a moment for her to shut the door, Sue's door opens down the row, and her miner steps out, showered and shaved. He sees us, smiles a bit at me in complicity, lets his eyes wander a moment to Petra. He nods to her as she turns, then he's gone, walking off down the verandah.

Petra smiles at me. 'See?'

I smile back, but the truth is I don't really like to have us grouped in anyone's mind with them. Why? Bloody snob, I suppose. They're doing their best in this bloody place, the best they can . . .

•

The rains of the night have left the world waterlogged. We walk along the track that leads towards the village, and the red earth is runnelled with small streams. Fresh white sand glistens in patches, and the bases of trees are deep in water. The grass seems to grow while you watch it. It seems a miracle of life and fecundity, a world that springs into being like some conjuring trick. By the track there is a castor-oil plant that I've been watching the last week. It seems to unfurl new bronze leaves overnight, and I swear it's grown three feet in a week.

Suddenly Petra gives a small cry, points at the track in front of us. The water is coursing along the wheel ruts from some flooded creek and there, swimming down the track, are hundreds of tiny silver fish, no longer than your finger. We pause and stoop over them, watching them flash along through the shallows, between the stones and pebbles and tiny dirt banks. To see fish swimming along a road seems so outrageous that it's on a par with a rain of frogs, of little green martians – another sign that there is something foreign, outlandish, almost malign, about this awful country . . .

•

We spend the afternoon mooning about, not talking much. The sun comes out and it seems too hot to do anything. For a long time we lie side by side on Petra's bed, barely touching, half asleep, in some sort of peaceful limbo. About four o'clock she stirs, makes tea, and we sit quietly drinking it. Then I leave her to go back to the donga. I'm beginning to feel a bit guilty about leaving Stretch.

But he's sitting on his bed, dressed, playing crib with Jimmy.

I sit on my bed, wink at Stretch, and lie down. I feel very tired. Oddly, the events of last night, the fight, everything before I knocked on Petra's door, seem to have slipped away into the distant past . . . misty, suddenly unimportant.

I doze, dimly conscious of the voices of the card players.

At five Vic comes in, and they begin to get Stretch ready for tea. I sit up. Stretch has refused to use the bottle or the bedpan, and we've been walking him down to the ablutions when he needs to go. Now he's decided it's time to eat in the mess again. I know that he feels self-conscious at having meals brought to him on a tray.

With Vic on one side, Jimmy on the other, he makes it all right down the track and up the steps. With me tagging along behind, bruised and battered, it's like a bloody procession of invalids.

Something has happened.

Overnight the whole thing has changed. Up till now I've been largely ignored except by the few blokes from our donga. Now there are smiles, waves, everywhere. Before I'm in my seat three or four strangers have come up, said a word, patted my arm, grinned . . .

'How's the knuckles, cock?'

'Christ, you look awful, Jack!'

'Good on yer, mate.'

And once: 'Seen ya in '65 mate, that day you give Hudson a bath . . .'

Very strange.

I've somehow measured up to the cardboard cut-out, made the grade, passed the test . . .

We take turns cutting up Stretch's food. He gets his share of greetings, too . . .

'How you goin', shagger?'

'Use that fuckin' nose for a buzzer on a tram, now, mate . . .'

'You need a hand to lift you on, give us a shout, mate . . .'

'You know what they say – one pleasure, a thousand pains . . .'

Stretch grins and blushes a little, lowers his head over his plate.

Later, back in the donga, Vic puts fresh plasters on my hands, tutting away. 'Have to teach you how to punch one day, Jack.'

'Don't think so, Vic.'

He looks at me under his brows. 'No?'

I shake my head.

'No,' he says. 'Maybe you're right.' Then, after a pause, 'Don't reckon you're really cut out for this sort of thing, eh?'

I don't say anything.

'And a bloody good thing,' he says. 'Roll over, I'll give you a rub . . .'

And I lie there as his heavy strong fingers knead my stiff muscles.

•

In the morning it's workday again. I wake to pounding rain, sweat already pooling round my eyes, hair soaked and sticky.

I get up, very creaky, worse than yesterday, and stagger to the door. Rain, sheets of it, water everywhere, no relief in sight. A few solitary figures darting or trudging through the downpour.

'Jesus, what a fucking awful day . . .'

From behind me I hear Stretch move in his bunk. His voice has a clean, almost happy tone that seems to cut through the megrims of the morning.

'It's better than nothing,' he says.

And the words bite deep, shock me into stillness and silence. Then I turn and look at him, lying there on his bunk, dressed in a pair of old shorts, the sweat darkening his fair hair, his upper body encased in plaster and bandages . . . a boy in a dirty donga, bruised and beaten, no childhood behind him, Christ knows what in front of him, and not a lot of present in sight either . . . rain and more rain, and sweat and more sweat . . . in this awful place . . .

And: It's better than nothing . . .

I want to cry at the fucking wisdom of it, at the lovely clean soul of him, at the way he *knows* himself, and the world . . .

•

Curly finds me easy work, repainting the trim in the mess hall. It's very quiet between meal times, only the muted sounds from the kitchen, the drumming of the rain on the tin roof. The air-conditioners are working, humming away, but they might as well be shut off for all the good they are. The humidity is so high that the water in the screens won't evaporate, and all that comes out is a stream of moist hot air. They stir the air up a bit, but a fan would do that just as well.

I'm still stiff as buggery, but slowly freeing up. But although the old body is improving the mind is locked into a kind of stiffness. I feel easier somehow, because of Petra, but there's a brick wall somewhere in there, and I can't see over it. All alone here, my mind seems to chase its tail, round and round, and I give myself a headache. The paint smell doesn't help.

Something is happening to me, at last, but I don't know exactly what. It seems somehow that I'm getting smaller, the world is growing around me, other people, other things getting bigger . . . It's as if my own importance in the scheme of things is diminishing; yet I feel a certain relief.

And, I have to face it, the old man's death – suicide, I know it must have been – has changed things. How exactly, I can't tell. It's not, oddly enough, as though I've lost something, rather that I've found something new, that everything is in some strange way complete.

I still can't bring myself to think about him for too long – it's too painful. And I seldom think about Nance. When I do, every time she comes to my mind, it seems that she is younger, younger . . . I seem to see her, not as she is now, but as a young woman, a girl, almost . . .

But the most immediate image that comes to me when I think of the valley now is of Kate – that golden omnipresence in the landscape. She has spent less time there than any of us, yet it is of her the valley echoes . . .

She was the high and ebullient spirit that hung over my childhood, lent it a golden light, a light that spilled over on to everything else; neither true aunt nor grandmother nor older sister, but something of each, she brought a kind of half-elegant, half-vulgar filigree to the edges of life . . .

And still does, perhaps . . .

•

Stretch comes in to lunch, limping a little. He eats his lunch, sits afterwards talking with me, watching my slow efforts with the paintbrush.

'You didn't have to do that, you know,' he says at last, cutting through the idle small talk.

'What, mate?' But I know what he means.

'The squarehead.'

'He's got to learn sooner or later.'

'He was – you know – in the right . . .'

'Until he picked up that stick, he was.'

'Well . . .'

'Never mind, it's over now.' I hope it is, anyway. We haven't seen him since that night. The word is that he's off work and staying at home. 'What's happened with Sigrid? Where's she living?'

'Down the caravan park. Marjie – you know, the lady used to run the post office – went sick, got out to the Isa before the strip closed. Sigrid phoned her in hospital, moved into her van.'

'Ah . . .'

'I'm going down to see her tonight.'

'Oh, yeah?'

'After tea . . .'

It seems as if he wants to tell me something, but can't quite get it into words.

'You serious about her, are you, Stretch?'

'Yeah.'

'Well, why not?' No good telling him the usual crap, too old for you, you're too young to know your mind, those kind of things don't really count for Stretch somehow. 'I'd like to meet her some time – you know, properly.' I couldn't really care less, but it seems the right thing to say . . .

He brightens a bit. 'Would you?'

'Sure.'

He doesn't say any more, but he looks happier.

'That girl,' he says after a bit. 'The one at the post office, you knew her . . . you know, somewhere else, did you?'

'Yeah.'

'She's beautiful.'

'Keep your eyes off, shagger.' I grin at him.

But he looks serious. 'No, I didn't mean that.'

'I know.' And I do. He's changed, the old Stretch.

'Fuck this,' I say, and start to pack up my brushes. It's nearly knock-off time. 'Let's go and have a beer . . .'

•

I call for Petra at the quarters after tea, and we walk down the road, hand in hand towards the village. There's nowhere much to go, but it doesn't seem to matter. The night is warm, heavy, the rain not far away again.

We pick our way across the low part of the track where the creek has risen, and just beyond we meet another couple coming the other way. As they get closer I see that it is Stretch and his lady. They are walking very slowly, holding hands. He towers over her.

We stop.

'We were just going to turn back,' says Sigrid. Then, looking at me: 'You're Jack, aren't you?'

I nod.

'I want to apologise. I behaved badly the other night. I shouldn't have spat at Piet, called him those names.' There's a serious cast to her face, certain painful shadows in the twilight.

'That's all right.' I introduce Petra, and we all stand there like a quartet of awkward storks, not quite knowing what to do.

Sigrid breaks the silence. 'Would you like to come back and have a cup of tea? At the caravan?'

I look at Petra quickly. She smiles a little.

'Why not?'

So we troop along the track in the deepening darkness.

The caravan park is dark by the time we get there, too dark to see much. But I know it well enough. Some of the vans are bare and unadorned, temporary as only a caravan can be; others have awnings and little gardens and trellises covered with bougainvillea and the lush vines of New Guinea beans, the great pods lying fat and heavy among the leaves.

We reach Sigrid's van, which has a neat little terrace complete with pot plants and canvas chairs. Inside, the van is very neat and clean, and the air-conditioner, refrigerator type, is humming loudly, and the air feels chill.

It's a bit crowded, and we all stand around in the hard light feeling awkward.

'Why don't we sit outside,' says Sigrid. Her voice has only the lightest trace of accent. 'It's not as cool, but we'll be more comfortable . . .'

So we sit in the canvas chairs under the awning. Sigrid drops the mosquito curtain, and suddenly we are enclosed in a small canvas-walled world of our own. The only light comes from the caravan door. Petra sits beside me, takes my hand. Near the van door Stretch lowers himself into his chair, extends his long legs.

No one speaks for a little. But it's not an uncomfortable silence now. Sigrid comes out with cups, a teapot, slices of lemon. We sit and sip. It's all strangely peaceful, and almost home-like. Four people, two couples, visiting . . .

A fifteen-year-old boy (his birthday is only a week away) and his married mistress; a female schizophrenic and a special kind of bastard . . .

No, that's the *old* Bastard talking . . . not like that at all . . .
Four people, two couples . . . drinking tea in the dark . . .
God help me, I feel almost happy.

I can see, dimly, that Stretch has taken Sigrid's hand.

After a while Sigrid speaks from the patch of deeper darkness beyond the lighted doorway.

'John and I love each other,' she says quietly, undramatically; but there is a firmness and certainty that somehow rings true as a bell.

There's nothing much to say. But I say it anyway.
'God bless you both.'

Petra squeezes my hand, and I feel sudden tears close, and I'm glad it's dark . . .

●

'Come on,' says Curly, a day or two later, 'we're going out to the strip.'

I climb into the cab with him and Tony, the plumber.
'What's up?' I ask.
'They're going to try and drop some bread,' says Curly, jamming his hat down hard and starting the engine.

The stale bread ran out days ago. The cooks have tried baking it since then, but it's bloody awful; coarse and heavy and tasteless. And flour's short anyway.

It's raining, but only lightly, when we get to the strip, which is nothing more now than half a mile of red mud. Beyond, among the thin brush, a small mob of stringy cattle is standing, browsing on the coarse underbrush.

We sit smoking in the shed. Every now and then Curly stands up, looks at the sky, grey and lowering, glances at his watch.

At last we hear the distant drone of an engine to the east. Then we see the tiny dot against the grey, as the plane drops below the overcast. A wonder they could find us at all. Not a week passes without a pilot getting lost and having to cruise round until he finds a landmark, a station or a river or something. This bloody awful country . . .

The plane, a Beechcraft like the one that brought me in, silver and brown, circles once and swoops towards the strip. It seems as if it's going to try to land, but at the last moment the pilot levels out, and the plane rises again over our heads. And as it does a bundle leaves the plane, loops groundward, hits the deck with a muddy splash, bursts, and loaves of bread fly in all directions, rolling and skidding like cannonballs . . .

He tries again.

And again.

And again.

Four bundles of bread.

They all burst on impact, and the strip is littered with broken muddy loaves.

The plane circles once more, waggles its wings and departs.

Curly shakes his head, spits and gets into the driver's seat.

As we drive away I look back and see that the cattle have emerged from the scrub, sauntered on to the strip, and are munching away at the muddy bread . . .

•

Christmas is drawing near, and it seems a very strange prospect – for me, at least. Rain, heat, sweat, isolation. And there is no sign of the strip opening; it seems to be deeper each day in red mud. Even when the sun comes out it never stays long enough to dry the strip. Along the verges of the runway the octopuses of the paddymelon vines are clawing outward, spreading their vines in great clusters.

I was warned about them, God knows, but I'm entranced by their enticing succulence, the neat domestic pattern of their skins. I have to try one. Out one day near the lake I break one open, place a tiny bit of the moist pale green flesh on my tongue . . . Christ, the bitterness! I spit it out, of course, but the taste lasts for hours . . .

So, the strip stays closed. And there seems no hope at all of the roads being negotiable for weeks, well into the new year, anyway. So, for Christmas – and for Christ knows how long afterwards – we are on our own, tied to our own resources.

It seems to me that we – all of us up here – move in a series of circles, circles of all sizes, circles that overlap but remain separate. There is the small circle that Petra and I make, the one that Sigrid and Stretch make, Jimmy and Vic, the rest of the donga, the people in the staff quarters, the village, the mine, the whole place . . . all touching in some degree, all remaining separate . . . And there are more complex circles, too: Vic and Stretch and Jimmy, Petra and I and Stretch and Sigrid, Sigrid and Stretch and Vic and Jimmy, and so on . . .

And there are other circles, circles that belong in other places; Nance and me, Nance and me and Kate, Nance, me and the old man. Or his memory. These circles seem faint now, maybe even broken, and I don't know if they will ever re-form, or if they are dead and finished. That old part of my life seems a long way away, almost inconsequential at times, I have left it so far behind. You can never go back, I know, but sometimes you seem to pass and repass certain places, certain relationships . . .

•

Stretch's birthday is a few days before Christmas, and we decide to celebrate both occasions at once. Fifteen years old, and I often grieve for all the childhood that he never seems to have had. He seems more sober, older, these last weeks. I see the two of them, him and Sigrid, together, seldom speaking, usually holding hands soberly, solemnly, almost . . . there seems little enough joy in them, but a sense of purpose now, and dignity. They don't smile a lot, yet they both seem happy. But almost middle-aged, somehow.

There is a little problem about the birthday celebrations. Sigrid wants a small party in the caravan, and the boys want a big piss-up at the canteen. We compromise: Sigrid will cook a meal for Stretch's friends from the donga – Vic and Jimmy, me, Ice-cream and Ray, then afterwards we'll go to the canteen for the piss-up.

A day or two before Christmas, the morning of the real birthday, in fact, when I give Stretch his present – a new transistor radio that I've found in the store to replace his battered one – he tells me his news.

'Going to move into the van with Sigrid,' he says, 'after Christmas.'

'Yeah, you might as well . . .' Might as well make the most of it. Life seems uncertain enough at the moment.

'I'll be sorry to leave here, though,' he says, not looking at me.

'You're mad,' I say, although I know what he means. 'When it comes to a room-mate, there's no choice between me and Sigrid.'

He smiles a little, and I give him a grin, slap him on the shoulder.

But I'll be sorry to see him go, all the same. The room will seem empty for a while. But, as Stretch says, better than nothing . . .

•

On Christmas Eve we shower and dress in clean shorts and shirts and walk down the track to the caravan park. The day is beginning to fade, turn quickly into night, as it does up here. No long summer twilights, but a sudden curtain at the end of the day. Stretch has been at the van all afternoon, keeping Sigrid company. In fact they're not often away from each other and I don't see much of Stretch at the donga any more. Most nights he sleeps at the van, and often eats there, too.

We crowd inside the caravan, and although it's a good big one, we make it seem small, because there are nine of us.

We cluster round the small table, and Sigrid brings the wine out of the fridge – a few bottles that we've found hidden away in the canteen store. The taste seems so foreign, after months of nothing but beer, that there's a real festive feel to it. Only Jimmy and Ice-cream drink beer from Ice-cream's esky. Sigrid has cooked *klopse*, a kind of meatball with capers and lemon sauce, a great panful. It's wonderfully succulent and tasty, particularly after the mess food, which is fast losing whatever variety it may have had before the wet. Ice-cream is much taken with the *klopse*, eats three platesful, with potatoes and yams and carrots, and, already a little pissed, grows verbose in praise of Sigrid's cooking, eyes rolling in his thin, brown face . . .

'A good cook's a treasure, mate,' he tells Stretch, leering at Sigrid who is warm and smiling and slightly flustered at the compliments. 'Look after her, mate, don't you ever forget that now . . .'

The dessert is Stretch's birthday cake, a chocolate cherry cake, and Ice-cream is devastated by it. He even absent-mindedly accepts a glass of port, which he downs like beer, and then hands back his glass for a refill. There's a new light in his eyes, and a look of respect verging on awe when he looks at Sigrid. Like most hard cases, he appreciates the basic virtues.

We sit for a while over cigarettes and coffee, out under the awning, letting the dinner settle, talking idly. Petra is close beside me, laughing at Ray, who is telling an obscene but hilarious story about his introduction to shearers' pool, the old outback game with two bob in and the first one to jerk off gets the pot.

Finally it's time to leave for the canteen, and we switch off the lights, lock the van, and walk slowly up the track by the light of a couple of torches. We seem to have split up into new groups.

I can hear Ice-cream somewhere behind me, telling Petra that she's 'a ripper'. I find myself walking beside Sigrid. The darkness seems to give us a feeling of isolation from the others, as if the night is a wall that guarantees privacy.

'Thanks, Jack,' she says, taking my arm. 'For looking after John.'

'Funny,' I say, 'hearing him called John.'

'He's John from now on,' she says. 'At least when we leave here.'

'We'd all find it a bit difficult to call him John, now, I think.'

'It doesn't matter,' she says. 'Later he'll be John. When we've gone.'

'When will that be?'

I feel her shrug. 'As soon as the strip opens and we can get a plane out . . .'

'Any idea where you're going?'

'Not really – maybe the west, Mount Newman, Tom Price . . . somewhere where they don't know us.'

'There'll always be someone who knows you – you know what the industry's like.'

She's silent a moment. 'I don't suppose it matters . . . it's a new start, that's all, that's what's important, isn't it?'

'I guess so.'

We're silent for a while, picking our way down the track. I take her hand to steady her, and for a moment I'm very conscious of her body close beside me, her faint perfume, the touch of her skin, the swing of her body . . . feel stirrings, and almost immediate guilt. Never mind.

'We had a kind of arrangement, you know,' she says after a while. 'Piet and I. We could both play around a bit, as long as the other one never found out.' Pauses a moment. 'The trouble was, we never worked out what would happen if the other one *did* find out . . .' Then: 'You know how old I am?'

'Twenty-seven, twenty-eight?'

'Thirty-two.'

'Not far out.'

'You might as well say it . . .'

'What?'

273

'That there's too much difference in our ages, that it won't last.'

'Christ,' I say, 'how do *I* know – I've fucked up my own life so badly I've got no right to make judgements . . .'

'I know it won't last forever,' she says. 'When he's ready to go I won't try to stop him. But it might last a year or so . . . it might last longer . . . It might last even ten years . . . and that's a long time, isn't it?'

'That's a *bloody* long time,' I say, putting my arm round her shoulders, feeling the tremors, 'That's a bloody eternity, sweetheart . . .'

•

Christmas at Carbine Creek.

It's rain and sweat and salt tablets as the thermometer climbs over the hundred degree mark . . .

It's hangovers and crushed whities scattered everywhere in the suddenly lush grass, half submerged in the red mud . . .

It's fights and laughter and drunks vomiting outside the canteen; turkey and chicken and plum pudding and custard in the mess hall where the air-conditioners no longer work . . .

It's a longing for the new year, and the end of the wet . . .

And over it all, over all the drunken gaiety and punishing boozing and loudness and sentimentality, there is a kind of suppressed gloom, a feeling somehow of loss and loneliness.

The truth is that everything here is so makeshift, so temporary, that Christmas is only a reminder that another rootless year has passed . . .

•

On Boxing Day, Petra and I spend the afternoon in the dim, hot little post office counting stamps and aerograms and money orders, checking cash, balancing the great cumbrous Form 100 that she can never seem to figure out. Her attention span is better than it was, but she still has lapses. Despite the heat, it's quiet and peaceful in the little building, and we take our time. When we finish we stay there a while, drinking lemonade, and talking a bit, getting slowly sleepier.

'Do you think you'll go home, Jack?' she says. She's perched on the counter, legs swinging, a dark form against the brightness of the window. 'You know, when the wet's over?'

'Christ knows . . .' It's something I've put off thinking about. Because this is such a temporary place, everything else, life itself, seems temporary. Which is fair enough, I suppose.

'If you don't go home, will you stay here?'

'This place? Christ, I'd rather be in the clinic!' Oddly enough, I probably would, too, the way I feel at the moment.

'If we're going to stay, I'd try and get a caravan . . .'

I don't say anything.

'Would you move in with me, if I got a van?'

'I suppose so.' It sounds so bloody ungracious. 'Of course I would. I just mean, I'm not going to stay anyway.' I hoist myself up on to the counter. 'What about you? When I go?'

'I'll go wherever you go . . .'

There's no arguing with that; and I'm not sure I want to. But I'm so uncertain of everything, I can't seem to make up my mind to do anything; I just drift . . .

I think about Stretch and Sigrid, and Western Australia. But I know it would be just another place like this. Oh, maybe bigger, better run, but basically the same. And whatever it is that I want, it isn't that . . .

I take her hand, lift it, kiss her fingers. 'Something will turn up.'

She leans against me, her hair brushes my face and I feel the weight of her shoulder against me. I feel so bloody *responsible* for her now, and I don't know if I want that, if I can handle it. But what can I do in the face of her certainty, her clear commitment?

'Come on,' I say, easing myself back down off the counter. 'Let's lock up and go and see Stretch and Sigrid . . .'

So we go and find them, sitting there quietly under the awning of their van, like an old quiet couple who have weathered a lot of storms and wars. They smile when they see us, and the day feels a little better.

•

'There's gunna be some sick men about soon,' says Vic.

The clouds have gone for a while, the sun is out, and he and Jimmy and I are brushing the mould from clothes and shoes and setting them out in the sun for about the fifth time since the wet began.

'How's that?' I ask.

'The beer's running out,' he says, working his brush carefully round the welt of a pair of shoes. 'Come New Year they're going to bar people from taking it away from the canteen – have to drink it on the spot.'

'Yeah?'

'My bet is they'll ration it soon – maybe a couple of cans a day. They always stock up for the wet, but this year, with nothing coming in at all, the odds are she'll run out.'

'Worry you?' I ask.

'Not us,' he says, looking at Jimmy, who's whistling over an old blue suit . . . 'We can live with it, eh, mate?'

Jimmy grins at him. 'I reckon.'

'You mean some of them can't?'

He says nothing for a minute, puts down the shoe, picks up its mate. 'There's blokes here that are used to their dozen or so a day. Shut them off, they'll be sick . . . You ever seen it?'

I shake my head.

'Alcoholics,' he says, 'you just shut them off like that . . . well, I've seen men go off their heads, even die.'

'Christ!'

'Oh,' he says, 'there's a bit of hard stuff around, they'll drink that if they have to, it'll keep 'em more or less sane, but they won't be happy . . .'

I shake my head. 'Going to be a great New Year.'

'Been to the shop lately?'
'No.'
'Sugar's been rationed. They're getting low.'
I raise my eyebrows.
'Someone's been stocking up . . . they're gonna brew their own when the beer runs out . . .'
'You're joking.'
'No fear.' He shakes his head. 'There's gonna be some real jungle juice about . . .'

•

On New Year's Day there is a big shindig out at the lake: water-skiing, stalls, races for the kids, a barbecue, the works. Everyone seems to be going. The sun is out, and it hasn't rained for twenty-four hours. We don't feel like crowds, any of us, so we borrow Ray's ute, the six of us, and head out to the Holes; Vic and Jimmy, Stretch and Sigrid, Petra and me. There's a carton of beer, bought a day in front of the restrictions, a big bag of sausages to barbecue, a couple of loaves of bread that Sigrid has made, a bottle of tomato sauce.

We're packed in the ute, Vic driving, the two girls in the front, Jimmy and Stretch and I in the back.

A mile or two out the road, the hot moist air rushing past, the ute bumping on the rutted gravel, Jimmy leans over to me, shouts in my ear.

'You want to go for a run some time, Jack?'
'A *run*?'
'Yeah . . . you know, *training*.' He's grinning at me like a small, battered madman, his fine silky hair flying about his head like a halo.

'*Training*!' I can't believe it. In the middle of the *wet* . . .
'Got to get in shape.'
'What the bloody hell for?'
He just grins, and turns away, laughing as the wind takes him in the face.

•

The Holes, by some miracle, are deserted. Everyone seems to have gone to the nonsense at the lake. We drive in, park by the bank, spread ourselves, stretch our legs. Vic takes up his usual position with his back against a tree, legs stretched, a can in his hand. Jimmy and I start to gather sticks for a fire.

It's so quiet here, so peaceful, that it almost – almost – reconciles you to the rest of the country.

I stop by Vic's tree with a bundle of sticks. 'Vic, why aren't there any Abos on the job?' I've never thought about it before.

He shakes his head. 'They won't have 'em on a mining lease . . . too much trouble.'

And I remember the Rodeo Bar in the Isa.

'What about the stockmen on the stations?' The lease is smack bang in the middle of Waverly Downs.

'Oh,' he says, 'you never see them, except when they're mustering, or come in for one of the dances that the squatters put on in the hall.'

'Aren't there any tribal ones left?'

He sips, meditating. 'No,' he says, 'I don't think so . . .' Sips again, puts his can down beside him, begins to roll a cigarette. 'Wiped out long ago they tell me.' He squints up at me through smoke. 'They were the Kalkadoons, see? Very fierce, very good fighters. When the squatters moved in with their cattle, well, the blacks speared a cow or two, just to see, eh? Reckoned they were better than scrubby kangaroos, see? Bound to be a bit of conflict . . .'

'What happened?'

'Oh,' he says, 'in the end, after the whites had shot a whole crop, after they'd speared a few whites, well, they rounded 'em up, shot 'em all . . .'

'Just like that?'

He stares out over the still water. 'Ask Nermutt to take you out past Mount Oxide some time. Took me once.' He looks up at me again. 'There's a whole bloody hillside there that's nothing but a boneyard . . . still see the bones . . . that's where they shot 'em.'

I shake my head, move over to where Jimmy has started the fire. It gives me the chills just to think about it.

Our ancestors . . .

Contemporaries, more or less, with my grandfather, I suppose. While he's out in the scrub panning gold in the freezing winter, the canny old Scots up here are slaughtering blacks. Not that we didn't do it in Tasmania, and made a fair job of it too . . .

We let the fire die down until there are plenty of red coals and grill the sausages. The girls slice the bread and we sit in the shade eating, drinking. Almost comatose, I lie back and stare at the lace of leaves and branches against the sky. Petra sits beside me, her knees drawn up, staring quietly at the pool.

It's strange, I spend a lot of time with her. Stay with her at least a couple of nights a week. The customs of the quarters say it's OK on weekends and the occasional night. Custom and usage. Any more than that, and I suppose someone would suggest we move out into a bloody van. So, we see each other, make love, are happy enough, I suppose, and it's true I feel something I've never felt about another woman . . . but I don't feel that thing that I'm sure Stretch and Sigrid have . . . a kind of total commitment, a unity that seems to enclose them like a bright cloud . . . It's the broken circles, the broken circles back home, that somehow keep me from it . . .

Somehow I've changed about the valley, about home. Maybe it's the old man's death . . . When Petra mentioned it . . . going home . . . it didn't seem quite so impossible any more . . . not completely impossible, but not wholly possible either . . . It's almost as if he left a gap, and it's waiting there for me to fill it . . .

There's nothing really to fear there, I suppose . . .

Nothing to *fear*? Have I been *afraid*? Afraid to go back?

I suppose so . . . Face it, killer, gutless again.

Petra seems a little moody today, and doesn't talk much. I close my eyes, then open them as I hear her get up. She moves away, aimlessly, kicking at the thin grass with her sandals. I close my eyes again. If I could only bring it all into focus. Once I start to think about her, about going home, everything seems fuzzy, unclear. I think of Petra, and everything else drifts out of focus; think of home and Petra grows unclear . . .

I wake slowly. Been asleep nearly half an hour. Look around. Vic is still by his tree. Jimmy and Petra are walking slowly by the edge of the bank, tossing twigs. They seem to be talking, very quietly. No sign of Stretch and Sigrid. He must have taken her up to the other pools. I think of them up there in the buzzing silence, alone with the red rocks, the overhanging trees, the blue waterlilies. It seems so right, so good, that they should be there, in that place, but I feel a stab of envy that it's not me and Petra . . .

I get up, break the spell, go and get another can, warming now, and sit with Vic. Somehow I seem to gravitate to him now, more than to anyone else. There's a quality of solidity, of permanence and sense about him that seems to draw me.

'I've been lying there,' I tell him, 'thinking about going home. After the wet.'

'Where's home?'

I tell him.

'You're lucky,' he says, looking at me calmly. 'Lots of people haven't got a place like that . . . they're still looking.'

'You and Jimmy?'

He nods. 'I suppose so.'

'There's a reason I can't go back . . . why I haven't been able to go back . . .'

He turns a little, moving his back against the rough bark of the tree's bole.

I don't really want to look at him at the moment. I look across the pool to where Petra and Jimmy are sitting, dangling their feet in the water. 'It's my family . . . See, my father . . . well, he's also my grandfather.'

He says nothing for a moment, turns back to the pool. Then: 'That's a hard one, mate, isn't it? How long have you known?'

I tell him. I tell him the lot. The night Nance told me, the wrist, the clinic, everything. And sit waiting while he sips and smokes, and frowns out over the pool.

'Listen,' I tell him, 'I know all that stuff about it not mattering, about being what you think you are, how you see yourself . . . but it doesn't work somehow in practice.'

'I know what you mean,' he says. Then he's quiet for quite a while. Then: 'Jack,' he says, 'I think you're kidding yourself . . . I think you're playing games with yourself, mate.'

I have to look at him then, and although his face looks much as it always does, there's an odd sort of sadness about his eyes, very deep, a long way below the surface, but there all the same.

'Listen,' he says. 'I'm nearly fifty years old. I've got no trade, no real skills. I was never more than an average pug. I'm not dumb, but I'm not real clever. I'm queer, and all I've got is Jimmy. And I'll never be any different to what I am now – just older.' He pauses, shakes his head a little. 'You've got brains, you had a good job, you're young, fit, you've got all those lovely years of football to look back on. You've got a lovely girl who'd cut her fucking throat for you. OK, she's got her problems, but that doesn't change things.' He leans towards me a little, reaches out, takes my forearm in his big brown hand and squeezes. 'Listen, Jack, you've got all that. OK, you've got a fucked-up family background, *and you can't do anything about it.* And you've got all that other stuff, Jack, what you really are, and you've got that lovely girl . . . and Jack, that's *all* you've got . . . it's all you'll *ever* have, Jack, there's nothing else . . .'

He holds my arm for what seems a long time. Then he lets go and sits back against his tree. He looks tired all of a sudden, and I have this chilly, shaky feeling despite the heat.

'Don't play games with it,' he says. 'You play games with it, it'll all just run away like water . . . and you'll be just like all the rest of us . . .'

I sit saying nothing. I don't seem able to move, to speak, anything. Just thinking, over and over again: Well, killer, you asked for it, you asked for it . . .

Vic raises his head, looks back towards the rock face, and I look too. Stretch and Sigrid are coming along the path and into the open, down the last of the slope. They're holding hands, as usual, and walking close together. They're a little flushed and disarranged, nothing much, more a kind of air about them than anything specific, and I know that somewhere up there among the silence and the blue waterlilies they've made love – the flavour of it still hangs about them like a kind of magic that transforms the day. And I feel like crying . . .

But Vic smiles and his sadness is gone, and his voice is rich and thick and warm. He looks at me. 'It almost makes you believe in something, doesn't it?'

•

All of us together again and, suddenly, as the sun begins to move down in the sky, dipping towards the trees at the top of the rock face, we are all together again really and properly, and everything has changed. We're suddenly cheerful and laughing and light, and the day has been recovered somehow.

We are clustered round Vic on the grass, smiling, smoking, talking a little, of nothing in particular, when Jimmy jumps up suddenly, his eyes wide and bright, his face suddenly childish.

'I'm gonna swim!'

In a moment he's out of his skivvy and shorts, and his light, pale, tightly muscled body is launched like an arrow from the bank, held a long moment like magic in the still air over the dark water. Then he is gone in a great splash, and water, white and fine, rises in a shimmering spray.

We watch as he surfaces, blowing, splashes, throws back his suddenly water-dark hair and dog paddles away. He turns ten yards out, treads water. 'Come on!'

We laugh. But suddenly Sigrid is on her feet, unbuttoning her thin cotton frock, unhooking her bra, stepping sedately out of her panties. Her body is very brown – except for the white bands at breast and buttocks – slim, almost frail, but very womanly, and quite lovely in the late slanting sunlight. Suddenly I feel affection and admiration and appreciation – all those friendly, unnameable things, without the selfish stab of desire . . . She smiles over her shoulder, steps to the bank, and dives in easily, without fuss, begins to stroke slowly out towards Jimmy.

I'm on my feet then, laughing, and as I pull my shirt over my head I see Petra is up, too, slipping out of her jeans and blouse, and her body – less tanned than Sigrid's, but taller, fuller, stronger, with her fine mounded breasts, straight back and long legs – seems as familiar as a happy dream. And I take her hand for a moment, squeeze, and she is gone, leaving the bank in a flat swimmer's dive and gliding seal-like through the dark water to join the others . . .

The water hits me like a warm, soft wall. I dive deep, open my eyes in the heavy brownness, drive myself forward, breath held a long time. Slowly out of the dimness come the long swaying stalks, pale and unreal, of the three pairs of waiting legs. I surface beside them, blow water, tread, look back. Vic is laughing, leaning against his tree trunk, as Stretch struggles out of his shirt, wrenching it over his cast. His shorts drop round his feet. He stands a moment on the bank, grinning, then launches himself feet first into the pool. The splash is enormous and when the froth and foam die, we see him standing – he is tall enough to stand – on the bottom, waving his cast above his head. He wades slowly towards us. When the water is up to his neck he turns, pushes himself off in a kind of one-armed backstroke towards us.

And we are there, all five of us, treading water, my arm around Stretch, his cast held aloft like a kind of rallying point, watching Vic.

He shakes his head, climbs slowly to his feet, peels off his T-shirt, drops his shorts, and stands a moment, big and brown and hard-muscled under his plumpness, a chieftain if ever there was one. Without his clothes he seems to achieve greater dignity than ever. Even his heavy, dangling genitals have a kind of primitive grace. He lowers himself over the shelf and into the water, and plows towards us with a slow, old-fashioned crawl. We cheer, and move toward him with a slow threshing of smooth, wet limbs and gather about him in the darkening water.

And in the laughing and the splashing we seem to make a new circle, a circle that can never be broken, a circle that will hold us safe long past this day, and long past the night that is deepening about us . . .

'What were you talking about to Jimmy?' I ask Petra.

The rain drums on the roof of the quarters, overflows from the guttering, gurgles down the pipes, splashes into the drains . . .

I'm lying on the bed, tired, but pleasantly so, after the day at the Holes. Ten o'clock, and soon time to go to bed, to start another Monday.

Petra seems restless; sitting in the chair, smoking too much.

'Oh,' she says, lighting another ciggie, 'he was doing most of the talking.'

'That's not like Jimmy.'

'Well, he was . . . he was talking about what he and Vic were going to do after the wet . . . where he wants to go, all that . . . and about being in gaol. He says he'll never go back there again . . .'

'I know.'

'You know,' she says, stopping by the bed, sitting down beside me, 'he's not . . . you know, an idiot or anything. When he talks he makes sense. He's just like everyone else . . . it's just that sometimes, now and then, one of the circuits seems to go wrong, and then he'll wander a bit, repeat himself, you know . . . but there's nothing really *wrong* with him . . .'

'I know. He just got scrambled a bit.' I take her hand. 'Listen.' She looks down at me. There are faint hints of some unease in her face – not lines, a kind of tension. 'What's the matter? Are you all right?'

She jerks her hand away, gets up, moves towards the table, turns on the trannie. The ABC is all it will get, and she turns it off in irritation.

'What's the matter? For Christ's sake, tell me.'

She comes back, sits beside me again, leans over, kisses me. 'I'm sorry Jack.' Smiles. 'It's just that I've run out of pills.'

'Jesus!' I have a sudden vivid recollection of Paddy lying, thrashing, on the floor of the corridor . . .

'It's all right, really.' She takes my hand.

'No, it's not. Listen, what about Margaret? Can't she give you some?'

She shakes her head. 'She hasn't got any lithium. She's got some largactil for emergencies, she'll give me some of those if I really need them.'

'But, Christ, we can get on the phone or the radio and get a plane to drop some.'

'We will – if I really need them. But listen, Jack, the doctor told me . . . it depends which part of the cycle I'm in . . . I might be in remission, anyway, and nothing will happen.'

'And if you're not?'

'There'll be plenty of warning . . . I'm not going to go off overnight.'

'Well . . .'

'Don't worry.' She lies down beside me. Smiles. 'I'm just a bit, you know, worried, that's all.'

'So am I.'

'Don't be. Think of something else.'

'Like what?'

'How about this?' Her hands move, and she touches me. 'And this . . . and this . . .'

In the familiar mysteries of the flesh everything dissolves, and, deep inside her, her mouth on mine, her hands clutching me, I seem to have completed another circle, somehow; to have arrived at some burning kind of homecoming . . .

●

A week goes by, and there are three days with no rain at all. It seems that the weather may be improving, that soon the strip may open. Three days of heat and sunlight and the mud is drying slowly, traces of dust are visible . . .

Then the rain again, solid, persistent, maddening.

Everywhere in the north it's the same. Creeks and rivers

impassible, roads washed out, homesteads isolated, helicopter rescues, families living on their roofs, and nothing anyone can do about it . . .

We are really an island here, in more ways than one. We are actually a bit elevated, a score of feet or so, and this little patch of a few square miles stands above the floods. But there is now an air of real gloom about the place, and the realities of isolation are catching up with us. The phones are still working, and the radio, but no mails coming or going; and the diet is restricted. Mainly we get stringy Queensland beef, roasted until it's almost grey, baked yams and dehydrated potatoes, canned two-fruits and custard. All the canned milk is reserved for the kids, and no one knows how long the dehydrated stuff will last. There is still plenty of tobacco, but tailor-mades are running short.

The beer is the great concern of everyone. Even those who don't drink much are catching the unease. We are all on a ration of two cans a day now, and they have to be drunk in the canteen. Someone – a TA – was caught trying to pinch Bully's beer and was badly beaten . . . Bully can still have as much as he likes, of course.

All the air-conditioners have been shut down now to save power. The generators are run on distillate, and stocks are low. If they run out altogether, then the mine will flood as the dewatering pumps stop and the water rises in the decline.

Ice-cream and Ray Nermutt disappear for three days just after New Year and then show up, tight-lipped but looking pleased with themselves. 'Been walkabout,' is all they will say. But the strange thing is, they seem to have plenty of beer now. The fridge in their room is always full, no matter how much is drunk. They share willingly, generously, with us, but everyone else has to pay. The price is two dollars a can, and I have the feeling it's going to go up soon. No one else sees how they replenish the fridge: it's a continuing mystery. But nowadays their room is locked tight when they're at work, and for the rest of the time one of them is always there . . .

The result of the shortage is that the hard cases drink their two cans and switch to spirits. There's apparently a whole lot of black Beenleigh rum in the store, bulk in barrels. Christ knows why they wanted to buy that much, but the hard drinkers are into it every night, and growing more and more savage. It's rough stuff, and almost lethal for men who normally drink nothing but beer. Each morning there are very sick men about the camp; absenteeism is high, and every night there are fights . . .

Today the payroll drop is due, and for some reason the miners decide to take the afternoon off and go out to watch it. The rain is light, little more than a drizzle, but the strip is still deep in red mud. Stretch and I go out with Curly to watch. Stretch is getting restless and, despite his cast, is back on light duties. Out at the strip fifty or sixty miners are grouped in the rain, shorts and shirts soaked, rain pouring down their faces, hair and beards slicked by the water. A couple of bottles of rum are being passed round, and it's evident that they've all had a few before they started.

The plane is late, as usual, but at last appears in the east, over the hills, just under the overcast. It circles once, then comes in for the drop. There's a great cheer from the waiting crowd as the red leather satchel, with something over three hundred thousand dollars inside, leaves the plane, and hurtles down like a bomb. It's quickly obvious that the satchel isn't going to land on the strip. Instead, it disappears into the thick low scrub at the southern end. Immediately the miners take off, splashing and skidding through the mud. The paymaster is there with one of the clerks, and he looks suddenly apprehensive.

They get into their car and skirt cautiously round the end of the strip.

In the mean time the miners, now copiously spattered with mud, are into the scrub, stumbling and jostling, looking for the satchel. It takes a surprisingly long time for them to find it, and now the rain is coming down harder, so hard that from where we stand we can hardly see the end of the strip. A sudden crush of men surges out of the scrub, and it's obvious that someone has found the satchel. We get a quick glimpse of red through the mud, then the man holding it is down, and someone else has it and is charging off along the strip. A roar goes up, and the rest are in full chase. It develops into a mad game of football, with scrums and rucks and packs, with punches thrown, kicks given. No goals, just the madness of possession of that bundle of money. Slowly it deteriorates into a mud-clogged scrambling brawl, with men so coated that they're unrecognisable. Slowly the number of miners prostrate in the mud increases; slowly the pace slows, the enthusiasms slip away until the men are all standing round in the rain, the mud washing slowly off them in dull red streaks. The paymaster is now in a fit of apprehension. But in the end one of the gasping figures breaks away, picks up the bundle, walks closer and hurls it in the direction of the paymaster, who catches it in his arms. Immediately his white shirt and face are splattered, and he drops the bag. The muddy figures on the strip begin to laugh; the laughter grows as the paymaster picks up the satchel, looks quickly at the seals, hurries to his car and races away skidding and fishtailing in the mud.

As Curly drives away towards the town I look back and see the first of the miners trudging back through the rain, swigging on their rum bottles, reeling and skylarking as they come.

●

There is little business now in the post office as there is no mail. But the money box on the public phone outside has to be cleared and telegrams have to be attended to. So Petra spends her days there still, mostly alone in the hot little building. I drop in as often as I can, and spend all my evenings with her now. Because I'm worried. She says she'll be all right, but she's growing very restless, and her attention span is notably shorter. There are traces of that pattern that was disappearing when I first met her . . . the sudden breaking off of conversation, the sudden movement from place to place, the leaving things behind – cigarettes, books, everything . . . and that growing irritation and restlessness . . .

But she won't go and see Margaret, won't ask for pills.

'I don't *need* them,' she says. 'Just *leave me alone*!' Then bursts into tears and apologises . . .

I talk to Margaret.

'It's no good,' she says. 'If she comes along and asks, I'll do what I can . . . but I can't just give out chlorpromazine for you to slip in her tea. And I can't give it to her by force.' She shakes her head. 'Jack, if she gets really bad, then call me.'

'Do you know what to do?'

She nods, 'I talked to the doctor on the radio after you came to see me the first time. There's nothing they could do even in a hospital – just let it take its course, if she won't take drugs . . .'

And that's a bloody great comfort.

So there's nothing I can do but wait and watch, and hope that it will go away . . .

Knowing that it won't.

•

The next day the ambulance pulls up beside the culvert where we're working, clearing flood debris, and Margaret gets out, comes over, beckons me aside.

'I've called the doctor in Mount Isa. He's going to put some lithium tablets in the next payday drop,' she says. 'Petra should be all right till then.'

'Thanks, Margaret.'

'Let me know if anything goes wrong in the mean time, won't you?'

'Sure.'

'I'm afraid this sort of thing's a bit out of my line.' She smiles wryly. 'I'm more used to broken bones and red-back bites and alcoholic poisoning . . .'

She picks her way through the rubbish back to the ambulance and drives away, wheels spinning a bit on the muddy road.

•

That night I tell Petra about the drop, but she doesn't seem very interested.

'I really think I'll be all right, Jack,' she says. 'I think I'm in remission . . .'

But there's a distracted air about her, and she can't seem to stay still.

•

If no one else seems very cheerful, Jimmy does. Christ knows why. He's on night shift, and this morning after breakfast I see him head off in shorts and sandshoes, jogging out along the road. He waves, smiles.

'What's he up to? Why's he so cheerful?' I ask Vic.

'He's always like that when he's in training.'

'But what the hell's he in training for?'

'Don't really need a reason, do you?'

But I have the feeling that there's more to it than that, that Vic isn't telling me all of it.

He's not the only one who's secretive. Ice-cream and Ray are getting more cloak-and-dagger about their beer cache, wherever it is. They make mysterious pick-ups nearly every day, but never at the same time. The old ute starts up at all hours of the day or night – maybe five o'clock in the morning, or lunchtime or midnight, or lunchtime again – and comes back with a load of cartons. Sometimes it's away an hour, sometimes half a day. I've an idea that they drive around a long time to make sure that no one is following them. I calculate they're taking well over a thousand dollars a week . . .

But Christ knows where they're getting the beer from. It's something like a miracle . . .

•

Stretch and Sigrid are spending more and more time with Petra. They go up to her room, go walking with her, take her down to the van, to the picture shows that are re-runs of the two or three movies we've had since early December. They don't seem to mind it when she's short with them, when she ignores them, when she gets up and leaves without a word . . . they treat her as they would a sick child. Which I suppose she is . . .

I find myself looking for excuses to stay away from her. God knows I don't really want to, but I can't bear to watch her coming apart . . .

•

In some sort of self-defence, a kind of escape, I go running with Jimmy.

We head off one afternoon when he knocks off work, out along the road, cut across towards the lake. For the first mile I find it hard going, my stride uneven, my breathing ragged, a stitch starting in my side. Then, as we approach the wide plain that surrounds three sides of the lake, as the hilly ground gives way to flats and the clumps of spinifex disappear, I begin to fall into the old rhythm.

It's a remarkable thing. Everything suddenly drops into gear: shoulders, arms, legs, all moving properly, all coordinated; your breathing flattens out, eases, your mind seems to withdraw a little from your body, and you seem to be watching yourself from some place just above your head, near your left ear . . .

Everything is so smooth, so easy, and it seems that you can go on for miles and miles . . . and of course you can . . .

I follow Jimmy, a couple of paces behind. We cover about three miles round the lake's edge, past the launching ramp for the boats, and swing wide round a hummock and start back. Jimmy's still breathing easily, as if he were doing no more than a slow walk, and his knotted legs swing effortlessly, carrying him over the rough ground.

By the time we reach the camp I'm buggered; the rhythm has gone over the last mile, and the whole thing is pure agony. But he's fresh as a daisy . . .

As we head down for the showers with our towels, I ask him, still breathing a bit raggedly: 'Jimmy, what the bloody hell is this in aid of, anyway?'

He grins, winks at me from his battered face. 'You'll see, mate, you'll see . . .'

And he won't say any more. Life is getting to be full of bloody mysteries.

•

It seems that the wet has been with us forever. Already it's February, and no signs of improvement. The word is that there's a great deal of worry now about the distillate shortage. Everything but essential equipment has been shut down. The mill has gone to day shift only, and the big stockpile of concentrate has stopped growing quite so fast across the road from the mill.

Thursday is payday, and the payroll is dropped on Wednesday afternoon. That night, Margaret comes down to the donga, knocks on my door.

'Come in.' I hold the door open for her. She looks a little washed out, tired. There have been a lot of calls from the town, I know – kids sick, mothers edgy and anxious.

She hands me a packet. 'Here, you'd better have these . . . the lithium pills.'

I raise my eyebrows.

'I tried to give them to Petra – she wouldn't take them.'

'Why not?'

'I don't know. She just says she doesn't want them.'

I sigh, take the pills. 'I'll go up and see her.' I look at Margaret. 'She's not getting any better, is she?'

She shakes her head, 'You want to go up now? I'll give you a lift.'

It's not raining, and the night is filled with cloud-broken moonlight, the loud sounds of frogs and cicadas and Christ knows what.

There's a light in Petra's room. I knock, go in.

She's lying on the bed, smoking, her hair spread like a dark fan on the pillow. Her clothes are creased, and there are sweat marks under her arms. She doesn't look at me.

I go and stand beside her, offer her the packet. 'Here's your pills . . . you'd better start taking them, hadn't you?'

She shakes her head, moving it back and forth on the pillow, not looking at me.

'What's the matter? Why won't you take them?'

'I don't need them . . . I'm getting better.'

'You're *not* getting bloody better, you're getting worse.'

She stares sullenly at the ceiling, sucking on the cigarette.

'Look, people are doing their best for you – why don't you get off your bum and do a little bit yourself?'

She turns her head to look at me then, and I swear the look in her eyes is pure hatred. 'Leave me alone,' she says. 'Just take your bloody pills away, and leave me *alone* . . .'

So I put the pills on the bedside table and storm out. But I only get as far as the verandah. I turn and go back in.

'I'm sorry,' I say. 'Look, I won't say any more about the pills. If you don't want to take them, that's your business. I'll just sit here quietly for a while. Is that all right?'

She doesn't say anything, still doesn't look at me. I go over and sit in the armchair, pretend to read a three-month-old magazine. After a while she gets off the bed, makes two cups of coffee, brings one to me, rests her hand on my shoulder.

'I'm sorry, Jack,' she says.

'It's all right, love . . .'

She goes and sits on the bed, lights another cigarette. But in a moment or two she stubs it out.

'Do you want to go for a walk?' I ask her.

She shakes her head.

'Listen,' I say, after a while, 'you want to go out tomorrow night? They're opening the bar up here at the quarters for the night. There'll be music, people . . . What say we get Stretch and Sigrid and have a night out?'

'I don't care,' she says.

'You'll come, though?'

'If you want to,' she says.

A little later, when I leave, the pills are still in their packet on the table. Neither of us has mentioned them again.

•

No rain the next day – broken cloud, fleeting sun, sticky warmth. The workday drags on and, despite the let-up in the weather, there is an air of foreboding about the place. A time for omens, maybe; lions whelping in the streets, all that sort of stuff. But nothing happens. Payday, and we all go to the canteen, drink our two cans, and I try to cheer up. Vic is thoughtful, Jimmy talkative. Ice-cream and Ray are back at the donga, attending to business.

After tea, we shower and clean up, drink a can with Ice-cream. He won't charge us anything, just winks and says 'plenty more where this comes from'.

Eight o'clock and I head off up the track to collect Petra. We're to meet Stretch and Sigrid in the bar.

Petra's ready and waiting. She seems more cheerful than she was yesterday. She kisses me affectionately, talks quite brightly about nothing in particular. But she seems restless, and the package of pills still sits unopened on the bedside table. She fiddles unnecessarily with her clothes, changing into a dark-green linen skirt and a cream blouse, puts on a little lipstick, which is about all she uses.

Inside the bar we see the other two waiting. They're sitting in a far corner of the room, their glasses of beer in front of them. It's strange now to see beer in a glass. Tonight there has been a general dispensation, as much beer as you want to drink. Maybe it's the signs of the weather clearing, maybe they've reassessed the stocks. Whatever, it's made people seem a bit brighter. Sigrid looks very attractive tonight, and younger than usual. She's wearing a dark-brown dress of some thin, rustling stuff, and her hair is brushed and shining. Stretch looks much as usual: his new serious self with scars and broken nose. He still has his cast on, but it should be coming off soon.

There's muzak from the speakers, and soft lights, and women in dresses, and it's almost possible to imagine we're in some civilised place. The two Japanese trapped by the floods are here in their dark business suits and white shirts, sipping their beers and smiling toothily at everyone.

We start on our second drink, and the place begins to fill up. The level of noise is rising, and the air is thick with cigarette smoke.

I see Sigrid tense a little, and Stretch goes very still. Turning my head I see that Piet has come into the bar. But he doesn't look at us after the first glance; instead, he joins a small group of staff drinkers in the far corner.

It's mostly staff here, all the office staff, engineering and mining people, a few wives from the village. Margaret is at the bar with Beagle Boy, who grins and waves to us. No grudges there.

'Well,' I say to Stretch and Sigrid, 'it won't be long now, I suppose. Before you're off.'

She smiles and looks at him. He smiles back.

'We're going to have a few days in Sydney first,' she says. 'A kind of celebration.' She looks very happy.

'What are you celebrating?'

'Everything,' she says, still smiling.

'Ever want to go home again? Back to Germany?'

'I used to,' she says. 'I still miss Hamburg. But no, I don't think I'll go . . . not for a long time, anyway.' And she looks at me, and I know what she's thinking. There's a trace of sudden sadness in her face. When it's over, she's thinking . . .

Stretch seems to sense it, smiles his new, much older smile, reaches over, touches her hand. He's always seemed much older than his years; now he seems fully and finally adult. And I like him very much.

'What about you two?' asks Sigrid. 'Where are you going?'

I look quickly at Petra, shrug.

'Not going to stay here, are you?'

'No.'

'We'll go wherever Jack wants to go,' says Petra, almost sharply, and gets up to go to the lavatory.

Our eyes follow her through the crowd.

'Will she be all right?' says Sigrid.

'Buggered if I know . . .'

In a little while we see Petra across the room again, talking to Margaret and Beagle Boy. She takes a cigarette, puffs, butts it out after a few draws. As she moves on I can see Margaret frowning saying something to Beagle Boy. Petra doesn't come straight back, but wanders from group to group, stopping here and there, talking. One of the men from the office buys her a drink, and she stays to drink it.

She comes back at length, sits down, lights another cigarette.

'The Caribous are coming next week,' she says. Funny, a fortnight ago no one had ever heard of Caribous; now every office girl knows all about them. They'll be hauling distillate in drums. Even with the weather on the improve – if it stays that way – it will be weeks maybe before the roads are open.

Suddenly Petra's gone again, leaving her cigarettes on the table, moving quickly across to the bar to speak to some woman I don't know, one of the office people.

'She's talking a bit more tonight, isn't she?' I ask the others, who nod. It seems to me that she is beginning that terrible wind-up, the time of mounting activity, the build-up that I saw in Paddy, the build-up that leads to that shattering climax.

'Still not taking her pills?' asks Stretch.

I shake my head, and we are silent for a while.

It's after ten, and the room is crowded now. It seems a lot of the men have left the canteen and come up here. There are faces I barely know, mostly belonging to men in shorts and shirts, sandals, T-shirts. The noise in the bar is very loud now.

Petra comes back, sips at her drinks, smokes a little.

'I'd like to go into Mount Isa, shopping,' she says to Sigrid. 'When we can. You want to come?'

'All right,' says Sigrid. 'If we're still here.'

'That's right,' she says. 'You're leaving aren't you?'

Then she's gone again.

I can hardly bear to watch her now. She seems much worse than she ever was in my time at the clinic.

The others are silent too, and we're a very quiet island in all the noise. After a while Stretch gets up, goes to the toilet. When he comes back he is frowning a little.

'I can't see her anywhere,' he says.

I look around, but it's hard to be sure in the crowd.

'Maybe she's in the loo,' says Sigrid. 'I'll go and look.'

She's back soon, shaking her head. 'Maybe gone back to her room, do you think?'

Anything's possible. So I go and look.

The window is dark. I use my key, turn on the light. Empty.

Back in the bar I stand for a moment by the table. It's been half an hour. 'I'd better have a look around.'

'Where?' asks Sigrid.

'I don't know. Anywhere, everywhere.' The worry is growing, building in me. 'Listen, don't worry. She's just wandered off. She can't be far, I'll find her . . .'

They look worried too, as I leave them, push my way through the throng of bodies, the eddies of cigarette smoke.

I work my way carefully round the room, looking in all the corners. Nothing. Along the bar. Piet looks through me as I go past.

There's another door at the back, by the lavatories, and I push through it, out into the night. It's bright moonlight, with only a few scattered clouds, and light enough to read by. I'm on a path that leads along the side of the building, past the backs of the rooms. Everything is quiet out here, still. There is only a faint distant hint of the noise in the bar.

I stand there, light a cigarette, looking out over the strip of rough lawn to where the ground falls away, towards the gulley, the scrubby plain that ends in the golf course. The shadows are hard and dark among the small trees, the ground silver, everything looking odd and foreign and moon-bent.

As I toss away the butt of my cigarette I hear an odd noise from somewhere off in the scrub; a kind of muted thumping. It only lasts a moment. Then nothing. But it's too close to be a roo, and no one goes out into that scrub: it doesn't lead anywhere. So I walk slowly across the grass, towards the broken shadows. A feeling that is something like fear, a great apprehension, is beginning to grow in me. Suddenly, I'm trotting, then running, my feet not making much sound on the grass.

In a moment I'm stumbling over the broken ground, slipping as my feet hit the loose stones that cover the earth. Then into the trees, thudding uncertainly through the shadows, branches scratching at me. I stop for a moment, my breath loud in the still air, trying to hear something, anything.

To my right, towards the slope of the little hill . . . I'm not sure if it's anything at all . . . a kind of low whispering, a scratching . . . or nothing . . .

But I begin to move that way, more slowly now, walking, looking carefully about me.

And as I break free of the trees and into a clearing I see it. For a moment things are not clear; a small cloud is passing over the face of the moon and it's no more than a low clump of something that moves and writhes, close to the ground. Then the cloud passes, and I see that it is not one but several shapes, human. I stop, rooted to the spot. Something white, something moving . . .

There are three of them, and they have her on her back on the ground. Her skirt is gone, a dark anonymous strip on the silver ground, and her legs are pale as flesh can be. Two of them, heads bent, are leaning over her shoulders, one holding something in her mouth to stop her screaming. The third is between her legs, leaning down, hands inside the torn blouse . . . He is facing away from me and I can see that he is naked from the waist down, his pale buttocks clenching and pumping in the moonlight.

I'm running then, stumbling forward over the uneven ground, my mind a sudden panic of rage and fear and hate, and my hands are hooked ready. I know that I'm going to take him by the throat and squeeze until he is still and no more clenching and . . .

They hear me coming, and for a moment I see his face turned towards me in alarm, a face I know, brown bearded, teeth very white in his panting mouth . . . I know the face, the receding blond hair, have seen it, will never forget it.

Then one of the others jumps to his feet and I meet him and hit him once and he isn't there anymore. Then my foot hits a loose rock and I sprawl forward, hit my head on another rock, scrabble, trying to get to my feet, and then I see the one rise from between her legs and move towards me, and his legs and hips are bare and pale except for the dark shoe that swings at me . . .

I roll away and it glances across my temple. The pain shoots through my head . . . rolling, rolling, but not fast enough, and he is on me again, his foot swinging again, and I can't watch it. My eyes are on his penis, still erect and engorged, standing evilly in the moonlight, as the boot hits me behind the ear and my head explodes in a welter of red, surging pain and then there is nothing . . .

•

I come to, bleeding against Sigrid's dress as she cradles my head. Stretch is kneeling beside me with a damp cloth, wiping my face. I put up a hand, feel cuts and gravel rash where I have fallen, rolled. My head is a sea of pain. Nausea wells up, I turn aside and vomit. Spit, try to speak.

'It's all right, mate,' says Stretch.

'She's all right,' says Sigrid.

I try to struggle upright, and go out again.

The next time I come to, I'm lying on my bed in the donga, and Vic is there, standing massive and foreshortened above me. There's a cold feeling on my forehead, and I feel very sick. The sickness is not all from my bang on the head, but from the last vision before I blacked out. Before I can think much about it, I pass out again.

•

I wake slowly, the next time, my head thick, confused images moiling through my mind. My mouth is foul, and my closed eye is sticky. The events of the last night seem very distant, fuzzy. Only slowly do they come into focus. Finally I open my eyes. I'm in my bed in the donga, and Vic is lying on the other bed reading a western.

I stir, and he looks at me, sits up, puts down his book.

'How you feel?' He gets off the bunk, comes over.

'Fucking awful.' I try to sit up, but he presses me back.

'Stay where you are. I'll get you a cup of tea.'

I lie quietly, my eyes closed against the sunlight that spills in through the open door. It's hot already, and my headache is coming back. Margaret must have knocked me out with something. I realise that my mind is shying away from thinking about last night, about Petra. Instead, I find that I'm thinking about the old man. I realise that, despite everything, I loved him very much, that I miss him, that one day I'll have to do my grieving. And I realise something else, too: that, by dying, he's made it possible for me to go home. If I want to. Because, no matter how much I loved him, I could never go back while he was there, never face him, look him in the eye . . . and of course he knew it . . .

Vic comes back with a big mug of hot, sweet tea, props me up against his arm and puts it to my lips. I sip a bit, and feel the warmth clearing away the cobwebs. My headache is sharper now, but somehow better; my head a little clearer.

'How's Petra?' I take the mug, settle back. Vic squats by the bed.

'She's all right,' he says. 'Margaret's shot her full of something, and she's sleeping. Her mouth's bruised from where they jammed a singlet in it to shut her up, and she's got other bruises and scratches, mostly from the rocky ground, but she's all right.'

'What about . . . you know, the other, what they did to her?'

He shakes his head, oddly a little embarrassed. 'Nothing, a little bit of bleeding that stopped quickly . . . no real harm done.'

'I'd better go and see her.'

'No,' he says. 'Not today. No visitors for her for a day or two, and you've got to stay flat on your back for a bit.'

And the truth is that for some reason I don't really want to see her, not just now . . .

'What happened? Last night, after I copped the boot?'

He settles back on his heels, leans against the other bed, begins to roll a smoke. 'You were lucky,' he says, 'both of you. Stretch and Sigrid followed you out. They thought Petra might have gone to the van, and they wanted to borrow a car and find out. They were only a minute or so behind you when they came out the back door. Saw you break into a run, and they ran too . . .' He pauses, lights his cigarette, squinting against the smoke. 'The bloke who kicked you – Beach is his name – Stretch collected him, hit him a beauty across the face with his cast, laid him out. The other ones ran, but Stretch got a good look at them, recognised them. Sigrid – sensible girl – ran back to the bar as soon as she saw there was trouble, got a couple of men to come – one of them was Piet, oddly enough – and Margaret. Piet took charge, went after the others, the ones who ran away.

'What happened then?'

'Then you came to, went out again. They carried Petra to the dispensary, you back here.'

'And the others – Beach and the two who ran away?' I begin to feel something very deep and nasty stirring a long way down when I think of them . . . Beach, I won't forget him, ever – the way he looked there in the moonlight, and that boot exploding against my head . . .

'Beach,' he says, 'they locked him in the cool store behind the quarters. Piet and Stretch and a few of the others went after the other two, no-hopers named Kelleher and Bryant . . . found them trying to pinch a Landcruiser from the carpark . . . Christ knows where they thought they were going.'

'Where are they now?'

'Both of them locked in an empty room in the bottom row of dongas.'

'Is the strip open yet? When are the police coming out?'

Vic says nothing, and I look at him sharply. It hurts my head. He sighs. 'We haven't reported it.'

'What?'

'Think about it a minute, mate. This flood is in the news all over the country. A rape investigation in the middle of it all? OK, so they won't put her name in the papers. But she'll still cop it all. You want her to go through that? The way she is?'

He's right, of course. 'But what about medical reports, doctors, they'll have to report it to the police?'

'What doctors? Margaret says there's no serious harm done to anyone. So who's to know about it? Certainly not any doctors or coppers.'

I think about it for a moment. It seems all right. 'But what about those three bastards that did it?'

He smiles then. A smile of a kind. Not a nice one at all. 'Oh,' he says, 'don't worry about that. They'll be looked after.'

I look at him steadily. 'When?'

'Tomorrow.'

Tomorrow's Saturday. I realise that it's Friday today. 'Why aren't you at work?'

'Took a sickie.'

'Jimmy?'

'Gone for a run.'

There doesn't seem much to say. It all seems so neatly tied up, organised. But I don't want to think about it. I'm not sorry that I'll have to wait for a day or two to see Petra. And I start to feel suddenly tired, very tired . . . my eyelids start to close, and the last thing I do before I go to sleep again is wonder if Vic put something in the tea . . .

•

I wake again later in the day, when the sun is low in the sky, and the brightness no longer hurts my eyes. Lie there dozing for half an hour or so, not thinking about anything much. Towards five o'clock Stretch comes in, gangling and concerned, with a covered bowl of soup that Sigrid has made for me. He props me up, awkwardly, almost blushing, but very solemn.

'How's your arm?' I ask him. 'Where you hit that cunt last night?'

'All right,' he says, swinging it round to show me.

'They tell me you and Piet took charge a bit?'

He grins then. 'Yeah. Bit funny, that. He was almost friendly.' He shakes his head. 'He walloped those two a bit when we caught them.'

'What's happening? About the place? You know, the powers that be?'

'Nothing. Oh, everyone knows what happened, but they're keeping quiet . . . Piet talked to the manager, I think.'

And I know how it is, too. What they call the 'informal organisation', the grapevine. They all know, but because it's unofficial they don't have to take notice. As long as someone's looking after it, and as long as it's kept quiet . . . but who *is* looking after it? And what *is* going to happen?

Stretch stays for an hour or so, until Margaret arrives. She looks me over carefully, peers into my eyes, all that stuff, changes the bandage on my head. Stands up, looks at me.

'You'll do,' she says. 'You must have a head like a brick.'

'What about Petra?'

'She'll be all right.'

'Yeah, but what *about* her?'

'No real damage,' she says. 'Cuts and scratches, bruises, she'll be stiff and sore for a bit. A little bit of vaginal bleeding, but nothing much, no stitches or anything needed. Semen in the vagina – the one who kicked you was second in the queue – but she's on the pill, so no problem there . . .'

She's so cold-blooded about it that I feel a little sick. I suppose thinking of *that* – those fucking animals shooting off inside her, and her lying there not being able to do anything – that dark rage is still stirring deep down, and I know that sooner or later, maybe when the dope wears thin, it will come to the surface . . .

'When can I see her?'

'You can't.'

'What do you mean, I *can't*?'

'She's not here any more. A plane got in this morning, and I sent her back to the Isa. They'll look after her there.'

I'm stunned, speechless.

She sits down on the bed, suddenly much softer, less brusque. 'It's the best thing, Jack. It's not the rape – that's over, she'll take no harm, and no one in there will know about it. It's the other . . . the way she is, the pills, all that.' She puts her hand on mine. 'I just don't know enough to treat her, I haven't got the drugs. Oh, I talked to the doctor on the radio, I shot her full of chlorpromazine, but that's only a stopgap . . . she's got to have proper treatment . . .'

And I know that she's right.

'And better sooner than later,' she says. 'Get her out of this bloody place.'

'What will happen to her now?'

She stands up. 'The doctor thinks they'll keep her for a few days, a week or so. If she's well enough to travel, they'll put her on a plane home, with a nurse. Her own doctors, her family . . . she'll be better off.'

And back to Purple Brewster, I think, and Johnny Cash, and all the little old ladies and their weekly shock treatments . . . and maybe they'll plug Petra into a power point again, and blast her brain cells once or twice more . . .

'You know what they brought in on that bloody plane?' says Margaret, standing at the door. 'Twenty-six and a half cartons of beer. No milk for the babies, no medical supplies, nothing like that. Twenty-six and a half cartons of beer . . .'

'Why twenty-six and a half cartons?'

'That's all they could cram in around the pilot . . .'

And suddenly both of us are laughing, laughing and laughing, laughing until we can't breathe, can't speak, can't see properly . . .

The first of the few, the lone Beechcraft on its errand of relief . . . and the lone pilot hemmed in by twenty-six and a half carton of whities . . .

•

I sleep well, deeply and dreamlessly, and wake slowly, feeling lethargic. Saturday, and with the new five-day week no one is working. I hear the usual day-off sounds from outside – footsteps passing and repassing the donga, voices, radios.

My head is still sore, but very little ache left. I'm lucky that the bastard was wearing shoes and not steel-toed safety boots. And that I *have* got a hard head. Vic brings me breakfast on a tray, and a couple of pills. He seems quiet and thoughtful.

'How you feeling?' he asks, standing looking at me.

'Not too bad.'

'Feel like getting up later?'

'I guess so. Why?'

He shakes his head. 'Just a little job to do.' He won't say any more.

A little later Margaret comes in, gives me a quick check over. 'You'll be good as gold in a day or two.'

'Have you heard anything about Petra?'

She nods. 'Not much. She's all right, though.'

'What are they doing with her?'

'I'm not sure. They know what they're doing, though. They'll get her back on an even keel, first, then send her south.'

'When?'

She shakes her head. 'I don't know.'

'You think I could go into the Isa and see her?' I have the feeling that if I don't do something, make some move, she'll just drop out of my life again. And I don't want her to think, just because of what happened, that I've abandoned her . . .

'I don't think so,' says Margaret. 'There aren't many seats on the planes, only three a flight, and there are lots of people in front of you. She'll be gone before you can get there.'

'Could I phone her?'

'Listen, Jack, I don't think they want her to have any calls or visitors for a while . . . till she's better. OK?'

'OK.'

'I'll see you tomorrow. You can get up if you want to, you know.'

But I don't really feel like it somehow. After she's gone I just lie there dozing. It's close to eleven o'clock before Vic and Ice-cream come in.

'Come on, mate,' says Vic. 'On your feet, a little bit of urgent business.'

'What business?'

'You'll see.'

Neither of them will say any more. They bustle about, getting me on my feet and dressed. The bandage is gone from my head and has been replaced by a big strip of plaster.

Vic looks at me. 'Come on . . .'

Outside the sun is bright after the dimness of the donga and it hurts my eyes. Ray's ute is parked at the end of the row, and we get in. Ice-cream starts up, drives out on to the road that leads to the mine.

'Where are we headed?' I ask Vic.

'Not too far,' he says. 'You'll see.' They are both very quiet, withdrawn.

Ice-cream turns off the road and swings down a track to the right that leads towards the lake. Half a mile in he parks in the sparse shade of a small coppice of trees. There are several other vehicles there, and I'm getting very curious. But I know that it's no use asking any more questions.

We leave the ute and the shade and walk along the track, now little more than a thin trail of gravel between the thinning trees. Ahead looms a high, broken, rocky hill – a kind of bluff, gashed with small gorges. I know now where we are going: to the narrow defile that used to be the bed of Carbine Creek before they dammed it to fill the lake.

Around the last bend in the track and I can see it, a high concrete wall between two shoulders of rock. The gulley, filled with loose, water-worn shingle, widens a hundred yards below the dam and the old stream bed splits. There is a small island in the middle, a cluster of bulbous bottle trees, some undergrowth, the remains of an old paling shed, falling apart. There is a thin trickle of water in the channels, seepage from the dam and run-off from the rains. There's hardly a sound, only a few thin calls from the little birds darting in the tree branches.

Then, as we come closer, as the whole of the valley comes into sight, I can see that we are not alone. There is a cluster of perhaps twenty men, all from the camp: miners, millhands, TAs, drivers, mechanics. They're standing in a cluster beyond the hut, between the hut and the dam wall. And a few feet away from them is another group, smaller: only three men.

Beach, Bryant, Kelleher.

And I begin to have some idea of why we are here. And feel very queasy all of a sudden.

No one speaks as we approach. The three standing alone look calm enough, but apprehensive. As I watch, someone hands Beach a bottle – it looks like rum. He swigs, hands it on to Kelleher. They're dressed in the clothes they were wearing two nights ago, as far as I can tell; and Bryant and Kelleher, unbearded, haven't shaved.

The larger group breaks apart to let us through. Someone moves towards the three men, pushes them into line, takes the rum bottle from Bryant. They stand quietly, Kelleher, younger than the other two, clenching and unclenching his hands.

Vic stops, turns to look at me. 'They're all yours, mate.'

I look at him, incredulous.

'Go on,' he says. 'Get it done, get it over with.'

'What am I supposed to *do*?'

'Whatever you like. Anything short of killing or maiming them.'

'You're joking!'

'What do you think we're here for?' He's very cold and serious now.

'I can't do that . . .'

He takes my arm and draws me aside, speaks quietly. 'Listen, mate, you have to. I know you're still crook . . . But you're the one, and there's no getting out of it.' He nods towards Beach and the others. 'They're waiting.' And I see them watching me. 'Go on, for Christ's sake, it was your girl they raped . . .'

And then, for a moment, it all comes back to me, the happenings of that night . . . the vivid detail of it, Kelleher's face as he held her down, Beach coming out from between her legs, wet prick and all, and running at me and kicking . . .

And I walk towards them, not looking at Vic. I stand for a moment in front of Beach, looking him in the face, seeing again the way he looked that night, drunken and evil. He looks steadily back at me. And that dark sickness surges up from deep down, and I hit him in the mouth as hard as I can. He falls back on the shingle and I stand over him. All I can hear is my own rasping breath and the shingle creaking under his feet as he scrambles to stand up again and then he's standing there, a kind of sick look on his bloody face, waiting for the next one and his hands moving up a little instinctively to protect himself and being forced down again by the knowledge that if he tries that he'll be beaten worse than ever and I brace myself and start to swing and as I do I see the blood trickling from his mouth and the broken teeth as he licks at them and I turn away and stumble somehow past the big group of waiting men. Under a big bottle tree I drop to my knees and it all begins to come up, all the darkness and pain and disgust, and I vomit and vomit until there is nothing left and still the dry, horrible retching goes on, tearing me apart . . .

And then Ice-cream is beside me, holding me, his arm round my shoulders.

'There, there,' he says. Then: 'Here, mate, take a drink of this, it'll settle you down.' And he puts the rum bottle to my mouth and I suck at it. The raw, dark spirit burns my guts all the way down, but in a minute or so I feel better and I wipe the water from my eyes and wipe my mouth, and spit.

'Listen, mate,' says Ice-cream, his arm still round me, his dark, hard-bitten face close to my ear. 'Listen, this isn't for *you*, you know, all this,' and he jerks his head back towards the others, 'this is for *us*! We've got to *live* in these fucking places . . .'

And then I hear it, from behind us, a solid chunking, like a butcher's cleaver sinking into a side of beef, and I look over my shoulder to see Vic standing in front of Beach, holding him up with one hand and hitting him with the other . . . hitting him again and again . . . and the solid chunking sound goes on and on, and finally he lets Beach go, all battered and bloody, Beach falls to the ground and doesn't move. Vic moves on to Bryant and the chunking sound begins again, and I can see that Kelleher is crying now, his eyes closed and the tears running down his face.

I get to my feet somehow and begin to stagger away towards the track. Ice-cream is with me making soothing noises, and keeping his hand on my arm. Behind us that awful sound slowly fades.

Back at the ute I stop and lean against a tree.

'What happens to them?' I ask. 'Afterwards?'

'We'll clean 'em up, give 'em a tot of rum, and they'll be on the first plane out.' He spits. 'They'll never work again on any mining lease anywhere in this country. They're in all the black books now. And if they happen to sneak in anywhere, sooner or later they'll have an accident. And they know it.'

'Listen,' I say. 'Drive me back to camp, will you?' I'm feeling suddenly very tired, and my head has started to ache again.

We don't speak on the way back. I lie down on my bed, the door shut tight despite the heat, shutting out the day . . .

•

With the arrival of the RAF Caribous from Richmond air base, via the Isa, we seem to have become part of the real world again. Yet, oddly, we also seem diminished somehow, the boundaries reduced, drawn in, rather than expanded.

We all go out to the strip to watch them come in – Curly, me, the whole gang. They circle like two large, ugly, ungainly birds, then descend steeply, touch down on the red earth that is still damp despite days of sun, and haul to a stop in an incredibly short distance. The big doors at the rear of the heavy fuselages open, and our forklift trundles up the ramp of the first one to begin unloading the pallets of distillate drums. The cargo seems to be emerging from the plane's arsehole.

Christ knows how much this is costing the company. Plenty, I'm sure. But cheaper than having to de-water the mine and replace the drowned equipment.

There is a sudden shout from one of the gang. I look across the runway and see that after several pallets of drums the forklift has brought out a pallet of beer cartons. Not supposed to be there, strictly forbidden, but it's obvious that the RAF blokes have turned their backs for a moment or two in the Isa. They'll be heroes in the canteen tonight . . .

•

In the mess there is an air of excitement and bustle. Nearly everyone has been up to the canteen for a few beers already, and there'll be more later.

Despite the excitement, I feel flat, let down. I should be happy, God knows, at the prospect of getting out of this place. But where to go? What to do? I still shy away from the idea of going home. Sometimes I think maybe I should go west with Sigrid and Stretch. But then what about Petra? I can't just abandon her . . .

There is no sign tonight of Ice-cream and Ray Nermutt. Their room is locked and the old ute sits forlornly at the end of the donga. I ask Vic about them.

He winks. 'Gone. Snitched a ride on the last Caribou today.'

'Why?'

'Plenty of beer about from now on.' He grins. 'And I reckon there might be a few would get the idea they'd made a bit too much money on their two-dollar cans . . . so they shot through with their roll while the going's good . . .'

So, two gone, and the place a little smaller, a little emptier.

Suddenly Jimmy speaks. He has been quiet all through the meal.

'Now?' he says.

Vic nods.

I frown, wondering what's going on.

The mess hall is still crowded, but the evening meal is drawing to its close and there's a small crush round the tea urn. Jimmy stands up, moves away from the table, pushes into the crowd. He stands behind the man filling his cup, Nick van Ommen, a big Dutchman who works in the raise-climbing crew. As the Dutchman turns away, Jimmy jostles him, jogs his arm, spilling hot tea over the man's legs and belly.

'Hey! Look what you're bloody doing!' He's big, dark, good-looking and heavily muscled, with shoulder-length hair pulled back under a red headband. He looks in his mid-twenties, and very fit.

Jimmy looks up at him. 'You stupid frigging squarehead – you want to look where you're going.' And then, before the Dutchman can speak, can even open his mouth, Jimmy hits him twice – a quick, stinging left-right, and he's stumbling back with blood pouring from his nose, the teacup flying. He stops, carefully runs his hand over his face, looks at it, at the blood, and begins to move towards Jimmy.

But Vic is already moving in. He's gone from the table in a long, fluid glide, and now he's a long punch away from the Dutchman. But the mess manager, a pale heavyweight in sweated white ducks, is already between them, swinging an axe handle.

'You two want to fight,' he says, 'you fight outside.'

And Jimmy is laughing, watching van Ommen.

'Come on,' says the Dutchman. 'You want it so bad, let's go outside.'

'Any time,' says Jimmy, still laughing, shuffling his feet, loosening his shoulders.

'Outside, all of you!' says the mess manager.

Then the Dutchman, looking at Jimmy, looking down at him, begins to smile a bit wryly. 'You little runt,' he says. 'I bloody *ought* to hammer you . . .'

'You couldn't hammer a bloody tack,' says Jimmy. 'You're all piss and wind, just like all bloody squareheads.'

The Dutchman loses his smile. 'You'd last about two seconds, you skinny little fart!'

Jimmy is suddenly very still. When he speaks there's a kind of tightness in his voice. 'I've got a thousand bucks says I can last longer than you, squarehead.'

Everyone, even the mess manager, is silent now.

Then Vic speaks up. 'I've got a thousand more. How about it?' He looks at the mess manager. 'You hold the stakes?'

The mess manager nods slowly.

'Paynight?' says Vic, looking at van Ommen.

Jimmy rips open his shirt and begins to unbuckle a money belt.

'Well?' says Vic.

The Dutchman nods slowly, not taking his eyes off Jimmy. 'All right.' Then he turns his head to look at Vic for the first time, and there is a faint haze of puzzlement and uncertainty in his brown eyes. But he's committed now, and he knows it . . .

We go back to the donga, no one saying anything. I go in with them, into their room. Jimmy lies down on his bed, Vic and I sit on the other one.

Jimmy closes his eyes. 'How much altogether?'

'Two thousand from the Dutchman and his mates . . . another five gees, maybe, at about fives . . . who knows? I reckon maybe twenty-five thousand, plus our stake.'

'Then we can go, can't we?'

'Sure we can, mate.'

'And it'll be enough?'

'I reckon.' Then: 'Listen, Jimmy – you sure you can take him?'

Jimmy opens his eyes for a moment, looks at us, closes them again. 'Don't worry about it.'

I get up, go to the door. The tension is getting to me. Vic stands up, sighs, moves over behind me.

'You got a few bucks in your kitty, Jack?'

I nod.

'Get it on,' he says. 'There's plenty of money in the camp right now. Get yourself set, eh?'

•

We're sitting on a ridge, Vic and I, a long way out towards the lake. Work's finished for the day, and tomorrow is payday. Jimmy is having a final run, his figure a tiny distant dot by the lake's shore.

The sun is low in the west, and the long range of hills beyond the town is purple in the failing light. Vic opens a can of beer from his haversack, passes it to me, opens another, sips, sighs.

For a while we don't talk.

Then he breaks the silence. 'It's wrong,' he says. 'This thing, this fight. I know it, there's something wrong about it.' He grins at me a bit wryly. 'You know, like Jimmy's wronged hedge.' He sees my look. 'Oh, don't worry, Jimmy'll win all right. It's something else . . .'

He falls silent again, and we watch Jimmy's figure moving

along the distant shore in the deepening twilight. Finally Vic speaks again, not looking at me.

'I've always tried, ever since I was grown up, to do the right thing . . . you know? But I've never got anywhere, nothing's ever gone right. I'm nearly fifty, and all I've got to look forward to is more of the same.' He looks down at his can. 'If it wasn't for Jimmy, well, I wouldn't mind so much. But we've got to get away from this kind of life, this kind of place . . . he can't take it forever.' He looks up at me. 'You know, if we could get away to somewhere quiet, somewhere *permanent*, I think he'd be all right. It doesn't matter much where, just a bit of a house, nothing flash, a few acres, a bit of garden, maybe a few chooks and a cow . . . we could get a bit of seasonal work, we'd get by . . .'

He sighs and leans back against his rock, very big and solid and sad in the dusk.

'But we never seem to be able to get quite enough money together. Something always happens. Either the pay's not good enough, or we lose it in a card game, or the coppers grab Jimmy again . . .

'So this time, well, I've got to give it a try. Even if it doesn't work out. See,' he says, turning now to look full at me, 'I think I know, deep down, that it's never really going to work . . . that whatever we do, something's going to fuck it up . . . but I've still got to try, see?'

'Yeah, I see all right.'

'And this time, at least we'll have enough money . . .'

'You're that sure, are you? About the fight?'

He's silent for a moment. Then: 'I really feel bad about that Dutchman.' He looks at me. 'He's not a bad bloke you know.'

There seems nothing left to say. Darkness is flooding across the plain now, and Jimmy's figure is much closer, crawling slowly towards our ridge.

'You ever think about dying?' I ask Vic.

'Sometimes,' he says. 'Why, it worrying you?'

'I suppose so. I never used to think about it until the last year or so. Now I wake up every now and then in the dark and I get frightened. And with the old man going . . .'

He nods.

'What do you think happens, Vic? When we die?'

'Nothing, mate,' he says, watching Jimmy's approaching figure.

'Nothing?'

'That's it, mate. That's the best and the worst of it.'

'It's an awful feeling, knowing you're headed for . . . that, nothing.'

'You think so?' There's a curious concern, a deep interest in his voice now. 'Not so terrible. Listen, can you remember when you were, say ten years old?'

'Yeah.'

'Five years old?'

'Yeah.'

'A year old?'

'Maybe . . .'

'Remember the time before you were born?'

'Of course not.'

He nods then, as if his point is proved somehow. 'Well, that's how it'll be . . . just like the time before you were born.'

And as we sit there, waiting for Jimmy to cover the last hundred yards in the deepening darkness, I realise that somehow he might be right; that at least the idea has in it a certain comfort, a certain warmth, a certain expectancy even . . .

•

Payday comes round, just like everything else.

Vic and Jimmy aren't at the evening meal, and their donga door is shut. After tea Stretch comes down alone and we go to collect them. I knock on the door and Vic lets us in. Jimmy is lying on his bed, eyes closed. We sit beside Vic on the other bed. It's very hot in the room.

'You got your money on?' asks Vic.

I nod.

'What odds?'

'Fours.'

'That's not too bad . . .'

Jimmy stirs on the bed. 'Time yet?'

'Just about,' says Vic, and Jimmy opens his eyes, sits up, winks at us.

We all get to our feet. The room seems very crowded with all of us in there.

'Come on,' says Jimmy, grinning, 'let's go and get rich . . .'

•

There must be a couple of hundred men in the crowd that is gathered under the lights on the square of starved grass by the big movie screen with its flaking paint. The night is clear and starry, but there is a grumble of distant thunder from the north, and a few faint flickers of lightning low on the horizon. The wet seems finally to have withdrawn north to the Gulf.

We come out of the darkness, the four of us, pushing slowly through the crush to the place where the Dutchman is waiting for us. He's wearing shorts and singlet, and he looks very big and solid. Jimmy, in his hacked-off jeans and white shirt, seems by comparison almost thin and undernourished.

'You both ready?' asks the mess manager, who is also referee.

'Ready,' says van Ommen.

Jimmy nods and peels off his shirt.

'Right,' says the mess manager. 'You both know the rules . . . no rounds, no spells, nothing below the belt, no kicking, and she's over when one of you can't get up.' He waves his axe handle. 'You set then?'

They both nod, and the crowd falls back, leaving a wide space around them. There is a sudden silence in the night, broken only by the soft slither of feet on the grass as Jimmy and the Dutchman begin to circle about each other.

And then, suddenly, Jimmy moves; moves so fast that he seems to dissolve in a blur of pale flesh. He strikes the Dutchman twice in the belly, hard jabbing blows. Then, as the Dutchman's hands come down, Jimmy punches for the head – left, right, left again – and then he's away, as quickly as he has come. There's blood on the Dutchman's face. He falls back for a moment, then, head lowered a little, moves forward.

Jimmy waits. And when the Dutchman is close enough he drops his guard, rides the punch when it comes, slips inside it, hammers two swift punches to the belly, then two long lefts that open a cut over the Dutchman's eye. But as he moves away van Ommen catches him on the side of the head with a solid right that makes a sick *thunking* sound, and he stumbles for a moment. Then he's away again, dancing and weaving easily, and smiling.

For several minutes it seems to follow the same pattern. Jimmy slides in, lands a couple of punches, takes one, slips away again. He seems to be breathing easily still, while the Dutchman's chest is starting to heave a bit.

Then, as Jimmy moves in for another assault, the Dutchman swings a little wildly, catches him squarely in the ribs, and Jimmy grunts, seems to stumble, clinches. He clings for a long moment, head buried against the Dutchman, hammering. Then he breaks away, swinging one last punch at the cut over the Dutchman's eye.

But it seems somehow now that Jimmy is tiring, that the Dutchman's weight and reach are starting to tell. Jimmy seems a shade slower to attack, and he grimaces when the heavy punches strike him. The big man's pure animal strength and stamina seem to be carrying him beyond the power of Jimmy's punches, and for maybe ten minutes Jimmy takes more and more blows, his light frame jolting with the force of the bare-knuckle blows. His right ear is swelling badly, and his lip is gashed. Blood masks both of them now, and their skins are mottled with knuckled roses.

Then – quite suddenly – Jimmy is down. The Dutchman rushes in, but before he can connect Jimmy is up again and gone. And as the big man turns, Jimmy plants himself firmly, throws a long, looping right to the forehead that checks van Ommen; a left jab flicks blood from the cut eye, and a right loops up below the hollow of the jaw.

The Dutchman stands flat-footed a minute, seems to be on the point of collapse. They were very hard punches. Then he lunges, swinging. Two great blows strike Jimmy, lifting him almost from his feet, and the Dutchman is in and hammering, beating Jimmy down by pure weight and fury. Jimmy's face is very white under the blood. His lip is badly split, and his nose seems broken. His hands hang low and his shoulders sag. It seems then that only the strength in his sinewy legs, the bonus of all that running, keep him from falling.

The Dutchman pauses, then moves in deliberately. He swings once, and Jimmy catches the punch on his arm, rides inside it.

And then a strange mad kind of magic seems to take Jimmy. It's like nothing I've ever seen, ever imagined. There is a sudden glow in the air about him, an electric quality that seems to vibrate like a magnetic field about him. He ceases even to guard himself. His hands drop, his feet move squarer, and he lowers his chin. He moves forward slowly, catching and muffling the Dutchman's next punch; and he strikes the Dutchman twice just below the sternum, punches that seem faster than a whip crack, punches that seem to crackle with that mad electricity. And the power, the bull strength, seem to drain from the Dutchman's body. Jimmy rises a little on the balls of his feet, drops his right shoulder; he hits the Dutchman once under the ear with his right, and the Dutchman's legs buckle a little. I can see that his eyes seem faintly crossed. Jimmy hits him again in the same place, and pauses as the big man begins to stagger. Then he moves in deliberately, beating down on the protecting hands, striking again, again, again . . .

The first punch breaks the man's jaw.

The second – a short upward thrust with the heel of the hand – catches the nose and forces the head back.

The third – a long, wicked hook – takes the Dutchman in the throat.

Jimmy stands back then, trembling like an overdriven horse, wavering a little, smiling a blank and nightmare smile as he watches the Dutchman fall to his knees, moaning and gulping for breath. He waits – we all wait – for the big man to fall, to collapse. But he doesn't; he stays on his knees, groaning, blinded by blood, trying to clamber back to his feet.

The mess manager begins to move forward, but Vic touches

his arm, shakes his head, and he falls back again.

And gently, almost reverently, Jimmy steps forward, measures, swings once, hard and short, to the spot below the ear. And the Dutchman topples at last, lies on the trampled grass.

A great communal sigh rises from the crowd. I find that I have been holding my breath. Vic runs forward. But he stops a pace short of Jimmy, who is pale and bloody, trembling still.

'You all right?' asks Vic softly.

Jimmy nods. 'Just don't touch me for a while . . .'

'I know,' says Vic, and turns to the mess manager. 'Fair fight?'

'Fair fight,' says the mess manager, and begins to count out notes.

The Dutchman's mates are picking him up and carrying him away.

'Come on,' says Vic. He hangs the white shirt over Jimmy's shoulders. In a moment it is soaked with bloody patches. We follow, Vic and Stretch and I, as Jimmy walks steadily and delicately and unseeing through the silent crowd. And a hundred paces down the track, beyond the final telltale street light, he crumples and starts to fall. Vic, waiting, catches him, picks him up, carries him very gently towards the donga.

•

Inside the donga the air is hot and stale. Jimmy is supine on his bed. Vic kneels beside him. He works for a long time. First he sponges away the blood and sweat and dust, and washes Jimmy's bruised face. With an arm round Jimmy's shoulders he lifts him, tapes his chest with a wide strip of plaster. Then he cleans the knuckles and swabs them with mercurochrome, and tapes them too. With a needle and surgical thread from his kit he carefully stitches a cut eye. He pauses then for a moment, rocking back on his knees.

'You awake?' he asks.

'Yeah . . .' Jimmy's voice is hoarse and nasal, and he has difficulty in moving his puffed lips.

'I've just about finished,' says Vic. 'You want a drink?'

'Yeah.' Jimmy doesn't open his eyes.

Vic reaches behind him, lifts a tumbler to Jimmy's lips. Jimmy sips a little, lies back. 'How am I?' he says.

'Not too bad. A couple of ribs cracked, your nose gone again, a cut eye, a couple of teeth . . .'

'Knuckle's broke, too,' says Jimmy. 'I felt it go at the end there . . .'

'I know,' says Vic. 'Don't worry about it.'

'No.' Then: 'He took some stopping, didn't he?'

'He sure did.'

'But I wrapped him up, didn't I?'

'You bet, mate.'

'How much we get?'

'About twenty-seven grand, by the time everyone settles up.'

Jimmy opens his eyes for a moment. 'When can we get out of here?'

'As soon as you can travel.'

'Tomorrow then. Can we get on the plane?'

'I reckon.'

'We'll go south, eh?'

'Yes, mate.'

'And start lookin' for a bit of land?'

'Yes, mate,' says Vic. He gets to his feet, a big hard man, past his prime, in sweated singlet and old shorts. Stands there looking down at the thin battered body and the beaten puffy face. 'And we'll bloody well find it, too, mate.' He looks at Stretch and me, still sitting on the other bed, jerks his head. 'Come on, we'll let him rest a bit . . .'

Outside, the night smells fresh and clean. And I can't help thinking about what Vic said on the ridge, about doing the wrong thing, about things being the wrong shape. And I hope to Christ that he's wrong, that they'll find what they're looking for, whatever it is, even if it is only for a while . . .

•

The next morning we borrow Curly's ute, Stretch and I, and take the two of them out to wait for the plane. They're both dressed in clean, fresh clothes. The first time I've seen Vic in slacks and a proper shirt. He seems to look smaller in them, for some reason. Jimmy is in pain still, and this morning he can hardly talk at all. But there's a kind of peaceful look in his eyes that I've never seen before. Vic keeps close to him, touches him a little when there is no real reason to.

The plane is late, as usual. Old Tom turns up with the bus, but there is no one on it.

'How'd you manage to get seats?' I ask Vic.

'Money talks,' he says, giving me his slow grin.

We stand about in the shade of the tin shed, a bit uncomfortable, no one able to find much to say. Finally the plane drones in, and it seems odd after all the mud to see it trailing the plumes of red dust from its wheels again. It taxis over to the shed, discharges a couple of passengers and some sacks of mail, a few parcels. And suddenly it is time for them to go. Vic and the pilot help Jimmy over the wing and into a seat. He waves at us, grinning crookedly from his puffed mouth. Vic leans close to Stretch, whispers something in his ear, then comes over, shakes hands with me.

'Don't stay too long, Jack,' he says. 'This isn't your kind of life, mate . . .'

Then he's gone too, and the door closes, the engine coughs, roars, and they are taxiing away, roaring down the strip, rising into the bright air, leaving Stretch and me alone with Tom and the tired old bus on the dry, red earth with its tangle of green paddymelon vines.

The place seems suddenly very empty without them.

•

A week later Stretch tells me that he and Sigrid are leaving. It hits me then, this enormous sense of shock and loss. I've known it was coming, of course, but . . . not yet . . .

'When?' I ask him. I stop and lean on my shovel. We're spreading fresh gravel on the washed-out patches of the road.

'End of the week – Friday.'

There seems so little left to say, now that it is actually happening. I'm suddenly conscious of how much I'll miss the bugger. I can't remember when I've felt so close to anyone before . . . except for the old man, of course, but that was different. Stretch . . . the age gap doesn't seem to make any difference . . . he just seems closer than a brother now, and I'll miss him badly – that's the long and the short of it. But he's got to go. This is no place for him, for them.

There are no celebrations this time, no parties. A quiet dinner for the three of us at the van, a can or two, and the evening petering slowly out, none of us wanting to say the things that are on our minds . . .

•

There's a kind of restlessness now about the place. There are new faces everywhere as people come in to replace the steady flow of those leaving. No one seems exempt from the feeling of edginess. Even Curly snarls at me when I ask for time off to go to the strip with Stretch and Sigrid. I tell him to get stuffed, and go anyway.

I catch the bus and sit behind Tom as we rattle down towards the caravan park. The two of them are waiting with their suitcases at the gate, dressed in their best. Sigrid is wearing a tan frock, stockings, high-heeled shoes, her hair caught back with a saffron band. Stretch looks very adult in slacks and shirt, proper shoes. His face is still battered, and will always look that way now – this place has stamped him no less than it has stamped the rest of us. With him it is more obvious, that's the only difference. Standing together by the roadside, very calm, very much a pair, they still have that air of unity that has graced them from the beginning. It makes me envy them. Their world may not be the best of all possible ones, but it seems very much to me that they have a good chance of making it so – for a while, anyway. And that's better than nothing, as Stretch would say . . .

It's hard to talk on the bus as it rattles and bumps along the rutted road. And there seems very little left to say now, anyway. At the strip we stand in the shade of the shed, wordless and a little self-conscious.

A few minutes later there is a stir of dust away back down the road, and Curly's ute appears, bumping over the ruts. It slides to a stop outside the shed and Curly gets out, a little shamefaced, and comes over. He gives me a sort of half-smile, a small apology for his earlier churlishness, and shakes hands with Stretch. He doesn't seem to know quite how to deal with Sigrid, and I take her arm, draw her aside. I take the envelope out of my pocket, slip it into her handbag.

'What's that?' she says.

'It's the money I won on the fight. You two'll need it more than me, and Stretch wouldn't take it. So you'd better.'

'How much is it?'

'Not much.' There's a couple of thousand. My pay's been mounting up, and there's nearly twenty thousand in the bank back home if I really need it.

She says nothing, but looks at me with a small smile touching the corner of her mouth. 'Thank you, Jack,' she says. 'You've been good to John . . . he's going to miss you.'

'I'll miss him.'

She nods. 'I know he'd like to keep in touch with you. But we don't have any address you could write to . . . Could we write to you?'

'I won't be here much longer, I suppose.'

'No, I didn't think you would be . . .'

In the end, because I can't think of anything else, I give her the address of the hotel back home. And my real name.

She writes it down carefully on an envelope from her bag.

Curly waves quickly from the other side of the shed, stamps off to the ute, drives away without looking back. Stretch is looking after him, smiling. He turns towards us.

'He's not a bad bloke, Curly,' he says. 'Wanted to give me a few dollars . . .'

'You take 'em?'

He shakes his head and laughs a little.

'Perhaps you should have done . . .'

'We'll get by.'

'I wasn't thinking of you, I was thinking of Curly.'

He looks puzzled for a moment. 'Oh . . .' he says, and frowns a bit.

Then that damn plane is droning in again, and we're gathering up bags and suitcases and making those last-minute pattings and tidyings, and the wheels are kicking up the dust, and suddenly it's all over . . .

Stretch takes my hand, and we grip very hard for a moment. He smiles, turns away without speaking and picks up the suitcases. I give Sigrid a quick peck on the cheek. 'Look after him . . .'

Then they are walking towards the plane and I feel so bloody lonely that I want to cry.

They wave once as the plane races by and then they are gone. I'm left again in the red dirt with old Tom and the bus and the bitter paddymelon vines and the bright sunlight and I wish to Christ that I was going with them . . .

Petra has gone south, and there's nothing at all left here for me now . . .

And yet for some strange reason I still can't go . . . I seem bound in some way to this place. I want to go, but I don't know where, and I don't know why . . .

•

There is still work, and there are still the long walks in the bush. There are books from the library, new films from the Isa and new faces to watch, new voices to listen to; there are fresh vegetables and fruits again, and the temperature dropping and the air growing cooler. The world turns towards another winter, and still I stay.

The circles are gone now, all broken. And I seem somehow broken with them, all volition lost, all momentum gone.

The roads are open, the creeks are drying up. The first road train comes in and we hear of a small wonder. Three creeks out along the Isa road, the wet caught a semi loaded with beer and frozen chicken. The driver got out before the creeks rose too high, and the truck stayed there. When the water went down it was still there. Where its cargo had been, there were only chicken bones and maggots. No sign of the beer – even the cartons were gone. So that solves the mystery of where Ice-cream and Ray got their beer! *How* they got it across three flooded creeks and miles of sodden road is a mystery that we're not likely to solve now . . .

No news from Petra, not a letter, not a card. I could write, should write. But I'm unsure if she's back in the clinic or at home, and I never knew her address. Besides, I can't bear to put pen to paper for any reason. It seems to commit me to something, to pin me down somehow . . . And I can't seem to break out of this inertia . . .

February slips into March, and March into April, and weather takes on its boring winter perfection, its procession of clear, windless days and bright nights. I long sometimes for frost and wind and cold rain . . .

I long for something to *happen*, for something to pluck me out of my despair. For that is what it is. Yet what do I despair at? That people have left me, that circles have been broken?

From the beginning, circles have formed, been broken, lost, and new ones have been made . . . the ripples from them run like the ones we made that day in the Holes, the six of us, when we made our own bright circle, our talisman against evil and loss and despair . . .

April draws towards its end, and I realise with a shock that soon I will have been in this place for a year . . .

A year . . .

And I seem bound to it by my own inertia, an inertia from

which I can't escape, from which I can be rescued only by some deus ex machina.

•

On the last day of April the god moves.

At lunch in the mess hall someone hands me a telegram. I sit, stunned, looking at the yellow envelope, hardly able to believe it. It's addressed to JACK TODD, and I look at the name in some species of disbelief, as if it were an old coat that I've worn so long that it is in tatters, fouled and grimed and torn, and hardly worth the keeping any more . . .

Petra?

Stretch?

Who?

I tear open the envelope and read, my stomach dropping away, sickness and emptiness filling me.

KATE ILL, it reads, NOT EXPECTED RECOVER ASKING FOR YOU . . .

And signed – without love . . . NANCY.

How did she find out? It doesn't matter now . . .

There is a plane today that leaves a little after four. I pack my bag, collect my money, shake hands with Curly, and take my last trip out to the strip with old Tom in the battered green bus.

On the plane, as it rises in the clear afternoon air, I look back once at the small island of high land that is Carbine Creek, and then don't look again. For a while I look instead out at the wide land below that stretches so far on each side, so old, so broken, so hard . . . so big . . . and then I close my eyes and lean back, listening to the slow drone of the engine, knowing that I will never see it again, that I never *want* to see it again . . .

PART SIX

MARTIN GOGARTY – LAUNCESTON, 1903

Gogarty came ashore reeling a little, lubberly, still pale and uncertain from a rough passage through the equinoctial seas. He did not look back on the black hull and red funnels of the *Wakatipu*, but set his face steadily to the shore. Along the river bank he stepped, chafed and a little joint-sprung by the sea. He turned right into Tamar Street, the spring wind swirling in from the west round the smelter chimneys and wrapping him in a thick, claggy swirl of coke and soot and arid mineral dust that mixed with the rich yeasty smell of the brewery a block beyond the wall.

He stopped on the footpath, dumped his worn carpetbag at his feet, and stood teetering on the toes of his worn, bulbous boots on the blue dolerite setts of the gutter: a tall man, wide across shoulders, flat of belly, heavy of thigh, long of arm. His grubby collar was tall enough to discomfort his unshaven chin, his tie spotted and tied with less than precision, his thick-pomaded blue-black curls escaping fore and aft from the narrow-rimmed curly bowler that had seen too many brushings by a hundred or so; and his eyes, like small blue animals, flickered at the busy street from the burrows of their sockets. His tarnished watch-chain garnished his greenish weskit like a forgotten decoration.

He sniffed a little, coughed, spat, shuffled his feet; ran tongue over strong teeth. Sighed, picked up his bag, squared his shoulders. Scarcely ten o'clock, and two good hours to spend.

He passed through the polished doors of the Launceston Hotel, stepped to the bar, and ordered a pint of draught beer. Leaning down, sipping it, he fingered his tender chin and cheeks, burned and chafed, unused to exposure to the unkind air, his blue-black beard sadly missed. His face in the bar mirror seemed half-formed without it.

The bar was quiet, dim. He pondered a little on the ways of the world, on the usages that had brought him to this odd little place, to the necessity for shaven beard and unmanly caution. Ah, well, he thought, better than the bloody trenches and the rockdust. He'd had half a year in the deep defiles, blocked from the air by walls that towered above even his tall head, and knew that in two years of it he could well have been dead. He'd seen them, the unlucky ones, lungs rotted by the dust of the sewerage trenches, old at thirty, held upright in bed by pillows and bolsters, coughing, spitting, dying . . .

Not for him, not even if the money was good. The work he liked well enough, the feel of a smooth helve in his palms, the weight of the maul swinging, striking deadly full on the drill's bright-shined boss . . . Sweat and hard work and the good feel of the steel, true and clean . . . But the dust, the rock-dust, the lungs clogging so that Sydney-siders might shit in water-closets, their sewers built on the bodies of young men . . .

No, he thought, never again. Better what they had done. Dangerous, but the risk just that: a risk, no more; and he might be dead in a week if they had picked up the trail. But clean and quick at least, and worth the game . . .

He drained his glass, pulled out his old brass watch, picked up his bag and turned back into the bright street. He walked to the intersection, took his bearing, saw the clockless tower of the post office to the north and moved that way. A few minutes to noon, now, and he kept his eye sharp for Byrne.

Byrne spoke from a small, dark doorway set in the wall to his right. 'You made it, then . . .'

'Oh, aye,' said Gogarty, unstartled, used to Byrne's quiet ways. 'And no trouble, not a hint of it.'

Byrne stepped out into the sunlight. He was a smaller man than Gogarty, but wirily built with a hint of whippet muscles. His hands belonged to a much bigger man. He pulled his briar from a pocket, filled it from his pouch, lit and puffed, back to the wall a yard from Gogarty. He wore a threadbare serge suit of too-bright blue, a collarless shirt with thin stripes, a flat hat of shapeless felt. His face was lean and almost square, and from each side of a broken nose eyes as clear and blue as an evening sky looked out cautiously on the world . . . He had kept his large dark moustache, but his chin had met the razor. Still, Gogarty saw, the beard was growing back quickly, already a vigorous dark undergrowth. Byrne's right incisor was broken off, long ago, and he clenched the stem of his pipe there in the gap.

'Where did you stay then?' asked Byrne.

'I went up the Parramatta,' said Gogarty, gurgling the juice a little in his pipe. 'Slept in a barn, pretended I was lookin' for work.'

Byrne had left a week earlier, since they'd agreed to split up for safety's sake.

'And the money?'

'Only spent me passage money and the necessaries.'

Byrne's mouth twisted a little, as if in some faint familiarity with Gogarty's notion of necessaries. But he said nothing.

'Where you living?' asked Gogarty.

Byrne sent forth a cloud of white smoke, waited, licking his lips until two porters had passed by.

'Boardin' house,' said Byrne. 'A Mrs Axup, up in Elizabeth Street, ten minutes' walk away. Took a front room for six shillings a week. She'll put in an extra bed for you. Nice and private.'

'What's she like?' asked Gogarty, grinning.

'Respectable,' said Byrne, flipping his pipe at the footpath, squinting sideways at Gogarty. 'Too respectable for a sewer rat like you.'

*

Mrs Axup was a tiny white-haired lady in her seventies, her pink scalp glowing, her hands never still, her feet twinkling her from one end of her big house to the other. She quelled Gogarty with a single look, smiled on Byrne. A friend of Mr Byrne must be a gentleman, of course.

In the big front room with sunlight like clear water from the big bay window Byrne laughed aloud. 'She ran a drunk off two nights ago, your size and better . . .'

Gogarty said nothing, suddenly tired and hungry and a bit depressed, adrift in a strange city, a strange room, with only a friendly grave-digger for company.

He wrenched off his boots and lowered himself on to the bed set against the wall, beyond the one where Byrne's gear lay. He slept immediately, head thrown back, snoring lightly and melodiously.

When he woke it was late afternoon. Byrne was not in view. Gogarty rose, put on his boots, found the kalsomined outhouse in the yard, washed, took his pipe to the woodheap, and sat on the woodhorse meditating in a cloud of smoke.

There Byrne found him an hour later, as the house began coming slowly alive with returning boarders.

They ate, silent in a group of silent, steady eaters, and afterwards in the gaslit dusk they strolled a block or two round the city, digesting. At full dark, with a light chill falling, hints of a frost, they retreated to their big room, drew the curtains, lit the gas fire, and spread themselves, unbuttoned. Gogarty sprawled in the easy chair, Byrne cross-legged and neat in a bentwood.

'Well,' said Byrne. 'First things first.' He chewed on his pipe stem, slid a glance at Gogarty. 'Still got the money?'

'Of course,' said Gogarty, peeling back his shirt, unbuckling his money belt.

Byrne took out a heavy purse, unbuttoned his own shirt, exposed his canvas money belt. They slipped from their chairs, knelt on the thin carpet, and began counting out their sovereigns, notes.

Gogarty finished counting his pile and pushed it to Byrne, who added it to his own. Byrne blew out a thin stream of smoke, nodded.

'Four hundred and thirty-eight pounds and a few coppers,' he said. 'Not a lot.'

'More than I'd earn in two years with me hammer,' said Gogarty. 'And you in three, digging slots at Rookwood.'

'Not a lot,' said Byrne, 'for what it's got to do, for how long it's got to last . . .'

They were silent a while, looking at the pile of notes and coins as if it might hold an answer to their problem.

'Ah, well,' said Byrne at last. 'If it isn't enough, it isn't enough, and that's all there is to it . . .'

'Listen,' said Gogarty, leaning forward, looking hard at Byrne. 'I'm not going to do that again. What we did in Sydney. No more of that for me.'

'Don't worry,' said Byrne. 'I said then, and I meant it, a one-off job . . .'

Silence again.

'Think they'll find us?' said Gogarty, looking at the flicker of the gas jets.

'No,' said Byrne, gathering up money, stuffing it away in purse and belts. 'Never. You know them – once outside the smoke, you're free. They keep to their patch.' He grinned. 'But we'd better be careful if we ever go back. They got a good look at us.'

Gogarty nodded slowly, remembering the back lane in Newtown with a single gas lamp that spilled light in their faces as they moved forward – him with the blackwood barrel stave, Byrne with his old Adams revolver – on the fat bookie and his bruiser. The bookie hadn't moved while they'd taken his bag. But the bruiser had, and Gogarty had hit him hard under the ear with his stave. Had broken it, in fact. And both the men had got a clear view of him and Byrne. But they'd expected that, allowed for it. Byrne had gone straight to the quay next morning, different clothes, his beard gone, while Gogarty, smarting from his blunt razor, had headed for the country to lie low for a week. It wasn't the police they had been afraid of, but the fat man's helpers . . .

'Well,' said Gogarty at last. 'What's next then?'

Byrne, back on his tall chair, uncrossed his knees, leaned forward and began to pack his pipe. 'Buy what we need here . . . stuff we can carry easy . . . head for the West.'

'How?'

'Well,' said Byrne, striking a light, 'we can take a ship to Strahan . . .'

'No!' said Gogarty, with energy, shaking his head. 'I've had enough bloody sea voyages to last me forever.'

'Good,' said Byrne, grinning his tight smile. 'Because I've got a reason for going overland, anyway. We'll take the train.'

'Listen,' said Gogarty after a while. 'How are we goin' to carry all our stuff into the bush? A horse?'

'I don't know,' said Byrne, tapping his front teeth with his pipestem. 'I'm not quite sure. There's no tracks there, see,' he said. 'And if the bush is thick – and they all reckon it is – then a horse is no good.'

'What then?'

'Carry it ourselves,' said Byrne, shrugging.

'Oh, Christ . . .'

'Wait and see,' said Byrne. 'Best we wait and see, mate.'

After they had knocked out their pipes on the hob, paid a last trip to the backyard, stood for a minute or two watching the fog rising from the river, seeping up into the city streets, they went silently back and crawled into their beds.

*

They stood at the top of a steep hill looking westward. The day was half spent, filled with pale spring light, soft clouds, a feeling of modest fecundity. Gogarty still carried his carpetbag, but, like Byrne, he also bore on his back a large leather pack. His battered bowler still sat atop his curls, but his suit was gone and in its place he wore brand new moleskins and a checkered wool shirt. Above his old boots, leather leggings hugged his calves. Byrne wore stiff riveted denims and a black wool shirt, a bluey coat rolled on his pack.

'How far now?' asked Gogarty, breathing a little heavily, easing his packstraps.

'Not far,' said Byrne. 'Just down the bottom of the hill.'

They started down the narrow gravel road that wound down the descending gulley, its banks riddled with rabbit burrows, its little creek clogged with willow coppices.

'Go on,' said Gogarty, 'tell me now, for Christ's sake – we're nearly there.'

'Wait,' said Byrne, secretive and smiling.

It seemed to Gogarty that the secretness had grown in Byrne since they had left the train at Deloraine and followed the road north and west, had grown inside him like a warm worm.

As they descended the gulley, the river valley began to spread out before them. The trees thinned a little, edging into green pastures still filled with dead-white ring-barked trees. To the north the valley opened towards the sea, spread into wide coastal swamps. As the hill slope eased, their road emerged by the river which ran slow and deep. Before them lay the rough piles and timbers of the wharf, stacks of milled myrtle and gum. The smell of the fresh sawdust, sappy and pungent, filled the air. The single berth was empty.

The road passed over the river on a narrow wooden bridge, lay straight for half a mile beyond. On the fertile flats where the pockets of scrub still lingered, a few heavy cattle grazed. A patch of oats lay like a velvet band, green and plush along the bank. The hills were still heavily timbered, but a tide of ring-barking was rising towards their shoulders. Here and there, along the road, in the expanding clearings, buildings huddled; most were of palings, galvanised iron; a few were more substantial, with roofs of tile or shingle, clad with dressed boards. A thin streamer of smoke emerged from a bark humpy.

Byrne stopped on the bridge, slipped his pack, leaned on the rail. He pulled out his pipe. 'Here,' he said. 'This is it, Martin, this is the place, old mate.'

Gogarty stood straddled on the coarse timbers looking about him, puzzled. 'What place, then?' He frowned. At times like these he seemed to lose the faint trace of brogue that mostly touched his speech.

'Where I'm going to build a pub,' said Byrne. 'When we come back.'

'Ah,' said Gogarty, not really enlightened. It seemed a dull and countrified place to him, not one for the great endeavours of men soon to be rich. He shook his head, thinking of more majestic schemes, hazy but urgent, which he might accomplish himself, schemes that needed only the yeast of gold to leaven them.

'It's a great spot,' said Byrne, disregarding him, sucking his pipe, peering down the dark river towards the estuary. 'Right on the main road, all the carriers pass. Not another pub for five miles, only that sorry humpy down the river.' He looked at Gogarty, a little amused it seemed at the bigger man's lack of response. 'Not for you, eh, Martin?'

'Not for me,' said Gogarty, shaking his head. 'I'll be looking for a little more life.'

'I'll marry,' said Byrne, sounding very certain of himself, 'and get sons, and live here till a ripe old age.'

'Why?' said Gogarty, a little querulous. 'Why this godforsaken spot? And why a bloody hotel?'

Byrne was silent a moment. When he spoke again there was a passion in his voice that belied the calmness of his face. 'I've never had a real home,' he said. 'Thirteen kids on a farm labourer's wage, everyone picking hops, and rags and oakum to make ends meet, and off to sea for me at thirteen . . . Nothing, ever, that wouldn't fit into a sea chest or a duffle bag, at sea or ashore, barmaids and harlots, minin' coal, slaughtering sheep, making bricks, loadin' drays, diggin' graves . . . nothing permanent, nothing solid . . .'

'Listen,' he said, looking at Gogarty almost fiercely, his hard, square face suddenly nobbled and rocky, 'I want something *solid*, see, Gogarty . . . something warm and *lasting* . . . I'll build a bloody hotel with a warm bar and clean sheets and good food and a friendly fire . . . and *I'll* be the one to stay in one place, and leave others to roam, to go passing by . . .'

He spat in the stream, shook his head a little. 'I'm thirty years old, more or less, as far as I know, and I've no more now than when I left home for the sea . . . bar the bookie's money, and that doesn't count . . . I need a *place*, Gogarty, that's what I need . . .'

Gogarty, a little embarrassed at the outburst, nodded. 'I suppose so, mate. Everyone wants a bit of comfort . . .'

'Comfort!' Byrne spat. 'It's not comfort I want . . . I told you, you bloody oaf, it's a *place* . . . and since I saw this place five years back I knew it was the one.' He knocked out his pipe on the railing, slipped it into his pack, shrugged himself to comfort in the stiff straps. 'Come on,' he said, 'let's get on with it, then, let's find ourselves some gold . . .'

And without looking again at Gogarty he set off at a good pace down the dusty road, his slight figure a little bowed under his load, but his legs pacing tirelessly through the dust.

In a moment or two Gogarty, sucking his cherrywood, his face cooling in the mild wind, set out after him, his long legs eating the distance between them. As he came up beside his companion he gave him an amused sideways glance. 'Are you goin' to have free counter lunches in your hotel?' he asked, grinning a little.

Byrne eased his frown, glanced up at the big man.

'Oh, yeah,' he said. 'Don't worry, you great Irish lump, when you've whored and drunk your share away, you come and fill your hungry guts at my bar . . . long as you've got the price of a drink left.' And he grinned, and his grin turned to a laugh. 'You know,' he said, hunching forward into his harness, 'I do believe we're going to be lucky, Gogarty, I do believe we're going to strike it rich.'

'I never doubted it,' said Gogarty. But a slight frown lay on his brow, the shadow of some small doubt, the merest whisper of future tribulations. But he shook off the feeling, and paced along beside Byrne, cheerful enough, even if only by an effort of will. Behind them the white dust settled again on the long road, whitened the grass on the verge, powdered the rough steps of the shanties that lay silent in the quiet afternoon.

*

Gogarty nodded with the rattling of the carriage over the points, with the soporific swaying of the train's motion. Now and then he raised his head, glanced out the window at the bush streaming past, or at Byrne across from him in a corner seat, his back to the engine. They were alone in the carriage. Byrne was busy at his calculations, pencil and paper on his lap, Gogarty yawning in the rocking world of heavy varnish, stiff horsehair seats, brass foot-warmers and netted luggage racks. Through the window, the vista of forest, of deep dull green, of misty rain and brown peaty streams seemed interminable. At last Gogarty stood up, braced himself against the gentle lurching, dropped the aisle window into its panel, stuck out his face into the cold air, blinked and shook his head. The train whistled sharply, and a new rain of soot flew along the line of carriages. Hurriedly Gogarty withdrew his head, closed the window again, sat down.

'Don't you think,' he said to the silent Byrne, 'that it's about time you told me a bit more about this bloody river? Where we're goin' to find the gold?'

Byrne looked up, pencil poised. 'Why now?' he said. 'I told you, once we're on the track, in the bush . . .'

Gogarty jerked his head at the smeared pane, spattered now with sparse raindrops. 'Aye, but look at that out there . . .'

Byrne glanced out the window, leaned back. 'What about it, then?'

'That's the stuff we're goin' into?'

'I guess,' said Byrne, 'somethin' pretty like it.'

'Then how the hell,' said Gogarty, 'are we goin' to find a single little river in all that?'

Byrne smiled at him. Tapped his forehead. 'In here,' he said, 'I've got it in here.'

'How come,' said Gogarty, still unsatisfied, 'that others haven't found it, then, if it's so easy, and there's gold there?'

Byrne was silent for a while, eyes turned to the window. 'I'll tell you this much,' he said at last. 'It's been tried and passed over . . .'

'How's that?' Gogarty was puzzled.

'Well,' said Byrne, 'it's only a small river, and it flows into a bigger river. There's no gold in the big river where the little river flows into it, and there's no gold in the little river for three or four miles upstream. And there's no gold in the little river ten miles up, and none even further up, where it rises.' He looked at Gogarty expectantly. But Gogarty said nothing, just went on looking puzzled.

'See,' said Byrne, 'about five miles upstream from where it joins the big river, there's a series of deep holes, too deep to pan or anything else. And these holes act like sinks . . . so no gold that washes down goes any further . . .'

'If it's too deep to pan,' said Gogarty, 'how are we goin' to manage?'

'Ah,' said Byrne, leaning back, bringing out his pipe. 'We don't need to. See,' he said, puffing, 'upstream from the holes . . . there's about three miles . . . of riffles . . . and in the riffles . . . that's where the gold is.'

'But why isn't it upstream too? Where they tried?'

Byrne shook his head. 'There's a lead somewhere just above the riffles, likely. Maybe even washed out, worn away, by now. And the gold's only downstream of that. Between the lead and the holes, see?'

And with that, Gogarty had to be content, for Byrne would tell him no more. But a little later, he returned to the attack from another angle.

'How do you know this fellow was tellin' you the truth?' he said, watching Byrne carefully.

Byrne sucked on the stem of his pipe, his thick brows almost meeting over his nose as he squinted at Gogarty. 'I don't *know*,' he said. 'But I'm sure all the same. I've told you before; he was dying, and he knew it, and he hadn't anything to gain by telling lies . . .'

Gogarty desisted, turned and stared out the window. To the west, grey rain-sodden mountains were beginning to appear from the broken cloud. He wondered how much longer it would be.

He could understand Byrne's secretiveness well enough. There was little reason for him to trust Gogarty; they knew each other no more than casually until the night in the Dawes Point pub, when, both a little drunk and both more than a little disgusted with their lots, they had shared a few small confidences. And one thing led to another, and within a week Byrne had broached the matter of the gold . . .

He'd heard about it, Byrne had said, from a watchman at the cemetery dying of consumption. He'd been a digger on all the fields, but never made a real strike until he went to Tasmania in the eighties. He'd found the gold then, all right, in this odd little river. But his mate had drowned in a spring flood, their gear had been washed away, and he'd crawled countless miles on a broken leg to safety. Now, he told Byrne, he was lame and dying, and had never found enough money or a partner he could trust to go back . . .

And why Byrne? Gogarty had asked. Why choose Byrne to tell his secret to? Byrne had been slow to answer that one. Because, he had said at last, they had both come from Kent; because they had both been at sea; because the old man had come to like Byrne; because Byrne had done some small favour for him; because, finally, the old man had perhaps seen in Byrne some faint echo of his own youth . . .

Whatever, he had told Byrne; and a fortnight later had taken to his last bed. Byrne had dug the grave at the end of autumn.

After that, Byrne had said, he'd waited, waited ... until he could see some way of raising the stake to go and look, of finding a mate to go with him, a mate with the nerve and the guts ...

So that the exercise with the Newtown bookie had had two purposes, not just one: the money was important, vital; but also Byrne could watch Gogarty, and see if he was made of the right stuff ...

Well, thought Gogarty, letting his eyes wander to Byrne's figure, still worrying his paper, licking his pencil, here we are, and it wasn't too difficult, taking the money from the fat man; in fact it was so easy that sometimes he knew that he could fall easily into the trap of seeing the world as a whole string of fat men with no muscle to hold their own money ...

'Come on,' said Byrne, putting aside his pencil, bringing out a packet of bread and cheese from his pack, a knife, a bottle of stout. 'Let's eat ... then we'll go over the lists.'

So they ate as the train rocked south and west, closer to their goal; ate and drank, and when that was finished, pored over Byrne's lists, smoking their stubby pipes.

Flour, that was clear ...

Tea, and not post and rail ...

Not sugar, but treacle for its cheapness, and the tins would be useful ...

Currants, for duffs and brownies ...

Onions, carrots ...

Baking powder and salt ...

Lard and bacon ...

Jam ...

And billies and pans and a tin of biscuits for the tin, which would make a camp oven ...

Mugs and plates ...

A pick, shovels, spoons for crevicing ...

Skinning knives, a saw, wire and twine and a canvas fly ...

Rubberised ground sheets, gumboots, a sledge-hammer and rope ...

Nails and bolts and an adze ...

Pans, most important of all ...

And so it went on, as the day drew out, as the rain came again and faded behind, as the train rumbled over trestles and through tall forests and over button-grass flats. On and on, pencilling in, crossing out, pricing, adding up, revising, reworking, taking off and adding on . . . Adding on and on, until Gogarty began to wonder, not only if they would ever be able to carry it out of the shop, let alone into the bush, but if they could ever pay for it . . .

Finally, with the shoulder of Mount Black behind them, they leaned back, smiling at each other, a new light in their eyes, a new excitement. And then the light went out and the train roared into the Argent tunnel. When it came out, sweeping in the grey afternoon towards Melba Flats and Zeehan, they were suddenly grinning, grinning like madmen, laughing, roaring, clutching at each other like two drunken swaddies, lost in their sudden, mad certainty of gold . . .

*

Across the last of the flats that were studded with the white stars of flag lilies the train flew, and steamed finally to a stop at the station. Gogarty and Byrne stood on the platform in a sudden burst of afternoon sunshine, looking about them, sniffing, staring. Passengers left the train, headed for the horse-drawn coaches from the hotels or loaded their luggage into cabs. Behind them, Mount Read soared beyond Dundas township; to their left Mount Zeehan rose, grey and bare behind the Oceana mine. To the south, a mile away, smoke rose in the clear air from the German smelter.

They made their way back to the guard's van, found their luggage already on the platform. They shrugged into the heavy packs, picked up their bags and stepped out into the road. It led straight to the west for half a mile before swinging northward. They took the footpath and began the long trek up the slope.

'Where we going to stay?' asked Gogarty, beginning to sweat under his load. The sun was in his eyes.

'Somewhere cheap,' said Byrne. 'We'll do as much shopping as we can tonight, get a good night's sleep, off again in the morning.'

They trudged on, past the hotels, the provision merchants, hardware stores, churches, schools, contractors, the stock exchange, the newspaper office. As the street curved back to the left under the lee of a steep bank, a small bluff, they saw the red-brick School of Mines, on the right, the post office, and beyond that the Grand Hotel, tall and elegant, and behind its façade the entrance to the Gaiety Theatre.

'How about that?' said Gogarty, nodding, beginning to feel the wear and tear of the straps on his shoulders.

'We'll see,' said Byrne, cautious and watchful. The streets were crowded; businessmen in trim suits and neat bowlers, miners in muddy oilskins, housewives, carriers – the miscellany of any big town. Here and there, outside the ubiquitous hotels, women strolled. Gogarty eyed them surreptitiously.

'Want a little bit of fun, big boy?' called one of them, seeing his hungry look. Gogarty frowned, blushed, risked a glance at Byrne.

'Go ahead,' said Byrne, 'if you want to be pissing fish-hooks for the next six months . . .'

Gogarty lowered his head and plodded on.

Outside the Grand they stopped, staring at its proud façade, at the wide arches and the tall balconies, the bow windows and flagpoles.

Byrne, leaning heavily into his pack, poked his head inside the main doors. He withdrew hasily, retreated to the kerb.

'What's wrong?' said Gogarty.

'Christ,' said Byrne, 'you know what they're chargin'? Eight bob a day! A *day*!'

Gogarty laughed. 'Go on,' he said, 'it's only for one day . . . let your head go.'

'Eight bob a day! I'll be spanned if I do . . .'

'Then I'll be seeing you,' said Gogarty, and swung into the doorway. Inside, he was overcome by the dimness and the smells of furniture polish and beer and cooking meat; he stopped, gawked at the great stairway, at the wide corridor ahead lined with plaster columns topped with flowers, interspersed with heavy varnished chairs, a narrow carpet runner down the centre. Three doors led off to the right – the bar, the dining room, the billiard room. Billiard room indeed, thought Gogarty . . .

A neat man in suit and cloth cap sat halfway down the corridor, reading a newspaper. He glanced up at Gogarty, sniffed a little, raised his newspaper again.

'Can I help you, sir?' said a rich voice behind him, and Gogarty turned to see the lady, all dressed in rich maroon stuff with white collars and cuffs and a dainty apron. She was tall, handsome, perhaps forty. Gogarty smiled at her, smiled and smiled and smiled . . .

She smiled back, and by the time she had produced a key for him, and written his name in the register, he was sorry almost to find that Byrne was behind him again, his face tight with disapproval.

Upstairs, they followed the lady along the narrow corridor between the rooms. The floor was polished to a gloss, the brass knobs bright, the matting dustless. A room each, it was, and Gogarty preened a little at the unaccustomed privacy, while Byrne still sulked at the expense.

Alone, Gogarty took off his boots and lay on the bed, hands behind head, his gear spread on the spotless linoleum, his feet raised clear of the counterpane, and daydreamed a little of the lady in the apron . . .

Then Byrne broke his dream with the pencil and paper, and Gogarty groaned and followed him down the stairs.

Byrne would not take a drink until their purchases had been made, and so Gogarty sulked for a little in his turn. But it wasn't long until the growing pile of foodstuffs and equipment began to lighten his mood and set a glint of excitement in his eye. He prevailed on Byrne to add a dozen tins of condensed milk to the list, and some raspberry jam, a penny dearer than the melon . . .

Byrne too made his last-minute additions – needle and cottons, a yard or so of calico . . .

The grocers, the hardware store, the chemist . . .

The load grew, and they had to engage a cab to trot it from one place to another.

Eucalyptus oil, and pencils, and adhesive tape; linament and chloradyne and epsom salts . . .

A sieve, sou'westers, gumboots . . .

Wool socks, and twine and a whetstone . . .

Plates and mugs and spoons . . .

Waterbags and candles . . .

Wire and matches . . .

Extra tobacco and nails . . .

And finally, a bottle of brandy for 'emergencies', despite their agreed rule of no grog in the camp.

Back at the Grand, they secured the use of a shed for their provisions, and retreated upstairs to wash. Cleaned, combed, dressed in their creased best, they went down to the bar, drank a couple of pints, sauntered like gents into the wide dining room with its spotless table cloths and bow-legged chairs, its shined silver and fluted green breadholders. Gogarty eyed the brisk waitresses in their black frocks and white aprons and high-piled hair. Winked at one, was rewarded with a blush, and grinned furiously. Byrne shook his head, bent over his Windsor soup. They ate roast beef with yorkshire and three veg, and wine trifle with whipped cream, took a port with their coffees, and retired to the billiard room to smoke their pipes.

And Gogarty began to realise the possibilities of being rich . . .

'You going to have a pub like this?' he asked Byrne seriously. Byrne shook his head, eyes on a sharper in a check suit making a shifty break at the table. 'Not so flashy,' said Byrne. 'More homey, like.'

'Girls like those in the dining room?' Gogarty twitched his head.

Byrne was sardonic. 'I'll have enough kids so me own family can do the dirty work.'

'Shagger Byrne,' said Gogarty, and grinned.

Byrne puffed away, smiling, now that the day's business was done. 'Listen,' he said, 'you want to go for a walk? Look for a bit of fluff? I'm goin' up to check the lists again, pack the gear for the morning.'

'You don't want a hand?' Gogarty made himself sound solicitous.

Byrne shook his head. 'Off you go . . . I'll wake you in the morning, early.'

So off went Gogarty, first to wander about the back door of the hotel, hoping for a sight of the girl who had blushed. But he didn't see her, and the others who came out were met, or went in pairs and threes, and pretended to ignore him. So in the end, he wandered off into the likelier parts of town. And finally, back near the station, in a slightly less salubrious establishment sandwiched in an angle between two sets of tram tracks, he found a smiling girl in a spotty green dress with sandy-gold hair who let him buy her several glasses of port, and who, when the night was well away, permitted him to walk her home to a shared shanty near the Silver King, allowed him to kiss her, did not resist too much when he would accompany her inside, and was gentle and friendly with him when he was insistent. He left at midnight, both parties satisfied, Gogarty with his well-being, she with her sovereign.

He woke at dawn, from a dream of soft thighs and smiling lips, to find Byrne standing over him, square and sardonic.

Gogarty realised with satisfaction that his mouth was dry and that his head ached. The last hangover, he thought, for a while, and I might as well make the most of it . . .

'Top of the morning,' he said to Byrne, and threw back the covers.

*

'That's a real brogue you've got sometimes,' said Byrne.

The train churned its way through the heavy morning, northward again, the broken cloud and mist drifting and re-forming over the bush, lying blanket-like in gullies, flying like frayed rags on the slopes of the mountains.

'Ah,' said Gogarty, 'it's a way of laughin' at me old man, really.'

'How's that?'

'He never got nearer to Ireland than Circular Quay, but he'd picked up the tongue from his father, me grandfather, who came out from the old country before me father was born. Me old man, well, he seemed to think it made him something special, almost a foreigner, like . . . I just picked it up so I could mock him.'

'What did he do for a livin'?'

'Oh, fettler, blacksmith's striker, roadmender, whatever came along. What about your people? With a name like yours you'd have some ties with the old country, eh?'

'Oh, yes,' said Byrne, watching the trees through the window, the thick green of tall myrtle broken here and there by the pale succulence of celery pine. 'Oh, yes, a connection, all right . . .' he turned and looked at Gogarty. 'Nearly starved, me grandfather did in the big famine of '48. Emigrated to Canada, found it wasn't to his liking, went back again . . . not to Cork, mind you, but to Kent . . . bloody *Kent*.'

'What'd he do there?' asked Gogarty, sticking his feet up on the other seat.

'Bloody nothing,' said Byrne. 'Poled off me father and mother, went chasing women, cadgin' drinks, a bit of poachin' on the side . . .'

'Your father?'

Byrne shook his head in disgust. 'Farm labourer . . . and you know what that means . . . long hours and short commons, and touch y' cap to the gentry . . .'

They lapsed into silence as the train rocked its way northward, along the shoulder of Mount Black, the jagged peaks big and grey and menacing above the cloud on their right. The day was warm enough, but there was a dampness in the air, a dampness not dispelled by breeze or movement, a kind of thick moistness that clung to the pearly land, the thick, heavy forest.

Gogarty closed his eyes, lay back, his head thudding lightly in time with the train's progress. He smiled a little to himself, thinking of the previous night, cozening his hangover with dried apples bought on the way to the station. Byrne had not wanted to stop the laden cab, but he'd jumped off anyway, grinning, and run into the grocery. Eat enough of them, he thought, and in time they'd cure the worst hangover.

He opened his eyes after a while, looked out the window. The line ran now in a long, wide valley between mountains, a plain of shale and tea-tree and low scrub. Mount Farrell loomed to the right. Not long now, he thought.

Five minutes later the train drew into the siding. Gogarty flung open the heavy padded door and jumped down on to the gravel platform, moved to the guards van, waited for the porter to toss out their gear.

It piled up, up, up, the heap growing as he and Byrne watched. There were bags, boxes, bundles, rolls, packages.

He looked quizically at Byrne. 'How we goin' to manage all this?'

'We'll see,' he said. 'When we get to Tullah.'

They dragged their belongings off the platform as the train wheezed and moved off, carrying them in instalments towards the horse-tram that waited fifty yards away. The wooden lines stretched off into the bush, leading west, curling into the deep, wet growth of bush.

His hat pulled a little down over his eyes, Gogarty smoked his pipe, leaning back in the rough seat. The air was clean now and smokeless, the cinders and soot of the train vanquished, left behind. Only the wet, fecund smell of the bush met his nostrils, and pipe smoke, horse sweat, manure, saw timber, leather . . .

The slow trip took an hour.

They drew up in the township, tiny after Zeehan, but big enough. Everywhere mud, ring-barked trees, fresh piles of timber for the diggings; shanties, bark huts, shingled cottages, a couple of rough hotels. As the tram dragged off towards the stables, they stood in the mud beside their gear, looking about them. It seemed to Gogarty that for all its mud, all its roughness and half-finished air, this place was still civilisation. After all, he thought, it's got people . . .

'I've never been in the bush before,' he said to Byrne.

'Nor have I,' said Byrne. 'Not to worry, it can't be worse than the sea . . .'

Unreassured, Gogarty followed him as he marched through the mud towards the nearest hotel, an edifice of rough-sawn boards and canvas awnings, with a galvanised-iron roof that was rusting already.

In the bar Byrne bought two pints from the publican, engaged him in quiet conversation.

And, yes, they might eat their midday meal at the pub.

And, yes, they might leave their gear in his shed for a few hours. All care but no responsibility, mind . . .

So they drank their pints at the bar – a single thick plank of blackwood a yard wide – filled their pipes. Byrne lit his pipe, stepped on the match.

'We might as well get started,' he said.

The sun had broken through the rags of cloud, and the two men were in a light sweat before they had moved half their pile to the shed. When they had finished, Byrne turned to look around the yard, stood staring at an old handcart with high, wooden-spoked wheels. He went to find the publican again.

'Come on,' he said when he came back. 'Let's load up.'

They stowed their gear as best they could in the small cart, lashed it down, took their positions at the pole. Immediately they moved, the thin rims sank into the mud. They were both sweating heavily by the time they reached the branch track that led westward into the woods.

Half a mile along, taking a blow, Byrne looked at the sun, pondered for a moment, spat. 'We might make five miles,' he said, 'before it's time to camp. Then five miles back with the cart, five miles out again . . .'

They plugged on, the track winding through the thickening bush. It rose and fell with the land, diving after a mile or so into a long, tunnelled run where the ferns and trees grew high overhead. There it was dim and mossy, and smelt of earth and water and leaf mould. At last, in an open patch where a small stream crossed the track, Byrne called a halt.

'This'll do,' he said, and grinned at Gogarty. 'We'll camp here the night.'

They walked slowly upstream beside the little creek until they found a fold in the ground that was sheltered and hidden from the track. Slowly, sweatily, they hauled their gear up to the hollow, laid it carefully out of sight. Then they went back to the track, swung the cart round, and began the trudge back to the town. Gogarty was silent now, his muscles protesting at the long haul. He was sweating freely, and although his hangover was gone he had a great thirst, and stopped at every runnel to drink. Byrne would smile at him, spit, suck at his pipe, wait calmly. Gogarty felt a little shamed that with his bulk and long legs he was tiring faster than the other man. By the time they had reached the hotel, put the cart away, he had retreated into sullenness.

To his mild surprise, Byrne led the way into the bar. Sweaty, tired, muddy, Gogarty followed him.

Byrne ordered pints and – again to Gogarty's surprise – whiskey. They stood a moment, glasses in their hands, looking at each other. A clear smile broke on Byrne's face, and he lifted his glass. 'Good luck to us, then,' he said, and tossed back his whiskey. He drew a sharp breath, wiped his mouth, took a draught of beer.

'And good luck again,' said Gogarty, and drank, his sullenness forgotten in the warmth of Byrne's smile; in the prospect before them, in a confidence that welled up suddenly inside him. 'When we come back, we'll buy the bloody hotel!'

They drained their pints and, laughing, left the bar, stepped off with a will along the track. Byrne began to whistle softly as they walked.

*

By nightfall the camp was shipshape; groundsheets spread under the canvas fly, blankets folded, stores sorted, counted, checked; a small, hot fire burning, a pile of dry shell wood beside it; a billy boiling, a pan sizzling; water, shelter, warmth, all accomplished; and a sense of order, of purpose. Gogarty, slicing spuds, looked up to watch Byrne for a moment as he squatted at the edge of the firelight, carefully sorting the provisions, making them up into manageable loads. His face as the flame caught it was intent, focussed. Gogarty smiled a little, lifted his eyes, watched the last of the light fade above the trees in the west. A great feeling of happiness and an enormous fondness for Byrne rose suddenly in him.

He dropped the potato slices into the hot fat and was rewarded with a great cheerful sizzling . . .

*

Later, when the night was clear and chill and the fire warm, Gogarty, fed and filled with well-being, his pipe drawing, raised again the matter of the river.

Byrne rolled sideways, opened his blanket roll, took out a small square of paper. It was a map, well thumbed now and dirty from the track. He drew himself up, squatted, leaning forward, the map on his lap, the firelight spilling red over the creased paper, beating up into his dark bearded face.

'Well,' he said, 'we're far enough on the track now . . .' And he shuffled his buttocks a little on the dry leaf litter, moving closer to Gogarty.

Gogarty moved to his knees, lowered his head, rested a forearm on Byrne's shoulder and looked down at the map. It was carefully drawn in Indian ink, smudged a little in places, but clear enough. But it made no real sense to him – it was just a haphazard network of rivers and streams, here and there a schematic peak, a cursory range. There were no names, no distances, no scale.

'You've got to know the key,' said Byrne. 'No use making it too easy for anyone sees it that shouldn't.' He pointed at the lower right-hand corner of the map, at a crudely drawn mountain. 'See, that's Mount Farrell, and that little dot, that's Tullah. We're headed nor'west . . .' and he laid the map on the ground, took out his pocket compass, set it on the map, twisted the paper a little until its compass rose was oriented with the swinging needle. 'So we're headed away from the Mackintosh River, up towards that one, see? And that's the Huskisson . . . well, we cross that and we go on a bit . . . the next river's the Wilson, but we don't cross that, we follow it north till we get to that valley, see, just to the south of that mountain . . . that's Mount Ramsay . . .'

'What then?' said Gogarty, frowning over Byrne's finger, blunt and muscular, as it moved across the blank spaces of his homemade map.

Byrne was silent for a moment.

When he spoke, there was a hint of uncertainty in his voice. 'This is where it gets a bit ticklish, accordin' to the old fellow . . . see, this country's riddled with little rivers and creeks . . . and we've got to pick the right one . . .'

'And how do we do that?'

Byrne began stuffing his pipe. 'Well,' he said, his fingers moving like blind moles in this tobacco pouch, his eyes on the fire, 'accordin' to the old fellow, you can't miss it. First, you go up the river . . . that's the Wilson . . . until you're due west, by compass, from the tip, the highest point on Mount Ramsay . . . then you go back downstream, counting creeks flowing in from the left, the east. Our creek's the third of any size . . .'

Gogarty was doubtful. It all sounded a little too easy. 'And that's all?' he said. 'How do we know we've found the right one?'

'There's a big celery pine, dead, fallen across the mouth of the creek, the old fellow said . . . a real big one, can't miss it.'

'And it'll still be there, after all these years? Not rotted away, or burned, or washed down by floods?'

Byrne looked at him quickly, then back into the fire. 'We'll find it,' he said. 'If nothin' else, we'll find the three deep holes . . . if nothing else, we'll find the *gold*.'

'Might take us a while,' said Gogarty equably.

'It's going to take a while whatever happens,' said Byrne, reaching forward to stir the fire with a stick. The flames leaped for a moment, throwing red light on his black beard that had grown now to a thick, glossy pelt. Gogarty, watching him, fingered his own sparse bristle. 'We'll do it slow,' said Byrne at last. 'We'll take our time, we'll do it right.' He looked sharply at Gogarty. 'Right?'

'Right,' said Gogarty.

'And we'll come back rich men,' said Byrne. 'Right?'

'*Right!*' said Gogarty. And they both laughed.

'But what about the gear?' said Gogarty, suddenly serious. 'All the food, everything . . . we can't carry it all, can we? Not on our own selves, not on our backs . . .'

Byrne tapped his teeth with the stem of his pipe. 'What I reckon we'd best do,' he said, 'is find a good place to stash most of it, take enough to do us a week or so, and find the creek. Then we'll come back, pick up the rest, pack it in a load at a time.'

'How far do you reckon it is? To the creek?'

Byrne grinned at him. 'Well, maybe only thirty miles or so.'

'That's all?' Gogarty was surprised.

'That's as the crow flies . . . might be two, three times that far over the ground . . . we'll see.'

'What do we do tomorrow then?'

'Find a spot to hide our stores, get ready for the next day.'

Gogarty lay back, cushioned his head on his rolled coat. 'Home for Christmas,' he said.

'Maybe the next one,' said Byrne. 'This year we'll be eatin' our Christmas dinner in the bush, for sure.'

They were both silent for a time. Then Gogarty, eyes firmly on the bright stars, asked: 'Tell me, what's the price of gold?'

'Not sure,' said Byrne. 'Not to the pennyweight. About three and a half quid an ounce, I reckon.'

'Ah,' said Gogarty, a little dreamily, 'that's better than three bob a pennyweight . . .' He turned his head, looking at Byrne's hunched, dark figure. 'What's an ounce of gold look like, Jack? How big is it? You ever seen one?'

Byrne shook his head. 'Never.'

'How'll we know if it's real gold when we find it?'

'Don't worry,' said Byrne. 'We'll know.'

'Christ, I hope so,' he said, and his face fell into a worried frown. 'All this, to come all this way and everything, and not know what to look for, to miss out . . . Oh Christ, that'd be awful, Jack.'

'Don't you worry,' said Byrne, turning, his face dark and earnest, but confident in the light of the dying fire. 'We'll know it when we see it.'

But Gogarty wasn't easily reassured, and he lay for a long time frowning at the stars before the growing chill and the dead fire made him retreat to his blankets. As he drifted finally into sleep, Byrne was still hunched over the embers, sipping at his cold mug of tea, small grey streamers of smoke from his pipe drifting up into the darkness.

*

Gogarty woke to mist and drizzle, a world that had turned overnight to grey. The beads of moisture lay like pearls on his stiff blankets. He turned his head slowly, found that Byrne was already up, the fire lit, the billy beginning to boil. He rose stiffly, slipped into his heavy boots, yawned, peed steamingly on to the wet leafmould, spat, squatted by the fire. Byrne, a groundsheet draped poncho-like over his shoulders, his floppy hat dark with moisture, handed him a mug of tea. He sipped, warming his hands on the hot enamel. Byrne prodded the bed of embers with a stick, picked up the pan, scooped a little lard into it, set it on the coals. When the fat was smoking a little, he dropped bacon rashers in, stirred them with a stick. While they were cooking, he scraped the ashes away, exposed a flat damper, broke the great charred lump in two, put each half on a plate, speared bacon rashers on to them, handed one plate to Gogarty, took the other himself.

'What's this?' said Gogarty, poking suspiciously at the hard lump on his plate, sniffing at the fragrant broken edges.

'Bunghole,' Byrne said, his mouth full, and took a swill of tea.

Following Byrne's example, Gogarty broke open his damper, slid bacon rashers inside, picked it up and began to munch. Nodded, mouth full, at Byrne. 'Good . . .'

They did not speak again until they had finished eating and the pipes were drawing.

'What's first?' said Gogarty, flipping water from the brim of his bowler, scraping crumbs into the fire.

'Wash up,' said Byrne. 'Pack up, hide the stuff in the scrub. Look for a place not too far away to hide it.'

'Jesus,' said Gogarty, looking round him at the sodden bush. 'We're going to get wet in this lot.'

Byrne laughed, stood up, began to gather the dishes and mugs. 'Gogarty, me boy, it's my bet that you'll be more wet than dry for the next year.'

And Gogarty, despondent, went to roll up his blankets and take down the tent fly.

*

They found a small hollow a hundred yards upstream where they could safely leave their stores, hid them under canvas and dry leaves, then took their lightened packs and set off into the wet bush, heading northwestward. The drizzle had now changed to a slow rain, not heavy, but persistent. Their upper bodies were dry under the thick bluey jackets, but they were soon wet to the waist from the soaking rain and the sodden underbrush.

For a time they made their way through open bush. But soon it began to thicken, tangled coppices of trees closed around them, and great walls of fern sprang up. The track disappeared into a kind of chill jungle. They plowed on, visibility down to no more than twenty paces, sometimes less. Everywhere the air seemed filled with water, until Gogarty felt that he could hardly breathe without drowning. The land began to fall away into a deep valley, and on the steep slope the ground itself disappeared from sight. They walked knee-deep, waist-deep in fern fronds, their feet slipping off rotten logs hidden by the foliage, on rocks, into sharp hollows in the ground.

It seemed to Gogarty that they had been walking for hours, although they seemed to make little progress. The bush about them was grey and featureless and looked no different from when they had started out. Gogarty was beginning to breathe heavily, to sweat uncomfortably under his heavy coat.

Finally the bush began to clear a little, and they came to the edge of a kind of rough meadow. The grass was coarse and tussocky, but the walking was easy after the thick bush, and Gogarty began to whistle. Then he noticed that Byrne was frowning.

'What is it?' he said.

Byrne didn't answer for a moment or two, but peered around him suspiciously. 'Funny,' he said. 'Blood funny.'

'What's funny?'

Byrne had stopped now, was staring at a large tree that stood on the edge of the forest, an old tree, gaunt and misshapen, its two main upper limbs twisted into a curious shape.

'Shit!' said Byrne, and spat.

Gogarty stopped beside him. 'What's the matter?'

'We've been walking a bloody circle, that's what's the matter,' said Byrne, disgusted. 'That bloody tree, see? I remember it just after we started.'

'We can't have been,' protested Gogarty.

'Bloody well have,' said Byrne, walking slowly off towards the forest edge, disconsolate in the rain. 'My bloody fault, should have used the compass.'

Five minutes later they had found the creek and in half an hour were back at their camp site.

The rain was coming down harder now.

'Let's get the shelter up,' said Byrne, 'and the billy on, and something in our bellies . . .'

Gogarty went happily enough about his small tasks, cheered for some reason by this evidence of Byrne's fallibility. As long, he thought, as it doesn't extend to the gold, to that bloody map . . .

They decided that as they had wasted the morning, they might as well wait for the next day to try again, when the weather might be better. So they sat under their dripping tent-fly watching the raindrops pool slowly in the drainage ditch around their island of shelter. They drank their tea, smoked their pipes, and in silence watched the grey world turn to water.

*

The morning was filled with light and mist and green promise. Steam rose where the sun touched the undergrowth and spiralled towards the clear, pale sky. Gogarty, waking after a night of restless half-dreams, looked about him with wonder at the new day; it was as if he had gone to sleep in a tired, dreary world and woken in another land entirely, one of sunshine and smiles. He rose, wondering and grinning, to find Byrne returning, dew-sprinkled from the bush.

'Where you been?' he said.

'Just looking,' said Byrne, self-conscious, aware that aimlessness was not of his character.

'Ah,' said Gogarty, understanding immediately. It was that kind of morning.

Byrne whistled as he started breakfast, and Gogarty smiled inanely at the day.

They set out again, this time true-directed by sun and compass, their packs light, hearts light, eyes bright. The underbrush was still sodden, and soon they were wet to the knees, but it did not trouble them. The world was too full of promises for quibbles, and they forged on like boats driving into a sea of green, obedient to their compass needle, to the coursing of the sun, the drift of the wind. They passed by gulleys filled deep with tree fern, over ridges of mountain laurel, through deep passes of dogwood and musk, sassafras and cheesewood; sank to their ankles in deep sphagnum beds, skidded on steep patches of sodden leaf mould, staggered on rocky bottoms and clawed over mossy boulders. A couple of hours out they passed across a mossy, sag-strewn plain and entered the corner of a thick myrtle forest. They both stopped a few paces in, stunned.

It was a world of green light, of tall myrtle trunks that speared upwards, their canopies keeping most of the daylight at bay; what found its way down in bright shafts illuminated the trunks with a green, soft, eerie glow. For every surface – trunks, fallen logs, earth, rocks – was covered with a thick growth of luminous green moss. Moss clothed the world, hung in strange strands from the branches, confused the perspective, led the eye into mirrored naves and dark cloisters. Over everything lay the heavy, damp, fungal smell of the rainforest, a flat and heady muskiness . . .

Gogarty was transfixed; wanted to do something extraordinary – kneel, pray, sing, cross himself. He glanced quickly at Byrne's solemn face, then away; for even Byrne seemed not unaffected.

Gogarty realised with a start that he wanted the forest to make some sign, to achieve some magic completion that would explain mysteries, hint at salvation . . .

To see a naked woman standing there, green light on her body, he thought, still, still, but promising . . .

He turned away, broke the spell, and after a moment or two shrugged his pack higher, moved. Byrne took a step, faltered, took another; Gogarty followed, eyes on the ground, and they were away, threading their way into the mysteries, eyes flicking sideways at possible visions. But the forest kept repeating itself, showing new vistas that were only subtle distortions of the old . . .

After a while Gogarty refused to be drawn.

They climbed a steep slope, crossed a ridge where the trees thinned, saw a quick vista of distant mountains, a little snow lingering on broken summits, and plunged down again, now into less magic vegetation, into a jungle of underbrush and fern that seemed strangely natural after their encounter with the green of the deep forest.

An hour later they stopped by a peaty creeklet to boil the billy, smoke a pipe.

Then on again, deeper into the land, deeper into forests and lost glens and hidden valleys.

In the middle of the afternoon they startled a wallaby in a thick clump of dogwoods; the first sign of company on the ground.

By the time they slept that night, exhausted but pleased with themselves, Byrne called their progress at ten miles or more.

The days lay before them, a serenity seemed somehow to be overtaking then, and they both fell asleep smiling.

And woke stiff and sore, to forge on.

*

A bad day, four hours to cut their way a hundred yards through almost impenetrable scrub . . .

A good day, steep and thick, but eight miles . . .

Two bad days, and maybe close to the river . . .

A foul day, turned back by a swamp . . .

A better day . . .

On, on . . .

*

It took them a month to find their creek.

They crossed the Huskisson with some difficulty, after Byrne swam a rope across and they ferried their small provisions. By then they had wasted two days looking for a safe ford, but the river was still swollen with melting winter snows.

By the time they had struck north, heading for the sometimes visible Mount Ramsay, they had both grown a deal leaner and harder. Their beards were rough, greasy, filled with twig and leaf-mould, their clothing was torn, mended, torn again; their boots were pale and pulpy from constant wetting in creek, moss, bog. Their hands and wrists were scratched, cut, insect-bitten; their nails torn, black; their lips flaked and cracked. Their eyes were sharper, harder, less prone to casual waverings.

They spoke less, and sometimes went for hours without a single word between them.

*

By the second week, Gogarty's piles were an agony to him, and whenever the two men came to a creek, he would remove boots, socks and trousers, and despite the icy chill of the water, would lower his pale fundament into the stream, breathing out a long-drawn sigh of something between agony and relief as the chill water shrunk the offending veins, anaesthetised the pain. When the cold became too much for him he would take out a tin of bacon fat and carefully anoint his rear. Rinsing his hands, leaving the water, he would grin as best he could at Byrne, smoking on the bank, and say with a small smile: 'The way of the transgressor is hard . . .'

If Gogarty grew hard, then Byrne grew harder. Tough and sinewy in the beginning, without flab or spare flesh, he seemed to thrive on the mild hardship, his muscles turning to something resembling the knotted roots of the tea-trees that grew on the banks of the creeks. He seemed never to tire, always to have a ready reserve of strength for emergencies. And if his body grew harder, his mind seemed to Byrne to grow harder still, to marshall both their energies, to keep them strung against the stress of the day, to hold them hard against the wheel of exhaustion, day after day . . .

He seemed almost to blossom in the forests and swamps, to find new ways of exhibiting his reserve of skills, of improvisions.

Rations were very low by the time they had passed the Huskisson, and it was Byrne who, sitting by a game path in the dusk with his old revolver, had brought down a large wallaby. They had fallen on the fresh meat, half-charred by their small fire, with silent ferocity, glancing occasionally at each other's bitten, filthy faces in conspiracy and congratulation.

It was Byrne who woke easily in the mornings with first light, and coaxed a neat fire from the ashes, set the billy to boil, portioned out their small meal of cold damper and raisins.

It was Byrne, with his seaman's eye, who found birds'-nests and, with his seaman's knack, climbed the trees. They ate the eggs raw, on the march, sucking them with relish.

It was Byrne who, when the seams of Gogarty's breeches gave out, took out his housewife and sewed them neatly together again.

It was Byrne who led, who directed, who made plans and decisions. It was Byrne who led, Gogarty who followed.

And by the time they reached the valley to the south of Mount

Ramsay, Gogarty had passed beyond his awe, had grown a little tired of it. Yet he could not argue, even to himself, that it was not as it should be, knew better than *that*. But all the same . . .

*

Turning west they found Wilson River, twisting, winding, cutting its way through beds of curved, water-worn rock, through gulleys filled with ferns and fallen logs. It was deep and quiet in parts, diffused and noisy in others; always difficult, unpredictable, hard to follow. Impossible to follow closely, to trace yard by yard. They withdrew, followed its course doggedly from a distance, hacking their way through thickets and dense underbrush, slogging through swamp and over sodden plain. The slowly rising ground led them to the sloped shoulder of the mountain, and there, in fitful sun, they eased themselves northward, Byrne checking the compass every half hour, until at last he called a halt. He turned his sweating face, grimed and brown, to Gogarty.

'That's it,' he said.

Gogarty dropped to a log, pulled off his hat – now more a kind of tribal head badge than a hat – wiped his face, closed his eyes a moment. But Byrne had already turned away, was striding downhill through clumps of tea-tree, mimosa and cutting grass, towards the thickening forest where the river lay. Groaning, Gogarty stood up and trudged off after him.

They camped that night by the river, in a gloom of myrtle and tall sassafras, cooked up their thin brew of tea, their shrinking measure of flour, the last slivers of bacon. They sat in silence beside the brown water of the river, listening to the noises that pass for silence in the bush; the tinkle and rilling of water, the call of birds, the small movements of unnameable animals, the creak of a moving deadfall, the brush of wind in the ferns.

'Tomorrow,' said Byrne, hunched over his pannikin. 'We'll find it tomorrow . . .'

'We're awful low on food,' said Gogarty, who thought that he would have turned back days ago if he had been alone.

Byrne said nothing. He stuffed his pipe with a handful of crumbs from his pouch, offering none to Gogarty, whose store had run out at noon.

The fire died, the day died, and after a little they both crawled into their damp, pungent blankets, pulled the rank fabric over their faces against the midges, and pretended to sleep.

*

They argued interminably – or at least for ten minutes – over the third creek when they came to it.

It was little more than a runnel, a yard wide, edging lazily out of a low swamp into the river. It had no proper banks, only sedgy margins. In the end, after changing sides more than once, they agreed. No. Go on.

Half a mile on they found it at last, after almost missing it. They had been forced to cross to the far bank of the river by impassable clumps of cutting grass and heavy deadfalls, and the mouth of the hidden creek was covered, almost totally concealed, by undergrowth, ferns, dead tea-tree. Only the change in current, the steady swirl of water into the river, betrayed it.

'Look,' said Byrne.

They stood, rooted, knee-deep in muddy shallows overhung by a great bluff of undergrowth and ferns, struggling to push their way through an eddy of driftwood and fallen rubbish. Beyond the slow swirl of water against the far bank Gogarty could see the faint shape of a great log, almost hidden by the vegetation, only here and there a hint of silvery grey showing through.

They both plunged forward, regardless of the depth of water. By mid-stream it reached almost to Byrne's chest, over Gogarty's waist; then began to shallow slightly. The bottom was sandy, unsilted. Holding his axe clear of the water, Byrne stood at the edge of the stream, swinging at the obscuring brush. Gogarty began to force his way in towards the log, breasting the thick crush of vegetation, digging his feet deep. Sweat ran down his face, forming muddy runnels. He found a foothold, an old stump, a handhold, a broken branch, and swung himself up, boots scrabbling on the slippery trunk. In a moment he was seated astride the fallen tree, feet dangling, above the level of Byrne's head. The hidden stream flowed strongly below the concealing underbrush and reeds, making a small bow wave on Byrne's chest.

'Give us the axe,' said Gogarty, reaching down.

He swung it high, twisting the blade as it struck, sending a wide chip flying. He bent forward, staring at the fresh kerf. He took the axe one-handed, cut a delicate chip off the honey-coloured wood and handed it down to Byrne, who sniffed, rubbed it, looked up and nodded.

'Celery,' he said.

Gogarty reached down the axle handle, hauled Byrne up beside him. The sun was out, almost overhead, beating down on the river bed where no breeze found its way. They sat side by side on the log, muddy, sweating, grinning, looking upstream at the tangle of brush that hid the creek's course.

'What do you think?' said Gogarty.

'I think this is it,' said Byrne, nodding slowly.

'What next, then?'

'Got to make sure,' said Byrne. 'Means we have to find the three deep holes.'

'How far up are they?'

'Christ knows,' said Byrne. 'Come on . . .'

They slid down off the log, and were immediately thigh-deep in water, the tall undergrowth obscuring their view.

'Let's see if we can find the banks,' said Byrne.

They pushed off in different directions, bulling their way through the reeds and ferns, under the snags of overhanging branches. Soon they were lost to sight of each other. Gogarty, with no sense of time or direction, blundered into the south bank. He called to Byrne.

'Found anything?'

'No – it's all swampy.'

'Over this way, then . . .'

When Byrne joined him they began to make their way along the bank. The true stream was only a dozen paces wide and quite fast. On back eddies insects buzzed on the surface of the brown water. On each side the dark cliff of trees stretched upward, merging into the heavy forest. Slowly the bed of the creek widened, and the water shallowed until they could watch the weedy rocks under their feet. The trees withdrew a little from the banks, and they found that they could walk with some ease. The river curled a little to the right, and as they rounded the curve they could see a wide, still pool under a dark, high rock. Beyond, the creek rushed, falling over a low weir of tumbled stones.

'This might be it,' said Byrne, and moved off into the scrub. He chose a tall, thin tea-tree, felled it with a couple of blows of the axe, trimmed it quickly, and brought it back to the stream. The trimmed spar was a good fifteen feet long. He moved cautiously along the bank towards the pool, testing the depth of water as he went. Slowly the pole plumbed deeper and deeper in the water. Each time he drew it out the waterline was higher on the pale bark. He stopped a moment, nodded towards Gogarty. Then he went on. By the time he reached the mid-level of the pool he could no longer touch the bottom, even by dipping his arm into the water. He raised his eyebrows at Gogarty, grinned. 'First one,' he said.

They went on, clambered over the weir, followed the stream, now running a little faster, deeper in the bush. The trees closed over them again, the banks steepened, and soon they were struggling against the current in a deep ravine. They could no longer see the sky. The insects rose from the damp banks and closed around them in a cloud.

For half an hour the stream wound up, without sign of change. No deep pools, no break in the dark bush.

The next hole, when finally they came to it, was nothing like the first. Instead of a sudden drop in the stream's bed, there was a slow and gradual deeping and narrowing of the stream. The water rose only slowly up their thighs, and they had gone some distance before Gogarty noticed the change. Over the next few hundred yards it deepened still further, until they were forced to take to the banks. If the beginning of the pool was gradual, its end was sudden. The water shallowed suddenly, flashed and foamed over a series of boiler plates, and twisted out from the trees into a bright, sunlit glade. They moved carefully along the banks. Byrne cut a new stick, took a dip, and found the water almost too deep for the pole. Then they were in sunlight again, and a light breeze caught the edges of the clearing, touched their faces. Gogarty found himself moving a little faster.

They almost missed the third pool. The creek, after the boiler plates, was smooth in the sun, dark and peaty, with little turbulence. At the far end of the glade, where the shadows began, the water deepened quickly, then shallowed again. Gogarty was already past the pool, for it was only a dozen feet long, when Byrne plunged in his pole, called to him.

'Look!'

The pole had disappeared, Byrne's hand was underwater.

'I can't touch bottom!'

Gogarty dropped his pack, yelled in jubilation.

Byrne slowly sat down on the rocky bank, staring at the surface of the gliding stream, took off his hat, wet it, and put it back on his head. Water dribbled down his face, trickled through his beard and whiskers. He released the tea-tree pole, which bobbed to the surface, floated off with the current until it snagged between rocks fifty feet away.

Gogarty realised suddenly how hot, how tired, sweaty, filthy he was; how hard the morning had been, how bitten he was, how bright the sun, how cool the water. He dropped to the bank, unlaced his boots, wrenched them off. Tore off socks, stood up, dropped his breeches, pulled off his shirt. Naked except for his battered bowler, his body white but for tanned forearms and face, he took three steps and launched himself into the air above the pool, saw in the last moment before he hit the water Byrne's grinning face. Then the water closed over him and the sound, the great explosion of his entry, was lost in the sudden, cold, brown silence as the daylight receded above, as his limbs spread and his downward movement slowed . . .

The pain, when it came, was fierce and terrifying, and caught the muscles of his right thigh, so that for a moment he believed that he had been taken by some terrible monster of the pool, some lurking horror that had sunk hooked fangs deep into his flesh. Then the pain, the awful pain, swept into his calf muscles, his feet. The other calf began to lock as well, and he knew it was cramp.

He came to the surface, face crimped in agony, mouth open, gulping, and as he sank again quickly he took in water, a burning cold fire. Then the sunlight was gone, the black water closed over him again, and the pain bit deeper, twisted his legs in fierce spasms, reached upwards to his back muscles, edged towards his belly . . .

he felt himself fainting, felt the weakness sweep him as he fought to control the paralysing agony . . .

He surfaced again, thrashing madly, furiously, yet aware that he was making no inroads on his incapacity, that he was weaker every second, more locked by the pain, less able to see, to think, his throat burning, his lungs bursting . . .

Instead of the brown of the pool, he now saw only a wavering blackness, and a reddish haze that began to build behind his eyes . . . and he knew that if he did not soon find an end to the pain, then he would die . . .

He came to the surface for the third time just as Byrne's body, still clad but bootless and hatless, speared across the pool at him. Then, the pain blazing still in him, unaware of Byrne's entry into the water, unaware of most things now except his almost extinguished body, his failing will, he was caught by some magic and torn surface-wards . . .

Byrne had caught him on the third descent, by his long black hair, had twisted it in his fist, backed water, hauled . . . and slowly, convulsing, flailing, Gogarty had come to the surface, had breathed, had even essayed a faint watery cry . . .

He turned then towards the new pain, flailing still, and as his face came clear of the water, Byrne let himself float in under the wild arms, struck Gogarty with his brick-hard knuckles on the bridge of the nose. Gogarty immediately went limp, slumped in the dark water.

He came to himself on the bank, belly down in prickling grass, spewing water, the world a faint and wavering outline of trees and wild, wet figures that danced in slow and stately nonsense about the clearing. He closed his eyes, vomited again, and fainted once more . . .

*

Propped shivering in the sun against a tree trunk at the edge of the clearing, he watched Byrne make camp. He felt quite distanced, and very weak, not at all involved. His body lay shivering and protesting, but his mind was quite clear and calm, and infinitely logical.

In the first clear, cold logic of his weakness he knew that he would hate Byrne as long as he lived.

That Byrne had saved him from death, that was only the final and capping insult, the last tribute to Byrne's excellence, his infallibility, to the unending catalogue of his superiority . . . He had led Gogarty, bullied him, taught him, and yet there was a strange disjunction, a lack of love somewhere in all his transactions that Gogarty began now to appreciate . . . it was not that Byrne despised him, Gogarty – that was clear and true enough – but that Byrne despised the whole world . . .

And it seemed wrong to Gogarty that Byrne's scorn of the world should be evinced in such a cool and smiling fashion.

'Hey!' he called.

Byrne looked up from the task of building the fire.

'Come here . . .'

Byrne knelt beside him. 'What is it, mate?'

'Why did you bring me?'

Puzzlement drew the dark brows down.

'A pack horse, eh? Any big strong halfwit would have done, eh?'

Byrne shook his head, patted Gogarty's shoulder. 'Rest a bit, mate, you'll feel better when I get some tea into you.' He got up, went to his pack, rooted for the whiskey bottle, uncorked it, held it to Gogarty's mouth. Gogarty drank and coughed, eyes watering, looked up at Byrne.

'You're just so bloody *competent*, aren't you?'

Byrne smiled a little, shaking his head again, took a sip of the spirit, closed the bottle. 'If I was so bloody great, would I have ended up digging corpse holes in Rookwood?'

'But you'll end up rich, won't you? A rich hotel keeper, rich and respected and all that . . .' The warmth of the whiskey began to spread from his belly, and he felt suddenly enormously tired.

'We'll both be rich,' said Byrne, still smiling his white smile in his black beard, as Gogarty slipped away . . .

*

In the morning, feeling fragile and ghost-like, Gogarty rose from his blankets and in the warm dawn went and stood by the pool, staring down at the brown water, his blanket draped in ecclesiastical fashion about him. Bird sounds, a little slow and sleepy in the gathering light, came to him from the thick forest, and the water shrugged its almost silent way past the brown scooped rocks at his feet. His mind seemed strangely blank, as if this new day was the beginning of something, some watershed in his progress in the new land. He rocked a little, bare toes curling in the dewy grass.

In a little while, behind him, Byrne rose and began stirring the ashes of the fire, doling meagre tea for the billy, breaking left-over damper, tidying his blankets. Gogarty took no notice, stood engrossed in the creek, in the silent bush, in the sense of life renewed. He sensed footsteps behind him, and Byrne put into his hand a full mug of dark, unsweetened tea, squatted, pipe in mouth, by Gogarty's feet. The smell of pipe smoke, of sleepy flesh.

'Will you be right?' said Byrne. 'Today?'

'Oh?' said Gogarty. 'Ah?' Sentience and sense slowly coming back.

'Will you be right? To go upstream?'

'Oh, yes,' said Gogarty, sipping, raising one leg stork-like to scratch the other shank.

'How do you feel, then?'

'All right,' said Gogarty, still sipping, eyes still fixed on some other distances.

'Aches and pains?'

'Not so's you'd notice,' said Gogarty. And then he became increasingly conscious of strained muscles and beaten bones. His nose bridge ached.

'Well,' said Byrne, standing up, 'we'd best eat and break camp.' He turned to look full at Gogarty. 'We're close to the riffles now. We should take a look, find a camp site.'

'Yes,' said Gogarty. 'Of course. Take a look, find a camp site.'

'After breakfast,' said Byrne, looking a little anxiously at Gogarty.

'After breakfast it is,' said Gogarty, still sipping, rocking a little dreamily on his toes.

Byrne shook his head lightly, walked away.

*

Underway, his now lightened pack seated like a familiar ape on his back, Gogarty's dream-like mood fell slowly away, and his body began to complain again; of hunger, of bone aches, of itching bites, of grit and grease and of being too long alone in the bush with Byrne. But he followed silently up the course of the creek.

By the time they had gone a mile he was in some kind of rapport with the day, and noted how the creek changed its pattern once more, began to broaden out between wider banks, how the bush began to thin a little, the land to flatten out. As the creek widened, rocks began to show here and there, glistening tips bright in morning sun. Then, quite suddenly it seemed to him, there was no water in the creek bed, only a narrow trickle here and there, and for the rest only damp sand, bare rock. He stopped, frowning. Byrne turned, came back, spoke to him.

'There must be another tributary somewhere . . .' Still frowning, he began to pace across damp mud to the far bank, to poke in the scrub with his tea-tree staff. 'Here . . . there's a spring or something.' Byrne came back through the drying shallows, shambling a little, frowning beside Gogarty. 'What happens,' he said, 'I think what happens is this . . . Somewhere upstream there's a fault of some kind, maybe the riverbed collapsed, dropped a few feet . . . so that in winter, with lots of water, this creek's full and running high . . . then, in spring, summer, the water level drops below the top of the fault . . . the water's diverted somehow into a channel . . . that spring the other side feeds the bottom of the creek near the river all year round . . . and in summer there's this dry stretch in the middle . . .'

Gogarty looked at him, trying to comprehend. He looked away, at the drying creek bed. 'You mean we're there?' he said. 'This is it?'

Byrne nodded, screwed up his face ferociously. 'I think so . . . not far anyway.'

Gogarty, looking round, felt no elation. The place looked no different from half a hundred spots he had seen in the last week. Was this the magic place? He shook his head, disgusted. 'I don't know,' he said.

Byrne turned away, began walking upstream. Gogarty, for want of anything better to do, followed him.

They covered perhaps a mile, or a little better, the creek bed widening slowly, until it covered perhaps thirty feet or so, bottom still damp, ridges of dull sand and steps of low rock. The banks were steep, but reaching only waist height, little more. And beyond the banks, past a shallow band of scrub, lay the beginnings of the rainforest. In places the myrtles reached down to the stream, their new bronze foliage sparkling with light, their dark green tops spreading high overhead. In indentations in the bank, man ferns grew clumped. In one place there was a sizeable clearing, covered only with occasional sags and clumps of cutting grass. Small myrtle seedlings speared up in a miniature forest from the edges of the clearing. Here Byrne left the creek bed, clambered up the low bank, sat there. He let his pack slip, took out his pipe. Gogarty climbed up beside him.

'Well?' said Gogarty. 'What now, Jack?'

Rubbing tobacco in his palms, Byrne said nothing for a moment, then, packing his pipe bowl carefully, he began to ponder, his words slow and exploring.

'Well,' he said, 'first of all, we start packing our stores in, eh? . . . Then have a good look at the creek . . . all the way up, eh? . . . What then? . . . Water, I reckon, have to find water . . .' He lit his pipe, raised his head, looked about him, squinting at the empty bed of the creek . . . 'No water in the creek, so no water for panning, see? And I doubt if the dirt'll ever get dry enough for dry-blowing, see? . . . Too much soakage.'

Gogarty frowned, gazing down at his ragged boots. 'So what do we do?'

Byrne seemed a little at a loss for once. 'Find out if there's any gold, if we're in the right place, I suppose.'

'How?'

'Try a pan . . .'

'But there's no water.'

'I filled the billy at the spring back there.'

'Well . . .' Gogarty was oddly reluctant now to attempt the final test.

'Come on.' Byrne scrambled on to the bank, undid his pack, took out the panning dish, one of two they had bought in Zeehan. 'Bring the water.'

Gogarty took the billy of water as Byrne slipped back down the bank holding the pan and a spoon.

'You pick,' said Byrne when they were standing together in the creek bed. The world seemed to Gogarty to have gone oddly silent. He could hear only a faint ringing in his own ears.

'What do you mean?'

'Pick where we start.'

'Oh.' Gogarty gazed about him at the vacant rock and sullen sand. There seemed no promise anywhere, no sign. He looked directly down at his own feet. 'Here.'

Byrne stooped, began spooning sand from behind a rock riffle into a dish. He held the pan for Gogarty, who poured a little water over it.

'More,' said Byrne.

Gogarty poured again.

Byrne began a gentle swishing of the pan, a cautious rotary motion, eccentric, slurrying the sand and water until it swirled in a dark mass in the tilted pan. He tipped cautiously, slopped a little liquid, swirled again, slopped, swirled. Paused.

'More water.'

Gogarty poured again.

Byrne swirled, spilled, swirled, spilled. Until finally: 'There.'

Gogarty bent, and peered at the inside of the pan. Only a faint line of sandy detritus lay now in the bottom crevice of the pan. He peered more closely. Yellowish, with darker flecks, tiny grains of . . .

'Gold?' said Gogarty, disbelieving.

'Maybe,' said Byrne, cautious.

'What do you mean?' said Gogarty. '*Maybe?*'

'We'll test it.' Byrne came to his feet, walked quickly to the bank, to his pack. He lay the pan down carefully. 'It's a bit rough,' he said, taking out a small package, opening it, withdrawing a glass phial and holding it to the light.

'What's that?' said Gogarty, who had never thought of tests, had imagined the gold in good coarse lumps that would look like gold, and nothing else . . .

'Aqua regia,' said Byrne. 'Nitric and muriatic acid mixed.' He took an empty phial, carefully scraped in a little of the residue from the pan and poured acid into it. He closed the cap, shook, shook; opened his fist, held the phial to the light. There was no change to the contents. He nodded, poured a little water into the phial, capped it, shook again. Holding it in his closed fist, he looked up at Gogarty, a bony grin tight on his face. 'Pray . . .'

Gogarty could not take his eyes off Byrne's closed fist. He felt tremblings in his belly, a dryness at the throat.

Byrne opened his hand, held the phial to the light. Gogarty noticed that his fingers were quite steady.

Gogarty bent and peered. The liquid was clear, with only a little translucent gravel faint on the bottom. He looked quickly at Byrne's face, found a dawning grin.

'Is it?'

'Gold,' said Byrne. He settled back on haunches, setting the phial down. 'Pretty certain. We need other tests, but the best way's a proper assay.'

'But you're pretty certain?'

'Bloody certain,' said Byrne. 'She's there all right.'

Gogarty found that there was a certain weakness in his knees. He sat down carefully beside Byrne, pulled the pan towards him, stirred the tiny streak of mineral with his finger. 'How much is there, you reckon?'

Byrne, smiling now, looked at the pan. 'I don't know . . . maybe a pennyweight . . . three or four bob's worth.'

'That much . . . Christ!' The reality of it left him speechless, almost.

'How much water's left in the billy?' asked Byrne.

'What? Oh, maybe half . . . What, you goin' to do another pan?'

Byrne laughed, shook his head. 'Boil her up, make a cuppa . . .'

Gogarty looked a little crestfallen, turned back to the pan, to finger the dirt again.

'Don't worry,' said Byrne, going to find twigs for a fire. 'You'll see plenty of that.'

*

They sat on the bank, the pan between them, sipping tea.

'There's not much tucker left,' said Byrne. 'We'll have to start back tomorrow.'

'I suppose so,' said Gogarty, still slightly stunned by the gold.

'It'll take us a while to pack everything in . . . couple of weeks at least.'

The thought of it filled Gogarty with repulsion. 'What if someone else finds the gold while we're gone?'

Byrne laughed. 'Jesus, it's been here all these years . . . why should someone find it now?' But there was a faint hint of worry in his own eyes too. 'We'll get back as quick as we can. Listen, first of all one of us has to go into Zeehan, get a proper assay done.'

Gogarty nodded.

'A few extra things we'll need . . .'

'Like what?'

'Brass screws, some canvas, stuff like that.'

'What for?'

'Wait and see . . .' then seeing the frustration in Gogarty's eyes, 'We'll have to build some sort of rig . . . maybe a sluice.'

'Can't we just pan it?'

'And have to carry every pan of water maybe five miles? How far do the riffles go?'

Gogarty was silent.

'Look,' said Byrne, 'there's miles, maybe, of these riffles . . . and no water until next autumn, right?'

Gogarty nodded, reluctantly.

'Well, I think what we should do is collect the dirt from the riffles, store it ashore. Make a permanent camp, build a good sluice. Then, when there's plenty of water, next autumn, we'll treat all the dirt at once.'

'That's months away,' complained Gogarty, feeling deprived of instant riches.

'What's a few months? Anyway, can you think of a better way?'

Gogarty was silent.

Byrne punched his arm. 'Come on, don't be a mug – how long were you digging shit pits in Sydney? More than six months, eh?'

Gogarty nodded, a little sullenly.

'And what did you make out of it? Fuck all, eh?'

Again Gogarty nodded.

'In six months,' said Byrne, earnestly, intently, staring into Gogarty's face, 'we'll both be rich men.'

And slowly the smile dawned on Gogarty's face, a smile that was reflected by the one on Byrne's face. The twin smiles deepened, broadened, until they were gaping at each other.

'Rich!' said Gogarty.

'Rich,' said Byrne.

'*Rich!*' shouted Gogarty, springing to his feet, beginning to dance a little, a kind of nervous stagger, on the sward. '*Rich!*'

And Byrne was on his feet, too, prancing a little, jogging his small wiry body. '*Rich!*'

In a minute they were reeling inebriated over the soggy flat, before the backdrop of the dark, silent myrtles, their laughter floating up to the clear sky, their feet beating a sodden tattoo on the ground, their mouths black gapes of pleasure as they revolved in their mad dance . . . and as they danced they shouted, their voices rising in point and counterpoint beyond the tall myrtle tops.

'Rich! Rich, rich, rich.'

'*Rich!*'

*

For eight days Gogarty had been packing stores and equipment in to the river. He was sore, sweated, and increasingly disillusioned. The loads seemed to grow heavier, more awkward, the track steeper, longer, boggier. They had marked a new track, a more direct one, from their Tullah depot to the creek above the holes, and had begun the carrying. Byrne had been with him for two days, then had gone off, early one morning, to have their dirt assayed at Zeehan. Gogarty had struggled on alone, his resentment increasing as the hours passed, as his imaginings grew more fervid, as he envisioned Byrne alone amid the fleshpots of Zeehan, indulging his pleasures. Gogarty thought often and longingly of the ginger-haired girl from the Queen end.

By the end of the eighth day the last of the stores had been shifted from the depot to the halfway mark. He had taken the track in short stages, moving fast on the backtracking, sometimes covering as much as forty miles in a day, half of it loaded heavily. His piles had grown active, and for much of the time he was in severe discomfort – he would not call it pain, dared not, in case he took too much notice of it. He would stop at every creek he crossed, pull down his ratty trousers, sink his buttocks into the water, re-anoint himself with tallow – the bacon fat had run out – re-belt his trews, and push on again. He found himself towards the end of his lonely portaging in a perfect lather of haste, imagining that the flats, the riffles, had been found by someone else, that their claim might be disputed by others stronger, more numerous, than they. Then, in a morass of reaction, he would fancy that the assay would be poor, that it would show no gold at all, that all their troubles would go for nothing. And when he lay alone at night, rolled in his blanket by some smouldering fire that would never seem to burn properly for him, he would cover his head to shut out the strange small noises of the bush. He – great clumping Gogarty, young and strong and robber of bookmakers – was afraid of the foreign darkness. And he knew that he needed the presence of Byrne, the reassurance of the smaller man.

On the ninth day, with the sun shining strongly between showers of rain, he came quickly down a long tunnel under tall trees, overgrown with vines and rambling ferns, moss under foot, and out into a small clearing where two logs made a rough bridge over a little creek. And there – there, smoking on the bank, fire alight, billy boiling – sat Byrne.

Sweating, tired, filthy, Gogarty thought for a moment that he might kill Byrne, so cool, so unarduous did he look, so much at ease, a perfect picnic of a sight, smoking in the wilds, leaning on his elbow, his hat flopping gently as he waved off flies . . .

Gogarty stepped down into the sunlight.

'You might have brought a load,' he said ungraciously.

Byrne did not speak, but smiled, jerked a thumb at a great bundle propped beyond a tree trunk, a bundle bigger than any that Gogarty had carried himself. He felt mean and small and bitter at himself, and liked Byrne even less. He covered his discomfiture as best he could by further surliness.

'Well?'

'Well what?' Byrne was grinning.

'How did it bloody *go*?'

'The assay?'

'Of *course* the bloody assay!'

Byrne said nothing for a moment, spat, trying to keep a straight face.

'For Christ's *sake*!' shouted Gogarty, making a quick movement towards Byrne.

Byrne laughed. 'All right! Hold on! Ninety-seven per cent! *Ninety-seven per cent*! How's that for jam, eh?'

'Jesus . . .' Gogarty sank down, propped his buttocks on a log. Looked at Byrne. 'Really?'

Byrne nodded, solemn now. 'Really . . . the rest is a bit of impurity in what they call the platinoid group . . .'

'There's nothing wrong with it, then?'

'Not a thing.'

'Jesus . . .' Gogarty was speechless for a moment. Then: 'How much did it cost?'

'The assay? Ten bob . . .'

'That's a lot.'

Byrne laughed, shook his head, bent over the fire. He lifted the billy-lid, tossed in a handful of tea, took the billy off the fire, stood it on a warm rock. He went to his heavy pack, opened the flap. 'Here,' he tossed a small blue tin to Gogarty.

'What's this?' Gogarty picked up the flat tin, read the label. 'Lanoline?'

'For your piles,' said Byrne. 'Supposed to be good for 'em.'

Gogarty was momentarily shaken, moved, that Byrne had bothered to do this small thing for him, and troubled by his feelings of guilt and ingratitude. He stuffed the tin away, out of sight, in his pocket. 'Thanks.' And after a moment. 'What else did you get?'

Byrne tapped the billy with a spoon to settle the leaves, poured tea into two mugs. 'Brass screws,' he said. 'Wire, canvas, more candles, more rope . . .'

'Ah,' said Gogarty, a little disappointed.

'And something to celebrate with,' said Byrne. He went again to the pack, withdrew a bottle of Watson's whiskey, pulled the stopper, poured a little into their tea.

Gogarty grinned a little slyly, raising his mug. They toasted each other silently.

Three days later, by dint of hauling from morning till dark, they had their gear all stored under a canvas sheet on the creek bank. There was no sign that anyone had been there in their absence.

*

They took a day's break, then, to look the creek bank over, and to choose a camp site.

'We need a flat space a good bit above the water level,' said Byrne, smoking thoughtfully after breakfast. He rose, walked over to the bank, inspected the bed, now quite dry except for a little seepage in the deeper cavities. 'Not too far from a spring or soak . . . timber for firewood and building . . .' He came back, settled himself on a rock by the coals. 'This bank seems flatter than the other one . . . if we could find water somewhere . . . otherwise we'll have to move back downstream to where that creek runs in.'

'You want enough water to pan, or just cooking and so on?' Gogarty was sprawled, hat over eyes, pipe puffing.

'Just for what you might call domestic purposes.'

'Well,' said Gogarty, 'we'll just have to look for it, eh?'

'Right,' said Byrne, 'and when we find it, then comes the hard work . . . building a hut of some sort, cutting firewood for the winter – it'll be a wet, cold job next year, working a sluice – building the bloody sluice itself . . . then carrying the washdirt, storing it.'

'You know how to build a sluice?' asked Gogarty. ' 'Cause I'm bloody sure I don't.'

Byrne pondered a moment. 'I've seen pictures,' he said at last. 'I know the theory, and I reckon I can fudge one up.'

There was silence over the clearing for a bit. A currawong, tame and cheeky, picked at tea-tree buds by the clearing's edge. Gogarty lobbed a pebble at the bird, and it jumped, complaining, out of the way. 'It'll be a long time before we see any more gold, then, won't it?'

'That's right,' said Byrne. 'But it'll come with a rush when it does come.'

'What if someone gets here before we've finished? I mean we haven't registered a claim or anything. What's to stop them just taking over?'

'I am,' said Byrne, and Gogarty was startled by the intensity in his eyes. 'Any bastard tries anything I'll shoot him.'

Gogarty nodded solemnly, not sure whether he was reassured or alarmed.

'But no one will find us,' said Byrne. 'You'll see. To be on the safe side we'll do most of our cookin' after dark, when no one can see our smoke . . . and in the daytime we'll take care to use dry wood.' He spat into the grey ashes. 'No,' he said. 'No one'll come this way, no one's been this way since the old fellow, and there's no reason for 'em to come now.' He drank the last of his tea, flung the dregs in the ashes, stood up, 'Come on, me boy, to work, to work, you'll never get rich lyin' about like a bloody lord . . .'

*

It took them well into the second day to find a small spring a few hundred yards in from the river bank, high up on a small knoll, where the land began to rise towards the foothills of Mount Ramsay. The flow was small, but enough for their needs, and clear and potable. On the riverbank nearby they marked out their camp, and began to move their gear. When that was done, they began the other jobs. Gogarty wanted to begin collecting washdirt at once, but was persuaded by Byrne that they should first build their shelter, start the sluice. So they began by felling several big myrtles that stood well back from the river, hard work with their single axe, cutting the trunks into lengths as Byrne determined – six foot, ten foot, eight foot – from some master plan in his head. They set one twenty-foot section aside. Then came the hard work of hammering in the pair of steel wedges, splitting the sections into thin palings, thicker boards. When this was done they felled a tall peppermint gum for its bark, carefully cutting it free, spreading the sheets to dry under stones on the flat by the creek.

All this they did to the dictates of Byrne's master plan, a plan which he communicated to Gogarty only in dribs and drabs as time went by, a plan which left Gogarty in an increasing fury of irritation.

'For Christ's sake, I wish you'd *tell* me what we're *doin'*!' he would storm at Byrne as some new direction was taken. 'I'd work better if I knew what the bloody hell you were up to!'

But Byrne would only smile. 'I can't tell you what I don't know myself, can I?' he would say, with some amusement at Gogarty's rage. 'I'm just makin' things up as I go along . . .'

And Gogarty would go away grumbling, forced to be content with that, but disgruntled all the same, and with the growing feeling that he was, in Byrne's shipshape universe, no more than a beast of burden, a drawer of water and a hewer of wood . . .

*

Summer was on the land now, hot and bright, and they sweated hard every day in the windless cleft beside the dry bed of the creek. The campsite now was neat and shipshape, and they slept in their hut, a small construction of palings with a mud-chinked chimney and a bark roof. By the door was a crude bench where a washing bucket stood, with an old flour bag for a towel. Most evenings when the weather was fine they cooked outdoors at their old fireplace, now embellished with an empty biscuit tin that served as a camp oven. Their meals were not ambitious. Occasionally Byrne would take out his old cap-and-ball revolver in the dusk and shoot a wallaby for fresh meat, but mostly their diet was a monotonous one of porridge, 'bunghole' damper and 'brownie', rich with fat and currants and treacle. In the mornings they ate their damper hot, sometimes with bacon, in the evenings cold, with treacle. After they had eaten the flesh from Byrne's wallabies, they would make the bones into a soup with an onion from their small store, a little barley, and any edible greens they could find in the bush. Into this they threw small lizards and scraps of damper, and once the carcase of a parrot that Gogarty knocked from a branch with his stick. Soup nights were special nights, and the treasures from the pot were apportioned with meticulous care.

Their beards grew long, as did their hair, and their clothes more torn and threadbare. Within a month they were both much adorned with neat patches of canvas, cut and stitched by Byrne with his housewife. They grew progressively more speechless, learning each other's ways, accommodating to the unchanging routines of camp life, going about their dull appointed tasks without words.

By the beginning of December they had cut a great pile of myrtle firewood, salmon-pink billets stacked to dry behind the hut, against the wet and busy days to come. The hut was finished, and while Byrne carefully adzed the long myrtle boards that would form the sluice, smoothing them, fitting, resmoothing and refitting, Gogarty dug great ranks of pits about the edge of the camp, all in neat rows, each one three feet deep and three feet wide, each one covered with a steep bark roof to keep off rain. These were the storage pits for the washdirt. When these jobs were done, and Christmas was approaching – by their rough and ready count – it was time to move on to the business of cutting sheerlegs and levers for the sluice machinery. Gogarty, strictly instructed by Byrne, attended to this while Byrne fitted the sluice box together with his hoard of precious brass screws. When the job was done they laid aside the box and the spars, the box disassembled again to dry and season.

As the summer drew on, the temperature rose, the nights were warmer and the air was clearer. Heady scents of leatherwood and tea-tree blossom drifted out from the forest. They had lost track of the days, and reckoned now only by the sun and a rough estimate of the season. They agreed, when they started carrying washdirt, that it was the first or second week in December.

After his long impatience with the other preparations, Gogarty felt a fresh enthusiasm grip him when at last he could begin on what he considered the serious work. Byrne was still occupied much of the time with cutting spars for the sheerlegs, rigging them for trial, re-rigging, setting them aside with the skeleton of the sluice. Also, there was a canvas funnel to cut and sew, washdirt packs to make. Gogarty, to his shame, found that he was too clumsy and slow with the needle to be of much use, and settled disconsolately to drudge at camp duties.

One morning, when they had eaten their silent meal, and before the sun had properly cleared the tallest of the myrtles in the forest to the east, Gogarty took one of the washdirt packs, a sleeve of canvas that fitted inside his leather pack, and went to work in the bed of the river. He chose a narrow transverse channel filled with sand, now dry on the surface and only faintly damp below, and began to fill the pack. With a bark scoop and a tablespoon, he scraped the sand carefully, shuffling forward on his knees along the width of the riffle. After a little his knees began to complain at the hard pebbles and sharp rocks, his back to ache with the strain of bending. He went back to where Byrne was stitching by the dead fire, found an empty flour bag and filled it with dry leaves, tied the neck. This became his cushion, and from then on he carried it every day to the river bed.

He worked carefully and methodically all morning, scraping, filling, carrying, emptying . . . scraping, filling, carrying, emptying. The monotony he found not unpleasant, and long, slow dreams began to meander through his mind as he worked.

At lunch he said to Byrne: 'What will you do when you're rich?'

'Build my hotel,' said Byrne immediately, chewing on cold damper. 'I told you.'

'Yes, but what *else*?'

Byrne looked at him, frowning a little. 'That's enough.'

'Just that? Don't you want to . . . to . . . well, *do* anything?'

'Yes,' and Byrne smiled his self-contained smile. 'I want to build a hotel.'

'And get married?'

'That too . . .'

'After the hotel?'

'After the hotel.'

'And have kids?"

Byrne nodded.

'Nothing else?'

Byrne shook his head, washed down the dry cake with a draught of tea. Wiped his lips with the back of his hand. 'What else is there?'

Gogarty smiled a little pityingly, a little secretively. 'There's lots of things . . .'

'Like what?' said Byrne, packing his pipe. Tobacco was getting low and they were holding themselves to three pipes a day.

'Travel,' said Gogarty. 'I'd like to see a bit of the world.'

'It's much the same wherever you go.'

'Even if you've a bit of money to spend?'

Byrne shrugged indifferently.

'Well, I'm goin' to travel a bit, see a bit of life . . . you know.'

'Women?' said Byrne, a little scornfully. 'Wine, women and song?'

'A bit of that, for sure,' said Gogarty, smiling. 'For sure!'

'You'll blow it,' said Byrne, with authority. 'You'll go through it and end up broke and poxed. That's what'll happen.'

'And I'll come and get a free lunch off my old mate the rich publican, eh?'

'If you've got the price of a drink,' said Byrne, puffing quietly, gazing at the distant mountain.

And Gogarty was a little chilled, defeated, half-believing that Byrne meant what he said.

*

By evening Gogarty's back was aching, his knees were sore despite the cushion, and his fingertips were raw from scraping at the sand. And there seemed precious little washdirt in the bottom of the first pit for his day's work. Byrne stood over the pit nodding.

'Plenty of time. We've got three months . . .'

*

The next day they worked the creek bed together, scraping, filling, carting, emptying. Despite Gogarty's efforts, he suspected that Byrne was carting more washdirt than he was. But if he went any quicker he risked missing dirt. And he knew that the richest gravel was most likely at the bottom of the cracks. So he plugged on, trying to ignore Byrne's trips, trying not to count them against his own.

They worked this way for a week, and gradually the pits began to fill. But after two weeks they filled more slowly, for now they had cleaned out the creek bed close by, were moving further upstream. The weather stayed mild, except for a few dull chilly days late in the month. At some time they realised that they had passed

Christmas; but it did not seem worthwhile to make a fuss – they were both too immersed in their drudgery. Now it was the small tasks of the camp – cutting firewood, cooking damper, cleaning the hut – that provided a welcome change from the dull packhorse routine of the creek bed.

With January the hot weather began, and the sweat ran freely from both men as they trudged back and forth with their packs of gravel, stumbling a little on the uneven bed of the river where the rock ribs now lay mostly exposed. In the evenings, after they had rested, they would take small twig brooms – made by Byrne – and dust out the cracks they had worked earlier.

The last of the black powder for Byrne's old cap-and-ball pistol was gone, so there was no fresh meat. They discussed the prospect of making snares, but there were more urgent jobs to be done. So they subsisted on their diet of porridge, damper and tea. Once every couple of days they would fry up small johnny cakes and eat them in place of damper. Treacle was low, and they no longer sweetened their tea.

Gogarty knew that there would have to be one more trip for stores before the weather broke. But he did not raise the matter, afraid that they might not clear the gravel before the rains came again.

As the heat increased, as the trips upstream became longer, as it became harder to wrest the washdirt from the bed, so their tempers frayed. Small things wore and edged at them. Gogarty found himself longing to strangle Byrne each morning at breakfast as Byrne slurped his oatmeal, licked at droplets clinging to his beard. Byrne complained bitterly that Gogarty always short-salted the damper. Sometimes they would go all day without speaking. Only in the cool and quiet of the evening would they feel calm and sociable enough to discuss the work.

'Another week or two,' said Byrne one night, 'and I'll knock off, put the sluice together . . . don't want to be caught short later.'

Gogarty was silent, tense and angry inside. It would mean that he would be alone on the carting.

But by the end of the month they had filled all the pits, and had to dig more, and it seemed to Gogarty that they must have a fortune stock-piled.

'Can't we wash a bit . . . just to see? I'll carry the water.'

Byrne shook his head. 'Better not,' he said, a reluctant elder brother to an impatient child. 'If it's bad dirt, you'll be disappointed, if it's good you'll want to do more . . . leave it, it won't be long now.'

Gogarty, cheated, went off to sulk in the forest.

Finally, when the shortage of food forced them to action, they made the last trip to Tullah for stores. In the small settlement Gogarty looked longingly at the hotel, but Byrne ignored him resolutely. He was brusque and uncommunicative with the storekeeper. It wasn't until they were back on the track, heavily laden both of them with flour and oatmeal and bacon and treacle and tea that he spoke about it. 'It's silly,' he said, 'at this stage to risk anyone wakin' up to us . . . better not to speak to anyone more than we have to.'

Back at the creek, the weather seemed hotter than ever. The horizon was hazed and unclear, and the smoke of bushfires hung in the west. They worked now stripped to the waist, and their bodies were burnt brown. They were working a mile above the camp now, and the remaining pits were slow to fill. But they kept at it, trudged back and forth, silent and reduced by the heat to beasts of burden. Thirst troubled them, and at Byrne's suggestion they did not drink at all until after the noon meal; instead they sucked small pebbles to keep the saliva flowing. 'I know,' said Byrne, 'once you start drinking in the morning you can't stop . . .'

It seemed easy for him, but the pebbles never seemed to satisfy Gogarty, and he had to stop sometimes, faint and dizzy. Byrne seemed immune to weakness, and Gogarty began to hate him afresh.

Slowly, the weight of summer passed, slowly the heat left the bush, and the nights grew cooler. The sky grew clearer, less hazed, and Gogarty began to feel a little better, a little easier. Finally, one night, Byrne said to him: 'It's time to put the sluice together . . .'

And a rising excitement took Gogarty.

The next morning after they had breakfasted, they took the long myrtle planks from under their bark covering and carried them to the bank of the creek. Byrne sorted carefully through the heap of small foot-long strips that he had cut laboriously with his tiny handsaw. He lay them out along the base plank and took up his pencil.

As the morning wore on they worked together quietly, speaking only in monosyllables, Byrne immersed in the work, Gogarty subdued as if by the gravity of the operation. It was all very well to spend the summer porting dirt, but this was the actual machine that would make them rich . . .

Slowly the machine took shape. It was simple enough: an open, three-sided box twenty-five feet long, the ends open, the bottom set with small transverse riffle strips. All the joints, all the strips, were fastened with brass screws driven tightly into the myrtle, and the box was braced and reinforced with strips and angles of hoop iron nailed into position with brass tingles. The four iron rings that Byrne had brought back on the last trip were set towards the ends, spliced to heavy ropes looped under the body of the sluice.

It was two days before Byrne was satisfied with the strength and tightness of the job. Gogarty peered and craned at it, a little alarmed by the gaps that showed where the planks met.

'Don't worry,' explained Byrne with some patience. 'It's dry as a bone now. But when we wet it, the timber'll soak up the water and swell, and all the joints'll be tight as a fish's arse. We'll leave it now,' he said, 'get on with the washdirt—it'll only take a few hours to rig the sheerlegs when we need them.'

So they went back to carting the heavy packs of gravel, slogging up and down the ravaged bed of the creek, bent and sweating.

In the evenings now Byrne occupied his time with sewing by the firelight. He was making dustbags, small calico bags, closely sewn and with drawstrings, to carry the gold dust.

Gogarty would sit across the fire from him, smoking quietly, wordlessly, watching the bags come into being under Byrne's clever hands, as if by a kind of magic. He imagined them full and heavy with gold . . .

One night he spoke out into the silence. 'It's too good to be true, isn't it? Something'll happen, won't it?'

Byrne shook his head impatiently. 'Don't put the mockers on us . . . it'll be right. Why shouldn't it be?' And he went on stitching.

Why shouldn't it? thought Gogarty. Why shouldn't it? I don't know, I don't know . . . but it isn't the way of life for things to go too smoothly . . .

And the dark shadow refused to move from his mind.

*

They came now into a period of waiting, of impatience, of uncertainty. The first rain clouds rolled in from the west, dropped a thin shower, passed on. The first chill of autumn touched the camp in the early mornings and dew lay heavily in their shadowed clearing.

Yet the rains did not come. Their spring still flowed, and they did not go thirsty. But the rains did not come.

And Gogarty grew impatient, and sullen, and unbiddable. He took long walks alone, and on some days refused to leave his blankets until the sun was high. Byrne seemed to take no notice, went about his business as if all were normal. He had begun to lay out his poles and spars beside the big sluice on the bank, to make a start at lashing the gear together, threading ropes through blocks, measuring and calculating. And when he was not doing that he spent his time in the creek bed near the camp, prising small boulders from the creek, spooning out the gravel below them, adding it to the store. Neither of them wanted to leave the camp, to risk absence when the rain started and the sluicing began.

Yet the rains did not come.

The weather grew chilly, the nights sharper, the days greyer. They wore their bluey jackets most of the time now, and when not working they tended to huddle by the fire. Gogarty spent his time making sombre calculations about gold.

'How much will it weigh? The gold, I mean? To carry out?'

Byrne laughed. 'Not so much we'll have to leave any behind.'

'But how *much*?' Gogarty persisted.

'Christ knows.' Byrne sounded impatient. 'Depends how rich the gravel is . . .'

'But roughly?'

'Jesus . . . I don't know . . . but we could each easy carry a couple of thousand pounds' worth on our backs.'

'God!' The prospect stunned Gogarty. After a moment he said: 'What's the most money you've ever had? At one time?'

Byrne shrugged. 'I don't know. Maybe forty or fifty pounds after a long voyage.'

'Two thousand each . . .' said Gogarty, dreamy and abstracted.

He looked at Byrne across the dusty circle of the fireplace. 'I've never had more than a fiver at once . . .' He jumped up suddenly. 'Why won't it bloody *rain!*'

*

One morning, after the frost had melted and the sun was shining, Gogarty and Byrne were both kneeling in the creek bed gouging out rocks, collecting gravel. They worked in silence, Gogarty fifty yards or so upstream from Byrne. He worked lethargically, uninterested in the sand and grit that was so familiar to him that it no longer seemed connected with the promise of gold. If only, he thought, we could get a sight of it, maybe go downstream and do a bit of panning, anything to break the monotony . . . He shuffled his knees a little on his old flour sack, avoiding a damp patch, went on scraping at the hole where the rock had been. A little water was gathering slowly in the bottom, trickling down the side into the hole. His knees were growing damp through the pad of his cushion. He shifted irritably, gave up scooping at the loose sand as it grew wet.

Wet!

He sprang to his feet, his mouth open in a strangled cry. Looking upstream he saw a creeping moistness in the creek bed – fine, thin tails of water slowly moving downstream, dampening the bare rocks and darkening the sand. There was no depth to it, a mere long deepening stain. But it was water . . .

He shouted to Byrne, and they stood wordless for a moment watching it.

'But it hasn't *rained*,' said Gogarty. 'How can there be water?'

'Upstream,' said Byrne. 'It rained in the mountains. Remember the cloud to the north, the bit of thunder? It's started. Up there somewhere . . .'

'It's a mad country,' said Gogarty, shaking his head.

'Come on,' said Byrne. 'Let's get the sluice rigged.'

*

By evening the sluice was ready, the tackle rigged, the sheerlegs in place. The long timber box lay on the bank beside the creek, parallel to the stream bed four feet below. At each end a pair of tall sheerlegs stood, towering over the men; and from each sheerleg a long boom, anchored deep in the soil, projected out over the stream bed like a giant fishing rod. From the ends of the booms hung the blocks and lines to lift the sluice out over the stream. At the upstream end of the sluice box a canvas tube, sewn by Byrne, was fastened. From its mouth a line led up to a smaller boom projecting from the nearest sheerleg. Byrne had tested every lashing, every footing, and they had swung the sluice into the air, its weight easily borne by the two men.

But in the morning there was still no water in the creek, only the now familiar dampness of the sand and rock. The tall sheerlegs, the long coffin of the sluice box seemed to mock them.

The sky stayed clear, and it did not rain.

It did not rain that day, nor the day after.

It did not rain for a week, and both men by then had sunk into a silence so tense and murderous that they hardly dared break it with conversation. They ate their damper, drank their tea and smoked their pipes in silence, went to bed wordless, rose again without greeting . . .

They had no heart for work, for gouging the too-familiar creek bed.

And then on the ninth day the rain began. It started with a gentle swirling drizzle from the west, a mere misting that pearled their clothes, the grass, the ropes of the sluice tackle. Then, after an hour, it increased to light rain, steadied itself, set in harder, and, in front of a cold wind, blew rain hour after hour without a let-up. They sat in the hut now, by the wide bark fireplace, smoking, one of them leaving the hut every half hour or so to look at the creek.

There was no change that day, but when they woke next morning it was still raining, and over their porridge they nodded to each other wisely. The weather let up briefly in the afternoon, then set in again harder than ever. It grew quite cold, and they built up their fire. By late afternoon there was a trickle of water in the creek. It did not increase much before dark. But that night they both lay awake for a long time listening to the gurgle and splash of the rising water.

By morning there was a foot of water in the bed, and it was rising fast against the marked stick that Byrne had set by the bank.

'It's time to get set up,' he said, 'to get things ready.'

So they hauled on the ropes, swung the sluice clear of the bank and let it down into the creek bed where the brown water splashed over it. Within an hour or so it had started to absorb water, to swell and close the cracks. When they swung it back on to the bank in the later afternoon, it was much heavier, and tested their strength on the lines. By then they had laid out their tools, the shovel, the pan, the canvas buckets, and had opened the first pit, begun to move washdirt to the bank.

'Tomorrow,' said Byrne, laying an old sack over the first pile of washdirt, 'tomorrow for sure . . .'

*

All the next morning the rain persisted, although now there were breaks in it. But the top of the mountain was still covered by cloud, and the creek was nearly three feet deep, a steady stream of peaty water, cold and strong. By lunchtime it had almost stopped rising, and Byrne decided that it was time to test the sluice.

They swung out the box, anchored it in position a couple of feet from the bank and a few inches above the water, the upstream end higher than the other. Gogarty spread a shovelful of washdirt above the top riffle and Byrne slacked off the pipeline, let the mouth of the canvas pipe dip into the fast-flowing stream. A small tide of water rose, flowed through the canvas tube and down the sluice, and washed the piled gravel out, leaving the heavier parts behind the riffles. Byrne steadied the pipe, adjusted it to give a constant flow, tied off the line. With one foot on the bank and one resting on the rim of the sluice box, he began rocking it gently. At his nod, Gogarty shovelled a little more washdirt in.

They worked steadily for an hour. Slowly Gogarty began to grow more skilled at placing the washdirt and letting the water take it easily off the shovel; Byrne at rocking the sluice and regulating the flow so that the gravel was spread evenly over the riffle. When they lifted the sluice clear, swung it to the bank, it was sodden and much heavier. Carefully, using scrapers fashioned from old tin cans, they cleaned the riffles, deposited the settled dirt into a pan.

'Every day or so,' said Byrne, 'I'll unscrew the riffle bars, clean her out properly.'

'What now?' said Gogarty, straightening his knees, kneading his back.

'Get a bucket of water,' said Byrne, 'and we'll give her a final panning.'

So Gogarty hauled a bucket from the stream and poured the water gently into the pan while Byrne swirled, swished, swirled, spilled the lighter sand out on the bank. Finally, he poured off the last of the water and sat regarding the line of fine gold granules, a mass that seemed almost soft, liquid; so fine it was, the soft afternoon light touching it with bright yellow so that it gleamed against the black specks of grit and the grey sludge.

'Give her a little bit more,' said Byrne.

Gogarty poured, Byrne panned, and they both sat back on their heels, staring into the pan. The rain fell on them unregarded.

'Christ,' said Gogarty gently.

'It's there,' said Byrne, as if he had lately grown unsure. 'It's really there . . .'

And they smiled slowly at each other in the rain, smiles of relief and wonder, at the miracle that was happening to them.

'Come on,' said Byrne at last. He carefully decanted the precious slurry into an old treacle tin, stood up.

They went happily back to the bank, swung on the lines, heaved the sluice back over the rising creek. Byrne lowered the canvas pipe, began rocking as Gogarty spread the first shovel of dirt . . .

By nightfall they had put through another three loads, and they were soaked and sodden and ecstatic.

*

That night after they had eaten, they cleaned the frypan, spread the slurry from the treacle tin in it and dried it, stirring over the fire. They were very silent, watching the grains catch the light.

'You know,' said Gogarty at last, 'it really is yellow.' He raised his head, looked at Byrne's solemn, bearded face. 'I thought maybe it would be kind of black or something.' He lowered his eyes to the pan again. 'I'm glad it's yellow . . .'

'We'd better bury it every night,' said Byrne.

'Where?' said Gogarty, carefully, averting his eyes a little.

'Somewhere simple, close. Maybe right in the middle of the doorway.'

Gogarty nodded slowly. No one would be able to get at it there, disturb it, without being seen. As long as they were both at the camp. As long as one wasn't off somewhere alone. He frowned, struggled with the thought . . .

'Do you want to split it every night? Take your share?' asked Byrne, his voice non-committal.

Gogarty thought about it. 'Do you?'

'I don't think so,' said Byrne carefully. 'I think we should divide it up when we finish. That way we'll maybe make it fairer, even it out, like . . .'

Gogarty nodded slowly.

So they scraped a shallow hole right in the muddy entrance to the hut, buried the can, filled in the hole, stamped and scuffled over it until there was no sign of their digging.

They drank a last mug of tea, smoked a final pipe each. But they had little to say to each other now. The knowledge of the gold under the doorstep seemed to have sobered them.

Just before he fell asleep Gogarty decided that, although he trusted Byrne, when he had his morning shit he would somehow do it within sight of the hut . . .

*

The days fell quickly into the pattern of their gold-getting. Each man assumed his tasks without discussion. Each morning, wet or dry, frost or rain, they rose as soon as it was light enough to see.

Byrne built up the fire, Gogarty hauled the water. Byrne began porridge, Gogarty made tea. They ate, hunched in front of the hearth, seldom speaking, their faces intent and focussed on the day to come. Their beards were long now, their hair grown down over their collars. Although they washed each night in a basin of warmed water before the fire, they had taken on the air of tramps, with small tidemarks of grime where their daily wash ended – behind the ears, above the wrists – and their beards were lightly festooned with fragments of food. Their clothes were clean enough, being soaked by river and rain, but carried the stiff, crushed look of cloth dried too often before too hot a fire. Their boots were pale and pulpy, the original colour long bleached away by persistent soakings. Bacon grease and lard rubbed into the leather lent them a scullery odour when they were set to dry by the fire.

When the two men had eaten they would leave the hut immediately, pausing to scuff a final time at the excavation marks by the doors, ensure their obliteration.

Then Gogarty would take the shovel, the canvas buckets, and begin to cart the day's dirt from the storage pits while Byrne checked the lashings on the sheerlegs, the screws and nails of the sluice. Then they would begin work; hoisting the sluice out over the fast-running stream, adjusting it; Byrne dipping the mouth of the pipe, the water beginning to course in the sluice; Gogarty throwing in the first shovelful of washdirt, spreading it over the bars with a twist of his wrist; Byrne rocking, rocking . . .

Then, hoisting the sluice clear, settling it on the bank . . . cleaning the riffles . . . once a day unscrewing them, re-greasing the brass screws, reassembling them; then hauling out, dipping, spreading, rocking . . .

At midday, a bit of cold damper, a cup of tea, a pipe, huddled over the hurriedly rebuilt fire; or if the day was fine, sitting in the sun by the doorframe . . .

In the evening, stripping off sodden clothes, washing quickly, putting on the stiff dry trousers and shirts. Bluey jackets hung near the fire to drip and warm, boots in the corner where they would not char. Damper in the coals, perhaps a bit of bacon; or hot dough fried in lard; brownie, dark with treacle, studded sparsely with currants; once a treat of fresh meat, stew, steaks, soup, after Gogarty by chance had knocked down a wallaby at dawn with his shovel. Always tea, dark, bitter, strong . . .

And afterwards the nightly ritual of exhumation, examination, adding the day's washings, reburying, scuffing . . .

Then sleep as the fire died, rolled in blankets close to the cooling hearth, aching bodies sinking into dreamless exhaustion . . .

Autumn, with the last of the clear weather, passed away unnoticed. The deep frosts began, and the men worked for days on end, chilled and stiff, their fingers blue with cold, so numb that they could barely tie the knots that held the sluice steady. In the third month the frosts were so bad, as mid-winter approached, that they were forced to light a great fire near the river bank and retreat to it every few minutes to thaw frozen fingers and feet . . .

But mostly it was rain, cold continuous rain, that swept in from the west, hiding the hills, the sky, everything but the narrow compass of their camp in the clearing, a hundred yards or so of rushing, dark water. They stayed wet for days on end, their dry clothes blotting up water as soon as they left the shelter of the hut; they walked in water, worked in it, seemed to breathe a kind of air that was mostly water. They both developed permanent coughs, and the nights were studded with their private hoarse barkings.

There were no holidays, no rests. Once they were forced to stop for a day when, sodden with water, the sluice grew too heavy for the booms, and they had to cut new spars, heavier, thicker, pull them half a mile, lash them in place. That day they wrought in the sodden world of rain and mud and recalcitrant swollen rope. But before evening they had the new spars in place, ready for the next day.

Every day was the same, and after a time neither of them seemed to notice whether the sun shone, whether the frosts were heavy or light, whether the world still existed outside their narrow, muddy platform.

But day by day the hoard of gold dust buried in the treacle tins under the threshold of the hut grew . . . And that was all that filled their minds; there was room for nothing else now . . .

As the weeks passed, grew into months, as the months themselves passed, the two of them grew more silent, more taciturn. Byrne had long ceased to talk of his hotel, Gogarty of travels to wider worlds.

Both men retreated into a kind of bitter, grinding marriage with elements that needed no language. The flowing water that clarified their coldness, concentrated it, was the ultimate reality in their world. And each worried, unknown to the other, in case the creek should flood, find a new bed, and leave them high and dry . . .

It seemed almost, as the time passed, that they had lost the need for speech; their life was so simple, so clearly delineated, that speech at last had become superfluous.

Yet once – on what was to be their final day of sluicing – they argued bitterly, cursed and slanged each other with force and fury. It was over nothing much.

As they trudged to the creek bank after breakfast, through a thin, driving drizzle that chilled the heart worse than honest rain, Gogarty – head bowed, broken hat brim pulled down, hands like great dirty claws clasping his worn shovel – spoke:

'We should pan each lot as we clean the sluice, not leave it till night . . .' He spoke with certainty, as if no demurral was admissable.

Byrne glanced at him dully. 'Don't be stupid, we've done it the other way since we started.'

'It's the wrong way,' said Gogarty. 'Just because you're a bloody know-all, we're doin' it the wrong way.'

'Don't be stupid.'

'You're the bloody stupid one, you stuck-up bastard . . .'

They trudged on, stopped at the bank. Byrne stood by his rope; Gogarty made no effort to take his.

'We should pan each load . . .'

'If you don't haul on that bloody rope we won't *have* a load to pan at all!'

Gogarty, throat frozen and constricted in a mad unreasoning fury, grabbed the rope and threw his weight on it. The sluice jerked up at his end, almost slipped away into the river.

'Look out, you bloody idiot!' shouted Byrne, hauling quickly, reaching with his foot to steady the sluice.

They went to work silently, each intent on his own anger.

At midday, cupping his hot mug, peering steadily into the fire, Gogarty returned to his preoccupation.

'I still think we should pan each load as we do it . . .'

'Why now?' said Byrne, keeping his voice steady. 'It's worked all right up to the present. Why change now?'

'It's better,' said Gogarty, doggedly. He had come upon the conclusion, during his long hours on the shovel, that by panning each load as they cleared the sluice they would have a chance for a few minutes' rest. But he could not bring himself to tell Byrne of his reason.

'You're just bloody lazy,' said Byrne, guessing it.

'What!' Enraged at discovery.

'You want to sit on your arse half the day and let me do the bloody work, that's what!'

Gogarty sprang to his feet. So did Byrne, and they stood glaring at each other over the fire like snarling, bedraggled mongrels. At last Gogarty turned away, stumped off to the creek bed, where he waited in hot silence for Byrne . . .

*

The afternoon seemed to last interminably for Gogarty. He swung his shovel, carted his washdirt, evading Byrne's eye, yet trying to watch his face. But neither man weakened, neither man spoke except for the most urgent of matters. This irritated them both further. By mid-afternoon Gogarty was working in white rage, beginning to mutter and grunt under his breath. This Byrne ignored, his face expressionless.

There was only an hour of daylight left when the end came. It would be their last sluice load, and Gogarty was priming himself for a new attack on Byrne. He had stepped back to the decreasing pile of washdirt on the bank, begun to scrape it together, while Byrne stood in his usual post on the edge of the bank, one leg rocking the sluice, one hand on the sheerleg.

It seemed afterwards to Gogarty that everything happened in slow motion, that there had been time enough for him to warn Byrne, to do anything he wished. The whole progression of events seemed spread over long minutes, as he stood gape-mouthed with his shovel, watching . . .

At first it seemed to him as if the world was bending, twisting, the lines of reality distorting, as if he were in the course of being overtaken by some strange illness, the onset of some strange aberration of vision. The riverbank seemed to tremble a little, to sink away slightly, so that the level of the bank, the angle of the sheerlegs, the jut of the booms were no longer the same . . .

Even Byrne's body, partway between bank and water, seemed suddenly awkward, unsteady . . .

He realised then, a fraction of a second before everything collapsed, what was happening – that the bank of the creek on which they and their machine stood had been slowly undercut by the flow of the creek, by months of their weight. A deep crack was widening a yard back from the edge, smaller cracks appearing; the front of the bank was dipping, the bottoms of the sheerlegs beginning to move, to tear loose from their holes. The tops of the booms began to dip towards the water.

He opened his mouth to call a warning to Byrne, who seemed yet unalarmed, unaware. Then closed it again, thinking, serve you right, you know-all bastard, serve you right for all the shit you've poured on me, for all the donkey work I've had to do, for the bloody sneering way of you . . . let your bloody marvellous machine fall in the bloody river, and you with it . . .

And then the bank finally gave way.

The great ledge of earth slipped into the fast water with a single great splash, Byrne with it, sliding down with his feet under the sluice. The sluice was in the water with him, and the sheerlegs and booms fell slowly over him in a tangle. In a second or two the sluice and the bank had gone, dissolved into a flurried mess of poles and wet earth and white-crested brown water . . .

It had never occurred to Gogarty that Byrne might be injured. After all, the creek was at the most four feet deep; there was earth to cushion him, water to break his fall . . .

So he watched, at first with amusement, then with the beginnings of alarm, waiting for Byrne to reappear above the brown, roiled surface of the creek.

But there was only the mess of poles and rope and broken water, and the lower end of the sluice as it swung sideways to the current, still held fast by its ropes to the remains of the booms and sheerlegs. He started forward, then, sudden anxiety seizing him. And as he did so, he caught a glimpse of Byrne's face, white as paper against the slicked wet beard and hair, mouth gagging, eyes closed, as it bobbed for a moment to the surface under the bank.

Then Gogarty was slipping, sliding down the bank, into the cold, brown water feet first, reaching under the spume and mud and the tangle of rope for Byrne . . .

He worked out much later – from the nature of Byrne's injuries as much as anything else – what had happened when the bank gave way. As Byrne's feet had slipped, as he shot down, his legs had slid beneath the descending sluice box. The bank, almost liquid earth descending on him, had jammed him on the bottom, for all the world as if he were sitting on the creek bed with the sluice box in his lap. In a moment the sluice was swept away to the end of its rope by the current, but, despite the cushioning effect of the water, the great weight of the sodden iron-heavy box had broken both his thighs. Then the tangle of lashings and lines and sheerlegs had descended on him, pressed him down, down . . .

At first, because Byrne's body came free of the mess so easily, the bulk of the wreckage having floated free, Gogarty thought that he was uninjured. Hands under Byrne's arms, slipping and sliding in the slick, wet earth of the broken bank, Gogarty pulled the smaller man clear of the water and on to the bank. It was only as he laid him down on the grass that he noticed the odd angles of the thighs . . .

Byrne did not seem to be breathing and Gogarty did not know quite what to do. But as he watched, Byrne coughed weakly, began to vomit river water. He opened his eyes for a moment. Then, as he struggled to sit up, the pain struck him and he fell back, his face pale, his lips blue.

Gogarty squatted beside him chafing his hands, quite overcome by the disaster.

*

He squatted there, stunned by the enormity of it all, for what seemed to him like hours, but was in fact no more than a minute or two. Darkness was drawing in, a slow misting veil of rain closing over the land, and he knew that he would have to get Byrne under shelter. It seemed that dragging him would cause less damage than carrying, so he stood up, took him under the shoulders and hauled him across the sodden ground to the hut. He lowered Byrne's shoulders to the ground, lit a candle, then lay a waterproof groundsheet and a blanket on the floor beside the fireplace. He could not face the prospect of getting Byrne into a bunk – the thought of the loose, dangling legs unnerved him. He propped Byrne's head on a rough pillow of old clothes, began to stir the ashes, to build a new fire. When it was blazing, lighting the small, cramped spaces of the hut with wild flickerings, he shuffled across to Byrne on his knees, looked down at him. He was still unconscious, his face very pale. He suddenly seemed much younger . . .

Gogarty propped the awkward torso up against his knees, unbuttoned the sodden coat and shirt, worked them slowly off. Byrne groaned a little but did not wake. Gogarty looked at the soaked trousers and shook his head. First he untied the bootlaces, worked the heavy boots off Byrne's feet; then, from the pocket of Byrne's jacket, he took the sharp clasp knife and slit the heavy dungarees from waist to cuff, eased the material away from Byrne's legs and pulled it clear. He looked quickly, swallowing uneasily, at Byrne's thighs; both were lumpy and strange-looking, with knobs of bruised flesh where broken bone ends tried to penetrate the envelope of muscle. He turned away and fetched a clean, dry shirt which he managed to work on to Byrne's torso, then covered him with two blankets. He tended the fire again, set a billy to boil, found the brandy bottle in the jumble in the corner of the hut, took a sip, set the bottle down, sat in front of the fire, huddled close, clasping his knees, his mind a panicked confusion, shifting and evading, unable to focus for more than a few seconds on anything.

When the billy boiled he made tea and sat sipping from his mug, sipping carefully, conscientiously, as if it were the most important thing in the world. After a while he realised that he was shivering, still soaked from his dip in the river. He rose and changed his clothes, put on dry ones, went back to the fire. He did not feel hungry, nor especially tired, but quite drowsy now. He sipped at his tea, his eyes avoiding the still figure of Byrne.

At last Byrne groaned, stirred a little.

Gogarty, turning his head unwillingly, saw that Byrne was conscious, his face creased in pain.

Gogarty wanted badly to look away again, to evade the problem, thinking, I did it, it was my fault, I could have called out, could have warned him, couldn't I? There was time, wasn't there? It didn't happen as quickly as all that, did it? My fault, it was my fault . . . He forced himself to keep looking at Byrne, to put down his mug, move on his knees to squat beside the injured man.

Byrne tried to move, to sit up. He fell back, his eyes closed at the spasm of pain that crossed his face. Breathing heavily, he lay still for a minute or two before he opened his eyes again. When he did, they looked very dark against the paleness of his face.

'How bad?' Byrne's voice was little more than a whisper.

Gogarty swallowed, feeling iller than ever.

'How bad?' repeated Byrne.

Fixing his eyes on a spot at the bridge of Byrne's nose, Gogarty made himself speak. 'Both your . . .' Started again. 'Both your legs . . . broken.'

'Where?'

'Above the knee . . .'

Byrne closed his eyes, seemed to settle lower against the ground. After a little he opened his eyes again, looked steadily at Gogarty.

'Something else is broke, too,' he said, his voice almost a whisper. 'Something inside, in my belly, my chest . . .'

Gogarty said nothing, but found the brandy bottle, moved closer to hold it to Byrne's lips. Byrne shook his head slightly.

'Later . . .'

For a long time there was silence except for the small sounds of the fire, the whisper of the rain outside. Finally Byrne spoke again.

'You'll have to set the legs,' he said.

Gogarty was aghast. 'How? I've never done anything like that.'

'I'll tell you . . .' Byrne's voice was a little stronger now, as if he were summoning up reserves. 'And afterwards, you'll have to keep me warm, that's important, don't let the fire go out . . .'

Gogarty felt the end of the world approaching, an apocalypse of his own frightening inadequacy. He forced his attention to Byrne's words as he gave instructions . . .

'. . . and whatever you do,' said Byrne, don't stop once you start . . . and for Christ's sake don't crush my nuts.'

Gogarty nodded vaguely.

'Get started, then,' said Byrne, closing his eyes again. 'The longer you leave it the worse it'll be for both of us . . .'

So Gogarty, in a kind of dream, got up and went out into the darkness. He found the axe, went down to the creek. He could barely see the rushing water in the darkness, but he fumbled at the edge of the bank until he found the remains of one of the sheerlegs, a pair of spars that the creek had not carried off. He hauled them laboriously out of the water, cut the lashings free, measured off two sections. He dropped the axe, carried the sodden wood back into the hut. With the clasp knife he began to cut Byrne's wrecked dungarees into long strips. When he was done, he sat gazing blankly into the fire, his breathing shallow. Almost absently he took one sip, then another, from the bottle. Then he held it towards Byrne: 'You'd better have some . . .'

'No,' said Byrne, moving his head slightly from side to side, 'I don't think it'd be a good idea with my insides the way they are . . .'

'It'll hurt,' said Gogarty.

'And the sooner you bloody start the sooner it'll be over,' said Byrne with a sudden urgent temper. 'For Christ's sake *do* it!' His head flopped back on the makeshift pillow.

Feeling very sick, Gogarty stood up. He bent over, peeled the blanket away from Byrne's body.

'Do it just like I told you,' said Byrne, not opening his eyes.

Gogarty took the rough splints and lay two of them outside Byrne's legs. He attached them tightly at the calves with strips of dungaree, loosely at the thigh. Then he set the other two splints inside the legs, extending from groin to ankle; he attached these in the same way, fixed slipknots, then he sat down and unlaced his own boots.

'For God's sake mind my balls . . .' Byrne's voice was fading again, weak and thin now.

Gogarty moved until he was sitting on the ground facing Byrne, his right leg extended between both of Byrne's, the foot in Byrne's crutch. Gently he leaned forward, lifted Byrne's genitals out of the way, forced his bare foot firmly into the groin.

'Ready?' he said.

'Go on,' said Byrne without moving or opening his eyes. Gogarty took Byrne's left leg in his hands, fingers round shin and calf, close to his chest, lay back, settled his foot in the crutch, and began to straighten his braced leg, pulling steadily . . .

Byrne screamed and fainted, and after a momentary start, Gogarty strained harder, felt the two ends of the thighbone meet, grating. Wedging the leg under his arm, he hauled on the slipknots until the splints were firm and tight, holding the leg rigid, the bone ends butted. He changed legs and began again. This leg was more difficult – the bone ends seemed intent on not meshing, and Gogarty was sweating badly before it was done. He slipped out from between the splints, staggered to his feet, dragged the blankets over Byrne, then blundered out in the night to vomit copiously.

He came back, rinsed his mouth with the cooled tea, spat in the fire, threw more wood on it. Washed his mouth again with a swallow of brandy. Sat by the fire watching Byrne's motionless face, listening to the slightly ragged shallow breathing.

Suddenly the guilt which he had managed to keep submerged all through the bone-setting flooded over him like a great suffocating tide. He let himself slip sideways until his cheek was resting on the chill dirt of the floor. A few tears slipped across his cheek and pooled into mud. And he found that his guilt had been miraculously transformed to self-pity. What could he do now, trapped with a badly injured Byrne in the middle of the bush? What to do? How to escape? And why? Why? Why him?

He sat up, disgusted at himself, wiped the muddy tears from his cheek. At least, he thought, I can look after him. I made a mess of it, it's my fault all right, no doubt of that, and I'll give him all my gold, make him take it; but at least I've fixed him up, doctored him as best I can, even if he had to tell me what to do . . .

It never dawned on him that Byrne might die. Broken legs, well, it was serious, but Byrne was at the peak of strength, young, fit; he would heal quickly. And if they had to wait for a month or two, well, they had a dry hut, plenty of firewood. Food was getting low again, but he could make a lone trip out, pack a load back; he was big and strong, thank God, and it would turn out all right . . .

And he felt a little better after that, and found that he was very tired. So he made himself a damper, put it in the ashes to cook, made more tea and drank it while he waited. He was tempted to add a splash of brandy, but decided that Byrne might need it after all. And a sudden chill took him when he thought of Byrne's words . . . something broke inside . . . But he shook it off quickly as the fancy of a shocked and injured man . . .

He ate part of the damper before it was quite cooked, still a little soggy in the middle. And he had forgotten to salt the dough. But he poured plenty of treacle on it, and chewed greedily, washing the heavy mixture down with strong tea. Afterwards, he sat staring into the fire, smoking his pipe. It could be worse, after all, and he would make it up to Byrne, for sure . . . if not *all* the gold, then most of it . . . and he'd help him build the hotel, even. He had nothing better to do . . . he'd go travelling about a bit later . . . And he wasn't really sure if he would have had time to warn Byrne anyway, it all happened so quickly . . . he realised quite suddenly that Byrne was awake, and shifted his gaze.

Byrne's face was pinched and white, his cheeks hollow as if he had not eaten for days, and his nostrils were crimped, his mouth thin and stressed. His eyes were open, fixed on the low bark roof of the hut, lit only dimly now by the dying fire.

Gogarty edged nervously across to him. 'Anything you want?' he said softly. 'A drink?'

'Smoke,' said Byrne. And his voice seemed to come from a great distance.

So Gogarty packed Byrne's pipe, lit it, held it to Byrne's lips. But after a couple of puffs Byrne began to cough, and seemed to faint again.

Gogarty went back to the fire.

Later in the night, when he woke from a doze, and went to fetch more wood for the fire, he thought that Byrne was awake, too. But his eyes were closed, and it was difficult to tell . . .

*

Gogarty woke with a start, to find that it was full daylight, and the rain had gone. Bright, washed sunlight laid gold on the wet grass, gilded the mud, cast a bright path through the hut's doorway.

He stood up, stretching, easing stiff bones. Saw that the blankets had slipped a little, leaving Byrne's feet bare. They were a cold bluish colour, and he stooped quickly, replaced the blanket. Rising again, he found that Byrne's eyes, alert and pain-filled, were on him.

He stopped. 'How are you, Jack?' he said. 'You feel any better?'

Byrne coughed, stifled it in pain. Then he spoke, his eyes, dark in their sudden hollows, still fixed on Gogarty.

'Go east,' he said, his voice a faint ribbon of life, twisting and curling about his pain. 'Go east, a bit south . . . you'll come across the railway.'

'I'm stayin' with you, Jack . . .'

'Yes,' said Byrne, closing his eyes. 'But when the time comes . . .'

'You're gonna be all right,' said Gogarty, trying to reassure himself.

For a time Byrne didn't say anything. Then, his eyes still closed, he spoke again. 'You did a good job on the legs, mate . . .' Closed his eyes again.

Gogarty, his throat tightening with pity and despair, wanted desperately to own to his shame, to beg for some forgiveness, some discharge . . . But Byrne lay so quiet, so pale, that he turned away, tiptoed out into the sunlight.

In the afternoon Byrne spoke again.

'Funny,' he said, his voice a little stronger, 'the old bloke who told me about the gold . . . he broke his leg too . . .' and he attempted a kind of chuckle that petered into a cough that turned into a groan.

He did not speak again.

By evening he was deep in fever, shaking, sweating, groaning. When Gogarty woke in the very early morning from his deep sleep he saw that Byrne was still again, not shaking. He felt his brow, but it felt as hot as ever. Byrne opened his eyes, looked at Gogarty a moment, then quickly about the small hut in a kind of wonderment, as if he could not remember where he was. Then his eyes closed and he slipped away again. That day he groaned for hours, until Gogarty was forced to walk away into the bush so that he could no longer hear it. He tried to make Byrne drink, but the fluid spilled from his lips, and only made him cough. By that evening Byrne was quiet again. Gogarty slept deeply all through the night, and when he woke in the pre-dawn chill to stoke the fire, he felt something odd, something strange and frightening about the hut. It took him several moments to realise that Byrne was no longer breathing. He lit a candle and stumbled across the floor, stood peering down at Byrne. The face was stark, fallen in on itself, the skin marble-white against the frame of tangled beard and hair. His eyes were closed, his mouth open. When Gogarty reached down cautiously and touched the skin of the cheek it was cold and inelastic, and he knew that Byrne had been gone for hours.

*

By the third day Gogarty knew that he was going to die.

It was not so much that he was lost, out of food, wet and shivering; it was rather that he had the growing sense of some relentless doom closing about him, a circle of guilt and retribution drawing gradually in. An enormous pressure seemed to swell inside his chest, choking him, until he could hardly draw breath . . .

In the afternoon he collapsed in a huddle of muddy leaf mould by the banks of a small creek. He drank from the brown, sweet water. It was colder than ice, and quietened the raging thirst in him. Once he stopped moving the sweat began to chill on his body and he started to shiver. He stood up, staggered up the slope a hundred yards between the low trees, through small mossy passageways and under overhanging branches, until the air seemed warmer. He dropped his pack beside the trunk of a tall tree, unstrapped his damp blanket and wrapped it round his shoulders, hunched against the tree. For a moment he closed his eyes. But strange echoes in his head jerked him awake again, and his eyes snapped open. A small mist was beginning to creep up the slope from the creek bed. In half an hour it would be dark.

After Byrne's death he had waited a full day at the camp site, although his every instinct had been to run. He had waited, had moved silently about the clearing, prowling in his new aloneness like some dumb abandoned beast. In the afternoon he had dug up the gold, had set the treacle tins by the fireside, had sat watching them. Byrne's body lay at the edge of the firelight, a visitor slow to leave.

After half an hour, Gogarty had left the hut, taken his shovel, dug a narrow grave in the bush. There were tree roots, and he had to take the axe to them. He wrapped Byrne's body in a blanket, carefully tying the end over the white waxy face so that dirt might not touch it. He had a moment of revulsion when he picked it up, and stumbled a little as he carried the burden, strangely light it seemed now for its previous strength, across the clearing and into the bush.

After the hole was filled he stood for a long time beside it, smoothing it over carefully with the shovel blade, deferring as long as possible the true aloneness that was now his world. At last he turned away, went back to the fire, made tea, sat sipping it. He debated the matter of a grave-marker for Byrne; decided finally against it. On the one hand, it seemed wrong to leave him anonymous and lost in the bush; on the other, he felt some strange and inexplicable belief that the body would lie better unmarked and unfound.

He sat long by the fire, stirring only to throw a new log on it, to refill the billy from the bucket, to make tea. Through the long night he sat, almost motionless, staring at the ebb and flow of light in the embers, avoiding the sight of the dark and empty doorway. In his mind he turned his actions like coins, auditing, assessing, evaluating. Always returning to the unshakeable and adamantine conviction of guilt that underpinned his new lonely world.

If he had not sulked, if he had warned Byrne, then Byrne would be alive . . .

If he not allowed his accumulated ill-humours to overwhelm him, Byrne would still be alive . . .

The night outside the hut, the blackness at the door, the encircling universe of cold and scorn and anger, all were filled with the reverberations of his wrong-doing, his pettiness and his shame. The wings of strange birds seemed to beat silently in the shadows, and he dared not look behind him . . .

He was tempted to discard the gold, open the tins, untie the drawstrings of the calico bags, drain the precious grit back into the creek. But he could not bring himself to such sacrifice . . .

So he sat till dawn, shivering, staring at the coals, picking at his blackened and torn fingernails, scraping chance patterns in the dust at his feet . . .

And when the first faint light in the east broke above the trees, when the dark edge of the forest showed hard and clear against the pale, chill sky, he rose stiffly, lifted the heavy treacle tins into his pack, threw in a few random handfuls of food – raisins, half a damper, tea, salt – took his battered, almost brimless, bowler from a peg on the doorframe, and walked out of the hut into the advancing dawn. Behind him the fire still burned brightly in the frame of the doorway, the camp lay ready for the day, its tools and fittings waiting for men to use them, an air of cheer and domesticity in the day's beginning . . .

He did not look back, but kept his head turned resolutely towards the east, plowed into the bush, not bothering to look for tracks or easy passages . . .

East . . . and, as Byrne had said, a little south . . .

Or so he thought at the time, anyway, although afterwards he was never quite sure . . .

*

The first two days were a bad dream of wet forest, creek beds too deep to wade, mossy swamps, wide rough buttongrass plains. The sun was lost early on the first day, the sky covered by a high, chill layer of cloud so that the world was blanched to a grey monochrome, without light, without shadows, without colour. And without direction. He tried to keep a line to his march, but was reasonably certain that he was straying. Byrne, he thought, would know directions from the growth of moss on trees, from winds and birds, and no doubt from strange voices in his head . . . He found himself laughing aloud at this, for some reason . . .

He was now, under his tree, curiously untired; he felt no fatigue, only a kind of emptiness and occasional pangs in his belly. He had not eaten for three days. It seemed, and it seemed quite funny to him, that he had brought food and tea, but no pan, no billy, no matches. He could cook nothing, make no tea, light no fire . . .

He had chewed the raisins, thrown the rest away, smiling to himself as he did. That was before the world had begun closing in on him . . .

He had crossed a river on the second day, wading through the freezing waist-high water, kept moving, and had expected to meet the railway line at any time after that. But there had been nothing but more bush. And he knew that he must have swung too far north, that there was much further to go, maybe another river to cross . . .

Then, towards the evening of the second day, he had begun to have blank spots, whole hour-long spells when there was nothing, and he would come back to himself miles onwards, the bush about him strange and new, directions uncertain . . . he would stop, frowning, then plod on again . . .

And about that time he became conscious of Byrne, a long way behind him. Not pursuing, not threatening. Dead, stationary in his narrow, wet grave by the creek. Byrne as a silent screaming point in the forest, a keening essence that grew louder the further he went, a kind of high wailing that he knew would be with him forever . . .

And hour by hour, the further he walked, the further he stumbled and crawled, the louder the echo of Byrne's scream became . . .

His body grew weaker, and he had found that he had difficulty walking in a straight line. He stumbled a great deal, fell unaccountably. His light-headedness grew. Once he had come to himself to find that he was crouched in a kind of form in the bush, a flattened area where perhaps wallabies had lain, clutching in his fist Byrne's old empty pistol . . .

And he could not remember having brought it. He left it there . . .

He had a vague impression that on the third day he had crossed a river, hauling himself over a brown flood on a long, grey fallen log, clutching at lichened boulders . . .

But perhaps he hadn't . . .

It no longer seemed to matter.

*

During the night of the third day his thirst grew until it was almost unendurable. But he did not dare leave his nest of damp grass and branches and go to the creek bed for water, in case he could not find his way back again to his hide, to the battered pack with its cargo of gold . . . For some reason he did not think of taking the pack to the creek with him.

So he stayed where he was, raging with his thirst, listening to the whine of Byrne's presence in the bush far behind him, until the light of the false dawn showed him the shadows of the tree trunks, the pillars of the bush, the crystallising shapes in the mist . . .

When he stood up, lifted his pack, he found it almost unbearably heavy. He had not noticed its weight before, although he knew that there must be fifty pounds of gold there; but now the weight seemed altogether too much. He knew, though, that he must not abandon it, so he struggled into the harness and, bent over, staggered down to the stream to drink . . .

Later, as he climbed the hill on the far side, slipping and sliding in the red mud, the sun came up. There was no cloud, the morning was fresh, clear, almost spring-like. He slipped once more, and as he rose laboriously to his knees, the weight of the pack bearing him down, the first beams of the sun struck his face. And he realised dimly that somehow, through all the mist and rain and blank places and confusion, he had kept his face to the east . . . not perhaps with enough south in it, to be sure, but east all the same, and that somewhere not too far ahead must be the railway line . . .

And he went on with miraculous new energy, for a little almost sane, although the silent screaming was still reaching over all the miles behind. He seemed to float a little above his own wracked body, watching with some amusement the efforts of his tired legs to plow their way through undergrowth and swamp and scrub . . .

He seemed to go on like this for a very long time. But it cannot have been so very long, because it was only a little after noon when he came to the railway line.

*

He sat for a long time, pack still on his back, on one of the sleepers, his hands on the smooth polished metal of a rail. He seemed, now that he had arrived, to be at a complete loss. His energy was gone now, washed away by his accomplishment, and he knew that he would be able to go no farther. Byrne's scream was gone now, everything was gone. Only a great weakness remained, and legs that trembled a little as they lay, partly curled under him, in the crushed stone of the ballast. He watched the twin steel rails as they curled away, vanished between the tall trees of the forest to the south, and seemed in his weakness content to wait on events . . .

An hour passed, and another, and still he sat, staring at the twinned steel that slid smoothly away into the trees . . .

He felt a little warmth in his groin that soon chilled, and he knew that he had wet himself. But it did not seem to matter a great deal. Nothing seemed to matter, in fact, any more. All he had to do, he knew, was sit by the rails and wait . . .

So he waited.

And partway through the third hour, the bright steel under his palm seemed to tremble a little, ever so faintly. A mere hint of a tremor, a dream of motion, the faintest of hummings . . .

Soon it grew stronger, and he let himself fall sideways, moved his head with a groan until one ear was pressed to the icy metal. It was there: a faint grinding hum, the regular faint progress of some wheel, metal on metal. He smiled vaguely at the gravel before his eyes, the spikes, the grey wood of the sleeper . . .

The humming increased, grew into a resolute song, and in a few minutes a vehicle came into sight round the bend. It came from the north, behind Gogarty, and he did not see it until it was nearly on him. Then, conscious of some bulk in the vacancy behind his head, he turned.

It was a strange and peculiar object that moved towards him on the rails; a kind of large bicycle-frame welded to a double pair of wire-spoked wheels, with a chain-drive, pedals, curving handlebars. Perched on the seat, his shiny boots pumping slowly on the pedals, sat the railway inspector. He was tall, hawk-faced, clad in blue serge suit and glossy brushed bowler. His collar was tall and stiff, his tie neat and only mildly egg-spotted, and strung across his abdomen was a bright chain with a gold wafer that dangled and swung with his movement. He was holding the handlebars with one hand, while the other held a bitten apple. He was munching as he came, his level heavy brows pinched a little at the sight before him.

He slowed the machine to a halt, still munching, set the brake, and sat regarding Gogarty from a distance of ten feet. He raised his eyebrows, frowned again. Lifted his hand from the handlebars, rested it on the oilskin bundle lashed to the bar before him. Probed a bit of apple free of a molar with his tongue, frowned again. Tilted his bowler a little on his head.

'Where've you come from, then?' he said.

Gogarty gazed at him, unspeaking.

'Get yourself run over, sleeping on the line like that.'

Gogarty shook his head, wagged it vaguely in the direction of the thick bush to the west.

The inspector raised his eyebrows again. 'Come out of there, have you?'

Gogarty nodded.

'Lost and hungry, I suppose?'

Again Gogarty nodded.

The inspector paused to consider. Took another bite of apple; raised his boots from the pedals, placed them delicately on the wide bars above the front wheel. Nodded slowly.

'Well,' he said at last, 'I'm headed for Farrell Siding. I'd better give you a dink . . .'

Gogarty stared at him uncomprehendingly.

The inspector grew impatient. 'Come on, man, you've got this far, you can climb up on the bar, surely?'

Exhausted but suggestible, Gogarty climbed slowly and uncertainly to his feet.

'That's it,' said the inspector, encouragingly.

Gogarty, pack still strapped to his back, made for the front of the bike.

'Not there,' said the inspector. 'Round the back, man, round the back.'

So Gogarty went slowly round the back of the machine, climbed clumsily up on to the transverse member above the rear wheels, braced his feet, leaned wearily against the frame, head nuzzling the inspector's dark serge back.

The inspector reached into his pocket, drew out another apple. 'Here, nibble on that,' he said, passing it to Gogarty. Gogarty began to munch obediently.

'Well, then,' said the inspector, 'we'd better be on our way.' Then, almost as an afterthought: 'What's your name?'

Gogarty mumbled a little. The inspector turned his head again. 'What's that?'

Gogarty cleared his throat. 'Byrne,' he said. 'Jack Byrne.'

'Fine, fine,' said the inspector. 'We'd better be on our way then, Mr Byrne.' And leaned forward, swung his weight on to the pedals. The machine began to roll forward.

Gogarty clung tightly to the frame, pressed his head firmly against the inspector's back. 'My mate died in there,' he said.

'What was that?' said the inspector, turning his head a little, pressing harder on the pedals. 'I didn't quite catch . . .?'

'I said,' said Gogarty, not sure of the words until they had been spoken, 'I said that I'm goin' to build a hotel . . .'

'That's fine,' said the inspector, rising a little in his seat, leaning his weight harder into the pedals now, the wheels turning faster, the machine rolling away along the track. 'That's fine . . .'

And Gogarty clung dumbly to the armature of the machine as it carried him south along the steel rails, his head pressed firmly against the solid, serge-clad body, his eyes closed, the pack weighing as heavily on his back as the burden of survival weighed on his consciousness. The half-eaten apple lay forgotten, clenched in his dirty fist.

PART SEVEN

JACK BYRNE – DOWN

I wake to dull light, grey and cold, and for a long moment I can't think where I am, what I'm doing. Then it hits me. The chill of the morning air tells me that I'm home again. Home...

I pull the covers over my head, not wanting to wake, hoping that I can haul myself bodily back into sleep...

The trip back has retreated already into a sort of dream. The night at the Overlander, on the piss with one of the road-train teams marooned with a broken axle, the taxi in the dark to the airport; the slow dawn, the long hung-over flight to Brisbane; the slow feeling, as I flew further and further south, of the world closing in about me, of more and more people, more and more bodies... Can you get claustrophobic about the suburbs when you're ten thousand feet above them?

In the late afternoon, the wide grey ruffled carpet of the Strait below, the wide swing over the low grey hills, lower and lower, and I can see where the valley is, and the great sweep of coast, and then down, down, sweeping over the sodden green fields by the airport.

Stepping off the plane into the bitterness of the autumn air. The wind razoring at me as I walk across the tarmac towards the big, glass-fronted terminal. Still wearing shorts and shirt, and so bloody *cold* . . .

And they've lost my luggage. Somewhere it's missed a connection, and I'm trapped in my tropicals. I go up to the bar, drink a rum to warm myself, then hire a car.

Heater on full blast, the radio playing the familiar assinity of commercials – I'd forgotten how stupid they are – a great heaviness settling over me . . . wondering if I should call in to the clinic, try and find out about Petra, try and find her . . . But in the end sheer bloody inertia keeps me on the road to the valley . . .

Coming down the last hill, twisting through the curves, past the almost leafless hedges, the willow trunks bare and blazing like yellow neon down in the creek bed, the rain damp on the road, I had this sense of déjà vu, and remembered my last trip down the hill . . . the night I came to get my papers, the night I talked to Kate, the night I really began my geographical . . .

I pulled into the parking area in front of the hotel, a few cars outside. But no sign of anyone, all silent, still, cold . . .

Then through the front door, a light in the bar, the low mutter of voices under the football broadcast. Football, Christ . . .

I went straight back to the kitchen.

The light was on, directly above the pale, scrubbed table.

She was sitting there, Nance, dark head bent over a newspaper, a cup of tea at her elbow, a cigarette smoking in the ashtray. The kitchen had that air of buttoned-up readiness that always seems to hang over it before an evening meal. I could smell the joint in the big oven. Roast beef . . . and I felt desperately, hilariously homesick for grey stringy Queensland beef . . .

She seemed to sense me standing there, and looked up. She was thinner, her eyes seemed larger in her face, and very dark. The hollows under her cheekbones were deep, new lines around her mouth.

'So, you came . . .' Her voice sounded tired, flat, at odds with the spark in her eyes, a spark of almost mad impatience.

'Didn't you think I would?'

She shrugged, picked up her cigarette.
'How's Kate?'
'The same . . .'
'What's the matter with her?'
'It's her heart.'
'Can't they do anything?'
She stared down at the table, puffing at her cigarette. 'She's got pills . . .'
'Yes, but can't they *do* anything?'
'There aren't any miracles any more.'

I stared at her for a long time. She sat motionless, her hand holding the cigarette so still that the smoke rose in a straight, thin plume almost to the ceiling. At last she stubbed the cigarette out, looked up at me.

'Aren't you going to ask about him? About Terry?' There was a kind of suppressed rage in her voice, and her mouth was a hard line.

'No.'

'If it wasn't for you he wouldn't be dead.' I thought she was going to spit at me. Mad? God, she looked it. Mad enough to spring on me, claw me to bits . . .

I shook my head at her, turned away. Stopped at the door. Looked back. She was still sitting there, her face like something out of a bad dream.

'Kate still in my room?'

She nodded slowly, lowered her eyes, lit another cigarette.

'Listen,' I said. 'If you didn't want me back, why did you send for me?'

'Kate wanted to see you . . .' She didn't look at me.

'How did you know where I was? And my shonky name?'

She seemed to sneer a little. 'Someone rang me from Zeehan. They'd been up to Carbine Creek after the flood – to look at accounts or something. Saw you, asked some questions . . . thought I ought to know. Considerate of them, wasn't it?'

I felt small and childish all of a sudden.

A longish silence. 'Where do I sleep?'

She shook her head slowly, as if waking up. 'Anywhere . . .'

I left her there, went off up the stairs. Halfway up I turned back.

'Who owns this place now? Who did he leave it to?'

She raised her head, and the eyes were dull now, all the spark gone out of them. 'You do,' she said. 'He left you fifty-one per cent . . .' let her eyes drop to the table again.

I went out, back up the stairs. Outside Kate's door – my door – I stopped and listened. No sound. Turned the handle, very softly. Almost dark, a dim pink bedside lamp burning. I walked over to the bed, looked down.

It was a great shock, in a way. Because for a moment I thought she was gone. So pale, so still, her breath hardly perceptible. I could see that there was a lot of grey in her hair where the dye was growing out. And it seemed thinner, finer. Her skin had a dry, parchment look to it and her lips were a little cracked. She didn't stir, and after a minute I tiptoed out again. I was shocked. It was as if an old woman I didn't know was lying there in my bed and Kate was gone . . .

I went into the room next door. Shivered. Went across the corridor, tried the door of Terry's room. Locked. I went downstairs again. Into the kitchen. She hadn't moved.

'Where's the key to the old man's room?'

'What?' Her head snapped up.

'The key.'

'What do you want in there?' She looked as if I'd offered to burn the house down.

'I've lost my luggage. I need some warm clothes.'

For a minute I thought she was going to refuse. But finally she put a hand in the pocket of her dress, dragged out a ring with a dozen keys on it. Tossed it on the table. 'There.' She looked suddenly old, defeated.

I took the keys, went upstairs. Opened the door. It was too cold for ghosts, and I hurried into his old wool dressing-gown, the blue plaid, braided lapels, and went back to my room . . .

•

Defeated by the sprockets in my head, I finally give up the idea of sleep. The day is too obtrusive, anyway. I throw back the covers, flinch as the cold air hits me. Grab the old man's dressing-gown from the chair, wrap up. Why the hell did I want to take his dressing-gown last night? There's a perfectly good one of my own, maroon wool and silk trim, in the wardrobe. Eh? Badge of office, the new owner in residence? I don't know . . .

Oh Christ, the day slams in with thoughts of all the bumph and bullshit . . . solicitors to see, licensing people, banks, brewers . . .

Knock on the door. Tap, tap.

'Who's there?'

'It's me.' Nancy.

'Come in.'

The door opens, and she comes in, lean and competent and wide-awake, looks as though she's been up since five o'clock polishing the silver. Wouldn't bet against it . . . She's got a tray, coffee, hot milk, sugar.

'Thought you might like a cup of coffee.' Sets it down on the bedside table. Lingers a bit at the door. 'I'm sorry, Jack . . . about last night.'

'That's all right.'

'It's just that everything's been, you know, so uncertain.' But she won't look at me. Her hands are holding her elbows, fingers handcuffing upper arms, twitching, nervous . . .

'I'll be down soon.'

She sighs, turns away. 'There's porridge on the stove . . . I'll make you eggs when you're ready.'

'Ta.'

She's gone, the door closed softly behind her. I think of her rattling round in this great place alone, except for Kate upstairs in bed, and the part-time locals . . . not knowing . . . no certainty anywhere . . .

It dawns on me suddenly that for the past year I've been play-acting. All this geographical crap, kidstuff really, a kind of cowboys and indians, dramatising myself, crawling round in circles pretending that I'm a foofoo bird . . .

Now, I just don't know what I am or where I am. Except here.

And that's not much help. I have this feeling of *waiting*, of being just a kind of bloody egg, waiting to hatch or something. Bugger, get on with it. Downstairs, eggs and coffee. The porridge, I know, won't be that slop they serve in the mess . . . it'll be wholemeal with bits of dried fruit in it and brown sugar and a dollop of cream on top . . .

Oh, Christ, I'd like to stick a gun barrel in my mouth and pull the trigger . . .

After breakfast I shower and shave and prowl round, dressed in my old clothes, the ones I used to leave here for weekends. After a year of shorts and singlets and thongs I seem overdressed, weighed down. Snoop about, look in the cellar, the pantry, the bar.

Mid-morning: Nancy, making pies for the bar, hands floury as she rolls and pounds the dough, grinding it fiercely into the marble slab on the sink.

'How's business?' I ask her.

'All right.'

'It's bloody not.' I know from the amount of food in the pantry, the barrels in the cellar, that trade's down.

She stops her pounding for a moment. Her hair is dark as a crow's wing, and a drift of it slips free of her pins and hangs down beside her face. There's a little life in her skin from the violence of the pastry pounding. 'We're going broke,' she says. Goes back to her pastry.

'Really?' I say. 'Or just a figure of speech?'

'Really.' She stops work on the pastry, brushes back her hair, leaves floury streaks in it. Takes a packet from the table, lights a cigarette, sits down, stares across the room at nothing. 'It's been coming for a long time,' she says. 'Started really when they built the new road. But . . . you know, people knew Terry, they'd go out of their way . . . But now he's gone . . . well, they don't come anymore.' She glances up at me, a bit fiercely. 'Why should they? What's here for them any more? Bloody free pies on the bar counter? Rooms with no TV? No cabarets, no honky tonk? Why should they?'

I say nothing. Doesn't seem much to say.

'Another year,' she says. 'That'll do it. We'll be flat broke, have to sell up for what we can get.'

'No way out?'

She puffs on her ciggie, frowning. She looks younger, somehow, for a moment. 'I don't know,' she says. 'If we'd made some changes years ago . . . updated things . . . made improvements . . . but Terry would never do it, no matter what I said, no matter how I pleaded . . . it had to stay the way it was . . .'

'We'd still be off the main road.'

'Advertise,' she says, scornfully. 'You've got to spend *money*, that's what he'd never admit . . .'

'What'll you do?' I ask. 'If it all goes bust?'

She stubs out the butt. 'I don't know. Sometimes I don't care . . .' She looks at me suddenly, suspiciously. 'You're not interested in doing up the place, are you?' There's a sudden glint in her eye.

'Tell the truth, Nancy, I'm not much interested in anything at the moment . . .'

Her mouth hardens, and she looks down at the table, still and tense. Then she gives me one final look, scornful and bitter, and stands up, begins to roll out the pastry.

I turn away, go up the stairs, up the old worn blue carpet to see Kate.

●

She's awake when I knock. Her voice sounds very faint and distant when she calls out.

I go in. She's lying propped up against a pile of pillows. Teacup and saucer on the table beside the bed, morning paper lying unread beside them. She's very thin and fragile, skin almost transparent. Someone has done her make-up, and the colours look garish and grotesque, her face under the paint job is so pale and gaunt. But when I get closer I can see there's still a bit of life in the old girl, a faint spark deep down . . .

'Hullo gorgeous.' I bend over and kiss her.

She puts her hand on mine. I look down. The veins are heavy, blue, the skin slack and spotted. Not seventy yet, but she suddenly seems as old as death. Her lips look blue.

'On your back, as usual,' I say, sitting down beside the bed.

'Cheeky, as usual,' she says. There's a hint of a catch to her voice, a certain throatiness. But still the same old Kate under it all somehow. She squirms a little in the bed, her hand goes up, fiddles with the front of her nightie. When it goes down again, the front's pulled lower, the tops of her pale breasts partly visible. I want to laugh and cry at the same time.

She looks at me, smiling, for a bit. 'You came, then . . .'

'How could I resist?'

She turns away, a little, looks toward the window. 'It's over Jackie . . . I've had it.'

'You? Don't be bloody silly! You've got years in you yet . . .'

She shakes her head. Then smiles at me. 'I've always wanted to die in bed, you know . . .'

The smile's gone. 'But not like this . . . not on my own.'

Can't bring myself to smile. 'You won't be alone, love . . .'

She takes my hand, and for a little while we don't talk.

'I shouldn't have brought you back,' she says at last. 'You don't belong here.'

'Where else?' I ask her. Where indeed? You have to start from somewhere . . .

After a bit she speaks again. 'All that other stuff . . . with Nancy and Terry . . . it's nothing to do with you . . . nothing at all.'

'Maybe not before . . . but it is now.'

She shakes her head slightly, closes her eyes.

After a while I say, gently: 'I can't help it, Kate. Knowing makes all the difference, there's nothing I can do. You can't just unknow something, by wishing, can you?'

She opens her eyes then. 'Jackie,' she says, 'if only you'd learn . . . wishing . . . that's *everything*.' And she closes her eyes again. She suddenly looks very old indeed, and very tired. 'If people didn't *wish*, then they'd never have anything.' She opens her eyes a moment, and I can see there are tears in them. 'That's what life's made of, wishes . . . there'd be *nothing* if it wasn't for wishes . . . bloody *nothing*.'

She lies there quietly, a vein throbbing very slowly in her throat. I think she's gone to sleep, and I start to take my hand away. But the pressure of her fingers increases, so I stay there, both of us still and wordless and close, while the thin sunlight crawls down the wall by the door, and the old clock, the brass alarm clock that I had all my school days, ticks off the seconds of our lives . . .

•

My car, the blue Volvo, is in the shed. Christ knows who brought it back. It's up on blocks, the registration has been renewed. For something to do, to get out of the house, I check the tyres, get the old girl down on terra firma, go over her innards, reconnect the battery, start up. A bit sluggish, but then it picks up, ticks away like a lovely old watch. My only real luxury. Caused a stir in Zeehan. Above my station, should have had a Kingswood, not the done thing to have a better car than the boss . . . Christ, it seems so far away, so dim and misty, all that stuff . . .

Back the car out, take it for a run. A few miles along the road, then back. Park it in the yard and sit there, switched off, listening to the tiny clicking noises of cooling metal.

Can't put it off, home for nearly a week, and it has to be done. Look at my watch. Eleven o'clock. Do it now, do it today.

Go inside, change my clothes, get a pack of cigarettes, smoking more heavily now. Nancy somewhere about in the kitchen. Avoid her.

I phoned days ago, she's still in the clinic.

The day is grey, with odd sudden bursts of sun. But chill and bleak, for all that. There's a peculiar thick greyness to the clouds down here that you don't seem to get further north, a density. They seem to fill the sky like a wall . . .

The road begins to unwind, and gradually I slip back into the easy habit of driving. An hour, a bit more, and into the outskirts of the city.

Not knowing what to expect, what she'll say, what she'll do, how much things have changed . . . There's this feeling that I can't avoid of some sort of disaster hanging over us all, something terrible that will collapse on us if we make a wrong decision, stray the slightest hair off the track . . .

The clinic looks the same. As I go in through the glass doors I think of Rene the Runner, weaving through the dining room, past the wardsman and nurses, down the stairs and out into the street. Wonder if she's still running . . .

Up the shiny lino-tiled steps. It's already visiting hours, and there are sundries about, can't really tell the inmates from the visitors. Or from the doctors for that matter . . . One of the nurses looks at me curiously, half-recognising. But no other faces I know in the long corridor. The staff changes, the nurses get sane again, go off to nurse amputees and syphilitics in the main block . . .

Rather than asking, I prowl about, looking.

Not in the dayroom. It seems not to have changed at all. The TV blaring out the daily soaps, a nurse playing some complicated game with a couple of patients, a trio of old ladies drinking tea in the corner, four old fellows playing cards. Clattering from the kitchen as someone makes tea.

Out again, past the ping-pong table, past the nurses' station, the dispensary and the key cupboard. Wonder briefly what became of my key to the billiard room . . . lost it somewhere on my travels.

Glance through the doors of the wards. No one I know . . .
Poke my head into the occupational therapy room, empty.
No, wait . . .

Behind the door, in a chair by the wall, staring out past some dry and half-dead pot-plants, head bowed a bit, hands folded in her lap . . . Petra.

Feel a sudden chill, a shivering, as if someone has opened a window on a new and freezing world . . .

I step inside, slowly, quietly, watching her. She doesn't seem to see me, doesn't move. She's wearing a long, dark-red skirt, ankle length, crushed and crumpled. A white blouse, high at the throat. Hair caught back in a rubber band, loose and untidy about her face. And she's overweight, by at least a stone . . . She turns to look at me, and her face is puffy, little pouches of fat beginning at the tops of her cheeks under her eyes. Her lipstick too red and too sloppy . . .

She seems to cringe a little at the sight of me, and her eyes fill with tears.

I drop to one knee, put my arms round her, hold her tight. She's sobbing quietly.

I lean back, look at her. She has streaked her eye-shadow, and she's a mess. And I know that I truly love her, that I'm committed to her forever, and that I don't know how to help her.

'Don't cry,' I say, and she reaches up to brush away a tear from her cheek with one – too plump – hand.

'I'm fat,' she says. But her eyes are the same eyes, and it's Petra there inside.

'No, you're not, it doesn't matter.'

'I'll have to go on my diet again . . .' Then: 'I didn't think you'd come to see me.'

I hold her close for a moment. Then she pulls away again. 'I'll make you a cup of tea.'

'OK.'

She stands up.

'Hang on,' I say. 'Listen . . . are you all right? You know? What happened . . .?'

She pauses in the doorway, looks a little puzzled. Light dawns. 'Oh, *that* business . . . I don't think about it much . . . it's all right.' Then, suddenly, a little fearfully, 'It's all right, isn't it, Jack?'

'Of course.' I kiss her cheek. Tell the truth I haven't thought much about it either . . .

We walk down the long corridor to the dayroom. Despite the plumpness, the untidiness, she walks still with that poker-straight back, and I know that it's Petra all right. But she looks all gone to bits . . . And Christ knows how much my fault . . .

In the dayroom, we sit by the window. No one taking any notice of us. I squeeze her hand.

'I was going to make some tea,' she says.

'In a minute. There's no hurry.' We sit looking at each other.

She raises one hand, touches her temple, a movement almost of distraction.

'I'm moving out to the annexe next week.'

'You must be getting better, then.'

'Yes, I must, mustn't I?'

'Taking your pills?'

'Yes.'

Silence again for a minute or two.

She gets up suddenly. 'I'll get the tea.'

In a few minutes she's back, two cups, tea slopping a bit in the saucers. There's milk in mine, which I hate. I say nothing, sip it.

'How is everyone?' she says. 'Sigrid and Stretch? Jimmy? Vic?'

'All right,' I say. 'Everyone's all right.'

The silence descends again.

After a long time she raises her eyes from the table. 'What's going to happen?' she says.

'You're going to get better as soon as you can,' I say. 'Get out of this place. Then we're going to get married.' And it all suddenly seems simple. No, not simple, just the only way things can be.

She just sits there for a minute. A couple of tears begin, slide slowly down her plump cheeks.

'Oh, God,' she says. 'Oh God . . .'

I take both her hands, and we sit there looking at each other. I don't really know whether to cry or what to do. It doesn't seem real, I can't see any future, can't imagine anything. It's only a great frightening void. But there's no other way . . . Surely you should feel happy about it?

After a bit she stops crying. 'I've got nothing to wear,' she says, and grins a little.

I grin too, shake my head.

She looks down at her waistline. 'I'll have to get this weight off . . .' Then, suddenly looking at me with a kind of desperation: 'It's all right, isn't it, Jack? Really?'

'Of course it is,' I say. And hope I'm telling the truth.

But later, on the road home, the rain slashing down, the wipers slapping it away, the wheels trying to aquaplane on the slick road, the heater blasting warm air at me, the world seems to be closing in again, and thickening about me. Will it be all right? Christ knows . . .

It *has* to be, somehow. But how? I have this feeling again that I'm just waiting, held in some sort of suspension, without real power or purpose, waiting to be born . . .

•

'Where have you been?' asks Nancy, when I walk in through the back door. She's standing by the dining room entrance, smoking, watching Mrs Hemmings make gravy for the beef. She looks more than curious, a little suspicious, as if I might sneak off and sell my share of the pub behind her back.

I shake my head, look at Mrs Hemmings's broad back, atwitch with curiosity, walk past her, upstairs. I go into my room, take off my jacket, sit on the bed to change my shoes. Nancy follows me in, stands by the door.

No point in playing games. 'Petra and I are going to get married.'

No fireworks. She looks at me without moving, without expression. But her face is gradually tightening, going paler, till it's as hard and smooth as ivory. And as bloody warm and welcoming.

At last she speaks. 'That's marvellous,' she says, almost spitting it out, face getting a nasty, scraped look. 'That's bloody marvellous . . . you'll have a mad woman for a wife, a lunatic to run the hotel . . .'

'Tell the truth, Nance,' I say, 'I never really thought about the hotel. Running it, and all that. It's funny, I was just thinking of Petra and me . . . Guess I should have taken a poll, driven round and asked all the neighbours, mailed a questionnaire to everyone who's stayed here for the last ten years . . . You know, Will you come back to stay when we have a resident schizophrenic? Maybe the Licensing Branch won't like it either, or the brewery . . . Maybe I ought to check with the bank, too . . .'

And while I'm going on with this nonsense she's getting tighter and tighter, thinner and thinner, like a snake stretching, and I'm waiting for some sort of long finely drawn scream to issue forth, some unearthly wail of rage and spite . . .

But it doesn't come. She tears her eyes away, swivels round, stamps out, every movement a kind of ripping in the air. You can almost smell the ozone, the burning. And then she's gone. I lie back on the bed for a minute, stare at the ceiling. I don't feel angry or upset, haven't lost my temper, nothing, I'm just bone-tired. Have this feeling that everything, the world, life, the lot, is just a great dark nothingness all round me, stretching away forever, and at the centre there's just this one tiny spark that's Petra and me, and maybe it's going to go out and then there'll be nothing; but all the same, there's only that one single spark, all the rest is cold and lost forever, and if I can't keep it alive, then that's it, that's everything, that's all she wrote . . .

But there's another feeling too . . . a feeling that somehow the walls are closing in, the high white wooden walls of this bloody old place, closing in cold and tall and tight, and soon they'll smother me, and all of us . . .

I get up, put on my slippers, go out into the silent corridor, tap softly on Kate's door. Listen hard for her faint voice. Open the door quietly, go in. She's lying there, still and frail, against the pile of pillows in that pink light from the little lamp. She never seems to change, never seems to move. I don't go in to see her in the early mornings, I know she doesn't like to be seen until she's washed and brushed up and painted and sexified. But every time I see her, there seems to be less life, less *time* left in her face . . .

I go and sit on the bed, take her hand, kiss her cheek.

'Petra and I are going to get married,' I tell her.

She smiles. 'When?' A thin whisper, only an echo of the old Kate.

'When she's out of the clinic, lost a couple of stone.'

She smiles at me. 'She's lovely,' she says.

'How do you know?'

There's a little bit of a twinkle in the pale old eyes. Old? She's younger than the old man was . . .

'I spied on her when she came to talk to Nancy . . .' She frowns a little, faint shadows on her pale forehead. 'Have you told Nancy?'

I nod.

'What did she say?'

'You can guess . . '

'Never mind, she'll come round . . .'

'It doesn't matter.'

'No.'

•

Later in the evening I catch old Parkie on his way out after the daily visit to Kate. He looks very grey these days, with a kind of loneliness about him. I think he misses the old man. I'm inclined to be cautious with him now, I don't know just how much he knows, how much he guesses, about anything.

'How is she?' I ask him.

He stops on the verandah, yellow light from the streetlamp playing on his face. There's a bit of wind, the light dips and sways, throwing moving shadows over us both.

'Much the same,' he says.

'Worse?'

'Weaker.'

'What's the matter with her? Really?'

He pulls out his old-fashioned cigarette case with its raised gold shield and monogram, his father's, he told me once. Lights a ciggie, draws, lets out a long stream in the chill air. He's as tall as I am, thinner, with sad doggy eyes. He sighs. 'All men are created equal, eh Jack? Right?'

'If you say so . . .'

'Well, they're not. Not physically, anyway. Like bloody cars, a Rolls is good for a million miles or so. An Austin 7 a bloody sight less, eh? Well, people are like that, too, bodies. Kate's one of the Austins, just not engineered for the long haul . . .'

'Isn't there anything you can do?'

He shrugs, a very tired movement. 'Put her in hospital, I suppose. Stick things in her, take things out of her, dose her up, cut her up, give her all that pain and fear and disgust . . .' He looks at me quickly. 'You want that?'

'Of course not.'

'She's at home here. Family, friends, no pain. Look,' he says, 'the whole structure's just weak . . . it's at that stage where if you fix one thing, something else'll go wrong.' He flips his cigarette out into the dark where it lies like a small orange window in the night. 'Let her go,' he says. 'Sometimes that's all there is to do . . . just let people go . . . just let go.'

And he trudges off to his old Rover, his little black bag in his hand. I watch until his tail-lights have disappeared down the road, and there's nothing but darkness, the swinging streetlamp by the bridge, and the cold wind from the west. Then I go inside, back into the prison where nowadays we seem, Nancy and I, to roll round aimlessly like a pair of demented marbles bouncing back and forth off the walls.

•

At tea, she doesn't say any more about Petra. Eats silently, not looking at me. Now and then gets up to peep into the dining room. There are so few guests nowadays that she does the table-waiting herself. Tonight there's only a single couple, middle-aged Queenslanders, seeing the south in the winter, huddled at the table nearest the fire. When she has them set on their main course, she sits down again, picks up her fork, puts it down, pushes her plate away. Mrs Hemmings has gone, and it's very quiet. A few locals in the bar, the slow clack of eight-ball, the dribble of sound from the radio. Old Freddie no doubt sneaking a brandy while we're out of the way.

'They bloody disgust me,' says Nancy.

'Who?'

'The locals.'

'Why?'

She looks up at me, eyes dark and bitter. 'You know that none of the men who work about here ever take cut lunches? Their wives give them the price of a five-ounce beer and they come in here and gorge themselves on the pies and stuff in the bar.'

'Why don't you stop cooking it? Or charge for counter lunches? Everyone else does.'

She shakes her head, staring at the table. I know why she won't. Because the old man always kept it that way, and she won't change . . . other things, but not that. Or not yet . . .

'You'd put in a cabaret, wouldn't you? And telly? And jazz the rooms up? Motel stuff? Wouldn't you?'

She nods slowly, not looking at me. 'That's different somehow . . .'

'Why?'

She looks up, and for the first time it seems that she might be as hemmed in as I am, worse maybe, because there's nothing else, no freedom anywhere for her . . . 'I could cut something,' she says. 'You know, all at once, something big, exciting . . . But I couldn't just whittle away at it . . . it's just . . . *mean*, that way. You know what I mean?'

'I know what you mean.'

Maybe we're *both* waiting to be born. And Christ, it seems a bloody hard labour . . .

•

May turns to June, and the rains start. Gently at first, not at all like the Queensland downpours, but chill, insidious, slow; beginning as a light misty drizzle, building slowly into a solid, fine, soaking rain. Easing overnight, giving a false promise of frosts and fine weather, starting up again, heavier, but still not really heavy. Just continuous. Day after day, night after night for a week. We seem to be struggling about here in a thick gloom,

Nancy and I, in a kind of cold, soupy vapour that fills the empty rooms of the hotel, flows over into the kitchen, the bar, the lounge.

I drive to the city every week to see Petra. I'd be happy to go more often, every day, but she won't let me. Says that if I see her only once a week then I'll notice the improvement. See her getting slimmer, better. The truth is she doesn't seem to be improving much. Yes, I suppose she's lost a little bit of weight, and the nurses tell me that she's sticking to her diet. I'd like to see her more often, anyway, however she is; it's as if she's my link with something important – what, I don't know; sanity, Queensland, Christ knows . . . Despite the memory of the way it was, I still find myself homesick for that bloody place. Or maybe just for the people . . . Surely I'm not that bloody perverse that I'm homesick for *that* place . . .

So we rattle round, sharp edges showing, Mrs Hemmings primmouthed as if it's improper somehow to smile; Old Fred, redeyed and rheumy, half-pissed, sucking away slyly at the brandy, then turning hurt and doggy when we give him a stir . . .

Outside, water everywhere. The garden sodden, the woodstack wet so that the fire smokes; the river rising, nibbling at the blackberry banks, the bitumen of the road bracketed by twin streams that undercut the edges, pour down the hill and spill under the bridge. The sky lowering, grey, the sun not visible for days on end. The locals, morose over their small beers and free pies, solemnly depose that they've never seen anything like it . . .

And upstairs, in the room next to mine, in the room that used to be mine, we've put in a new Dimplex heater to keep the chill and the damp at bay. Kate seems to be growing frailer every day, sinking lower and lower as we draw closer to the shortest day. She speaks seldom now, just lies there and dozes. Takes little notice of any of us, not even Nance and Mrs Hemmings when they wash and primp her a little, put on her lipstick and eyeshadow. I sit with her often in the afternoons and evenings, hold her hand, a hand very pale and fragile now; her skin seems almost transparent. Sometimes I read a book through the quiet afternoons, but mostly I just sit there, her hand in mine, the light glowing on the bedside table under its pink shade, the rain, steady and monotonous, pouring down outside the window. The whole world seems grey, bereft of all colour and life . . .

One night, as we sit over our coffee cups and cigarettes in the dim kitchen after Mrs Hemmings has tidied up and gone, I say to Nancy, watching her dark, shadowed face: 'Had any more of your attacks?'

She looks at me sharply, takes a deep draw on her ciggie, blows out smoke in a thin, hard stream. 'No.'

Silence as we both ponder, not looking at each other.

'Why did you tell me, Nancy? Really . . .'

She doesn't say anything for quite a long time. Then, at last, when I've stubbed out my smoke, just about given up any hope of an answer, she raises her head, looks me straight in the eye.

'I've thought about it,' she says. 'There were lots of reasons, I suppose. At first I thought it was just to hurt you, to make you carry something too . . . but lately . . . well, I think it was mostly because if I died, and then *Terry* died, then there'd be no one that would know any more about us . . . but if you knew, it'd be alive for that much longer . . .'

And she starts to cry then, the tears spilling from her eyes as she sits there looking at me. And I get up and go round the table and put my arms round her, and she turns and rests her head against me, and just holds me and goes on crying for a long time; not a harsh crying, not hard or racking or anything like that, but just a gentle sort of crying, soft and easy, as if at last something inside her is flowing again after being locked in for a long time . . .

After a while she pulls away, wipes her eyes and gets up to put the kettle on. We sit for a while longer, drinking our coffee, smoking, not saying anything. And it seems that part of the strain, the hardness and emptiness, has gone out of the air of the old place at last. We never say any more about it, but we seem easier with each other now, easier than we've been for a long time . . .

•

At the end of June the rain slackens, there are a few days of frost and clear weather. Every morning the earth is frozen and sparkling, puddles covered with half an inch of ice, pipes locked solid, trees creaking as the ice splits their fibres. Each night the sky to the west, beyond the estuary, is a curtain of flame-like orange that seems to burn with the cold.

But it doesn't last, and with July the rains are back. From our sparse bar trade we learn that the district has had its yearly quota of rain already, and there's no sign of a pause. The earth is sodden now, and there is an uncertain sloppy feel to the pastures and the road verges; the ground is saturated, it's rejecting the water; banks and culverts are collapsing and trees are falling, showing muddy roots to the sky.

On one wet day that is like every other, a letter comes for me. The handwriting is unfamiliar, and the postmark says Goldsworthy, W.A. The single sheet of paper inside is covered on both sides with spidery continental handwriting. Sigrid's signature is at the bottom.

'Dear Jack,' she writes, 'we are both well and settled here with jobs. John is working in the mill, and I am in the accounts office. We both miss you and Petra and all our friends at Carbine Creek . . .' Stretch, she says, is living in the quarters while she is boarding with a fitter's family. They're saving their money, and a bloke in the drawing office is tutoring Stretch at night – he's going to go back to school and maybe try for an apprenticeship later . . .

It seems more like a sister writing about him, or a mother; but there's still that odd dignity, and it comes through the writing, jumps at me, and I find I'm close to tears, what with missing them, and thinking of that day at the Holes and all the rest of it . . .

'We both send our best love,' she writes at the end, 'to you and Petra. She's a lovely girl, and we hope that things work out for you two. Please write, as John misses you very much . . .'

So I go out in the rain, and walk for miles up the old road by the river, under the branches of the tall pine trees that have been there as long as I can remember. I try to get rid of this hard ache under my breastbone that seems anchored there, won't shift no matter how far I walk or what I do. It seems to me that so much has happened in the past year; so much that the past, the time before that, has faded, almost disappeared, doesn't matter much any more. And it seems that for a long time I've been on the brink of finding something, something important, that I'm on the edge of some discovery and it won't come, it's just beyond my grasp. I know that somehow Stretch and his girl have found it, that Vic and Jimmy have had it all along, and that if I don't find it I may as well go and jump in the big brown river . . . but I can't seem to cross that boundary, that line that separates me from whatever it is that I have to learn . . .

Truly, it doesn't seem to matter so much any more about Nance and Terry and what they did, and what I am . . . it's just faded into the background, something that I've learned to live with in the past year, that people have *taught* me to live with . . . What does matter, though, is that I can't seem to get engaged with the *future* . . . If I could only somehow see just a *little* way . . .

Marrying Petra? It's not that, I have to do that, that's just plain survival, because without her there's nothing . . . It's more, more . . . it's like this bloody rain; its greyness obscures the countryside, and there's something obscuring mine . . .

I'm blinded, somehow, can't see my way . . . depressed, disgusted, crammed stiff with self-pity . . .

So I walk for hours, all the way up past Logan's farm, across to Ertler's track, back across the sodden paddocks by the cheese factory, wet through, soaked, rain in my eyes, my mouth, my whole bloody soul . . .

Tired and wet and sorry for myself, and no closer to finding any answers, I lumber down the road towards the river and the pub . . . The lights are burning by now, although it's only four o'clock, and Parkie's old Rover is parked by the front door, sidelights on . . .

I stand at the front door, shuffling my feet on the big doormat, trying to shake most of the water off, struggling out of my jacket, and wondering about Parkie being there. Suddenly Nancy comes running down the old blue-carpeted stairs, her face strained, big shadows under her eyes.

'Kate's dying,' she says as she reaches the bottom. 'Where the bloody hell have you been?'

•

Upstairs, still dripping water, leaving muddy pools on the runner, I meet Parkie coming out the door of her room. He stops when he sees me, closes the door behind him, leans back on it. He looks very tired.

I don't say anything, just look at him.

He just nods.

'How long?'

He shakes his head wearily. 'Any time, son, any time now. She's overdue anyway . . .'

I push past him, open the door, stop.

For a moment it seems that she's gone already, she's so still, so pinched. There's that blue look, and the thinness about the nostrils . . . Then I see the covers move a little, a very little. I go over, sit on the chair beside the bed, take her hand. She stirs. Slowly she opens her eyes, closes them again. There's a faint pressure from her fingers.

I sit there for what seems a long time, an endless time, holding her hand. The daylight has long gone outside, and we're isolated in this pink soft island. My mind seems frozen, can't seem to function. But slowly, as I watch the gentle rise and fall of her chest, a feeling of something like peace drifts over me. And I feel warmer and easier than I have for days, weeks . . .

Parkie comes in a couple of times, checks her pulse, looks her over. She opens her eyes, tries to raise her eyebrows at him. I swear to God she's trying to flirt . . .

He goes out again, and we're left alone.

The old brass clock ticks away, eight o'clock, half past, nine o'clock . . .

Nance brings in a cup of coffee, puts it on the table beside me. She raises her eyebrows. I shake my head, smile a little at her. She goes away.

Kate is very quiet now, very still. The rise and fall of the pink cover is almost imperceptible.

The clock says nearly ten, closing time, when she stirs, opens her eyes, moves her head a little, looks slowly about her.

'Shit,' she says. 'Am I still here?'

I squeeze her hand, smile at her. 'What's it like, Kate?' I ask her. It seems suddenly a sensible and proper thing to ask.

She looks at me once, smiling a little, closes her eyes.

'Oh,' she says, 'It's so bloody *boring* . . .'

Ten minutes later Parkie comes in again. Bends over, feels her pulse, touches her eyelids, then places his hand on my shoulder.

'It's over,' he says. 'She's gone.'

It seems hard to believe. So gently, just slipping away. So gently and so quietly.

Give her a kiss on the forehead, still warm, and blunder out of the room. Next door I drag off my clothes, fumble my way, suddenly absolutely exhausted, into bed. Shed the odd tear or two, gentle, gentle, the rain coming down on the steep roof, slipping away, gentle, gentle . . . and sleep.

●

The day dawns in funereal brightness. Find myself wondering what sort of day it was when Terry died.

I've never been to visit his grave. Not yet.

Kate is gone – I mean her body – when I get up. Water everywhere, the puddles, the river, the dew, all reflect the light. It beats back at you, a cold brightness that seems to burn on the retina. The undertakers have taken her away. Why 'undertakers'? What do they undertake? Or whom? The sunlight goes to my head and, despite the loss, the thought of the grim rites of the undertakers, the indignities on the poor old corpse, you can't weep too long when the sun shines . . .

There's been enough weeping, anyway.

Is that all it is, in the end? Boring?

All gone then, the black soldiers, the gold lamé swimsuits,

Luna Park and port wine, and sleeping in on Sundays . . .

But I know what Nance meant – as long as I go on, someone who knew her, she'll be about . . . not a new thought, I suppose . . .

And will *I* find it boring? And will I worry about that last ride to the undertakers?

Never mind – she'll be back, the old Kate, tomorrow some time, when we take her over the river to the cemetery and lay her down. I'll take the fire myself, not that long darkness under the ground . . .

No point in ringing Petra, she never knew Kate.

Things to do on this bright morning. And Nance feels it too. By ten the kitchen is sparkling and she's started on the rest of the house, turning it over properly, shining brass, cleaning windows, vacuuming carpets. In the bar, I give old Fred a shove, get him started on the woodwork, the glasses. He's red and weepy-eyed, already had a glass or two in honour of the dear departed. Old drunks never die, they just get pissed earlier in the day.

I go out, find a broom, begin sweeping the yard; keep busy cutting wood, washing the Volvo for the morning.

I've just finished raking over the white gravel, still very soggy, when Nancy comes out, lips pursed, hair escaping in dark wisps from a red headscarf.

'Bloody Fred's half pissed in the bar,' she says, lighting a cigarette, breathing deeply. 'Will you go in and look after things?'

I've made it plain enough since I came back that I'm not going to be a drunk's labourer. But all the same, in I go, obedient and dutiful. Fred leaning on the bar, staring damply at the lone customer, a truck driver with the smell of pig-shit about him, a smelly wet truck outside. Eyes very red and weepy. The squint doesn't improve his looks . . .

'Fuck off home, Fred,' I tell him. 'Have a bit of a kip . . . be back by two, though.'

He looks blearily at me. 'She was a real lady, Jackie boy . . .'

Brandy fumes that'd cook an egg. Turn my head away.

'Listen,' I tell him, 'if I ever catch you pissed behind this bar again I'll kick your arse so hard your eyeballs'll drop out.'

'Real lady, a real lady . . .' He wanders off, wavering vaguely towards the door.

The character at the bar is grinning. I fix him with a beady eye.

'On the slops a bit early, eh?' he says, nodding towards Fred's departing back.

I walk along the bar until I'm standing in front of him, give him the beady eye again, a bit stronger. 'Bereavement in the family.'

'Ah.' He seems only a little abashed. Drains his glass. Puts it down, nods. 'Same again.'

'You've had two. You're driving.'

He looks at me carefully, nods slowly, picks up his change off the bar without a word.

Having asserted myself, I feel better, more at peace. The old piss and vinegar coming back. Lord of me own bar.

Light a cigarette, settle back in the bar corner and watch the sunlight stream in through the doorway, making a bright road across the brown lino. Christ, how many bars still have brown lino on the floor? The genuine old-fashioned slop shop is fast disappearing. All wall-to-wall and indirect lighting now . . .

Kate gone then.

All right.

What did she say . . . about wishes?

Wishes are all there is? Something like that. I have no wishes now, not right now, at this moment. Can't wish the old biddy back, can't wish you'd see her swinging out of a taxi again, flouncing in the front door, pay the taxi, there's a dear . . .

The truth about Kate is that she never hurt anyone as long as she lived, and you can't say that about many people. Never harmed anyone, never wished anyone harm. Too busy being loved, and making love, and loving people, the old Kate. Well, time to lay her in the ground . . .

Old Dick Wellard comes into the bar, eighty and spry for his age. Got his hat on, a good old Akubra with a sewn brim. Black suit, tie straight, tall boots polished. Nods at me, pulls a stool up.

'Morning, Jack.'

'Morning, Mr Wellard.' Call him Dick? Like buggery.

Pull him a ten without asking, set it in front of him.

Puts his money on the counter. I push it back. 'No charge today, Mr Wellard. Not for friends and neighbours.' An old custom I just made up. He nods, as if it's no more than he expected. Draw myself a small beer, set it on the counter. Me and Fred Brady, bushrangers all.

The old boy picks up his glass, sips, sets it down.

'A real lady,' he says, wiping froth from his moustache.

'I'll drink to that.'

'Won't see her like again.'

'You're right there . . .'

'Sense of humour, though . . .'

'You said it, Mr Wellard.'

'But a real lady, all the same.'

'A real lady. Mr Wellard.'

'Funeral tomorrow, is it?'

'That's right. Two o'clock, up the hill.'

He nods, satisfied. 'I'll be there.'

'You want a ride?'

He shakes his head. 'Young Alf'll be over to take us up.'

Sits for a moment, looking at his glass in his old heavy yellow hand, the knuckles like big old walnuts with seventy years of hard work. Raises his glass, drinks it off.

'Another, Mr Wellard?'

'No, thanks, Jack, I'll be off . . .' On with his hat, up off the stool, straight as big stringybark, and about as tough. A halo of brightness about him briefly as he steps through the door out into the sunlight. And for a moment I have this feeling that I've discovered something important, just in time, just before it's too late. But before I can recognise it, grasp it, it's gone. I feel suddenly very tired. It seems a long time till two o'clock. Outside, a small cloud drifts across the face of the sun, and the day turns grey for an instant. But only for an instant.

I take a towel and start to polish glasses, just to fill in time . . .

•

In the afternoon I go up to my room, lie down, doze for an hour. When I wake it's already growing dark, and soon a whole day will have passed since she died. I wash my face in cold water and go downstairs. There's no one staying in the house, no one in the dining room, and only a handful of locals in the bar. Everything very quiet. You can hear the old building creaking a little as the chill settles.

Mrs Hemmings has gone, and Nance cooks scrambled eggs for us, the way I like them, with peppers and ham and cheese, and out-of-season tomatoes sliced beside them. It's a quiet meal, neither of us has much to say. But there's no tension left between us now, it all seems to have faded away. Some strings stretched too far, too tight, then snapping . . .

'We'll close the hotel after lunch,' Nance says while we're drinking our coffee. 'Open the bar after the funeral. OK?'

'Yeah, right.'

'Jack?'

'Mmmm?'

'What are you going to do? About the hotel, everything?'

Sigh. 'I don't know. I really don't, Nancy . . .'

'You want me to leave? Leave the hotel to you?'

'I just don't know . . .' And somehow I seem too tired even to *try* to sort things out. Lethargic, as if the day's been too much . . .

'We can't go on much longer.'

'I know.'

After a little silence: 'Jack?'

I raise my eyebrows.

'It's all my fault . . . isn't it?'

'How do you mean?'

'If I hadn't told you . . . everything would have been the same as before, nothing would have changed . . .'

'I don't know . . . I don't think it's as simple as that.'

She picks tobacco from her lip. Still too many ciggies, too much coffee. 'It seems wrong, somehow.'

'What?'

'To sell the hotel.' She looks at me very earnestly. 'Terry felt so strongly about it . . . his father, that terrible time in the bush, losing his friend and everything . . . almost as if the hotel was . . . I don't know, a kind of luck piece.'

I shake my head. To tell the truth I'm sick to death of the bloody hotel, of talking about, thinking about it. I'm locked to it by this bloody curse, this entail that says I've got to look after the place because Old Jack Byrne lost his mate in the bush . . . Sometimes I wish he'd stayed in the bloody bush himself . . . no gold, no pub, no me, no nothing . . .

'After the funeral,' I say. 'We'll talk about it after the funeral.'

Outside, the night's dark and very still. Don't want to think of Kate lying in some cold bloody morgue . . . but can't seem to think of anything else . . .

I lie in bed for a long time before I finally get to sleep.

•

The weather is clear and bright, as cold in the shade as in the big chiller in the kitchen. The sunlight is a pale fire, the world lit in a daffodil hue. By noon the ice is almost melted, and the eaves are drip-dripping. We are on our own, the pub closed, a silent waiting feel to everything. Don't want lunch, but we make some toast in the big, quiet kitchen, Nancy and I, eat it standing. The silent, empty building is full of old ghosts, the air trembling in the stillness with the presences. All here today: Kate and Terry, old man Byrne, his long-dead mate, faceless and silent; and, strangely, it's as if Nancy is with them too . . . But not me, I'm not there, it's as if I'm somehow excluded from the clan of ghosts . . .

Upstairs I dress carefully, my best dark suit, smelling faintly of napthalene from the big wardrobe in the room where Kate died, my old room; shine my shoes till they're mirror bright; white shirt, dark maroon tie. Hair carefully combed. Look at myself in the mirror. Big man, dark and not too pretty. Bumps and lumps and a couple of scars. A touch of grey, very faint, at the temples, and that surprises me. But the most surprising thing of all is the look, an aura almost of sadness, of weighed-down gravity, stricken flesh, an ancient sorrow that's run marks into the face like cheap paint . . .

Not me, surely . . . I'm no tragic figure. But it's there all right . . .

The truth is, I look . . . surrendered.

•

Nancy is dressed in black, severe, fashionable. Small hat and veil. Handsome.

We go outside, get in the newly shined Volvo, drive the short distance to the church. Already there's a crowd there, perhaps a couple of dozen people. The Wellards, the Kennys, Herbert from the store, the Filleuls from the post office, a few farmers. Most I've known since I was a kid. Everyone spruce and uncomfortable, men in once-a-year blue serge, women corseted and crow-black, all in fidgeting families, waiting with self-conscious solemnity.

The parson's there, a young chap from the town, looking a bit High Church in his cassock and petticoat. Shakes hands with us, looks solemn and shepherdly, a thin muttering voice and pale eyes.

The tail end of the hearse is visible round the corner of the church and inside the coffin is already set on its trestles at the front. We queue in, settle ourselves. The smell of the place is stale and sickly, dying flowers and face powder and old sweat. The pews are old and worn, glossy with layers of varnish. Small stained-glass windows make patterns of the light – red, green, gold, blue.

I shut off my mind as the parson goes through his spiel. I stand, sit, kneel, look pious at the right places; but none of it sinks in. I can't keep my eyes off the casket, all red shining wood . . . mahogany, I suppose, with brass handles and baroque gewgaws that glisten cheaply and shoddily in the dimness.

There's a hymn . . . what I used to call Jesus songs, and hated when I was at Sunday School . . . and then it's over. The bearers move out into the aisles and pick up the coffin. We follow them out. There's a certain confusion in the small yard until everyone sorts themselves out. The coffin goes into the hearse, the mourners into the cars, and the parson is left stranded. His car won't start. We all stop and give him a push. With four strong pallbearers it's no trouble, and soon his Mini's chuffing down the road, across the bridge. We follow slowly in the wake of the hearse, and I watch the great pile of flowers on top of the glossy box. God, the old girl'd laugh at it all . . .

But I don't feel like laughing. And I don't feel much like crying either. I just feel like a prisoner going off to the mines, a life sentence on my back . . .

The cemetery is a joke. On a shelf above the river flats, it's tiny, and unfenced except for a couple of strands of wire to keep the stock out; but at the front there's this pair of great iron gates set in an enormous brick surround. Incredible. We go through the gates, park in the little weedy gravel area to the right. There's no more than a hundred or so graves in all, including the old ones, and the grass is long in patches. Blackberries have crept in despite the annual spraying, and a branch has broken off a big silver wattle in the far corner, and is lying across three graves. In the bright sunlight the marble sparkles and the red and grey granite shows blinding flecks of mica. The white chip gravel on the monuments is like snow. Beyond the wire fence the land drops away towards the river. Beyond that I can see the hotel, the church, the hill, the bare empty blue of the sky. It seems very cold and empty, and despite the slight warmth of the sun I feel the same. There's a certain trembly feeling in me now, as we come to the end of it, a nervousness at the horror of committing her to that dark slot halfway down the row. It gapes blackly in the light, and I don't like it much at all. And next to it is the clay mound that must be *his*. Oddly, I find that I can look at it now without feeling much at all.

The caretaker comes along, speaks to the undertaker who stands patiently in his striped trousers and top hat while we get ourselves organised. In turn the undertaker goes over and speaks to Kenny Weller, one of the bearers. They put their heads together and natter on for a couple of minutes. When the undertaker moves away, Kenny talks quietly to the other bearers. They nod wisely at each other.

I go over. 'What's the trouble?' I say to Kenny, who is red-faced, fair-haired. A tight collar constricts his thick throat. He looks worried. Scrunches up his face, squints.

'It's the bloody grave, Jack,' he says. 'All this bloody rain we've had. They had trouble digging it, and it's not too stable. We've got to be careful, that's all . . .'

Slowly the business takes shape. We form up behind the bearers who slide the coffin out of the hearse. It seems hard to believe that inside the box, on all that white satin padding, is old Kate, going quietly to the last long sleep.

The grave looks worse the closer we get. Damp, slick earth, oozing slightly. I don't want to look down into it, but as they let the bands out and the box drops the last few inches there is a slight splash. I wince and catch Nance's eye. She's very pale, standing there opposite me, the black shadowed slit between us, the top of the box just visible down in the hole. There's a horrible lump in my throat now, and I don't really know where to look. So I fix my eyes on the vacant blue sky to the west, beyond the dark pillbox of Nancy's hat, and try to close my mind to the high whine of the parson's voice . . .

And then, quite suddenly, the world seems to come unhinged. As I stand there, engrossed in trying to separate myself from the grotesqueries of the ceremony, the ignominy of the parting with the old girl, it seems as if the earth is turning faster and faster under my feet, as if the sky is drawing farther away. There is a sudden queasy feeling in my belly; and in my ears there is a faint sea sigh that seems to come from a long way away, but is really only the suddenly inhaled breath of a dozen mouths . . .

The truth is that I'm descending; taking a slightly faster and less-dignified passage than the coffin, but to the same destination. The sodden earth about the lips of the grave is slowly giving way, collapsing under my feet, and I'm sinking, sinking . . .

I can't believe it, even while it's happening.

And faster and faster I fall, until with a great rush and surge and a disgusting squelching and loud cries from above, my feet sink deeper and deeper, the wet earth closes round my calves, and my eyes, fixed till then on the sky, are suddenly staring at the horrified face of Nancy as she stands on her side of the grave's shore . . .

Then, as I watch, her shore collapses too, her shiny pumps sink into the wet clay, the whole bank sags, and she too descends, hands still clasped at her waist on her black patent leather bag, until she arrives at my level . . .

For a long moment we stand there staring at each other blankly across the half-buried gloss of Kate's coffin, buried to the knees in foul mud, prematurely reunited, the three of us, in that dismal crowded slot . . .

On the earth's surface they have been drawn back – all of them, even the parson – from the edge of the hole; and, except for the ragged frieze of curious and horrified heads above us, we are alone.

So for that long moment – and another and another, we're past counting – we stare at each other, Nancy and I, stare into each other's eyes; I try desperately to read something there, some meaning, some charm that will nullify this farce, enable us to find some answer, some dignity, allow us to *get out of there* . . .

And the longer we stand there, the worse it gets . . .

Under the horror, the awareness of the grotesquery, the despair, I can feel the beginning prickle of tears, and I can see that Nancy's eyes are wide with shock, her mouth slowly opening . . . to scream? To curse? To surrender?

It seems all too much.

Which of us starts, I don't know. But suddenly, all in a moment, we are both laughing, roaring, rocking, choking with laughter at the final inescapable comedy of our predicament. For half a minute? a minute? who knows how long? we stand there, bent and twisted with our laughter, weeping with it, cramped and aching with it, a pure and final desperation of laughter . . .

And as the tears clear, as the laughter slowly subsides, as the curious heads advance closer to the edge of the destroyed grave, Nancy and I look each other in the eye; and in that moment there flashes some spark between us, blue and sharp and clear, a spark of acceptance, of recognition that we are somehow, each of us, finally released . . .

And in that moment the world seems finally to turn itself inside out. The wrench of parturition has come, the shock and pain and delight are thrust on me; I know then, instantly, that I will give her my share of the hotel, that finally I am free of it, and of every other bequest of the Byrnes, that I am free at last . . . *free to go* . . .

And as I am freed, so am I also joined; Petra and I, somehow, somewhere . . . the last ties cut, off to God knows where – maybe Goldsworthy, and maybe Peru – the *where* doesn't matter, what matters is that there will be new circles . . . and the new circles will change and in turn make new ones, and in those free, bright circles we will find joy and grief and pride and love; and a spaciousness that will spread before us forever . . .

And a great joy takes me then, because I know that I am finally home, that I have found my place in the world, and it is not a narrow place like the valley, but a wide one, and a changing one, like a great river . . .

As the last of the laughter dies in us, as we smile at each other over the mired coffin, it seems to me that I am truly no longer there in that dark sunken bed, but rising high above it like a hawk into the clear, cold, bright air . . . and as I rise, higher and higher, so the earth grows wider, the tiny figures below grow smaller, the horizons expand until there is nothing but a great green plain . . . and as I fly higher and still higher the earth spreads wider and wider until at last I can see that it has no end, ever . . . and I know then that what is happening below is only a beginning, that there is no limit to the earth and to the wishing . . .

And, knowing that, it is no great problem to come back to the earth again, to reach over the muddy coffin and take Nancy's hand, to begin together the slippery and awkward climb up into the light.

MORE ABOUT PENGUINS
AND PELICANS

For further information about books available from
Penguin please write to Dept EP, Penguin Books Ltd,
Harmondsworth, Middlesex UB7 ODA.

In the U.S.A.: For a complete list of books available
from Penguin in the United States write to Dept DG,
Penguin Books, 299 Murray Hill Parkway, East Rutherford,
New Jersey 07073.

In Canada: For a complete list of books available from
Penguin in Canada write to Penguin Books Canada Ltd,
2801 John Street, Markham, Ontario L3R 1B4.

In Australia: For a complete list of books available
from Penguin in Australia write to the Marketing
Department, Penguin Books Australia Ltd, P.O. Box 257,
Ringwood, Victoria 3134.

In New Zealand: For a complete list of books available
from Penguin in New Zealand write to the Marketing
Department, Penguin Books (N.Z.) Ltd, Private Bag,
Takapuna, Auckland 9.